The Chemical Girl

ALSO BY THE AUTHOR

Diner Guys by Chip Silverman

The Block by Bob Litwin and Chip Silverman

Aloha Magnum by Larry Manetti and Chip Silverman

The Last Bookmaker by Bob Litwin and Chip Silverman

Ten Bears by Miles Harrison Jr. and Chip Silverman

Lucky Every Day by Chip Silverman

The
Chemical

CHIP SILVERMAN

BORDERLANDS PRESS
Baltimore, MD ❑ 2006

ISBN#1-880325-73-X

Typesetting and page design by E. Estela Monteleone

Jacket Art by Clark Calhoun
Author Photograph by Gail Wolven

Printed in the United States of America

Borderlands Press
POB 660
Fallston, MD 21047

800-528-3310

For The Chemical Girl,

Wherever She Is . . .

Acknowledgments

Special thanks to Renée Silverman for spending two fleeting decades tirelessly editing and re-editing the multiple versions of *The Chemical Girl*–a Herculean feat.

Also, thanks to Jeanette Hastings, Delene Carlee, and especially, Eileen Lesser for patiently transcribing tapes and typing and retyping the corrected manuscript over and over again.

My gratitude to Clark Calhoun for his original and artistic interpretation of *The Chemical Girl* as displayed on the book jacket.

To acknowledge everyone who contributed to this book, a twenty-year effort, is nearly impossible, especially for those who provided me with substance abuse education.

My heartfelt thanks go out to the countless colleagues, teachers, and patients who consciously or unconsciously mentored me over more than thirty-five years in the addictions field. To list them all would double the size of this book–if I could even remember each one.

I learned from the guys I grew up with at the playground, on the street corners, in the poolroom, and at the Diner; from college and graduate school educators, seminars, lectures, and conferences; from my coworkers at the Maryland Drug and Alcohol Administration, the Department of Health and Mental Hygiene, Greenspring Mental Health Systems, and Magellan Behavioral Health Care; from the legislators, council persons, politicians, mayors, county executives, and governors of Maryland; from the clients and patients in the public and private outpatient and inpatient sectors; and from the junkies, dealers, smugglers, and others who never came in from the cold. Thank you for the priceless and well-rounded education!

Preface

The Chemical Girl has been a labor of love *and* frustration since 1986 when I began writing it. During those twenty years, I have had six other books published.

This book is a historical novel. It contains fiction and fact. All references to the Len Bias saga–a tragic watershed event in the country's continuing struggle with drug abuse–are true. During the time that I was Director of the Maryland Drug Abuse Administration, I was on the College Park Task Force that investigated Bias' death. Not only was I privy to interviews and documentation presented to the Task Force, but once I decided to write this book, the setting of which was *the* event, I recorded critical individuals who were aware of most of what transpired and surrounded that tragic night of June 19, 1986.

The rest of the novel is a crazy ride filled with truth and fiction. It is the protagonist's account of what it was like from a bureaucrat's viewpoint to run a state agency charged with the treatment, prevention, and education of substance abuse and addiction. Administering those legislative mandates resulted in humor, frustration, cynicism, and despair; all for trying to help diseased individuals who had been labeled as criminals and whose treatment was sorely underfunded, underappreciated, and overwhelming.

As an escape from the stress of this seemingly hopeless job, I began writing for newspapers and magazines, and eventually, writing books. To the best of my knowledge, there has never been a novel that has looked at addiction from the bureaucrat's perspective.

"Work like you don't need money.
Love like you've never been hurt.
Dance like nobody's watching."

Satchel Paige
Hall of Fame Baseball Player

"'Scrub that thing, cover that thing, hide that thing.' That's what my granny always preached to the little girls in our clan," said the Chemical Girl as she raised her eyes and grinned.

She rose effortlessly, to my constant amazement. Here it was six p.m., and the Chemical Girl had been drinking since she'd arrived on the beach at ten-thirty this morning. Now, as we sat in our junior suite on the fifteenth floor of the beachfront Sheraton Fontainebleau Hotel in Ocean City, Maryland, waiting for the Deputy to return so we could go out for dinner, the Chemical Girl poured herself yet another drink–this one to wash down two .5 Xanax pills.

"What's that for?" I asked, somewhat disgusted.

"Prevention, Ted," she mused, spinning around in her light pink bikini. "You're a clinician. Alcohol gives me the shakes, so the pills which counteract that side effect are substance abuse prevention. See what I've learned from our relationship so far?"

"You need more than preventive help," I said.

"I've had lots of help. It's all bullshit," she said matter-of-factly. The Chemical Girl never responded in a loud, angry, or nasty way.

"The shrinks wanted me in psychoanalysis five days a week," she continued. "Quit work. Right. Spend all my time in their offices. They only want to fuck you anyway, physically and financially."

She was very therapy savvy. She was also very natural and very feminine. I'd met a lot of women over the years, but she was special, sensual, and intriguing. Only in her mid-twenties, the Chemical Girl had already lived, fucked, and drugged several lifetimes.

"I went from baby dolls to smoking weed to sex in a tree house when I was twelve years old," she had once confided. "I embraced drugs and sex as a religion and never looked back."

Someone was banging on the door of our hotel room. The Chemical Girl opened it as the Deputy burst in with two pizzas and a six-pack, which contained five Buds and a Diet Coke for me.

"Where the fuck have you been?" I asked, irritated. I didn't want the pizza. I thought we'd be dining out on some fresh Chesapeake Bay fish or soft crabs.

"At an A.A. meeting," answered the Deputy triumphantly as he placed the pizzas on the table in the center of our suite.

I was the Director of the State of Maryland Alcohol and Drug Abuse Administration, and he was one of four deputies whose specialty was information technology. But he considered himself *the* Deputy.

"Since when do you attend A.A. meetings? I thought the macho Hispanic mentality abhorred it. Not that you shouldn't go, and you could even take her as your guest speaker," I said, nodding in the direction of the Chemical Girl.

She paid me no mind as she deftly snapped open a beer and began pulling apart the pizza slices, placing them gently on paper napkins.

"Remember that black-haired waitress with the curly hair I was talking to at breakfast this morning?" the Deputy asked. "She told me she attends an A.A. meeting after work at the church near Shane's Pizza Pub on Coastal Highway. So I went with her. I do go to an A.A. or N.A. meeting every now and then to update my education on the importance of support groups…"

"Bullshit!" I interrupted. "You're going there to pick up women."

"Exactly," confessed the Deputy, biting into his pizza slice and smiling deviously at the Chemical Girl.

"How can you do that in good conscience?" I demanded. "The women there are so vulnerable." I slid off the sofa, walked over to the table, and eyed the pizzas: one plain and one with mushrooms and onion.

"Vulnerable. Exactly. I love it," said the Deputy. "I'm in the rooms as often as possible. Can't miss gettin' laid." The term "rooms" was jargon for A.A. and N.A. meeting places.

"Christ sakes!" I yelled at the Deputy. "You remind me of my old buddies in the '70s. They did the same shit at EST meetings." I turned away from the now cold pizza and retreated to the sofa.

"My dad used to attend EST," said the Chemical Girl, popping open her second beer since the Deputy had returned. EST, an acronym for Erhard Seminars Training was a growth-experience-based fad, one of many in California at that time.

Where did it go? I wondered. The booze had no effect on her beautifully proportioned body.

"What did your friends do at those meetings?" she asked.

"They'd go to the EST recruitment meeting over and over again. The one where people had to stay in a room without going to the bathroom for hours and blurt out thoughts and feelings they had harbored forever and ever. My pals would locate pretty chicks, sit next to them, and after an hour or so, they'd fake a breakdown or confess and say, 'God, I can't believe I'm doing this, but you're just so nice. I'd love to make passionate love to you over and over again,' or they might say something a bit cruder. It didn't matter. Whatever they'd say, it usually worked. If it didn't, they had plenty of time to move on to other unsuspecting and vulnerable women."

The Chemical Girl got up and brought me a slice of mushroom and onion pizza. She'd read my mind.

"Here," she offered, as she handed me the pizza and a Diet Coke. "Ted, there's nothing wrong with what the Deputy and your friends did. I love it. A.A., N.A., EST, whatever turns 'em on. You don't think the girls know what's happening?"

"Wait," I interrupted, my mouth full. "You two just don't get it."

"Oh, we get it," the Chemical Girl purred. "It's you who doesn't."

❑ ❑ ❑

At that time, I had been working in the field of chemical dependency treatment for almost twenty years. Substance abuse, recovery, addiction, codependency–I thought I knew it all, but I never did fully comprehend it; not until the summer of '86. That's when it all began to come together; when I began to get the what-fors, the whys, the why-nots, and the interdependency.

I'd been living vicariously for so long through friends, patients, lovers, smugglers, gamblers, addicts, and dealers that I never saw it coming.

The frustration, cynicism, and humor of the field had shielded me from it. They were my escapes and too many obstacles kept me from getting it. Too much philosophy, theory, spirituality, support groups, extended treatment time, twelve steps, The Big Book, The Little Book had blocked the bigger picture. But the summer of '86 opened my eyes and the catalysts were the Deputy, Len Bias, my estranged wife, some old friends, and the Chemical Girl.

I rose slowly, controlling my movements so as not to awaken the brunette who shared my bed. Some eight years earlier Candy. had been the ornament of my dreams, but the relationship did not wear well with time and no longer served my ego or stirred my fantasies. I watched her as she slept with her mouth open, mascara streaked under her eyes. She was still pretty and sensuous, but the turn-on days were long gone. A wave of nausea moved through my gut and lodged in my throat. *Was it last night's dinner and drinks, or the past five years of a deteriorating marriage?* I thought.

I had to get to the bathroom! I moved quickly from the bed and gently closed the door to my sanctuary. Tension escaped my body with the morning ablutions. The hot shower released me to thoughts of the coming day as I pushed the misery of my marriage to the back of my mind.

"Ted," she demanded, "are you ever coming out of there?"

I pretended not to hear and lingered an extra moment, though my hand was on the doorknob when she called out.

"Ted, Jesus, you asshole! I have to get in there and get ready! What are you, some fucking prima donna jerking yourself off?"

My hand gripped the knob, and I slowly turned it and sauntered past her as though she didn't exist.

❑ ❑ ❑

The Deputy signed out a large, nondescript station wagon from the State Motor Pool and drove it to our prearranged meeting place. He sped to within a few miles and slowed to a crawl, watchful of being recognized. As he carefully approached the house at the top of the tree-lined hill, he breathed more easily at seeing only another state car in the driveway. I signaled that all was clear and he entered the garage.

My friend, Ron, arrived several minutes later, approaching from another direction. He drove his mom's new Ford Escort cautiously for he was fearful not only of damaging her precious vehicle, but also of encouraging the wrath of Candy that he knew all too well.

We rearranged the wagon seats for maximum capacity. It would be the first of two trips and time was critical. We quickly filled the car with waiting cartons, formed a mini-convoy and dropped my belongings off at awaiting friends' homes.

Later Candy would ask in her demanding tone how I had removed all of my things without her noticing, and I would answer that I had done it over many months.

❑ ❑ ❑

GREENSPRING VALLEY, BALTIMORE COUNTY, MARYLAND
1976-1984

Bees. I hate bees…and wasps…and hornets! They're scary, they sting, and they hold you hostage in the summer. And when the summer ends and you drop your guard and think that the anxiety of being outside is over, surprise! They're still around; except now they're even more dangerous. They're mean because they know they're going to die soon, and they want to fuck every day and sting anyone who gets in their way.

After Candy and I married, we moved to Greenspring Valley in the country. The home and the land were spacious, courtesy of Candy's wealthy granddad who adored her. We soon had a swimming pool surrounded by a large deck. It was quiet, beautiful, and delightful…except for the bees, wasps, and hornets. I became obsessed with their presence and spent hours planning their demise. I hired three different exterminating companies to work almost around the clock keeping the insects at bay.

Despite my constant vigilance, a huge bees' nest grew beneath the deck. Candy discovered it by accident one morning and was "gang stung" by three of them. She, of course, went berserk.

"Ted," she demanded, "get rid of that fuckin' nest! I don't care how you do it, but it'd better be gone by tonight." Her tone as usual was serious and challenging.

"Don't worry," I assured her, "I'll see that they're destroyed before you get home."

Not knowing how to get rid of the nest and realizing that it was Sunday and the exterminators were probably off, I consulted with an old farmer who lived down the hill from us.

"Oregon, how do you get rid of a bees' nest?" I asked. Oregon was a small, gray-bearded man, forever in overalls.

"Ted," he said, stroking his whiskers, "it's simple. Ya take a corncob, douse it in kerosene, and stick it on the end of a pitchfork. Then ya wait 'til dusk, when they're all back in the nest for the night. Ya set the corncob on fire, and ya stick it up in the nest. It'll go up in flames and those babies will never bother ya no more. Lemme know how it turns out, buddy."

The project was more complicated than it sounded; at least for me. I didn't have a corncob, kerosene, or a pitchfork. And how was I to know when every fucking bee came home at night? But I was determined and Candy had thrown down the gauntlet. I spent the entire day preparing myself. I bought a pitchfork and kerosene. The salesman at the hardware store told me to wrap some rags around the end of the pitchfork to substitute for the corncob.

"And you better be careful," he warned. "If you don't burn 'em out on the first go-round, they'll come after you. Also, watch for the guard or scout bees as you're approaching the nest, or they'll get you, too. Make sure you protect yourself."

And protect myself I did. Even though it was ninety-two degrees with a hundred percent humidity at seven forty-five in the evening, no part of my body was left exposed. I donned long socks, thermal underwear, a flannel shirt with the collar up, sweatpants, and high-topped tennis shoes. Then I covered my face with a ski mask and sports goggles, racquetball gloves for my hands, and finally, my full-length Italian raincoat. I appeared to be a cross between Jesse James in *The Long Riders* and Colonel Erwin Rommel in the Afrika Korps in World War II.

I was now ready to proceed with the task at hand–elimination of the four-by-six-inch bees' nest beneath the deck. The heat, humidity, and layered clothing created heavy perspiration, steaming my goggles and distorting my vision, but I persevered. First I tied torn pieces of an old towel around the pitchfork. Then while holding it over a bucket, I drenched it with kerosene. Opening the gate leading to the pool and deck, I walked swiftly over to the bees' nest. Gingerly, I removed a wooden match, struck the side of the matchbox, and lit the end of the pitchfork. Flames immediately engulfed the towel parts, and without hesitation, I stuck the torch into the nest. More flames shot up. My heart began to pound and I shook uncontrollably. Sweat poured off my body in torrents as I endured the intensity of the heat.

Suddenly, I became aware that the fire had not died down although the nest had been destroyed. The wood it was attached to had caught fire and the flames were spreading quickly across the deck. I ran blindly to the garage and filled the bucket with water, racing back to the deck and dousing the fire. But the fire roared on and continued to spread. "Shit!" I cried, as I realized that the bucket I had filled with water was the same one I had poured the kerosene in a few minutes earlier.

Just as I began to panic, Oregon appeared by my side, scooping water from the pool with a different bucket and soaking the deck. I joined in and we formed a bucket brigade.

Within minutes the flames died out, and through the smoke and charred, buckling wood, I could plainly see that I had burned down at least one-third of the deck. Even worse, it had come within a few feet of the kitchen door.... Candy was going to kill me.

"Teddy," said Oregon as he placed his arm around my shoulder, "you did a helluva job here this evening. See, you accomplished your task, and the bees are dead. I'm proud of ya, but unfortunately you took out several hundred, maybe even a couple thousand dollars worth of deck. But war is hell! Oh, and Ted, you can get outta them silly clothes now. You won't get stung tonight by these bees, although Miss Candy may sting you pretty good later."

❑ ❑ ❑

A few years after my beehive arson job, I had another near-fatal bee encounter. I stepped on a honeybee nest while jogging and was stung over a quarter of my body. I became faint and nauseous. Candy, in a rare sympathetic mood, rushed me to a doctor who directed me to the Allergy Clinic at Good Samaritan Hospital, part of the Johns Hopkins Medical Complex. There, a doctor, who looked very much like a huge honeybee, tested me and confirmed my fears–I was highly allergic to bee stings and most other biting insects.

"You'll have to get allergy shots for a year," he explained, "and you'll have to keep a bee sting kit with you at all times. When you get stung, shoot the hypodermic into your thigh intramuscularly, and it'll ward off the allergic reaction."

Miraculously, from that point on, I was stung only once. But I religiously refilled the bee kit prescription long before it expired.

Actually, I worried about carrying the hypodermic with me because of my job with the Maryland State Drug and Alcohol Administration. It looked and felt awkward to be in possession of drug paraphernalia. But to save my life, I had no choice.

Because I traveled extensively throughout the state and across the nation consulting and lecturing at drug and alcohol programs, I convinced "Dr. Honeybee" at Hopkins to compile for me a list of the finest allergy doctors and experts on insect bites in the country whom I could call if I were stung.

Protection from that "worst-case-scenario" assured that I could continue the lecture circuit, hobnobbing with my fellow wizards in trying to bring about the downfall of the scourge of the twentieth century.

□ □ □

During those years, I headed the combined Maryland Drug and Alcohol Administration and, before that, the Drug Abuse Administration. In fact, the agency went through several identity crises. In the late '60s, the responsibility for drug and alcohol abuse was still part of the Mental Hygiene Administration. However, since advocates in these newly emerging fields did not wish addicts to be considered "crazy people," two entities were created. First there was the Alcohol Control Administration, followed by the Drug Abuse Authority. They were autonomous organizations, enacted by very different laws. In 1978, the responsibility for compulsive gambling was assigned to the Drug Abuse Administration. By the mid-'80s a merger began during which administration names changed annually. We were The Addictions Services Administration, The Substance Abuse Administration, The Chemical Dependency Administration, and, finally, The Alcohol and Drug Abuse Administration. Our overall responsibility was to provide treatment and prevention of substance abuse for all State of Maryland citizens, to which we gave our best efforts....

BOOK I

"The United States has an extensive history in the use and abuse of drugs reaching far back into the nineteenth century. When we are in the middle of a drug crisis, we tend to forget this history and assume that we must face our drug onslaught with no guideposts. Unaware of how we have overcome past drug problems, we are liable to panic."

David F. Musto
The American Disease

Chapter 1

OCEAN CITY, MARYLAND
Summer of 1972

Public attention began to focus on the drug abuse epidemic. The governor's aide and the director of the Drug Abuse Administration decided to personally intervene in a drug crisis in Ocean City, Maryland.

Drug dealers were selling a "sunshine pill" they claimed was LSD but was actually laced with strychnine. A couple of deaths and several dozen very ill kids resulted when unsuspecting teenagers bought and ingested the pills.

The governor's aide, the director, and I, then chief of Administrative Services, drove to Ocean City to investigate the crisis and determine a prevention strategy. We contracted a single-engine plane to fly along the beach towing a sign proclaiming "The Sunshine Pill Kills!" The media were alerted, and Sunday afternoon we stationed ourselves on the Boardwalk along with thousands of beachgoers eager to observe the event.

As the plane flew over towing our huge golden message, the governor's aide pointed towards the sky boasting proudly to the press of his strategy. The crowds on the sand shielded their eyes from the sun and looked up as the sign flew by. Suddenly the plane began to sputter, the engine stopped, and the sign became entangled in the wind. Within seconds the plane crashed headlong into the choppy ocean water. Unbelievably, cheers arose from the crowded beach.

We drove back to Baltimore in silence.

When I look back on that sweltering day in Ocean City, I sometimes wonder if it signified the first battle in the so-called "war on drugs" in Maryland. Perhaps it symbolized the frustration of the countless losses to come in our efforts to halt the drug scourge and to educate the public. We would launch optimistic attempts to counter drug abuse and then watch them sputter and die much like the little plane that day. But there were *some* successes, and very few dull moments....

❏ ❏ ❏

The Chemical Girl

BALTIMORE, MARYLAND
1974-1984

It was around my sixth year with the Drug Abuse Administration when I ran into Holt, an old neighborhood buddy, at a disco in downtown Baltimore. He was living in San Diego. We had grown up together in Baltimore where Holt often got high when we were barely teenagers. He would stand on the street corner waiting for the trolley that stopped at our junior high school, under the influence of cough medicine or pills he had found in his mother's medicine cabinet. Other times he drank Jack Daniel's bourbon at seven or eight in the morning. On this day twenty years later, he confessed to me that he had been doing a lot of cocaine recently. "It's great," he told me, "you should try it." I admonished him for using coke, but he didn't appear to care.

Instead, he smiled at me and said, "Well, Ted, you know, I got laid seven times last night with my girlfriend and two of her girlfriends." I did not respond since I wasn't even getting laid seven times a year.

In the '60s, Holt had been a small-time but world-renown international drug smuggler. He was very successful at the trade for many years, and acted independently until an organized drug ring thought Holt was becoming too competitive. They dropped a dime on him with Interpol and the FBI, and he was eventually arrested and convicted.

Holt served three years in a federal prison, and upon his release vowed never again to smuggle dope for a living. He continued to use drugs, but never sold them. After several years, however, he found it necessary to deal just enough cocaine and Quaaludes to pay for his personal use. Holt believed he had not violated his vow.

I saw him again in early 1984. He had graduated from snorting cocaine to freebasing it on a regular basis. Although he appeared to be slightly burned out, and seemed somewhat paranoid and schizophrenic, he had obviously not yet bottomed out from his excessive abuse of cocaine. I admonished him once again. My expertise in the field had grown since the last time I had seen him, but it didn't appear to matter to Holt.

"I'm going to tell ya how great freebasing coke is," he whispered. "Do you know I can lie on my bed and have multiple orgasms, ejaculating over and over again without even touching my prick?"

I remembered his earlier boast that he had gotten laid seven times in one night. Now he was having multiple orgasms!

A few months later on a drug lecture tour, I approached Dr. Sid Cohen, the "Godfather" in the field of addictions and an early leader of the National Institute of Drug Abuse. Sid was in his eighties and had experienced a number of drug epidemics. I nearly cried telling Sid Holt's stories. I asked, "What's going on here, Sid? Am I in the wrong business?"

"Don't worry, Ted," said Dr. Cohen. "You see, when Holt was getting laid seven times that night, that's seven times in the future that he isn't going to get laid."

It didn't make me feel better. Well, maybe a little better.

Then Dr. Cohen added, "About his report of ejaculating over and over again while freebasing coke, that's probably true. But those are orgasms he also won't be having in the future."

"Why?" I asked.

Cohen was a bottomless pit of knowledge when it came to drugs, alcohol, chemical dependency, substance abuse, and just about any other related topic. I relished my conversations with him and enjoyed his lectures immensely.

"You see," he explained, "there's a neurotransmitter in the brain called the dopamine. The dopamine stores all kinds of pleasures and rewards. Pleasures and rewards like eating a good meal, the exhilaration of running distances or completing a race, exercise, getting a raise at work, completing a task you're proud of, being proud of your kids, or in some cases, having sex.

"The dopamine gives off what we call a 'natural high.' It controls our reward and pleasure center. But cocaine acts unnaturally on the dopamine. I want you to look at the dopamine as a box full of all pleasures and rewards. All the thousands of pleasures and rewards are stored in this box. And they come out a little bit at a time when you have a natural high. But when you have a cocaine-induced, unnatural chemical high, these pleasures and rewards release themselves too quickly. That's why cocaine is the most seductive drug in the world.

"If I told you that I could provide you with instant gratification, super-abundant energy, intense feelings of sexuality, exhilaration, and extreme competence and confidence, you'd say, 'I'll take it.' That's the lure. That's why over twenty million people have taken cocaine. They surely never look at the negative aspects."

Then, as an aside, Dr. Cohen said, "Remember, the federal government announced in the early 1970s that cocaine was neither addictive nor toxic. Isn't that what the government said about marijuana in the 1960s? Those of us who work for the government have a great cross to bear."

Cohen was a master at going off on tangents and magically returning to the subject at hand.

"So the dopamine gives off dozens and dozens of pleasures and rewards all at once when someone is ingesting cocaine. The quantity and the quality of the cocaine, as well as the route of administration, will determine how soon an individual will bottom out, and how much pleasure and rewards they'll get during that time."

I was thinking about Holt. Sid continued, "But the paradox of cocaine is that in search of euphoria, the ultimate high, you always wind up with dysphoria, the ultimate low, which is why cocaine abuse is epidemic and not endemic. And, while this is the third cocaine epidemic in the last hundred years, it's the greatest one because we never before had millions of people involved with cocaine.

"You see, the more cocaine one does, the more pleasures and rewards depart the dopamine center. The box begins to empty out. And so you never achieve that initial high again. The next high is not as high. The duration is not as long. And eventually, over a period of months or years, again depending on quantity, quality, route of administration, and the physiological and psychological makeup of an individual, that person *will* bottom out. He will exhaust the dopamine center. All pleasures and rewards will leave that box, and the individual will no longer feel any form of pleasure or reward. He will become what is known as dysphoric or anhedonic, and will not enjoy pleasure."

Oh well, I thought, *Holt was still enjoying himself.*

Dr. Cohen continued, "When the dopamine is exhausted, a person becomes extremely despondent, often displaying suicidal tendencies. Many such people will attempt or even commit suicide.

"It takes years and years for the craving for cocaine to leave users, and it takes months or longer for the dopamine center to restore itself–for the pleasures and rewards to return. There will frequently be periods of depression, but eventually if a person stays off of cocaine and other stimulants, he will experience normal pleasures and rewards once again.

"Yet there are people who don't come off of cocaine no matter what. All you have to do is refer back to the monkey bar press trials in which cocaine was offered continually to monkeys. Although they would receive a slight electric shock, and monkeys do hate electric shocks more than anything; and although they would have food and a receptive female in the cage with them, the monkeys would still prefer the electric shocks in order to receive cocaine. They would keep pressing the bar for more cocaine until they died of exhaustion and starvation. This is similar to their primate friends whose number includes people like your friend Holt or even you. If I gave cocaine to everyone in this or any other room, ninety percent of you would not refuse it if it were offered a second or third time. And, of course, access to the drug leads to excess. That's the beginning of the road to addiction...."

❑ ❑ ❑

BOSTON, MASSACHUSETTS
June 1986

According to gossip, and later, legend, the following phone conversation took place:

"Doc, guess what? It looks like I'm gonna get picked number two in the country," said the big guy, elated.

"Everything great is happening," he continued. "Signing bonus, endorsements maybe for years from Reebok...I'll be playing side by side with 'The Bird'...and, dig this, I passed the piss test easily. Ya know I was more worried this time, but the Golden Field worked wonders again!"

Golden Field, a health food herb bought over the counter, a natural diuretic and laxative also successful in healing ringworm and cold sores. Simply mix the bitter-tasting powder with water and drink it. And, if you drink even more water afterwards, Golden Field flushes the system completely. This, plus the short half-life of coke, makes it easy for someone who has recently ingested cocaine to test negative just a few hours later in a urinalysis exam.

"Oh, and dig what else," the big guy, Len Bias, crowed, "I did the 'toot' with one of the Celtics. You'll shit when I tell ya who! Later."

OCEAN CITY, MARYLAND
June 13, 1986

The first time I saw the Chemical Girl was on the beach in Ocean City at the oceanfront Sheraton Hotel. She was lounging on a beach chair, wearing a very sleek and revealing black bikini, chatting away with two elderly gentlemen.

The Deputy and I had just returned from the first week of training for addictions counselors at the annual Education and Training Program at Salisbury State University in Wicomico County, approximately forty-five minutes by car from Ocean City. I was scheduled to address the Maryland State Bar Association Convention the next day on "The Continuum of Care in Adolescent Substance Abuse Treatment."

We had settled in our sand chairs and were closely observing the Chemical Girl when our friend Dancing Dave appeared. Dave was a real estate agent who had hit the jackpot in the Ocean City resort boom of the mid-1970s and now worked only on occasion. He derived his nickname from his habit of nonstop dancing in Ocean City night spots–not only on the dance floor, but wherever he happened to be; by the bar, talking, drinking, whatever. Dave was tall and thin with straight bleached-blond hair. Always smiling and sporting a golden tan, he epitomized the aging Beach Boy. As he sat down on the clean white sand and removed his Walkman earphones, he immediately took notice of the Chemical Girl who had risen from her beach chair and was strolling casually by us towards the ocean.

She was about five-feet-four-inches tall with auburn hair and an angelic schoolgirl look. She couldn't have been more than twenty-four years old, yet seemed quite sophisticated. Dancing Dave shouted out what he thought were some appropriate lines to get her attention, but was completely ignored. We laughed and turned our attention to more mundane issues.

That night, the Deputy and I found our way to the packed Samantha's Nightclub on 46th Street and the bay. Around twelve-thirty a.m., overhearing an unusual conversation behind us, we turned and observed the Chemical Girl speaking with two very muscular college-age boys. We picked up on the discussion as she responded to a question one of the boys had posed. "Why, are you guys voyeurs?" she asked. Obviously unfamiliar with the term, they asked her if she was French. The Chemical Girl, noticing my attentive stare and the large smile on my face, looked me straight in the eyes and asked me what I was laughing about.

Quickly brushing off the two hulks, she began an incessant discourse with me about her life. She was stunning and I bought her a drink and began to listen. Later I asked the Chemical Girl for a dance.

The band had taken a break and the popular D.J. "owned" the dance floor. The lights and sounds pulsated through the see-through floor to the bodies of the dancers gyrating to the music.

The Chemical Girl appeared to dance in a trance, oblivious to my moves. She was wearing a black halter top and miniskirt, with her bare and darkly tanned midriff exposed. The lights seemed to bounce off of her glazed eyes as her body kept in perfect sexual rhythm to the music.

Before last call was announced, the Chemical Girl had asked me at least five times if I had any cocaine. She never asked my name or what line of work I was in. Obviously she thought I looked like a cocaine dealer or at least a user.

Actually, hanging out at these resort bars was an extended form of outreach for my job. I should probably have been earning compensatory time for it since I was the head of the Maryland Drug and Alcohol Abuse Agency. Well, I liked to think of it as outreach, and it certainly helped me understand drug trends and patterns....

For a guy in his mid-forties, I did alright in resort nightclubs. My weight and height were average and I looked much younger than my age. I had long, wavy dark brown hair, a good tan, and sharp Mediterranean features. Internally though, I was in trouble. The hereditary traits of high blood pressure, clogged arteries, and high cholesterol were beginning to wreak havoc, not to mention the stress of too many years in the drug field and the toll of a nasty separation from my wife.

At one point during the night the Chemical Girl glanced at my wedding ring and asked, "Why are you here? You're married!"

Laughing, I told her, "I didn't come to the bar to get married."

Even though I'd been separated for about a year, I found that wearing a wedding band was an effective form of protection. It gave me a reason to tell a girl to get lost in a gentle way, not that it ever happened. More likely I didn't feel as rejected since I'd convinced myself it had to do with the ring. Surely it made many women feel comfortable. And in those sexually-transmitted-disease-phobic times, it probably alleviated a lot of the fear of herpes and AIDS since many single ladies felt that a married guy didn't mess around...much.

But all the Chemical Girl was interested in was whether or not I had cocaine, and if so, why I wasn't sharing. I'd probably be asked this dozens of times during the course of the summer, just as the summer before; but never in the semi-desperate, yet classy, and almost seductive way that the Chemical Girl asked.

❑ ❑ ❑

When the Deputy and I explained our line of work, we were often mistaken for narcs. We had to be very, very careful.

"No, we're not in enforcement," we would insist. "We're in *treatment*. We *help* people, and sometimes even get people out of jail and other trouble."

As it turned out, we ended up hearing a lot of confessions. After we explained the term "confidentiality" and how it governed us, people felt free to confess their problems and even those of their friends'. We were often able to refer people to treatment or to intervene with other issues, although some people simply wanted to get things off their chests. Many would go through the denial process, explaining that when they were ready, they would seek help. From these experiences, the COPYIR program was born on the beach in Ocean City, Maryland.

COPYIR was an acronym for Counseling Outreach Program for Youth in Resorts. Acronyms were popular in the health profession, especially in the substance abuse field, and were instrumental in creating effective programs. Actually, the acronyms often took more thought than the type of program, modality, or treatment.

During the summer months, Ocean City became the second largest city in the state of Maryland and the number one per capita alcohol and drug problem area. A significant number of people vacationed there to blow off steam or to get high, stoned, and bombed. And since on any given weekend the crowd increased to between two and three hundred fifty thousand people, it created some very challenging times. So in the summer of '86, we implemented an innovative and cost-effective program.

We selected experienced counselors from statewide public treatment programs and sent them to Ocean City on a two-week rotation basis. They would man a hot line, conduct prevention, education, crisis intervention, outreach activities, and brief treatment services. They also trained emergency services personnel on the Eastern Shore. It was a perk for the counselor and a great management tool for the treatment program director. It was also an effective way of keeping a lot of kids out of jail since the ultra-conservative thinking on the Eastern Shore, similar to that of the Deep South, was more bent on punitive than therapeutic measures.

It was early June when we launched this pilot project. Most of the counselors we chose were from our methadone maintenance programs; people who were used to dealing with the most difficult and transient of clients. It was a great busman's holiday for them. Their condo was paid for and we gave them twenty cents per mile for travel reimbursement, which didn't amount to a hill of beans since there were only ten miles of highway at the resort. We also gave them about fifteen dollars each per day for meals, which couldn't buy breakfast in New York, but could buy a lot of food on the Eastern Shore. We designed tee-shirts for the COPYIR program and developed a hot-line number, 289-LIVE.

The program almost didn't get off the ground because the mayor was adamantly opposed to it. He was livid over the public relations and advertising segment of the program, which called for the use of a small plane flying over the beach towing a message. This was the easiest and most effective form of advertising in Ocean City. There was also a less expensive method of advertising where a boat sailed close to the shoreline along the packed beach with a message displayed in blinking lights. The COPYIR program planned to utilize these two advertising campaigns to alert the public that there was a hot-line number available. It would read: *For a drug or alcohol problem, call 289-LIVE.*

When I called the mayor to discuss his displeasure, he threatened to have me fired by calling the governor or my boss, the secretary of health. Before he even got into any in-depth explanation of his opposition, I told him that it didn't matter who he called.

"This is a state problem," I said firmly, "not an Ocean City or Worcester County problem. I've got the responsibility, and unless you prefer to wait for people to start dying from drug abuse and be embarrassed at the height of the vacation season, you should go along with the program. Or at least give me a better explanation as to why you don't want it!"

I tried to reason with him. "Look, I own property on the shore and I've been coming here for thirty years. I'm concerned about the image of the resort, too." I owned one-sixteenth of a condo with my estranged wife.

The image of Ocean City was the mayor's major concern. Finally he confessed to me, "Alright, here's what's happened. Two weeks ago, a plane flew over the ocean advertising free pregnancy tests. Word quickly spread, and it upset so many of the parents of our female high school and college work force that almost a third of the girls were called back home. Their parents figured that if Ocean City was offering free pregnancy tests, sex must be rampant."

The mayor added, "And on top of this, if we flew a plane around advertising a drug hot-line number, it could further destroy the family image of our town."

I understood his apprehension, so I decided to make a deal with him.

"We won't have the plane or the boat with the hot-line message," I bargained, "if you'll cooperate with us. Let our people train the emergency services workers, the police, and the firefighters. Agree that we can have flyers posted throughout the town, that we can advertise on radio and television, that we can have billboards with the hot-line number, and that we can give seminars and lectures to all of the motel and hotel operators, bar owners, restaurant owners, and summer workers about drug and alcohol abuse."

He reluctantly agreed. "Just don't use that damn plane or the blinking boat!"

We decided to fully implement COPYIR that Fourth of July weekend with hopes that if it proved to be successful, we would run it from Memorial Day weekend through Labor Day the next year.

As we left Samantha's, the Chemical Girl walked outside with us. She got into her car which wouldn't start, so she asked us for a ride. Since we were all staying at the Sheraton, about three miles north, it wasn't a problem.

In the car, she teased us. "I think you guys are dealers. C'mon, what are you selling? 'Ludes, flakes, coke, grass, smack, acid…?"

"Christ, are you off base," I said. "But you really do know your drugs. What are you, the Chemical Girl?"

She smiled and fell silent. The name stuck.

We entered the Sheraton and took the elevator to the fourteenth floor. Her suite was directly below ours. When the elevator stopped, she stepped out, said good night to the Deputy, and pulled me out with her.

The Chemical Girl led me into her room where we sat and began to talk. Two hours later, we were still talking, and I had the distinct feeling that this was about all I was going to get out of the night–talk.

At some point, the Chemical Girl asked me again if I had cocaine or any other drugs, and suggested that I order some vodka from room service. I explained that the hotel stopped serving liquor at midnight.

Then, the Chemical Girl opened her handbag and removed a vial of cocaine and about ten orange pills. When I asked what type of pills they were, she told me they were Xanax. Xanax is a benzodiazepine, an anti-anxiety drug similar to Valium, although you can perform everyday functions somewhat better while using it. A number of patients in my methadone programs were currently abusing Xanax.

The Chemical Girl quickly snorted all of the cocaine and swallowed a handful of Xanax with two glasses of red wine she had chilling in the suite's small refrigerator.

It was tough to get a word in edgewise with the Chemical Girl, who chatted away nonstop. I finally blurted out, "Look, Miss, it's late and I've gotta leave...."

Ignoring my comment, she abruptly stood up and asked, "Which bathing suit do you think I should wear to the beach tomorrow?" The Chemical Girl had a unique way of changing subjects in midstream, and after observing the number of pills she'd ingested, I could understand why.

Unsteadily, the Chemical Girl walked into the open closet and removed her clothes. Her body was unbelievable, and she was uninhibited and quite comfortable in her nakedness.

She put on a hot pink bikini and paraded around for a few moments as I strolled toward the bed. I took my clothes off and got under the covers.

"That looks great," I said. "You look gorgeous. And pardon me again, but what's your name?"

"Lola," she whispered.

The lights went out, the bikini came off, and she crawled into bed next to me. We made love for what seemed like an eternity, but was probably more like forty-five minutes. The Chemical Girl had more orgasms in those forty-five short minutes than I had achieved in a lifetime.

Being a light sleeper, I was wide awake fifteen minutes after I closed my eyes. I looked over at the Chemical Girl who was in such a deep sleep that her snoring forced me to roll her over to the other side of the huge king-sized bed. The sex had been so good that I wanted to light a cigarette, but I didn't smoke. So, I lay awake and watched her. She had finally stopped snoring.

I sat up in bed for a while and around six-fifteen a.m., I decided to go upstairs to my suite, shave and shower, and prepare to speak to the Bar Association. Before leaving her room, I went to the bathroom, and when I returned to her bedside, I noticed the Chemical Girl was very still, even for a sleeping person. I tried shaking her to wake her, but she didn't budge. In a panic I thought, *Oh fuck, maybe she OD'ed!* I mean a dozen pills, cocaine, and wine, not to mention the seven drinks she must have had at Samantha's. She wasn't stirring. I shook her and talked loudly to her to no avail, so I decided to get dressed and split. She could be dying or dead, and I didn't need this aggravation, not in my position. I gave her a little kiss on her cheek and prayed she wouldn't die...at least not until I returned to Salisbury. I wiped my fingerprints from everything I could remember touching, just in case. Hoping no one would see me leave her room, I cautiously returned to my room to prepare for my presentation. The Deputy's loud snoring welcomed me. He hadn't undressed and was sprawled across the bed.

❏ ❏ ❏

After my speech at the Ocean City Convention Center, I returned to my room, slipped into a bathing suit, and went out to the beach in front of the Sheraton. Thank God the Chemical Girl, bedecked in that hot pink bikini and Vuarnet sunglasses, was seated comfortably in a sand chair next to the Deputy soaking up the rays. She hadn't died after all.

The Chemical Girl had an eye-stopping tan, but curiously no bathing suit tan lines. I discovered later that she frequently sunbathed nude in a tanning bed–yet another addiction. She also informed me that the intense heat of the beds often gave her orgasms and she was sorry when the tanning session ended.

She waved me over and for the next few hours, as the Chemical Girl and the Deputy sipped frozen strawberry daiquiris, we soaked up the sun, talking nonsense. She still hadn't asked my name or what I did, nor had she asked anything relevant of the Deputy who by now had fallen asleep.

Before long the Chemical Girl and I left the beach and went up to her room. We made love again, but this time slower and more sober–at least for me–and it was even better than before. She was the most sensual, sexual woman I had ever been with in my life. She paraded around in the nude with no inhibitions or embarrassment, as if she were wearing a parka.

She reminded me of a "Nexus Six," the ultimate synthetic replicate-android in the movie *Blade Runner.* The Nexus Six female in that film was specifically designed to please men, and it appeared to me that the Chemical Girl had been created for that same purpose.

Later that evening the Irish Chemical Girl and the Hispanic Deputy discussed the heredity factor of their drinking habits, while imbibing like it was the end of the world. I had developed a slight cough and tickle in my throat making it difficult for me to sleep, but I hardly noticed since the Chemical Girl kept me aroused again for hours that night.

The next day we sat on the beach until two in the afternoon before the Deputy and I departed for Salisbury. As we drove inland, I realized that I didn't even know how to reach the Chemical Girl. I wasn't even sure of her last name in spite of her incessant discourse about her early affairs, her work, her Oriental boss and his obsession with her, and a myriad of other innocuous topics.

Likewise, she didn't know my full name, occupation, or how to reach me. It appeared that our relationship was going to end up as just another quickie-resort sexual encounter. It was the kind you reminisce about when you get old, except that I was already old.

Reading my mind, the Deputy said, "I have a funny feeling you're going to see her again." And as we sped towards Salisbury State University to begin the second week of training for the drug and alcohol counselors in the Mid-Atlantic Region, I quietly hoped that the Deputy's prognostication would come true.

Chapter 2

Cᴏʟʟᴇɢᴇ Pᴀʀᴋ, Mᴀʀʏʟᴀɴᴅ
June 18-19, 1986

When he returned from Boston, two former teammates were waiting for Len Bias to join them for dinner, but the big guy said, "I have to go empty my lizard." He wanted to get laid, so he told his admiring buddies, "I'll be back. Wait for me."

The guys hung around waiting for him to return, but when Bias didn't show up, they went out to get some snacks.

After they got back to the dormitory, one went to sleep and the other talked to his girlfriend on the phone.

❑ ❑ ❑

"Let's party!" the big guy ordered, finally returning to the dorm with his main pal. Len Bias was their hero–whatever he said, these guys did.

After the teammates hauled some beer and cognac into the room, they settled around a huge mound of cocaine piled high on the table. It was extremely pure coke that didn't get any better. Some called it "dealer quality." Others called it "White Christmas."

How much the big guy had ingested earlier was anyone's guess, but the real partying was about to begin. Hours of instant gratification lay ahead, and no one would fall asleep despite the late hour.

Hit for hit, everyone began doing the coke. They bullshitted about Boston, sharing stories about what had happened there, and celebrating the big guy's success.

❑ ❑ ❑

At first they thought the big guy was joking around and faking convulsions. Then they realized he wasn't. The next few minutes became a nightmare of mass panic. Bias' main man was on the phone to his mom who had some nursing background. Someone called 911. A teammate was on the floor performing CPR on Bias as his terrified friends looked on in horror.

The powdery white cocaine mound disappeared even before the big guy died. While his friends took turns trying to resuscitate

Bias, the main man had packed up the coke. During the chaos, the cocaine found its way into the glove compartment of Bias' car.

While teammate Terry Long waited for a ride to the hospital, he began to clean up the room. It was not to hide evidence or obstruct justice; he was just nervous and congenitally neat. He took empty beer bottles and other trash out to the Dumpster, and by the time they left for the hospital Bias' room was spotless.

❏ ❏ ❏

Hours later an assistant basketball coach named Oliver Purnell received a call from head basketball coach Lefty Driesell who suggested, "Clean up the room." But Purnell never went to the room. He instinctively felt that it would be a bad move. It wouldn't have mattered anyway since the room was already clean.

❏ ❏ ❏

OCEAN CITY, MARYLAND
June 21-22, 1986

The Deputy's prediction proved accurate. The next weekend after driving from Salisbury to Ocean City, registering at the Sheraton, changing into our bathing suits, and walking out to the beach, there sat the Chemical Girl. She lifted herself halfway up from her sand chair and eagerly waved us over. To my delight, she too had returned.

Three hours later The Chemical Girl and I left the beach. For the next ten hours, from six p.m. until four a.m., the Chemical Girl and I made passionate love. Me to the tune of four orgasms; her, as usual, an insurmountable number.

I still had what now appeared to be an infection in my throat. I couldn't eat or sleep, and I was over forty and Jewish. To have one orgasm a week was okay, two a night was unbelievable, and four in one evening was pushing it to the outer limits. While mounted over the Chemical Girl, banging away for the fourth time that night, I conjured up some very ominous images. I thought, *Oh God, don't let me die coming this fourth time*. I could see the newspaper headlines: DRUG CHIEF FUCKED TO DEATH IN OCEAN CITY MOTEL. AUTOPSY REVEALS ABSOLUTELY NOTHING

LEFT IN HIS SYSTEM! Not a very good news story to follow Len Bias' death.

❑ ❑ ❑

The next day with the radio blaring, the Chemical Girl and I were lounging on the beach in our rented sand chairs, while the hung-over Deputy sprawled out on a beach towel. I told her that I only played FM radio in the summer. Listening to rock and roll was my way of rejuvenating.

Lamenting the past year with my separation, discontinuance of regular exercise, and the stress of the burgeoning drug and AIDS problems, I had a confession to make to the Chemical Girl. "I've gone from a fourteen- to a fifteen-and-a-half-inch neck size, from a thirty-one-inch to a thirty-three-inch waist size, and from six-feet-five-inches to five-feet-nine-inches tall." She laughed, noting my very average height.

Although it was only two in the afternoon, the Chemical Girl and the Deputy had each consumed a Bloody Mary, two draft beers, and a strawberry daiquiri for breakfast and lunch. They loved the way the intensity of the sun and the humidity amplified their noontime highs.

"Do you ever get high?" she teasingly asked me.

"No," I said matter-of-factly, "I'm more of a social drinker."

The Chemical Girl laughed. "No, I mean with drugs."

"Oh, not any more," I answered. "I tried just about everything years ago, but it was more out of curiosity. I don't like anything controlling my mind or me. Never did. And drugs do that, so it was actually more the risktaking, and…well…uh, I probably got laid over a hundred times in the early '60s just by hanging around druggers. Sex was the real lure to me back then. Fortunately, I didn't have the addictive disease."

"Gee," said the Chemical Girl sadly, "that's too bad."

❑ ❑ ❑

Ocean City's lifeguards were among the finest in the nation. Every other city block, from the old part of town for ten miles up the beach to the Delaware line, there were lifeguard stands.

Since the U.S. government established a Life Saving Service in Ocean City in 1878, strong, well-built men and athletic women have manned the beach, saving lives and enforcing beach ordinances. The job was demanding, but the perks were great. With the exception of sports and entertainment celebrities, no other profession attracted more groupies or beautiful women than lifeguarding.

In the summer of 1961, my old neighborhood buddy, Holt, and I were lifeguards for a brief stint; less than two weeks to be exact. A little deviousness on our part and a shortage of "a few good men" got us the job. A friend of Holt's named Casey Peters, a high-ranking member of the Beach Patrol, fixed it so we were hired without taking the grueling two-mile ocean swim test around the pier and the flag signal examination.

Back then, Ocean City's main beach scene was from the inlet across the Route 50 bridge into town to approximately 17th Street. Although the Boardwalk continued for about seventeen more blocks, not many people beached there or swam that far.

Unfortunately for Holt and me, we were given the lifeguard stands on 14th and 16th Streets where very few sunbathers, swimmers, or groupies congregated. It was also unfortunate for those who ventured into the ocean and drowned because we weren't paying attention. Holt was unable to watch anything because he was usually stoned out of his mind. I was quite nearsighted at the time and unaware of it, and there was no way I could see a head bobbing up and down or one which had gone under for the last time. And to make matters worse, we had no idea what the flag signals from the other lifeguard stands meant. On occasion Holt would get up and wave the flags as though he knew what he was signaling. God knows what he said.

We lived at the Modern Apartments on 1st Street across from the bridge that led into Ocean City. Coming across the Route 50 drawbridge was the only way to enter Ocean City at that time. Holt and I lived with seven other guys and one girl in an apartment that was too small for even three people. Although we worked different shifts, we all had to sleep at night, and it was very uncomfortable.

A week and a half into our job, during which time Holt showed up at his lifeguard stand about five or six days, and I showed up eight, we were summarily fired. But the lifeguard experience, which we embellished over the years, made us proud to have been members of the Beach Patrol; and part of the history of the Ocean City Life Saving Service.

Today, there are well over a hundred lifeguards working the

Ocean City beaches during the summer months. However, decades ago when the lifeguard Beach Patrol was organized, only six members were needed to oversee the bathers. Public bathing from the late 1800s until the 1930s was allowed only in front of the Life Saving Station.

Since very few people could actually swim by the turn of the century, bathers either held on to or were attached to ropes tied to the pilings of the Boardwalk. This was especially true for youngsters and women.

The pier was built over eighty years ago, and it was the first structure ever built into and over the ocean. Originally designed to have refreshment stands, a pool hall, and a dancing pavilion, the pier now housed more and more refreshment and game stands. The dance pavilion was still there, but the skating rink and other amusements like the movie theater were gone. These attractions had been a major plus to the resort in the early 1900s.

The Boardwalk, originally only two blocks long, was also constructed during the turn of the century. After the summer season, the boards were removed and stored until the next summer. Around 1912, the first permanent Boardwalk was created.

The Chemical Girl strolled the Boardwalk in Old Town toward the pier. Dressed in tight black jeans and a revealing white blouse, she was waiting for Backfin Molly, her cocaine connection at the shore. Molly earned her "Backfin" nickname by cleaning and eating steamed crabs faster than anyone else.

Backfin Molly was running her usual "a little late" as she drove recklessly toward the bridge into Ocean City. She lived in Snow Hill, the county seat of Worcester County, about twelve miles from the ocean.

The Chemical Girl waited patiently for Backfin Molly, knowing she had no other trustworthy source in town. She passed the old Fun House and stopped to read excerpts from the John Barth novel *Lost in the Fun House* on the outside wall. An attraction there formerly called "Laughing Sal," whom Barth had called "Fat May, The Laughing Lady" in his book, was in a state of disrepair now, although it used to attract millions of resort-goers. The Fat Lady would rock back on her heels and shake her Jell-O-like body around. Recorded laughter blaring louder and louder from a speaker brought people rushing over to gaze at her in the Fun House years and years before in Ocean City.

Finally, Backfin Molly arrived. She epitomized the legacy of the working women of Ocean City. Besides selling drugs during the day, she worked as a waitress at Philip's Seafood House in the evenings. She also sold real estate in the winter and rented many listings during the spring and summer.

Backfin Molly's lifelong role model was Ella Phillips Dennis, an old woman who built the Dennis House, a majestic hotel in Ocean City decades ago. Ella was a very strong-willed, outspoken woman who once proclaimed, "Ocean City is seventy percent built by women, run by women, and the men are all henpecked."

Backfin Molly had short curly hair, a rotund build, and stood almost six feet tall. Twice divorced, each marriage had produced two children and no child support.

The granny glasses she'd worn since the mid-'70s rested on her nose. Backfin Molly had a ring on every finger and an over-sized diver's watch on her right wrist. Her face was tan year-round, and she had the rosiest cheeks on the beach.

The Chemical Girl was three years Backfin Molly's junior and at least a head shorter. They could have been a big and little sister team as they strolled the Boardwalk. Every now and then they'd stop in a restaurant or a hotel restroom to snort cocaine, and from time to time, they'd have a beer at a side-street tavern.

The girls had met years before when the Chemical Girl worked the summer season in Ocean City before her senior year in high school. They were bussing tables at The Crab House on 23rd Street and Coastal Highway and were both fired for showing up stoned on the same night. Quaaludes were the rage back then, and the two young ladies had an insatiable appetite for drugs.

Later, the Chemical Girl moved in with Backfin Molly, who was going through her first divorce. Her kids were one and three at the time, and in return for babysitting the children, Backfin Molly gave the Chemical Girl free room, board, and drugs.

They'd maintained their friendship since the late '70s, except for a brief period in 1982 when Backfin Molly caught the Chemical Girl with her estranged second husband dancing at the Rusty Rudder in Dewey Beach one night.

"Sorry I'm late. Got caught at the drawbridge," said Backfin Molly. "By the way, I heard you've been running with a new boyfriend. You've been seen with him at Samantha's Nightclub, the Ocean Club, and the Paddock." She pulled out a one-by-two-inch piece of folded paper that contained cocaine. "It's a hundred and a half."

"Inflation up this month, huh?" asked the Chemical Girl. "And yeah, I did meet this older guy who's kinda nice and different in a good way."

"Look, girl," said Backfin Molly firmly. "Who you hang out with is your business, but I heard he's a narc…. This is much better shit; seventy-five percent pure!"

"He's not a narc," laughed the Chemical Girl. "He treats people or something like that…. Seventy-five percent what? Baking soda, mannitol, ephedrine? Please don't bullshit me."

"I swear," said Backfin Molly.

"Oh, right," said the Chemical Girl sarcastically. "It's different when you swear to it. I believe you now."

They both smiled and wandered over to the legendary Thrasher's stand to purchase some French fries.

"I went up to Harbor Place in Baltimore one time," said Backfin Molly, "to try the new Thrasher's, but the fries just weren't the same. I guess the ocean air, salt water, and maybe thirty years of grease buildup on the deep-frying baskets make the difference."

The Chemical Girl paid for a large cup of fries and poured vinegar, salt, and pepper over them, a traditional way to eat Thrasher's fries. She and Backfin Molly shared.

"How do ya know the guy's not a narc?" asked Backfin Molly.

"Because he swore it to me, Molly," the Chemical Girl joked. They giggled loudly, almost dropping their French fries.

❑ ❑ ❑

That evening, the police and ambulance lights flashed brightly across Coastal Highway as the Deputy and I approached 118th Street. We were returning to our hotel from a very late dinner at Nick Idoni's House of Ribs in North Ocean City when we saw the accident.

To the passengers of the car that initiated the chain reaction and to the victims who followed, it probably seemed like an eternity. However, the accident was over within eight or nine seconds, or less.

"Look at that guy hoppin' around out there. What the fuck is he doing?" exclaimed the Deputy.

I peered through the window and immediately recognized Tim Wood, the photo editor for the *Eastern Shore Gazette*. Tim had lost his leg when he was six years old in a bus accident and had lived the next thirty-some years with a prosthesis. He was not ashamed or embarrassed by being an amputee, and moved around with such ease and confidence that he was oblivious to the stares he often received.

Tim had made his "bones" as a photojournalist in the Middle East. During the hostage crisis, he was one of the few photographers allowed into Iran and Lebanon to photograph just about anything he wanted. To the Arabs, amputees are Allah's special children, and Tim was considered a saint in the Moslem world. When he returned from the assignment for the *Washington Post*, he resigned and moved to Ocean City.

Wood was busily snapping pictures of the accident scene as the Deputy pulled the car over to see what had happened. It was a revolting experience. I had trouble looking at the dead and injured, especially since we had just eaten. The sights and sounds of an accident chilled me to the bone, although I'd seen many. But to Tim it was business as usual. This was what he did for a living, and he did it well.

"Hey, Teddy-Boy!" yelled Tim, never removing his eye from the lens of the camera. "How's it going? What brings you down here this early in the season?"

"We're working at Salisbury State," I answered. "I usually see you up there. What's the matter? Are we bad news, small news, or no news?"

Tim shot every possible angle of the accident scene and then walked over to his Volvo station wagon with the Deputy and me in tow. I introduced him to the Deputy and a couple of nods and some brief remarks later, he had slid gracefully into the front seat, prosthesis and all. He told us he had to make a deadline and was off. I shouted to Tim that we were staying at the Sheraton, and he said he would give us a call if he had a chance. He wanted to catch up with me and see what was going on in the drug world.

❑ ❑ ❑

The phone was ringing extremely loud. Perhaps it was the alcohol, or the fact that the Deputy and I had only been asleep for a couple hours, but the sound was shocking. I lifted the receiver to stop the ringing and was about to throw it against the wall when I heard the distinct voice of Tim Wood.

"Ted. Good morning. How ya doing?" he said cheerfully in his New England accent.

"Tim, it's not a good morning. It's too early. What's up?"

"I've got something very interesting to talk to you about. Why don't I come over and catch a little breakfast with you and your deputy?" he asked.

"Tim, I hope you're talking four or five hours from now. It's quarter after five in the morning!" I pleaded.

Tim laughed. "Alright, I'll give you guys a break. I'll see you in about an hour in the dining room at the Sheraton."

The Deputy and I stumbled in to the hotel restaurant to meet Tim at our agreed-upon time. He was sitting at a table overlooking the beach watching the sun come up. It was a beautiful sight–the Atlantic Ocean, the white beach, and schools of dolphins leaping in and out of the water.

"There's no way I can sit here," said the Deputy. "The fuckin' sun will kill me. My eyes ain't open yet. I can't take this. Why do I have to be here? Wood, already I don't like you."

"Come on," I insisted in a whisper, "sit down. I'm sure you're going to find Tim very interesting and intriguing."

We sat down and looked over the menu as the waitress appeared with our desperately needed coffee. After some social amenities, Tim took out vivid photographs of the accident the night before.

"Oh no!" cried the Deputy. "How do you expect me to eat breakfast and look at these pictures? Are you fuckin' crazy?"

Tim laughed and scooped up the pictures. "It was just for shock effect, fellas," he began. "What I've got to tell you, I think you'll find fascinating. It will provide reinforcement for this program I hear you're trying to implement in Ocean City."

Tim spoke to us as if conducting a class. "It was a strange set of circumstances. When you consider what happened, you'd have to admit that everyone involved in this accident was purely random. They were there by chance. It started off with four drunken teenagers in a Jeep. 'June Bugs,' summer kids, speeding north on Coastal Highway up past the Carousel Hotel. Two people were crossing the street. The kids who were drinking and driving hit these two pedestrians, knocking them into the traffic traveling in the other direction on Coastal Highway. Then a couple of cars hit the pedestrians again, and they went flying. One car bounced up onto the curb in front of a bayside strip shopping center before hitting three other pedestrians.

"The four kids in the Jeep that veered out of control were killed along with two of the pedestrians. All told, there were thirteen injured and six killed. Now here's the kicker, guys. All nineteen people involved had a blood-alcohol level higher than the legal limit in this state, and some had drugs in their systems; this according to the docs in the hospital who took their blood samples."

"Whew!" bellowed the Deputy. "That's beyond random, man, and tough to believe! What were the ages of these people?"

Tim told us, and it was scary. "The teenagers in the car who were killed ranged in age from fifteen to nineteen. The two people hit crossing the street were a couple in their mid-fifties. Those were the six who died. As for the people involved who were driving the two cars on the opposite side of the street and the other unfortunate ones who were hit when the car went up on the sidewalk, the age range was from twenty-one to sixty-two."

"I find it hard to believe that *everyone* had either alcohol or drugs in their systems, Tim. Are you sure?" I asked.

Tim looked me straight in the eyes and said, "I'm not bullshittin' ya. I know the police and the doctors very well, and I'm telling you that's what happened. That's what the tests showed, and that's what you're dealing with."

The Deputy was impressed. "I agree with what he's saying, Ted. I think Tim's right. I mean, yeah, it's random, and yeah, it seems like a great coincidence, but let's face it. What do people come down here for? To relax, blow off some steam, and get high and wasted. It doesn't matter if it's legal or illegal. Besides the alcohol, some have prescription drugs they're abusing and shouldn't mix with alcohol, and many others have illicit drugs. Which again, you can't say is unusual in a playland resort like this one. I think this only reinforces the need for the COPYIR program. It gives us tremendous support. And as you know, I've been somewhat skeptical about the program."

The Deputy asked to look at the photos again. I guess his nausea had passed. As he sorted through them, he stopped and asked Tim what picture they were using for the front page of the newspaper.

"I think we're going to use this one," Tim said, pointing to the photo of the Jeep overturned on the sidewalk in front of the Carousel. You could make out most of the Carousel sign and the hotel in the background.

Tim continued, "I'm sure the owners of the Carousel aren't going to be too thrilled about the picture. They'll feel the public will perceive them as having something to do with the accident. That's how these places are. But that's my best photo shot of what happened."

"I was the house detective at the Carousel years ago," said the Deputy. "Back then when there was hardly any traffic out there, these kinds of accidents never occurred."

Surprised, I chirped in. "I never knew you worked at the Carousel. I thought you were a golf pro in North or South Carolina back in the '60s."

"I was," said the Deputy. "Hell, Ted, I did more than one or two things in my life; especially during the '60s. I ain't like you, just being in the dope field all my life. Variety is the spice of life, baby cakes. I've even got some law enforcement experience.

"After the army, I was a cop in Ocean City. Then, the following summer, I was a house dick at the Carousel with my dog as my sidekick. Don't you remember my dog? The real mean Doberman I had years and years ago? I've shown you pictures."

"Oh, yeah," I said. "The one you took with you after you got out of the army in Germany."

"Yeah," said the Deputy. "It was very rare for them to let you keep a dog that was part of the service."

"What kind of dog did you say it was?" asked Tim.

"A reddish-brown Doberman. I called him 'Red' and he was nasty as hell. He was always with me and I even rented him out on occasion.

"When I was house dick at the Carousel and all those developers were building lots of high-rises up and down Coastal Highway, I'd get a hundred extra bucks a week to rent Red out. We used to find that dog with swatches of bloody clothing in his mouth. Even found a finger once."

"That's disgusting," I said. "Here you're complaining about the accident pictures and now you're talking about something like that. Why don't you tell Tim what happened to Red?"

"Well," said the Deputy, "if you really want to discuss him. By the way, Tim, you're obviously not embarrassed by being an amputee. You're even wearing shorts so everybody can see your fake leg. You don't wear shorts in the winter, do ya?"

"No," said Tim amused.

"I'm an amputee too, but most folks don't know it," said the Deputy.

"Where?" Tim inquired. "Arms, legs?"

"Some people may not define me as an amputee, but I only have one ear," the Deputy said quietly.

I took over the conversation with Tim. "You see, he's always worn his hair very long and shaggy. I know it might look a little silly for a guy who's a bureaucrat to wear it…"

The Deputy broke in. "Hey, it was my ear, so I'll tell the story! Not you. What happened was this. I woke up early one morning with Red sleeping in bed with me. He was lying on my leg and as I tried to get up, I said, 'Red, come on, move. Get outta here!' I kind of kicked him, and he bared his teeth and started growling at me. I told him firmly, 'Don't you growl at me. Don't you do that.' I smacked him in the face and he gave me this quizzical look like 'Don't you ever do that again, motherfucker.' Then I felt bad and started to stroke him on his backside. Next thing I knew, he leaped up and snapped off my ear. Bit it clean off. I jumped up, grabbed my rifle, and shot Red right between the eyes."

"My God!" exclaimed Tim Wood. "What happened? Anyone hear it?"

"Yeah," said the Deputy. "My mom heard it. Wanted to know what was going on upstairs. Like there's a lot of gunfire usually going on in my bedroom. I mean, can you believe that? She simply asked what was going on instead of running upstairs to see. I yelled down to her that I had killed Red. Her only response was 'Tear down the shower curtain and throw it around the dog right away or else there'll be blood all over the place, and I'm not about to be scrubbing it up!'"

❑ ❑ ❑

COLLEGE PARK AND UPPER MARLBORO, MARYLAND
June 20–23, 1986

Rumors of illicit drug use by Len Bias surfaced immediately, but were denied by his teammates and University of Maryland officials. They said it would be totally out of character for Bias to use drugs. Besides, he was drug tested by several National Basketball Association teams.

Maryland basketball coach Lefty Driesell became the focal point of the news media.

On Sunday, June 22, a *Washington Post* article contained statements by the cardiologist who was called in by the emergency room physician at Leland Memorial Hospital. The cardiologist was the first to see Bias and allegedly confirm cocaine use.

Frustrated by a lack of cooperation by the University of Maryland at College Park, and fueled by continuous speculations of rampant drug abuse on the campus, the Prince George's County state's attorney impaneled a grand jury to look into Bias' death.

The state's attorney, in the middle of a close re-election campaign, targeted both the Maryland basketball coach and a mysterious friend of Bias', Brian Tribble, in the investigation.

❑ ❑ ❑

SALISBURY STATE UNIVERSITY
SALISBURY, MARYLAND
June 23, 1986

"I'd like to preface my remarks by reminding you that cocaine and coca are not magical elixirs that automatically transformed Charlie Chaplin into a ferocious fighter in the 1936 movie *Modern Times*, nor is it the monstrous evil that automatically transformed Sherlock Holmes into a paranoid psychotic in the 1976 movie *The Seven Percent Solution*. Rather it's simply a substance with certain chemical properties and behavioral ramifications. I don't believe that the images in the movies and elsewhere that we have of cocaine use are anything but reflective of the patterns of use in society, and the problems seem to be related more to the dosages and the patterns of use throughout history than to the nature of the drug itself."

I was giving one of my cocaine lectures on a myriad of issues, many of which I had "lifted" from my colleagues on the circuit, to several addictions counselors who had chosen my class from among three seminars offered four nights a week.

"Did you ever notice how druggers are always telling you that their cocaine is at least eighty to a hundred percent pure? Well, what's interesting is that cocaine hydrochloride, the crystallized substance you snort up your nose, can never be greater than eighty-seven percent pure. Thirteen percent *must* be the hydrochloride, which is the salt, not the cocaine. So you can never have any more than eighty-five to eighty-seven percent pure cocaine in a gram of coke. But all the users and dealers say, 'Oh, I know mine's a hundred percent.' If you ask them why they think that, they tell you, 'Well, I bought it from Eddie, and Eddie wouldn't lie.' Of course not.

"Very rarely does one see more than twelve to twenty percent pure cocaine in a gram or more. It's usually been 'stepped on, cut,' or diluted a number of times. On occasion, if an individual is making a big purchase, he might get what is called 'dealer quality' cocaine which is about seventy-five to eighty percent pure.

"One of the more undesirable effects of cocaine is that you can't turn your head to parallel park after you've been snorting it," I joked as I saw the Deputy walk in and take a seat in the back row. He'd heard the lecture before, and was only there to remind me that he was ready to go out drinking.

"Isn't it funny that you always know how much cocaine you've done because you usually do it all? There's no way to snort just a little and put it away. Cocaine breeds greed. You can't get your mind off of its very compelling allure. Let's say you did some cocaine and then you put the rest away in your room. The cocaine will call out to you to take more. So never be alone in a room with it.

"The comedian, George Carlin, used to say, 'A toot of coke makes you feel like a new man; but the problem is that the new man also wants a toot.'

"Coke is a sex drug, but that diminishes with the quantity ingested. There's usually only sexual arousal in low doses." *Christ*, I remembered, *not when it came to my old buddy, Holt.*

"There are basically five types of cocaine users: The *experimental* user who will use cocaine less than ten times; the *social-recreational* user who likes to share the drug and do it mainly at parties, and who represents eighty percent of the cocaine-using population in the United States; the *circumstantial-situational* user, who uses cocaine for performance–like a student who has to stay up to study, a lawyer who has to defend a lengthy case, or a housewife who has to perform a lot of household chores; the *intensified* user who uses the drug at least once a day for relief of a persistent disorder such as depression; and the *compulsive* user who is psychologically and physiologically dependent upon cocaine.

"The four stages of cocaine use are euphoria, dysphoria, paranoia, and cocaine psychosis.

"Around sixty percent of all cocaine addicts also have a history of alcoholism in their families...." My mind began drifting as I thought of the Chemical Girl and her family history of addiction.

❏ ❏ ❏

OCEAN CITY/SALISBURY/BALTIMORE, MARYLAND
June 24, 1986

Many University of Maryland current and ex-athletes worked in Ocean City. The jocks I spoke to right after Bias' death indicated that there was a lot of cocaine use among the basketball players, and that Bias was not the *innocent* the public wanted to believe. I decided to explore the drug trends at the University to find out more about just what the athletes were abusing. So, during an afternoon break from lecturing at Salisbury State, I drove back to Ocean City. I was also looking forward to a little time in the sun.

Prime sun time was from eleven in the morning until three in the afternoon, daylight savings time–a great way to get cancer on a good day! And since I planned to fool God and not die of a heart attack like most of my family had, cancer seemed the perfect way to avoid it.

On my way, I stopped by a payphone on Route 13 just outside of Snow Hill, Maryland to check my messages at my Baltimore office. I usually called four or five times a day, and I think the secretaries hated me for it. They thought I was actually checking on them. The receptionist advised me to contact my boss, the secretary of health, or her assistant as soon as possible. I was transferred to the assistant and told to drive back to Baltimore immediately to attend a two p.m. autopsy press conference on Len Bias. And, yes, it would reveal that Bias had died of a cocaine overdose.

I told the assistant I'd never make it to Baltimore by two p.m. even if I averaged ninety miles an hour. "Then fly up from the Salisbury Airport," she ordered, "but you damn well better be there!"

Some heavy soul-searching hit me when I reached the Route 50 intersection. If I turned right from Route 13, it would be toward the beach–sun, music, girls, and some well-deserved relaxation. If

I turned left, I'd have to drive like a madman to get to the airport before the last plane to Baltimore took off.

Aw, fuck it, I thought. *There'll be other sunny days.* I turned left and sped to the Salisbury-Wicomico Airport.

A thunderstorm struck just as the tiny aircraft took off, and I began to cough. It was that nagging cough that I had suffered with for a while. I felt certain that the plane was going to go down and cursed myself and the secretary's assistant for guilting me into making this trip for a seemingly foolish press conference.

The plane landed safely in Baltimore, but my cough was growing worse. Maybe it was a viral infection. I made a mental note to check it out when I returned to Salisbury for my evening lecture.

I reached the press conference at one-fifty p.m. It was being held at the University of Maryland's downtown Baltimore campus where the Law School, the School of Nursing, the School of Social Work, and the Medical School were located. My destination was a second floor conference room in the medical examiner's building. Autopsies were performed on the first floor.

As I entered the building, I realized I had a three-day growth of beard. I was also wearing dirty khakis, tennis shoes, a sport coat that I'd worn every summer for ten years, and a faded yellow cotton shirt. The security guards stopped me twice, thinking I was trying to crash the press conference.

The secretary of health's assistant approached me as I walked into the conference room, saying they had given me up for lost, but thanking me profusely for getting there, as if I had a choice. I was now coughing miserably, and I think the assistant felt sorry for me. I felt sorry for missing the beach time. It was ninety-five degrees and sunny when I left. The assistant sent me to the front of the room to sit with the medical examiner, who would soon shock the world with the news that Bias had died of a cocaine overdose.

Leonard Bias, All-American. Returning from a press conference in Boston as the Celtics' number-one draft pick, he had agreed to a big contract with Reebok, and was preparing to negotiate a multimillion-dollar deal with the Celtics to play alongside the great Larry Bird. Perhaps Len Bias would lead them to future National Basketball Association titles. The next day he was dead.

Wires were everywhere as I tightroped my way to the front of the press conference. I couldn't believe the number of television cameras, radio people with tape recorders, and reporters from newspapers and wire services. The noise was deafening with amplified media chatter. On my way to the front, several reporters shot dirty looks my way. They must have thought I was some jerk from a local news service.

I sat to the left of the podium where the medical examiner would brief the press. As I settled comfortably in my chair, a newsman asked me why I was there. I explained, "I run the Drug Abuse Administration for the State of Maryland. I was requested to be here in case there were questions concerning drugs–specifically cocaine."

He said he was with the *New York Times* and, puzzled by my appearance, asked, "So like you're a manager in the drug abuse field?"

"Yes," I coughed uncomfortably. "I'm not a typical bureaucrat. You find out a lot about drug trends and patterns by being on the street."

The reporter leaned forward and continued his questioning. "So you're on the street a lot?"

God, I thought, *I've been waiting for that question my entire career*. I turned to him and said, "No, I am the street!" I instantly regretted saying it. I must have sounded like an asshole. The *Times* reporter simply stared at me. I could have sworn he whispered "schmuck" under his breath.

He moved two seats away, saying, "I'll talk to you afterwards."

The medical examiner arrived at two-fifteen p.m. The public information officer informed me that there were over 130 members of the media, international television, radio, and newspapers there. "This is the biggest press conference ever held in the state. Bigger even than the one after George Wallace was shot," he said. "But don't get nervous."

I really wasn't worried. I kept looking at the sun coming through the windows and started sweating. The medical examiner, dressed in a three-piece suit and sporting a full beard, appeared to be cool. He had probably been downstairs performing autopsies in the cold rooms.

Somberly and dramatically, he announced to the press that Len Bias had died of a cocaine overdose. He explained in clinical and forensic terms how he had determined that Bias' death resulted from a lethal ingestion of cocaine.

As soon as he finished reading from his prepared statement, the medical examiner was inundated with questions from the media concerning the autopsy. The assembled newsmen and newswomen also began shouting out questions about cocaine and its pharmacological, psychological, physiological, moral, social, ethical, and legal aspects. This was not his area of expertise.

It was now my turn. The public information officer scurried me to the center of the table and I began a discourse on cocaine. After twenty-five minutes that seemed like hours, the medical examiner, public information officer, and I thanked the press.

It was a madhouse as news people raced to payphones and satellite hookups to get their stories out. Remembering that I had lost a full day of sun, I thought only of getting back to the beach.

The secretary's assistant thanked me profusely and ushered me into a taxi to the airport. I called the Deputy at Salisbury State University and informed him that I'd be there in time for my evening lecture. I asked him to try to locate a doctor to treat my sore throat.

As the plane took off, another thunderstorm began violently rocking the plane. To make matters worse, a twelve-year-old boy sitting behind me threw up on my back as we approached Salisbury Airport.

That night, radio and television were full of the news of Len Bias' shocking cocaine-related death. The Prince George's County state's attorney planned an investigation. The University of Maryland at College Park would go on public trial. It was a tragedy that the University would suffer because Len Bias had died there. Having had no experience with a crisis of such magnitude, the public relations department at the school failed to deal appropriately with the packs of reporters.

For the next few days, all that was heard on television and radio or read in the newspapers related to the Len Bias press conference, over and over again. I received telephone calls not only from around the country, but even from relatives traveling in Europe and Japan. They told me that they were appalled watching the international coverage with me looking like a disheveled bum. But my parents and other members of my family liked it. I'm sure, however, that my estranged wife hated it, having never liked my getting any attention.

❑ ❑ ❑

SALISBURY STATE COLLEGE
June 25, 1986

When I awoke the next morning I couldn't speak. I had the

worst sore throat I had ever experienced, and I was scheduled to talk to the media all day. Telephone calls from reporters poured in to Salisbury State where we were still conducting our counselor training. When informed that I had lost my voice, the reporters believed I was stonewalling them, or that I'd given an exclusive to someone else. They were furious.

One of the local addiction counselors and the Deputy drove me to a clinic called "Instant Care," where a group of incorporated doctors promised patients instant care. An hour and a half later I saw a physician's assistant. A real doctor finally examined me two hours after I'd passed through the Instant Care doors. He prescribed an antibiotic, recommended cough medicine, and told me not to talk. I tried to explain to him the importance of responding to reporters about Bias, but the doctor was already on his way to another examining room, providing more instant care.

It took a half hour to fill the prescriptions at the Instant Care Pharmacy next door. I went back to the university, canceled my lecture for the evening, and tried to rest. But I couldn't sleep.

Every time I dozed off for a few moments, I began to cough. After taking more of the recommended dosage of the antibiotic and cough syrup in an attempt to jolt my system, I became even sicker. Trying to recall who told me to do that in the first place, I later remembered the Chemical Girl had suggested it.

Chapter 3

The June Bugs had descended like a swarm upon Ocean City. They were high school graduates and college kids who came to work and play in that first month following the end of classes.

Although they hailed from numerous states, the majority lived in Maryland, and the predominant beach gossip concerned Len Bias' sudden death. A great number of students who attended the College Park campus professed to have known Bias well. Most lied.

Many were amazed that someone could actually die from cocaine. And while the Chemical Girl and I exchanged pleasantries and small-talk, the beach chairs and blankets close by debated cocaine use.

"I had these chest pains on a few occasions," said the nineteen-year-old sophomore from Washington, D.C., "and twice my buddies rushed me to the emergency room at Holy Cross Hospital in Silver Spring." He was albino looking with curly blond hair, but the sun had burned his body to a bright red, and zinc oxide dotted him from head to toe.

Sharing the albino's blanket were two male college friends and a dark-haired, well-tanned coed from Baltimore. She interrupted the albino. "I've had rapid heartbeats many times after doing coke, but I took some Valium and felt better right away."

The albino continued, "I knew Leonard pretty well. He was in one of my classes last year. This news makes me sick. Plus I'm a Celtic fan and…"

The pretty coed interrupted once again. "Ya know, I don't give a fuck about basketball or freaky drug deaths, and I don't really care if I die or not. I'm still gonna do cocaine!"

❑ ❑ ❑

Holt called to compliment on how I looked and spoke on national television after the Len Bias press conference.

"But don't think for a second that Bias' death will curtail the push to legalize drugs," insisted Holt. "It's all political. Hell, because of the archaic drug laws, I've been an outcast, a political prisoner…."

"And you're full of shit," I responded. "His death and the deaths of hundreds more would only be the tip of the iceberg if drugs were legalized."

Holt and I debated drug legalization, with neither of us giving an inch.

Usually his arguments dealt with the assumption that we'd lost the war on drugs, that doing away with the black market would drastically decrease the crime associated with drugs, that England's heroin maintenance program worked, and that marijuana was harmless.

Unfortunately, there has never truly been a *war* on drugs. World Wars I and II were wars. Korea was a conflict and Vietnam was a police action. The annual cost of the Vietnam police action was thirty-nine billion dollars. At this point, we'd never spent even a third of that on enforcement, treatment, prevention, and education combined.

In order to totally do away with the black market would mean to give drugs away twenty-four hours a day, seven days a week–and not just cocaine and heroin, but every other illicit drug. If not, there'd still be a need for the black market.

There are no blueprints defining the precise means by which legal distribution could be administered or paid for by those who support the legalization of illicit drugs. There would have to be strict quality control, assurances of adherence to approved dosage levels, not to mention extensive security to prevent diversion.

The need for funds for education, prevention, and treatment for abuse problems would be even greater. Medical care and welfare costs would likely increase, and law enforcement costs would remain high.

There would still be a black market associated with legally available drugs, especially if dosage limits or requirements such as treatment attendance were required. There already existed a significant problem associated with the diversion and abuse of legally prescribed drugs. It was difficult to envision a legal distribution system that could accommodate the powerful and addictive drugs that abusers found most appealing.

If one reviewed the history of the U.S., they would discover that between the 1880s and 1914 drugs were legal and regional problems were equated to anarchy. That was why the Harrison Narcotic Act was passed. When drugs such as heroin, cocaine, and marijuana were legally available in this country, it was the alarming spread of addiction that gave rise to initial regulatory controls.

The British experience with dispensing heroin to addicts was in fact a failure. The resulting tolerance, theft, and resale of heroin for profit created dramatic increases in addiction, especially among the young. It also became clear that physical complications and overdoses were not eliminated through free distribution.

And as for pot being referred to as harmless, disorientation and impairment of perception related to marijuana use often had devastating effects. Particularly vulnerable were adolescents who, in the process of forming stable personalities, had their critical thinking processes essentially turned off by its use. Marijuana impaired short-term memory, slowed the learning process, interfered with oral communication, and often caused temporary confusion and delirium. Enough research had been completed on marijuana to identify several serious health hazards, including lung infections, cellular damage with impaired immune responses, and negative effects on the reproductive system. It was inappropriate to label marijuana a "soft" drug, and the efforts towards its decriminalization were very misguided.

When I finished debating with Holt, his retort was always, "Fuck you, Ted. You're arguments are strictly political!"

❏ ❏ ❏

SAN FRANCISCO, CALIFORNIA
June 29, 1986

Don Rogers, a defensive back with the Cleveland Browns pro football team, died of a cocaine overdose just ten days after Bias' death. The news coverage was quick to speculate on the cause of death, and the autopsy results were analyzed even faster than usual. The public and the media weren't nearly as upset as they were over the Len Bias death.

Approximately 150 people nationally were killed by cocaine intoxication in the nine days between the deaths of Bias and Rogers. But no one would ever learn of these tragedies because the victims were not celebrities. They were just people who didn't know that as good as the coke made them feel, it was deadly.

Maryland's medical examiner compared data with the San Francisco medical examiner. He was informed that Rogers had suffered seizures and fell into a coma. His blood cocaine level was 5.2 milligrams per liter, less than Bias' level of 6.5.

❏ ❏ ❏

BALTIMORE, MARYLAND
STATE OFFICE COMPLEX

Belinda Gray burst into my office. "The rural health officers are balking at your memo to have mandatory AIDS training for all local health department staff, especially addictions personnel."

"Why?" I asked. The Deputy and I were in Baltimore for the day to catch up on our budget work and visit two inner-city drug clinics.

"Same old shit," she answered. "They're uncomfortable with anything dealing with sex and drugs. Words like homosexual, condoms, unsafe sex just blows them away."

Belinda headed up my Field Staff Division. She was a shapely, tall black woman in her late thirties. Headstrong and aggressive in her early years with the administration, she had mellowed somewhat. But in private, Belinda still spoke her mind.

"Are you going to cave in to them, Ted?" she challenged.

"No. This stuff's too fuckin' serious. Tell them to do it or else…"

"Or else what, Ted? They don't care what Central Office says."

"Yeah, you're right, Belinda. Put the word out to their managers that if the AIDS training doesn't go off as planned, I'm going to stop passing drug and alcohol funding through the health departments. I'll open it up to competitive bids. Not only will they not operate the programs, but they'll lose the indirect cost. And that'll kill them."

"Very good, Ted," she said as she walked out of my office. "We've been a little worried lately that you'd lost your balls…."

❏ ❏ ❏

The Deputy was out of the car in an instant. He loved to mix it up in confrontations and scuffles. At six-foot-two, tall for a Hispanic, he had long prematurely gray hair and a quarter-inch white beard. The Deputy was slightly overweight with a beer belly, but had well-defined muscular arms. Skipping three steps at a time, he reached the altercation outside the door of the Northeast Baltimore methadone clinic in seconds.

We were in "Beirut," the nickname the police gave the area around North and Greenmount Avenues. The place not only looked like downtown Lebanon, but the frequent gunfire was reminiscent of the Mideast powder keg.

I locked the car. Who wouldn't in this neighborhood? Cautiously I approached the hassle where two counselors were trying to keep Johnny Bop from entering the clinic. Johnny had pulled a knife and the Deputy was in the middle of the fracas.

"What's this about?" I demanded. "Johnny, put that knife away!"

Johnny Bop was a forty-five-year-old Jamaican heroin addict. He'd been on methadone for over fifteen years and had been thrown off all twelve programs, at least twice, that he had attended in the city. A convicted felon and very prone to violence, he was an amazing survivor, considering most narcotic addicts seldom live past forty.

"They shorted me on my dose again, Mr. Ted," he said in his clipped Caribbean accent. "I'm tired of it. I'm gonna kill that fuckin' dispensin' nurse!"

Johnny finally put his knife back into his hip pocket and tried to reenter the clinic. Reed, one of the counselors who was fed up with Johnny's antics, shoved him hard enough to cause him to fall backwards down the steps.

As I attempted to help him, Johnny got up shakily and screamed out, "You're dead, motherfucker!" He pulled out his knife again and without opening it threw it at the counselor. The counselor ducked as the closed weapon shattered the top portion of the glass door.

Johnny rushed the counselor and drove him through the remaining shards of glass in the door. The Deputy and I tried to subdue Johnny Bop. Glass and blood were everywhere as a police cruiser pulled up to investigate and ultimately arrest Johnny.

The program's medical director, Dr. Foreman, came out to check on everyone. Reed had suffered a cut on his leg and some abrasions. The other counselor, the Deputy, and I were covered with Johnny's blood. The doctor bandaged Reed's injuries and escorted us into his office.

"Wash the blood away immediately," he ordered. "Then I want to check each of you for open wounds."

"Why?" asked the Deputy.

"Because Johnny has AIDS-related complex, otherwise known as 'ARC,' and we can't be too careful."

Fortunately, no open wounds were found on the two counselors, me, or the Deputy.

"Christ," I mumbled to the Deputy as we were leaving, "if we're gonna die from AIDS, I can think of a lot of better ways of getting it than from a street-fight.

I was still having problems trying to convince numerous health officials, legislators, and the public at large of the efficacy of the controversial drug, methadone. Complaints abound that methadone maintenance was just another form of addiction, genocidal to blacks, and that the programs were a breeding ground for crime.

Advocates responded that methadone maintenance was a treatment and not a cure, that one could detoxify in twenty-one days any time they desired, that it was the most successful treatment modality for narcotic addicts, and that crime dramatically declined when patients were on methadone. And we questioned how it could be genocidal to blacks when two-thirds of the methadone patients in the U.S. were white.

After over twenty years, methadone was becoming the most studied drug in the history of mankind. When taken in the prescribed dosage, there were no physical or psychological side effects, regardless of how long one was on it. And now with AIDS and other needle-sharing diseases, including various strains of hepatitis, methadone's place was more crucial than ever. I stopped trying to convince the legislature of the health and humanitarian aspects of methadone treatment and played to their real concerns.

Unless elected officials were in recovery or had a significant other with an addictive disease, they viewed drug and alcohol addiction as willful misconduct. And when it concerned chemotherapy–opioid replacement or substitution therapy–like methadone, they were either outraged or skeptical. Forget that since the early '50s, addiction was recognized as a disease, and methadone had been the treatment of choice for narcotic addicts as early as 1963.

The heroin-addicted patient, not unlike an insulin-dependent diabetic in need of daily medication to relieve the suffering due to their medical condition, was forced to stand in line on an almost daily basis to receive his or her "medication." And only during a mandated time period, usually six a.m. to eleven a.m., could that medication be dispensed. How desperate must these individuals have been to suffer such indignities as their loss of privacy and subjection to unprecedented rules that perpetuated the stigma of narcotic addiction.

"How do these patients feel when they're on methadone?" asked an ultra-conservative senator from Western Maryland during a legislative budget hearing.

"It makes them feel good and gives them relief," I answered.

"Oh, that's not good," responded the senator.

Since crime and the economy impacted more on the senators' consciences and constituents, I cited a study indicating that crime days decreased by eighty-seven percent when heroin addicts were on methadone maintenance. Two Baltimore researchers, Dr. David Nurco and Dr. John Ball, as well as Temple University, had interviewed thousands of narcotic addicts in seven cities and found that heroin addicts committed crimes 287 days a year. However, when being treated with methadone, the crime days dropped to forty-seven.

That was enough positive information for most of the legislators, but I continued to explain the additional benefits. Addicts need a hundred dollars a day, 365 days a year, to support their habit. That requires stealing five to ten times the sum of money they would receive from the fences that purchase the addicts' stolen goods.

"Let's keep it simple," I'd tell the Senate Budget and Taxation Committee. "Three hundred sixty-five days times a hundred a day is roughly $36,000 a year to purchase their dope. Suppose we've got a sympathetic fence, a rarity, who is paying a third for the stolen merchandise. That isn't happening but it makes the math easier. Three times a hundred a day times 365 days is over $100,000 per addict. Now multiply that by the 65,000 narcotic addicts in Maryland."

"Jesus Christ!" exclaimed the committee chairman. "That's billions of dollars."

"Correct," I said. "And on methadone that number decreases by eighty-seven percent."

Case closed. My treatment budget was never cut, but every year I still had to defend it.

❑ ❑ ❑

The Deputy and I drove back to the Eastern Shore. We stopped at a traffic light after crossing the bridge into Cambridge, and a wasp and a bee flew in through the open driver's and passenger's windows. I didn't realize it until a minute or two later, so I screeched to a stop at a Roy Roger's and leaped out in panic.

"What the fuck are you doing?" yelled the Deputy. "Are you out of your mind?" He mumbled something in Spanish, obviously curse words, which he did only when he was disgusted with me. Born in Mexico, but raised in the U.S. from the age of six months, the Deputy had no accent and rarely spoke in his native tongue.

At this point, I was rummaging through the Dumpster in search of a piece of newspaper that I could roll up and use as a weapon.

After finding some, I ran back to the car.

"I'm gonna save our lives! Get out of the car! There's a wasp and a bee. I can't believe it. Two at one time. God knows what could happen to us!"

The Deputy was laughing as he casually stepped out of the car. "I'm only getting outta here," he said, "because you're gonna so enrage those insects that they *might* just sting us."

I danced around frantically for nearly twenty minutes dueling with my adversaries. Finally cornering the bee, I killed it, smashing it a dozen times to make sure it was dead. I used a small hand towel I had in the backseat to swat my victim out of the car.

The wasp was another story. I couldn't find it. Forty-five minutes passed, and the Deputy was becoming impatient and disturbed. "Enough already. Let's get in the car and get goin'. I'm sure the wasp will turn up later."

"But you don't understand," I explained. "I'm not gonna find the wasp. The wasp is gonna find me while I'm driving, and it's gonna sting me in the back of the neck or the jugular vein, and it's gonna fuckin' kill me. I gotta get my bee sting kit out of my toiletry bag in the trunk."

The Deputy grabbed the rolled newspaper from my hand and calmly sat down in the car. He swatted at the air, but the wasp did not emerge. Then, lo and behold, out of nowhere, it appeared, flying crazily, bouncing off the seats and the back window.

Finally, the Deputy swung as hard as he could with the newspaper, grazing the wasp's wing. Then he grabbed the towel, rolled his arm inside, and punched the wasp as hard as he could, shattering the car window and seriously wounding the wasp. Amazingly it was still alive when it hit the ground and attempted to crawl away. Without hesitation, I stomped on it several hundred times.

"Great work," I complimented. "I guess we can go now."

The Deputy had a puzzled look on his face. "Ted, you've got to cool it with the fuckin' bees and wasps. We just broke the window of a state-owned car and it looks like it's gonna rain. I think we need to find an auto glass store as soon as possible."

"*We* broke the glass?" I asked as we started to laugh.

❑ ❑ ❑

VIENNA, MARYLAND

Just outside of Vienna, Maryland the Deputy parked the car by an old shack about 200 feet from the road. He walked to a rickety porch where he was warmly greeted by an old black man.

"How the hell are ya, my man?" asked the Deputy. "Got anything for me?"

The black man slowly stood up from his broken-down rocking chair and walked into the shack with the Deputy in tow. An old sign on the side of the building in poorly-lettered black print read *Duck Decoys and Hunting Equipment*.

Five minutes later, the Deputy came out to the car and asked me for fifty dollars to buy a duck decoy.

"Why do you need another fuckin' decoy? You must have more than the allowable limit," I joked as I began to cough.

"Just loan me the fifty. This one's a rare find, and I've gotta have it," the Deputy insisted.

I loaned him the money, still coughing, and he went back inside the shack. He carried on with the old black man for a few more minutes before getting back in the car with a brown shopping bag.

"Ya know, Ted, I just bought what I think is an original Lem Ward for $400..."

"Wow!" I interrupted sarcastically. "You really think it's a Lem Ward?"

He laughed. "It's an investment, and I could probably sell it back in Baltimore for twice the money. But in time, it'll be worth three or four thousand dollars. As a matter of fact, for another hundred bucks, I'll give you a third interest in it."

"No thanks," I declined. "Just give me my fifty bucks back some day."

The Deputy was a collector of duck decoys and model trains. To him, they were investments, although in the dozen years that we'd been friends he had never sold one train or duck decoy. He must have invested between fifty and a hundred thousand dollars in the trains. The top floor of his garage was filled with elaborate train tracks, model train sets, and other related accessories. There were even more trains stored in several built-in closets on the first floor of his garage and some hidden in his house. Every Christmas, he'd invite the neighborhood kids over to see his model train displays, keeping them spellbound for hours.

The Deputy also collected wives and daughters. Although only forty-three years old, he'd been married three times and had six girls, two from each marriage.

Youngish looking and ruggedly handsome, the Deputy could have passed for a man in his early thirties. He possessed an infectious smile and was well-liked by both men and women.

Before becoming one of my deputy directors, he had a varied employment record. After a stint at the University of West Virginia on a baseball scholarship and a tour of duty in the army, he became an assistant golf pro, first in the Carolinas and then at a public link just outside Washington, D.C. in Bethesda. Two years later, he worked for local racetracks in Maryland, overseeing the parking lots. The salary was poor, but the tips were huge and probably went unreported. The Deputy worked the tracks full-time for six years and made enough money to purchase a big house, begin investing in and collecting his trains and duck decoys, and pay alimony and child support.

It seemed that the Deputy felt the need to get married every six years, and each failed marriage resulted in alimony and child support for a wife and two daughters. Although still married to his third wife, the relationship had grown extremely rocky and violent. She had a nasty temper that was further fueled by the Deputy's unacceptable late-night behavior.

Rarely would the Deputy go home before midnight when he was in town, usually parading in around four a.m. smelling of liquor and pussy. His spouse would explode every few months, pouring extremely hot water over his head as he laid sleeping, trashing six of his vintage Lionel trains, changing the door locks a number of times, or cutting the arms off of dozens of dress shirts, as well as the crotch areas of all of his dress pants. The results of their many confrontations over several years had left the Deputy with six KOs, and somehow, two more daughters.

There was also twelve-year-old Junior whom the Deputy called his son. Five years earlier, the Deputy had brought Junior home. Where the boy had come from was a mystery, but everyone speculated that he was the result of a tryst that the Deputy had engaged in long ago. The Deputy's current wife told me that Junior was the son of the second wife's neighbors who had been killed in a car accident. The boy had been living at the second wife's home because no relatives had come forward to care for Junior. A foster home was all that loomed in his future. The Deputy had been very friendly with the neighbors, and since he'd never had a son, decided to informally adopt Junior.

Whenever I stopped by their East Baltimore County home to pick up the Deputy, he would be driving Junior around in a sophisticated go-cart or "desert rat" as they referred to it, which he had bought for his son for Christmas for $2,000. The desert rat could reach speeds of almost fifty miles per hour.

As if all of this wasn't enough, the Deputy also had a collection of stray dogs, and when he or Junior drove the go-cart, the dogs would be freed from the yard to chase the desert rat. There were six dogs of varying size, pedigree, and temperament. They adored the Deputy and his family and were friendly to neighbors and strangers, except for one of his dogs and one visitor.

Justice was a big yellowish-brown mutt who resembled Old Yeller from the movie. But unlike Old Yeller, he could be vicious and was seldom let out of the yard. He had taken a terrible dislike to our friend, Ron Epstein, and would growl and snarl at him every time he visited the Deputy's home.

Ron loved to visit the Deputy, being a model train groupie who thought that the Deputy's collection was the ultimate. Ron had his own train set years before and never forgave his parents for selling it when he was a teenager.

Ron also worshipped the Deputy for his magical way with women. He marveled at the Deputy's ability to "wheel" women in bars, and loved to go out with him. Ron seldom scored with normal women and could only be assured of a sexual conquest by paying for it. The Deputy also impressed Ron with his drinking prowess, consuming incredible quantities of liquor without getting drunk. Ron got wasted from only two beers.

❏ ❏ ❏

ATLANTIC CITY, NEW JERSEY
July 4, 1986

Ron called me from Atlantic City where he was spending the Fourth of July weekend. "I'm staying in a nice suite at Resorts," said Ron. "The chick I'm with was comped by the casino because she's a bodybuilder in a competition here. She won the preliminaries last night and is in the finals this evening."

"Thought you were only into hookers," I remarked.

"Well, I am," said Ron. "I met this girl through some dyke

broad. She hustles other girls, but the bodybuilder, Alice, is her main squeeze. I pay on an 'as come' basis. Anyhow, since I came up here on the gambling bus from Baltimore, and the room and food is free, it's a wash. There's only one thing…"

"C'mon, Ron," I pried, "what's the problem?"

Ron was silent for a moment before confessing in a whisper, "She's a bedwetter. I woke up this morning in a sea of piss…. And I mean a huge sea of piss. I don't know how to deal with this. Do I confront her or what? She acted like nothing happened–just got up, showered, and carried on as usual."

"Hell, just talk to her about it or sleep on the sofa after she falls asleep. Anyway, what's she look like, Ron?"

"There's no sofa here, Ted. When I first met Alice two years ago, she was in her mid-twenties and much more feminine looking. But now, well, she's still cute, but…"

"Man," I laughed, "she's probably on steroids. How's the sex?"

"Great," said Ron. "Gotta run now. She's back."

Ron hung up quickly as Alice entered the bedroom of the suite. She removed her blouse and slacks, tossing them casually over a chair. Ignoring Ron, she went into the bathroom with a glass of orange juice and a handful of pills.

"What are they for?" asked Ron.

"To make me a winner," said Alice. "They're steroids and hormones."

"Aren't they dangerous?" asked Ron. "Won't they cause you to look like a man?"

"Listen, Ron," said Alice, "I've gotta get ready for the finals and I'm in a hurry. If you'll sit still and stay outta my way, I'll explain the ups and downs of steroids and bodybuilding."

Ron watched Alice remove her bra and panties. He thought about last night's sex–how strong she was, the tightness of her pussy, and the size of her clitoris. Her clit was so big it reminded him of a turkey neck.

"If I can finish in the top three today," said Alice hopefully, "I'll get a chance for some magazine work as a poser. And if I'm really lucky, I'll get to compete on ESPN. Someday, with the right agent, I may even be good enough to do an exercise video, all because of the steroids and my dedication. The steroids help to deplete some of the estrogen in my system, causing water loss between my skin and muscles, making the muscles become fuller and bigger. And the hormones make my bones grow. Got it?"

"Yeah," said Ron, "but what about the bad side effects?"

Alice was posing and flexing in the mirror. She opened several bottles of what looked like heavy oils.

"Side effects are what we call risks," said Alice. "There are always risks in anything if you want to succeed."

Alice slowly and seductively massaged the oils on the insides of her legs and around her buttocks, much to Ron's delight.

"Over the past year, I've noticed my jaws have gotten broader from the male hormone, testosterone. I have some hair growing on my face, my voice is a little deeper, and I stopped having my period. Oh yeah, and my clit has become much bigger, but I don't know if that's good or bad."

"What's that stuff you're putting on?" asked Ron, noticing how enormous her jaws had gotten since he'd first met her. It gave her a dog-face look, so he decided to call her Dogface Alice. But never in front of her.

"Dyo-derm," said Alice. "Perception is as important as the actual build. I use a tanning booth almost daily. This dye makes my skin even darker, and along with the baby oil, it accentuates the muscles and creates shadows. With the proper lighting, I look bigger and more muscular than I am. Shit, if I was a black woman, I'd look even better!"

"Uh…Alice…ya know there *is* another side effect," said Ron hesitantly.

"Yeah, what's that, Ron?"

"Well, uh, it's kinda awkward and difficult for me to discuss."

"Hey, babe," exclaimed Alice, "you're a whoremonger degenerate and I'm a pill-poppin', bisexual slut. What can't we discuss?"

"Okay," said Ron quietly, "it's your bedwetting. You didn't even acknowledge or apologize for it this morning. I thought you acted quite cavalier about it…."

"Hold on a minute, asshole," Alice retorted. "I'm not a bedwetter, and I don't know even what 'cavalier' means.

"Look, see this stuff I'm using? It's a very heavy-duty dye that clogs my pores and makes me sweat a lot in my sleep. When I wake up in the morning, I'm usually in a pool of dye-laced sweat which looks like urine, Ron. I'm sorry. I'm just used to it happening. But, hell, a degenerate like you, I'd figure you'd be turned on by the pee!"

❑ ❑ ❑

Ron was obsessive-compulsive and anal retentive–a bit fucked up to say the least. He smoked dozens of packs of cigarettes weekly, though never inhaling.

I advised him that he could still get cancer, referring to a Johns Hopkins School of Public Health study of pipe smokers who developed lip and tongue cancer. Ron said it was a bogus study and didn't apply to him.

He drank four beers every weeknight to wash down his salted peanuts and chunks of cheese. A cocaine, marijuana, stimulant, and barbiturate abuser; he insisted the drugs were only an enticement for his prostitutes. His weekend nights were spent prowling for hookers on Baltimore's infamous Block and on South Broadway near the Inner Harbor. On these nights, he easily consumed over a dozen or more beers with the degenerates downtown.

In all the years I'd known him, I never saw Ron exercise or do anything healthy for himself. I warned him about the toll that his lifestyle would take on his body, but he ignored me and continued his deadly obsessions. Every year he'd have a physical and the result would sicken me. Like my friend Holt, Ron's cholesterol level was under 150, his blood pressure was 110 over 70, and his heart rate was that of a teenage athlete. He could've been an astronaut, except he was too old and was afraid of heights.

As careful as I tried to be with my health, I was on blood pressure medication, had a rapid heartbeat, and a cholesterol level of 270. I wanted to give up on many occasions.

Ron made others around him uneasy and nervous. He had married a cute, petite young lady named Lorna from the Washington, D.C. suburbs in the early '70s whom he'd only known for several months. Within a year of the marriage, Lorna developed agoraphobia, the fear of leaving one's house. Ron really didn't care since it gave him more freedom to run around. He had grown bored with Lorna only months after their wedding. He could not enjoy sex with the same woman day after day. Compassion on his part was rare and he refused to hug anyone–especially after sex.

Before long, Ron felt that Lorna needed to work or at least shop for groceries. The agoraphobia was costing him too much time and money, so he had a psychiatrist visit her regularly to no avail.

Shortly before their breakup, Ron convinced me to help him attempt to shock Lorna into recovering. Devising a plan to trick her into leaving the house, he figured once she was out the front door, it would be easy to keep her from going back in.

The plan was to have two of our friends dressed as utility company employees come to the house as Ron was about to leave for work. The men were to warn them of a nearby underground gas leak and insist on their immediate evacuation. I was to stop by while this was happening to drive Ron to work, and together we would keep Lorna out of the house.

The plan worked well initially. The fake utility guys came and nearly forcibly put Ron and Lorna out on the street. Then I arrived to hustle them into my car. Lorna was numb with shock and seemed okay until she began to step into my idling 1970 Datsun station wagon.

Suddenly Lorna panicked and began to run back to the safety of her house. Ron grabbed her, but she escaped. I jumped out of the car and tackled her on the front lawn. She started kicking and punching at my arms and face until I lost my hold, so Ron pounced on her.

The fake utility workers were still on the porch laughing and cheering us on. Lorna finally realized it was a hoax. At this point she was screaming, kicking, and biting as we called to the guys for backup.

Lorna broke loose again, her overcoat covering her nightgown falling away. She ran toward the back of the house to avoid the fake utility men blocking the front door.

The yelling and screaming increased. It was seven-thirty in the morning and kids were on their way to school while neighbors left for work. The scene was unbelievable. Although Lorna succeeded in retreating to the back door, it was locked. Dodging Ron and me, she headed back around to the front of the house. Concerned neighbors began calling out about what was going on, and some even came over to watch.

Lorna's nightgown got caught on something and was suddenly ripped away. She crawled, screamed, and stumbled her way to the front porch and finally entered the house, by now totally nude. Once inside, she quickly bolted the front door.

Ron stayed away for the next several days. When he finally returned, he discussed divorce with Lorna who insisted on keeping the house. Her parents were wealthy and more than happy to help her. She didn't want alimony or anything to do with Ron ever again.

Years passed, but Lorna never again ventured outside the house; not even to get the newspaper from the front steps. She used a metal coat hanger to hook the paper like a fish.

OCEAN CITY, MARYLAND
July, 1986

At breakfast in the Sheraton Hotel's dining room overlooking the beach, the Deputy and I shared the local newspapers.

"Says here," I began, pointing to a front page article, "that 335,000 people were in Ocean City over the Fourth of July weekend. Did it seem that crowded to you?"

"Hell," said the Deputy, "traffic is always a nightmare here in the summer. And where they get these crowd estimates from is probably the same place you come up with your figures for the number of addicts in Maryland."

"Don't be a smartass," I countered. "My numbers are the reason we are awarded such a substantial amount of federal money. You know the feds formula for treatment dollars is tied to the population data for the addicts."

The Ocean City mayor, who had been having breakfast with the Sheraton's owner, approached our table. "How's the new program going, boys? You're not gonna make any waves, right? No pun intended."

"No sir, Mayor," the Deputy responded. "As a matter of fact, I was just comparing your holiday crowd guesstimates with Ted's number of state addicts, and I can't figure out who's a bigger bullshitter."

The mayor sat down and smiled. "Ted's a way bigger bullshitter. Our numbers are within ten percent and represent demo flush figures. Your agency comes up with seat-of-the-pants stuff."

Demo flush figures were gleaned through an intricate formula derived from the amount of sewage that ran through Ocean City's wastewater treatment plant. The sewage consisted of every toilet flushed, shower taken, load of laundry done, and sink of dinner dishes washed. It was then divided by a number based on an average of gallons of water used by a beachgoer in a twenty-four-hour period. Very complicated.

The formula was developed in 1972 when the town fathers needed to come up with genuine population estimates to justify building an Ocean City hospital. Counting cars passing over the Bay Bridge and monitoring hotel occupancy rates didn't suffice. So two local doctors developed a formula based on the length of the sewer system, the diameter of the pipes, the difference between overnight and day visitors, and a number of other variables.

"I won't argue your assessment of Ted's figures," said the Deputy, "but I've got some questions about this demo flush formula."

"Fire away," said the mayor confidently.

"Okay," the Deputy began, "suppose you drank too much, you've got diarrhea, or you don't shower. Say you pee in the ocean, you're constipated, or you've got a weak bladder…"

Cutting him off, the mayor laughed. "Enough. It's all factored in. Now, Ted, let me ask you how on earth you come up with your estimates on the number of addicts in the state of Maryland?"

"We use an extrapolation of treatment data, arrest records, and emergency room statistics for our incidence and prevalence study every four years. And we conduct a school survey of sixth, eighth, tenth, and twelfth graders every two years."

"But, Ted," asked the mayor, "I read where you say that addicts are world-class liars, so how can you determine who's telling the truth?"

"We factor it in the formula," I said with a smile.

"How do you differentiate social and recreational users from addicts?" asked the mayor.

"It's a simplified definition taken from a long explanation of addiction. Basically, to be defined as an addict you have to meet three criteria: obsessive-compulsive behavior, inability to stop using, and continued use in the face of danger and/or adverse conditions. It applies to any form of addiction—drugs, alcohol, eating, gambling, smoking, shopping, exercise, sex…you name it. The longer definition was developed by Dr. David Smith of the Haight-Ashbury Free Medical Clinic in San Francisco."

"Who's he?" the mayor asked.

"In the late '60s, fresh out of medical school, Dr. Smith went into the streets to treat drug abusers and alcoholics for free, in spite of the fact that the California Medical Society threatened to revoke his license. He set up a clinic, conducted research, and became one of the top experts in the world on treating addicts."

"Teddy," the mayor joked, "you need the demo flush to deal with all your bullshit extrapolations. Gotta go, boys."

Chapter 4

My nagging cough continued. Although the doctor changed the antibiotic, I wasn't getting better and I couldn't sleep or eat very well. However, it didn't hinder my sexual performance with the Chemical Girl at the beach on weekends.

As time passed, I began to lose weight. My first thought was that I had AIDS, and the second, cancer. Third, I figured a possible pending nervous breakdown. Then I decided not to think at all.

Around my third or fourth week spending time with the Chemical Girl, I discovered that she tended to be a tad selfish. We had gone out to dinner, and by the time the food arrived, I had no appetite at all and suggested that we take a walk on the Boardwalk to get some fresh ocean air. I had become almost delirious from the cough and a combination of self-prescribed cough medicine, antibiotics, and a little too much alcohol. For a moment, I thought I was going to pass out and felt extremely nauseous. I tried to remain calm, but realized there was no way I was going to make it through an evening out.

We drove back to the Sheraton and, still feeling very ill, I told the Chemical Girl that she was on her own. She became agitated and upset, and viewed the fact that I was sick and wanted to be alone as rejection.

"Look," she said firmly, "if you want to off me, just tell me. Don't lead me on and don't fuck with me. I've been through all that before."

I tried to explain to her that I was truly under the weather. I even gave her money for taxis and drinks, but she was still upset. I begged her to just let me go to my room and rest, promising sex later that night regardless of how I felt. I also reminded her that I liked her company a whole lot. Reluctantly and in a huff, she left, getting the hotel van to drop her off at Samantha's Nightclub.

Around two-thirty in the morning, the Chemical Girl reappeared. Her sensual movement and alluring scent created such an amorous atmosphere that I almost stopped breathing–but my cough managed to kill the moment. As sick as I was, I knew I'd have to perform for her or she would feel rejected once again. So we made love for the next couple hours, and the delirium and nausea disappeared, replaced by my heightened and desperate attraction to the Chemical Girl.

The next morning at breakfast, I questioned her about her insecurity and feelings of rejection, explaining again that I was honestly extremely sick. She told me that she had engaged in a number of affairs with men who would react in a similar way when they were about to break off the relationship. She was afraid the same thing was happening with me. I was glad to hear that she considered us a relationship because she was so sensuous, so vulnerable, so…chemical that I wanted to keep this liaison going on for as long as possible.

❏ ❏ ❏

The Chemical Girl worked for a very mysterious Eurasian entrepreneur named Arthur Lo Ming. He was born in Singapore to a father from Shanghai and a former English nun from Liverpool. His family moved to Hong Kong, and in the early '50s relocated to America, settling in Baltimore.

The family owned a small Chinese carry-out in a predominantly Jewish neighborhood. They sent their son, Arthur, to the finest public schools in the city and later to a very prestigious private Catholic college. He received his bachelor's degree in 1962 and attended graduate school at a small state university where he attained a master's degree in business administration.

Lo Ming was five-feet-ten-inches tall with jet-black hair and yellow-tinged skin. There was only a minor slant to his eyes and very little of Lo Ming's appearance and character were Asian.

He was soon hired by a bank in Baltimore as a minority recruit. The quite racist bank's owners loved to proudly boast that they followed the rules and hired minority employees–the minority employees being only Arthur Lo Ming. They lavished praise upon him and assisted his rise up the corporate ladder to success.

Lo Ming found his niche in the banking industry and devoured any information he could find about it. He learned from the bigwigs how to put major banking deals together, and soon devised a way to siphon funds from the bank. After five years, he left with quite a nest egg tucked away. His crimes were never discovered.

From there, Lo Ming began an import-export business, traveling extensively around the world forming syndications to fund many remarkable deals. He was the consummate middleman with an income anywhere from one to three million dollars a year. There were times, however, when some of the deals failed and he lived on a shoestring budget for months before a new and usually clever deal revived him. Somehow, he was always able to keep his head above water in spite of living quite lavishly and very over his head. He loved to spend, purchasing only the finest objects, and abhorred anything discounted. By this time, Lo Ming, ashamed of his middle-class family, had pretty much kissed them off.

Fresh out of high school at sixteen, the Chemical Girl went to work for Lo Ming in one of his six offices spread strategically throughout the Baltimore-Washington region. After a couple years, she became the general manager of all of Lo Ming's holdings, traveling the world over, far beyond her wildest dreams.

To the Chemical Girl's credit, she had put together some of the more successful of Lo Ming's business ventures. She had an uncanny ability to work with men, regardless of where they were from–the Third World, the Orient, and even the Middle East where most men frowned upon working women. She was able to communicate positively and effectively with these people and to inspire their integrity, loyalty, and respect. The Chemical Girl was the ultimate manipulator.

By the mid '80s, however, Lo Ming's businesses had started to falter. Unsuccessful venture followed unsuccessful venture, and by the time I met the Chemical Girl, she never knew if she was even going to get paid.

She explained that this had happened before, but he always seemed to rebound. "It hasn't been this bad for three years, though, and the businesses and Lo Ming are in serious debt. I spend my days on the phone placating Lo Ming's creditors from all around the world. They have faith in the fact that I'm still working with him, and it seems to keep them from going after him legally."

Aside from their working relationship, Lo Ming was madly in love with the Chemical Girl, but was not particularly romantic. Very direct and brutally obnoxious, the Chemical Girl was forever fighting off his crude attempts at affection, and was somehow able to control him. He often shared drugs with her, thinking they would entice her into bed with him. Unfortunately, when he was close to "capturing" the Chemical Girl, he passed out.

The Chemical Girl was still a virtual captive of Lo Ming. She lived from paycheck to paycheck, squandering all of her savings on drugs and a lavish lifestyle. She desperately needed Lo Ming's handouts.

❏ ❏ ❏

Lo Ming was known as a "player." Having traveled extensively around the world and befriending many high government officials in Third World countries, he was a broker who profited from deals involving selling goods from one country to another. Lo Ming middled wheat deals between the Saudis and the United States, packaged deals for toilet seats made in Japan and sold to the United States, and brokered fertilizer shipped to Red China from Argentina.

Most deals were consummated over the phone by Lo Ming or the Chemical Girl. Due to the negative attitude toward women in many of these countries, the Chemical Girl could only speak to specific people or deliver messages. Almost every phone call required a bribe with payoffs to bankers and government officials in other nations.

Seldom were any shipments made after the first payoff. It was only following secondary and tertiary payoffs that goods would be shipped, and that was not even always the case.

If the fertilizer from Argentina cost $50,000 and was sold to China for $250,000, Lo Ming would make about $200,000. But the amount of the payoffs would ultimately reduce the profit he made; not to mention that if he made three million dollars a year, he somehow managed to spend six.

Lo Ming had been very lucky meeting the right people, whom he usually easily impressed. And he was also fortunate to have the Chemical Girl working with him. However, his luck, but not his spending habits, was changing rapidly.

❑ ❑ ❑

Unlike the Chemical Girl, Lo Ming had no concept of cocaine quality. When he wasn't in the office, which was most of the time, the Chemical Girl would replace the mounds of cocaine in Lo Ming's stash with vitamin B-12 powder. When the stash became low and there were no typical adulterants to use, the Chemical Girl improvised by crushing up Tylenol tablets and watching Lo Ming snort them up his nose.

"I only do this stuff because of you," Lo Ming would say from time to time. "I spend $2,000 or more an ounce on your dope and you don't seem to appreciate me! I think I'll have to exclude you from our next trip!"

Lo Ming consistently punished the Chemical Girl by threatening her with no more travel, but she didn't care. Other forms of punishment included his constant interrogation of her expenditures from checking accounts on which she was a signatory, not buying her extravagant three-hour lunches, discontinuing her "pin" money, or making her actually work a portion of the day–his version of Chinese water torture.

After a couple of days, Lo Ming would apologize to the Chemical Girl, going so far as to promise to be circumcised and even find a way to grow body hair for her. He bought the hair-growth product minoxidil in Hong Kong since it was not FDA approved in the states at the time. He stripped in front of her at the office, pouring it over his body.

Not impressed, the Chemical Girl simply laughed, telling him, "Pour it on your cock and maybe it'll grow."

❏ ❏ ❏

OCEAN CITY, MARYLAND
July, 1986

My lovemaking sessions with the Chemical Girl were always lengthy. She was impressed and questioned how I could last so long.

"Most men," she said, "whether they're fifteen or fifty, come too fast. How do you do it? Do you beat off before you see me?"

"I just enjoy pleasing women, especially you," I lied. Embarrassed that my estranged wife had taught me how to extend the sex act, I certainly wasn't going to tell the Chemical Girl.

❏ ❏ ❏

My wife Candy was originally from Texas, and her lineage extended back to the defenders of the Alamo. Candy's granddad was a former wildcatter and had made it big in the oil business. He gave her a substantial trust fund to live on, allowing her to choose any career that made her happy. She had beautiful, wavy dark hair; big, round brown eyes; full rosy lips; and a body that defied description. She was five-feet-seven and weighed 133 pounds, and was so firm and well proportioned that she appeared fifteen pounds lighter. "Awesome" was an understatement. She was so taut that if she stood in the eye of a hurricane, absolutely nothing would move.

She attended the University of Texas in Austin where she quickly became the head cheerleader and won the title of "Miss U.T." In her sophomore year, she fell in love with the captain of the University of Alabama football team and transferred there for her final two years of college. Within a year, she had become head cheerleader at Alabama, too.

Candy also received an education in alcohol and drugs in college, and could drink most men under the table. Through her football connections, she was introduced to a wide variety of stimulants. Initially, the players used them only during games, but soon progressed to using them at practice just for fun. The pills made Candy and the athletes feel "up," and the alcohol brought them down when they became too up.

After graduating, Candy returned to her home in Houston where she went to work for a major real estate developer. In the early '70s, she moved and accepted a temporary assignment in Columbia, a new town in Howard County, Maryland. She never returned to Texas or the football captain. Bored with the monotony of the business world, Candy moved to Anne Arundel County, Maryland and joined the police force.

I met her while she was training to be a police officer. She was standing at the bar in a popular Baltimore disco called "Girard's," wearing a green mini-dress and the highest heels I'd ever seen. They made her legs look beyond belief. A stilt-walker couldn't have gotten around in those heels, but she whirled around like she was barefoot. We hit it off quickly, dancing until the place closed, and drove to her apartment in Annapolis.

Although the eighty-mile roundtrip to her place was geographically undesirable, just to be seated near her was worth driving to Canada blindfolded. I wasn't exactly sure that I would get down with Candy, but I didn't care. Her aura was intoxicating. After she kissed me a couple times in the car and pressed her body against mine in the elevator leading up to her apartment, I was confident that one of us would have an orgasm before the night folded.

I cursed myself bitterly for not drinking more. It seemed that a lot of alcohol made me last longer. As soon as we entered her apartment, I asked to use the bathroom, also believing that relieving myself would make me hold out longer.

When I walked into her bedroom, Candy was naked on top of the bedspread with her legs tucked under her, sitting on her ankles. I was still wearing my new suit and dress shirt. As I sat down on the edge of the bed, she suddenly threw me down and started kissing my face and neck while my hands hungrily explored her legs, buttocks, and breasts.

I knew I was in deep trouble. There was no way I wasn't going to ejaculate fast. Real fast. I feared that I would "pop my nut" before I even undressed.

I leaped up, tearing off my clothes, trying to think bad and innocuous thoughts so as not to come too quickly. I pinned Candy down and kissed and licked her everywhere, praying that she wouldn't touch my overly engorged prick. If she did, I would be "Ejaculation-ville." Just when I thought I was in control, my mouth found her pussy, which had been shaved cleanly to my surprise and delight. My tongue explored every crevice. I gasped for air only occasionally, knowing that if my prick just grazed the sheets, I'd be history. Never had I been so excited.

I tried thinking of things unrelated to sex to distract my mind and prolong the experience–my parents, lacrosse, being chased by bullies in junior high school. Nothing worked.

I decided it was now or never and swiftly entered Candy. Fifteen seconds later, maybe ten, I was finished. I tried to hang in there, hoping she hadn't felt me come, and thinking that maybe I could resurrect the hard-on. But it wasn't happening. Even worse, I got soft so quickly my dick slid right out of her.

Humiliated, I managed a smile. "Go get me a towel, stud!" she said sarcastically, and continued to tease as I tried to speak. "Nice self-control."

As I began to conjure up an excuse, she started laughing and dashed quickly to the bathroom.

When Candy returned, she comforted me. "Ted, you have the tools, the attitude, and the knowledge. All we need to do is practice technique and mental control. C'mon, let's practice for a while."

A year later, we were married–and we practiced for a couple more years.

Candy worked long and erratic hours as a policewoman, and there was nothing better than fucking a woman in uniform. She climbed the ladder of success rapidly, soon rising to detective. So athletic and skilled was Candy that she awed her fellow officers, even becoming the sharpshooting champion of the county. I joined her in her exercise regimen just to keep up with her from a physical standpoint.

By the end of the '70s, Candy, having had enough of law enforcement quit the police force and opened a string of fitness centers, enjoying immediate success. Our life together, however, was not enjoying the same degree of success.

❑ ❑ ❑

LAS VEGAS/BALTIMORE/THE CATSKILLS/BALTIMORE
February 1983-August 1985

We had been married for over eight years and the first three years were okay. The last few weren't very smooth. Fortunately, we never had children, most likely because we were both too selfish.

Candy was a controlling individual whose career and lifestyle *always* came first. Mine was merely an afterthought, but I didn't mind so much because I had a tremendous amount of freedom for a married guy. Sure, it was like being a bird in a gilded cage, but it was a great type of freedom, nonetheless.

Traveling extensively, Candy worked long hours. As long as I was there when she came home or I called in from wherever I was, everything was fine. But Candy didn't reciprocate. She would call in once a week when she was away and seldom called from her office. It was basically her show, but I didn't really mind being a part of it. Naturally in the small community where we lived, there were rumors about Candy, but there were always rumors about the pretty women. Some false and some, well....

I, however, remained one of her greatest supporters. But to her, my interests were secondary, tertiary, or probably less. So after a few years, I became disenchanted with the marriage. I knew that leaving the relationship would definitely cause me a great deal of grief. Instead, I became involved in a number of liaisons, trysts, affairs, and quickies–more quickies than anything–and convinced myself that it was the best of both worlds.

Although I wasn't proud of myself, I didn't feel all that bad either. I wasn't sad, nor was I as happy as I thought I should have been. But I let the marriage continue. It was only during verbal and sometimes violent confrontations with Candy that the thought of separation or divorce entered my mind; although I did often lay awake at night, semi-dreaming about being free and not answering to anyone.

I did leave on a few occasions, but they were brief and usually followed an argument. The first time I split was the day before I was to attend my older brother, Phillip's, third wedding. He'd moved to Las Vegas and was marrying a "change girl," a woman who provided change in a casino to the people who played the slot machines. My cousin, Mason, and I were to fly out the next morning. The previous night Candy and I had a huge argument over whose turn it was to clean the kitty litter box. Since we had four cats, this was an issue which sparked many arguments throughout our married life.

One thing led to another, and I stormed out of the house telling her I was never coming back. I didn't really know where to go, so I drove to a Holiday Inn parking lot and slept in the car. I was wearing a sweatshirt, sweatpants, a jacket, and tennis shoes with no socks. Fortunately, I had remembered my wallet.

The next morning I picked up my cousin and we drove to the airport. He didn't seem to suspect anything, but he did find it odd that I wasn't too upset when I opened the trunk and calmly lied, "My goodness, I must have left my luggage at the house. I'll just borrow some of my brother's clothes."

On the flight out, we had a number of personal discussions, one centering on his divorce that had taken ten grueling years to finalize. Although I had never before discussed my rocky relationship with Candy, I could no longer hold back after hearing Cousin Mason's story. I told him about the previous night's argument, and admitted I had run out without packing. He laughed for the rest of the flight.

Family from all over the country was in attendance for Phillip's wedding. There was a prerehearsal and rehearsal dinner planned before the wedding ceremony, a Friday through Sunday affair.

I pleaded with my cousin to keep my problem a secret, and I told my parents, also in attendance, that I had forgotten my suitcase. Much to my chagrin, I discovered that Candy had hysterically called Las Vegas, informing everyone that I had not returned home the night before. I was then forced to tell my family about the argument. Naturally they sided with me, taking me out and buying me clothes. I probably enjoyed the wedding more than my brother since I ended up receiving more attention than he did.

The second time I left home was after Candy returned sooner than expected from a trip to New York. I had gone to the grand opening of a friend's bar and didn't get home until three o'clock in the morning. My wife, neither mannerly nor warmly, blurted out, "Where have you been and who have you been with, you son-of-a-bitch?!" That was one of the nicest things she said all night.

When I tried to explain for a change that I was innocent, she wouldn't hear from it. She grabbed my suit jacket, ripping the pocket which held my glasses and intentionally breaking them. In the struggle to retrieve what was left of my glasses, she inadvertently, or probably purposely, cut my hands with the broken glass, and also sliced the side of my cheek. I wrestled her to the ground and tried to hold her down, but she was too strong. An ex-cop and a great jock, there was no way I could restrain Candy in any kind of fair fight unless I really hit her. Since I would never punch a woman, I knew that the best thing for me to do was to pull her hair and run out of the house, which over time, I became quite adept at.

Grabbing my now lensless glasses, I raced down the steps to the driveway, jumped into my car, and drove away as she pursued me and punched the side of the car.

A decent athlete at one time, I no longer kept myself in the kind of shape necessary to outdistance or outfight my wife unless I dealt with her as I would a male adversary. And then it would have been close.

I stayed out that night in the same parking lot at the Holiday Inn and decided that sleeping in cars certainly wasn't my cup of tea. However, adamant about not going home, I moved into my parents' house for the next week.

They were almost as bad as Candy, wanting to know where I was going, where I was coming from, when I was coming home, and what I was doing every second of every day. So I went home with my tail between my legs, almost feeling a need to apologize, although I felt strongly that I had done nothing wrong.

My parents were devastated by the fact that another divorce in the family would create more embarrassment for them and their friends. It was Old-World thinking–you stayed in a marriage no matter what.

I left on other occasions, even moving in with Ron once. He had lived in the same apartment since he left his agoraphobic wife in the early '70s. Now fifty years old, it hadn't been cleaned since he moved in. Dust rested upon dust until it had changed to a solid form, and the kitchen sink and bathtub was black from never having been scrubbed. I managed to stay there for eleven days before I nearly lost my mind. However, to save face this time I used a fake suicide attempt by my mother, who loved to pretend that she was going to kill herself, as the reason I went back to Candy. Surely, I couldn't leave Candy if my mom was threatening suicide over it.

I needed to justify going back with Candy in order to spare myself the humiliation that my friends and extended family were sure to heap upon me for returning to her once again. By this time they recognized the futility of my marriage. They had never been that enamored with Candy, anyway, nor had she ever been enamored with them.

So I returned home to try and salvage our sick relationship, although I had a funny feeling when I walked in the door that I was definitely going to leave again soon–for good.

After I was back with Candy for about a month, she and my mother got into a ridiculous argument over a chopped liver recipe. As a result, Mom told me crying, "You should have let me kill myself."

Three months later while attending a drug treatment conference in Aspen, Colorado I got into a conversation with one of my psychiatrist roommates. I confided to him that I had a very troubled marriage.

"You're pure textbook, Ted," he casually explained. "Within the next couple of years, you'll probably leave, but not in anger, shame, or guilt. And it won't be over an argument or a confrontation." He recited alarming statistics about how most marriages ended in divorce, and how the vast majority of those who remained married weren't truly happy.

He continued. "It's not the '50s, the '60s, or even the early '70s any longer. You can divorce and start anew. Someone in the marriage is going to be unhappy, maybe even for the rest of their life. The person who didn't want the divorce may never get over it; but the person who stays and longs to leave is doomed to a life of depression."

He suggested that it may be one of the reasons I was having problems with high blood pressure and an ulcer.

Respecting his knowledge and advice, I methodically plotted my split. A month before I planned to leave I began to take, piecemeal, clothing and other objects that I wanted to keep. Amazingly, Candy never missed a thing until the day that I departed when I removed the rest of my clothes and a number of pictures, plaques, and citations from the walls.

Two trips later in my state vehicle, a station wagon driven by the Deputy, and Ron Epstein's mom's car, my belongings had been distributed to different friends' homes. A coworker let me use his cabin in Western Maryland as a retreat for a couple months. This way I could be alone and not blame my parents or my friends if I went back to Candy again.

I called Candy at her office, informed her that I had left again, and hung up quickly. She raced home and confirmed the worst. This time, seeing the bare walls in my home office, she knew I was serious. She rushed over to my parents' house and cried her heart out to them.

Feeling somewhat guilty, I spoke to her on the phone, saw her on occasion, and even gave her some money; although I was living from paycheck to paycheck. I left her the home and all the money rationalizing that if I were nice, she'd be nice. I didn't realize that this kind of rationalization in divorce was quite irrational.

I had a couple of girlfriends for a year prior to this…maybe a few years…well, maybe a little longer. They were mainly divorced women who were not looking for anything permanent. If I visited that was fine, and if I didn't that was fine, too. We knew the relationship was purely physical, and we were using each other for our own selfish purposes.

Jan was one of these women, whose home was not far from where Candy lived. Jan had long red hair, porcelain skin, and bright green eyes. At five-feet-seven-inches tall, she was built very well.

I knew Jan as a teenager, although I was several years older. We never really got it on, but we had come close. We lost touch for about fifteen years, and then I bumped into her at a mall on the outskirts of Baltimore City. Even wearing a purple business suit and very large sunglasses, I knew it was Jan the moment I set eyes on her. I recognized her husky voice and irresistible sexuality.

We had a pleasant conversation, and she told me she was divorced with two sons. She asked me to give her a call sometime—anytime. A week later, I gathered up the nerve and called her. Having told her I was married, we met in an obscure restaurant outside of the city. After lunch, she invited me over to her place in Owings Mills, in Northwest Baltimore County, where we spent the next two hours in bed.

We had a continuing series of trysts for a few years, and she was the one I felt most comfortable with out of the various affairs I was carrying on. We were never in love, but we had an excellent rapport and I felt she understood me.

Early one morning, four weeks after I separated, I left Jan's fourth-floor apartment. About to enter my car, I noticed that all the tires had been slashed. I raced back to the apartment and called the police.

Upon their arrival, the officers asked me if I had any enemies. I explained that I was recently separated, and before I could even finish, they advised me, "It's probably your wife."

I asked them how they made that presumption, and one officer answered confidently, "In ten out of ten cases it's the wife. Slashing tires is a woman's thing, and it usually happens to a boyfriend or a husband who leaves a woman, or one who gets into an argument with a woman."

I decided not to press charges or file an insurance claim. Still feeling a little guilty over the split, I figured my punishment would be paying for new tires and keeping quiet about what had happened.

I didn't say a word to Candy about the tire-slashing episode for months. I figured that if she had done it, she would inadvertently ask me something incriminating; but the conversation never came up. Even though Candy was the number one suspect in the tire slashing, when I discussed this with Jan, she admitted that she had recently split up with a boyfriend known for his violent and bizarre behavior. "And, my ex-husband is always concerned about male figures in the house for this reason," she added.

Jan also recalled an argument she had with some guys who had moved into the apartment beneath hers. They played very loud rock and roll music late at night, which she had reported to management. The guys found out and were very pissed off at her.

This information helped a little because I didn't want to believe that Candy would resort to messing up my car. After all, it was still in her name.

A series of other coincidental events began occurring at an alarming rate, and I was growing slightly paranoid. I sensed that someone was following me and watching my comings and goings. I figured it had to be Candy using her ex-cop skills and connections, but again, I didn't want to believe it. There were always the other possible suspects.

Chapter 5

OCEAN CITY, MARYLAND
July, 1986

"Look here," motioned the Deputy to the Chemical Girl. "Ted's in the newspaper *again*." The article in the Baltimore paper high-lighted the latest drug fad–a highly addictive form of cocaine known as "crack." There had been several drug arrests on the Eastern Shore of Maryland reaching into Caroline County near Federalsburg. A segment of migrant workers were trafficking in "black-tar" or "tootsie-roll" heroin, very potent marijuana, and now crack.

In the article, I was expressing my concern about crack's avail-ability on the Eastern Shore. Being such a large playground in the summer, Ocean City was destined to have a problem with this drug since it was cheap and potent, and was being marketed to the usual vulnerable adolescent and young adult populations.

"There's a lot of money to be made in this business today. I'll tell you that," said the Deputy, shaking his head.

"Yes indeed," I agreed. "The economics of trafficking cocaine are just mind-boggling. You're talking billions and billions of dol-lars because cocaine is much easier to smuggle. It's amazing." With that, I began a discourse on how the Colombians had replaced the Mexican marijuana traffickers, and from there had extended their marketing to include cocaine. They had, in effect, set up the only successful multinational, multibillion-dollar industry in Latin America. I wasn't sure if the Deputy was paying attention any longer.

"Ted," said the Deputy, "if you hadn't left your wife every-thing like a fool, we could be investing what money you had and probably be on the verge of making our own fortune."

"You *are* kidding," I said. "Why would I want to risk getting involved in any kind of illegal activity, even if it was a one-time-only shot? I'm not lucky like you. Only insane people want to deal drugs and live with the constant paranoia and risk. Why…"

"You're not hearing me out, Ted," the Deputy interrupted. "I'm not talking about cocaine or dope; I'm talking about duck decoys. If I had what you left Candy…and don't tell me you did it so you'd never have to deal with her again. You still deal with her all the time. I could corner the decoy market with that money right now and in a few years we could retire. We'd have the greatest collec-tion around because I know just who to buy from and how to go about it. I've got experts who can identify the forgeries, the counterfeits. Listen, if you took out a large personal loan, we could still work it out. Tomorrow I'm going to take you to the Woodcarving Championships at Convention Hall."

"You're not taking me anywhere like that," I responded adamantly. "And why don't *you* borrow the money? Why should I?"

"Ted, let me enlighten you a little bit about duck decoys. You've been giving me your opinion about dope, and I'm always listening to your historical lectures. Now you pay attention to me for a change. And stop gawking at all the fuckin' bikinis." In my boredom, I had begun glancing around the beach.

"It wasn't that long ago when collectors marveled at a decoy worth a hundred dollars. Then the price jumped to a thousand bucks, and nobody ever imagined in their wildest dreams that duck decoys would sell for $10,000 each. But now there are some even more expensive price tags around. I know of a William Bowman 'Clover' duck that sold for fifty grand, a Joe Lincoln 'Hissing-Head Goose' that sold for ninety grand, and a Crowell 'Canadian Goose' that sold for seventy-four grand. And very shortly I think we're going to see some of these decoys going for over six figures. This isn't the norm, but about a month and a half ago, a Lincoln Wood Duck sold for $205,000!"

I was now only half-listening to the Deputy, but when he said $205,000, my ears perked up. "That's certainly a lot of money…but it doesn't mean that if you see something at this convention that I'm not attending, anyway, or that every time you make me stop on the Eastern Shore and loan you money to buy one of these birds, somebody is going to sell us a $200,000 decoy. Hell, I'd like to see you get even $3,000 for a bird you pay a hundred dollars for…. And not only that, if I were still married, my wife would never give me any extra money, let alone give it to you. I mean, you're not one of her favorites, you know."

"Not one of her favorites? None of your friends has ever been one of her favorites. She's hated every one of your male friends!" the Deputy reminded me loudly. "And you know what? None of us was that crazy about her because of the way she treated us like scum, wondering why you were even hanging with us."

The Chemical Girl, suddenly interested, smiled and asked, "Why *did* your wife hate all of your friends, Ted?"

"Not all my friends, just my male friends, and they were usually the guys I grew up with or worked with. And she wasn't alone in those feelings. Clinically, I think you can trace a lot of marital arguments to external spousal relationships. The male friends are disliked by the wife, and the female friends are disliked by the husband. I'm more familiar, of course, with women who dislike their husbands' male friends."

"Why is that?" asked the Deputy

"Probably the majority of women, my wife included, initially want to be buddies with your male friends. But once you get married, they feel threatened and jealous of the camaraderie or male bonding. They don't feel that their husband talks to them or confides in them in the same way they do with their male friends; especially when they go to a ball game or out drinking with a buddy. Women tend to view this as a threat when it really isn't; unless, of course, a guy turns gay and starts fucking and blowing his buddies...but we're not talking about that. What we're talking about here is normal male friendship.

"So what happens is this," I continued. "A guy doesn't want to arouse his wife's anger, so he starts seeing his male friends on the sly, like an affair. After he's been sneaking around doing that successfully for a while, he convinces himself, *Well, Christ, if I'm going to get in trouble for seeing my male friends, I might as well see a broad or two or three on the side, too.* And bam, then it's all over."

The Chemical Girl was laughing. "I don't know. I understand what you're saying, but I don't buy that one should lead to another. I've seen it happen with husbands and wives before, and I just don't get it."

❑ ❑ ❑

BALTIMORE, MARYLAND

After returning from Ocean City, I received a phone call at three a.m. from a Maryland legislator. Senator Brown, chairman of a very powerful budget subcommittee, from Howard County was calling. This was not uncommon. I often got calls from the governor's office, from legislators, and from media people. They always seemed to phone between midnight and six in the morning. Drug addiction was not a nine-to-five problem.

Senator Brown was in a panic. His nephew had taken PCP and the senator's sister was in a tizzy. She felt that the boy was uncontrollable and needed hospitalization and detoxification. "Get him out of here. Get the police," she cried in the background. "Get some treatment people…but by all means, keep it a secret."

"Ted," he told me, "you've got to take care of this kid immediately."

"But," I yawned, "it's three in the morning. Can it wait until six?"

"No, Ted," he bellowed in his chairman's tone. "You have to handle it now!"

"Okay," I said reluctantly. I could hardly open my eyes, although I should have been used to these intrusions by now.

"Oh, and Ted, do us a favor please," added Senator Brown. "We'd like to have the young man cured by the weekend. We've got a big family wedding, and we don't want any embarrassing situations."

"Cured?" I asked, holding back what I truly wanted to say. *What the hell*, I thought. *What's the sense of trying to explain to him that there is no such word as* cured *in this field. We provide treatment. People are in recovery forever.*

Some people actually used to say "cure." The last person who uttered it publicly was the clinician for David Kennedy, the late President's late nephew. The clinician boasted, after treating David for a cocaine problem, "This young man is now cured." Two months later David Kennedy died of a cocaine overdose in Florida. It was the last time the word "cured" was ever used by professionals in the treatment field.

❑ ❑ ❑

PCP had not yet become a serious national problem, but it was a major local problem in Maryland. We were not very proud of this, but the Baltimore-Washington corridor was the world center for PCP manufacturing and distribution. It had been that way since the very early '70s.

My first experience with a person on PCP occurred in 1971. I was summoned to the Baltimore City Jail to investigate a crisis. A student from Johns Hopkins University, who had a number of unpaid parking tickets, had been arrested and jailed. A cellmate offered him what he thought was pot. Unfortunately, drugs *can* be obtained in jail, and are probably of a better quality than those on the outside. There's an ingenious drug distribution network on the inside.

In any case, the student smoked the joint, not knowing it had been laced with PCP. He had an almost instant negative reaction and ripped his eyes out of his head. The story received not only local, but national attention, and the student became sort of a cause célèbre in the PCP crisis.

The first experience of most users of PCP is generally quite unpleasant, and they often have bad side effects. This is unusual since one of the main reasons people take drugs is because of its reinforcing effect–it feels good and you want to use it again and again. Yet people keep using PCP because it's a cheap drug with a macho reputation trafficked primarily by outlaw motorcycle gangs. There is occasional violent and bizarre behavior associated with PCP users, but most people who abuse it just become catatonic, sitting and staring into space.

After the Hopkins student removed his eyes, he went on the lecture circuit speaking about the evils of drugs, particularly PCP. The PCP epidemic went away, the trauma of this incident having had a profound effect. After a few years, the former student wasn't useful anymore from a prevention perspective, but his horror story stayed with the public for a couple of years to follow.

Many people knew that PCP was first used as an animal tranquilizer, but it had such adverse effects that even veterinarians eventually considered it inappropriate. When government researchers experimented with army recruits and reserves in the '50s and '60s with PCP, it resulted in a number of very fucked-up veterans.

PCP is a very dangerous drug that's inexpensive to make. It is often produced in clandestine labs, and one doesn't have to be a world-class chemist to manufacture PCP. There aren't a lot of world-class chemists who are members of outlaw motorcycle gangs, anyway. PCP manufacturing and distribution started in Southern Pennsylvania. The outlaw bikers were eventually driven out of there and into Maryland by the state police and the feds. Later, they were forced out of Maryland and into D.C. and Virginia where PCP is still very popular.

Second to Maryland in demand for PCP is the San Diego area, followed by the San Francisco Bay area. It is customarily sold in the form of sprayed parsley flakes stuffed into an empty film canister. In many instances the manufacturers will also spray Raid, an insect repellent, on the PCP to produce an even better high. However, the primary reason for using Raid is because they are out of some of the chemicals that are needed to make the PCP.

PCP became popular yet again in the late '70s. A young man in Anne Arundel County, Maryland, high on PCP, stabbed his infant son about twenty-five times before throwing him out of a fourth-story window. The man said the devil spoke to him through his kid instructing him to kill the baby. Of course, the story was headline news, and the new epidemic slowed and finally ended.

PCP made another comeback in the mid-'80s, and until another horror story comes along, people will continue to abuse it.

❏ ❏ ❏

EAST BALTIMORE COUNTY, MARYLAND

The Deputy bounced up the steps, opened the unlocked front door, and announced to no one in particular that he was home. His wife, daughters, semi-adopted son, and mother lived together in a white stone corner house in the East Baltimore County section of Dundalk. Since the Deputy seldom called home to advise of his whereabouts or when he would be arriving home, he was never expected.

Had I ever during my married years not called in my whereabouts or showed up on time for dinner, Candy would have shot me. But the Deputy lived by his own rules. To him, phoning home was a remote afterthought, and he viewed my frequent calls to Candy as the ultimate in being pussy-whipped.

No one responded to the Deputy's "Hello, I'm here!" shouts as he put away his briefcase, unloaded his pockets, and checked his mail, which had been unceremoniously strewn over his bedroom desk.

The Deputy relieved himself and went to the kitchen where he unconsciously opened cupboards and the refrigerator looking for a bite to eat. Minutes later, his two daughters from his third and present wife entered the kitchen from the back of the house. They slammed the screen door, yelped with joy, and leaped upon the Deputy, hugging and kissing him.

While they talked and played, the Deputy's mother strolled into the room. Without even acknowledging her son, she told the girls that it was time for their bath. She took them out of the Deputy's arms and guided them from the kitchen.

"Dinner's in a couple hours," she called back. "I'll have a drink with you after I give the kids a bath. Your wife's mowing the lawn and wants you to help her. And don't go nowhere. I need some money!"

"How much?" the Deputy screamed back. But she was already running the tub water and could not hear him.

The Deputy opened the screen door and yelled out to his wife. When she didn't acknowledge him, he walked over and stood in front of the mower.

"Could you give me a hand?" she pleaded, beads of sweat running down her face.

"No, I'm too beat," he answered. "I'm busy, too. I have stuff to do and I don't feel like fuckin' with the grass right now. Damn it! I just got home!"

"You never feel like fuckin' with anything, including me," she barked.

"How come there's nothing to eat in the house?" he asked. "The refrigerator is about as dead as Kelso's nuts."

"Who's Kelso?" she asked.

"He was a great gelding racehorse," he said, noticing she still didn't get it. "Gelding! No nuts!"

"Oh," she nodded.

His adopted son Junior came skipping across the yard and announced that he, too, was hungry. The dog, Justice, approached from his pen near the garage as the Deputy's wife continued to struggle with the overgrown grass.

"Get the fuckin' dog out of the yard," she demanded as the Deputy and his semi-son walked back up the steps and into the kitchen.

"Hey, Dad," said Junior, "I know where there's something to eat." He motioned toward the living room. The Deputy looked over to where his son was pointing. In the china cabinet were two Twix Bars. The Deputy opened the cabinet and removed both Twix Bars. He ate one and gave the other to Junior, and then threw the wrappers into the trash can.

Five minutes later, hungry and tired, the Deputy's wife walked into the living room toward the china cabinet. Noticing the missing Twix Bars, she started viciously interrogating the Deputy about their whereabouts.

"I don't know what they were doing in there to begin with," he said. "Were they limited editions? Were they being saved for posterity? Hell, the kid and I were hungry."

The Deputy's wife continued to flip out. She ranted and raved and hollered so loudly that the daughters, who were being dried off in the bathroom by their grandmother, started crying. Justice, the dog, went berserk and jumped through the kitchen screen door. Junior darted upstairs where seconds later, so upset, he climbed out an upstairs window, leaped to the ground, and ran down the street.

Grudgingly, the Deputy said to his wife, "Don't get so bananas, okay? I'll go get you another Twix Bar for Christ's sake."

With that the Deputy hurried out to his car and drove to the 7-Eleven, only to find that they were out of Twix Bars. He proceeded to a High's Dairy Store and again there were none. At a Royal Farm Store, he was finally able to buy the last three Twix Bars. He ate one very quickly as he carried the other two out to his car and tossed them onto the dashboard.

As he started the car and headed towards home, the Deputy realized that he needed to chill out and made a turn on Essex Drive, pulling up to Joey's Bar and Grill. He walked into Joey's, saw some old buddies, and joined them for a couple beers.

The Deputy returned home over an hour later and placed the Twix Bars on the table, yelling to his wife, "All is well. Here are your Twix Bars!"

"Where have you been?" she yelled. "You can't tell me it took you that long to get candy!"

"Well, first of all," he explained, "I had to drive to about a half dozen stores before I finally found one that had your fuckin' Twix Bars. I was so crazed by then that I decided to stop at Joey's and get a drink. What the hell's it matter? You probably had them hidden in the china closet for God knows how long, anyway."

"You bastard!" she yelled. "You know how much I love Twix Bars."

The Deputy's wife walked over to the kitchen table, looked down at the Twix Bars, and went berserk again. The Deputy rolled his eyes and began muttering in Spanish.

"You motherfucker!" she cried out. "They melted! Where did you put them? You left them in the car while you were drinkin', didn't you? Probably right where the sun could melt them, and I'll bet you did it on purpose, you bastard!"

She started grabbing things and throwing them at him. The Deputy double-stepped it upstairs and put everything back in his pockets. He pulled a sport coat out of the closet, threw a couple of bathing suits in an athletic bag, and hurried out the front door.

BOOK II

"Understanding of addiction has not advanced much beyond what it was fifty years ago. Addictive behavior is attributed to weakness of character. The argument is a logical circle: if the treatment fails, the addict is responsible, and the failure is taken as evidence showing his weakness of character.

"How is it possible for the medical profession to learn nothing from fifty years of failure? The answer is that it is easier to blame . patients rather than wonder whether a treatment is at fault."

Dr. Vincent Dole
Pioneer in methadone maintenance
treatment of heroin dependence.

Chapter 6

My staff nicknamed my office "the morgue." Pictures of dead celebrities, mostly from the music field, who had died from alcohol and drug abuse, adorned the walls; and the walls grew more and more crowded as time passed. They were entertainers from the '40s through the '80s and included Billie Holiday, John Belushi, Elvis Presley, Judy Garland, Hank Williams, Frankie Lymon, Janis Joplin, Jim Morrison, and Jimi Hendrix. I had blown up album covers, posters, and magazine articles, and had them mounted on box frames.

Time and again when I returned after a couple of days away from the office I would find one or two pictures missing. If the original or negative was available I replaced them, or I would simply fill in the missing space with somebody else who had died. The latest pictures were of basketball's Len Bias and pro football's Don Rogers.

My staff and I also videotaped a television commercial–a spot panning the dead celebrities' pictures. We played some of their original music in the background while a voice-over stated their name, how old they were when they died, and what killed them. The public service spot ended with the comment, "Drugs were the last thing on their minds."

We aired three different spots: One aimed at the older generation that included Billie Holiday, Hank Williams, and Judy Garland; another geared to people who could identify with Jim Morrison, Janis Joplin, and Jimi Hendrix; and finally one which appealed to everyone with Elvis, Belushi, and others.

❑ ❑ ❑

After the dead celebrity TV spots first aired, I received a call from an old buddy Buzzy who owned a health food store, was a devout vegetarian, and dabbled in illicit drugs.

"Ted," he whispered, "drugs didn't kill those rock and roll stars. The CIA did. They wanted to teach the kids who were influenced by Joplin, Hendrix and even Mama Cass to stop taking drugs. It was all a grand conspiracy."

"Really?" I asked sarcastically. "But Buzzy, it didn't work. Kids took even more drugs after that."

"I know," he said. "Ted, be careful."

❑ ❑ ❑

BALTIMORE, MARYLAND
July 8, 1986

The governor called an emergency meeting with the secretary of health, the state police chief, the director of the Budget Bureau, and me to develop and discuss a strategy for dealing with both the Len Bias situation and the drug problem in Maryland. Reeling from months of bad publicity as a result of the savings and loan crisis in Maryland, the governor needed help. In the last year of a two-term, eight-year reign as governor, he was running for the U.S. senate seat and initially looked like a sure bet to win—except he felt the savings and loan crisis might hold him back. And the Len Bias tragedy could be his death knell. The meeting was a crisis strategy session, which could possibly help propel him back into the senate race.

During my years as head of the Drug Abuse Administration, I had been exposed to this governor on only a few occasions. On each of those occasions, he had no idea who I was. He knew my name but never connected it to my face. A year earlier there had been a drug prevention conference at the governor's mansion. My staff and I were going to show several public service TV announcements we had developed.

Before the governor and his cabinet arrived, we were having trouble with the television set and the VCR. It was either a blown fuse or a faulty wire. The governor's public information officer asked me to retrieve some new wires that were being dropped off at the gate of the mansion. When I returned with the wires, I accidentally bumped into the governor, who was rushing into another room. He asked me where I was going, and I told him, "The television isn't working. We're trying to get it repaired so that you can see the public service spots." He wished me luck and said he'd be over shortly.

We finally corrected the problem, and when the governor viewed the public service spots he was quite impressed. But I had the distinct feeling that he thought I was either the electrician for the governor's mansion or the health department, but not the head of the Drug Abuse Administration. This held true on other occasions, too. He once asked me how everything was going, patted me on the back, and complimented me with "I haven't had a bit of trouble with the television set since you were at the mansion. Thanks."

I didn't want to tell him who I really was since I was embarrassed about the situation. I did, however, tell the secretary of health, who laughed, but obviously didn't believe me. Later, she was convinced I was telling the truth when she saw the governor motion to me to adjust the television set at a governor's mansion function.

The Len Bias meeting was held in the governor's Baltimore office. I was running late, and when I entered the conference room, the secretary of health, the head of the state police, and the Budget Bureau director were already seated. We had outlined a good strategy and were ready to present it to the governor.

Since there was no seat left for me, I unconsciously stood next to the television set. Just then, the governor walked in, nodded to me, and asked if there was a problem with the set. The secretary of health could barely keep from laughing. The governor looked around the room and impatiently asked, "Where's Ted What's-His-Name? He's ten minutes late."

The secretary swallowed hard and answered, "He's been waiting to give his presentation, governor. Ted, why don't you begin?"

She pointed to me and I began to speak. I thought the governor's eyes would roll back in his head when he realized that I was not the electrician, but the head of the Drug Abuse Administration. Or maybe he thought I was an electrician who just knew a lot about dope.

We presented our strategy to the governor. Using a budget deficit appropriation, we would immediately implement three million dollars' worth of new programming, which included a cocaine detox unit for indigents; an intensive outpatient PCP program in Prince George's County where there was a PCP epidemic; prevention coordinators for all state subdivisions; additional treatment counselors; expansion of the Street Outreach AIDS Project; more methadone maintenance slots; and a significant increase in public awareness programs on the hazards of cocaine abuse. This was just for treatment and prevention. For enforcement, we requested six drug strike-force teams to be placed around the state, including fifty new narcotics police officers. The governor was impressed with the program.

Enforcement was still crucial. The governor had great faith in his colonel of the state police, George Brosan. Brosan was a near-mythical character in the drug abuse field. Before the state police position, he had been the resident agent in charge of the Drug Enforcement Administration in Maryland, Delaware, Virginia, and the District of Columbia. Prior to this, he had joined the feds after a stint as a customs agent at Idlewild Airport in New York. Brosan was the man who arrested Dr. Timothy Leary, the LSD guru, as he was reentering the country in the 1960s. It changed Brosan's life forever.

We agreed to form a task force to investigate the Len Bias cocaine death and the substance abuse problem at College Park. Headed by Ben Civiletti, former U.S. attorney general under the Carter administration, the task force would include a number of congressmen, state officials, and local members of the judiciary and legal profession, including the state's attorneys from Baltimore City and County. They would deal with the drug and alcohol abuse problem at the University of Maryland, and recommend programs for all of Maryland's public colleges and universities.

❑ ❑ ❑

Drug testing, especially urinalysis, became a major issue after Len Bias' death, not only on campuses, but in the workplace. Controversy arose on all sides. Employees, athletes, and students felt it violated their Constitutional rights. Employers, universities, professional teams, and other organizations worried about the validity of the tests.

"Instant experts," often inexperienced, came out of the woodwork. No one suggested going to the veterans in the treatment field who had been involved in urinalysis testing since the late '60s. There were only a handful of labs in the United States that could testify in court under oath that their urinalyses were ninety-five percent accurate or better. Questions were rife about probable cause, quality assurance, and punitive versus therapeutic actions following test results.

Drug treatment programs in the late '60s and early '70s, especially methadone maintenance and methadone detox, utilized urinalysis screening of their clients. They experienced a number of problems in the early years that led them to determine that test results should be used therapeutically rather than punitively. It was a better way to predict drug patterns and trends by observing the drugs that showed up positive on the drug screens. Treatment personnel also discovered clients' methods of cheating on the urinalysis. They had already uncovered what the instant experts of the '80s later rediscovered.

When I came on board with the Drug Abuse Administration, we were involved in direct treatment and were spending large amounts of money conducting urinalysis screenings in our outpatient programs. The methadone programs required more frequent mandatory random urinalysis tests than the drug-free outpatient programs. When funding was cut in the mid-'70s, a decision was made that urinalysis testing would be done only in the methadone maintenance and detox programs, and in the drug-free outpatient programs treating individuals either sent by court order or others already on parole or probation.

Personnel were my responsibility as chief of administrative services. The first job classification which I was asked to create was for employees who conducted the drug-testing urinalysis. My staff thought up a lot of titles, some for real, and others for fun. When they were finally decided upon, we couldn't remember if we had come up with them as jokes or as serious titles.

Someone who would watch people pee was a Urine Surveillance Specialist. Depending upon their experience at watching people pee, they were a Urine Surveillance Specialist I, II, III, or IV. Number IV was, of course, a Senior Urine Surveillance Specialist. Next in line was the Urine Surveillance Supervisor or Coordinator. The Supervisor of all the Urine Surveillance Specialists was called the Chief of Void Services. When we marched over to the State Department of Personnel to set up job specs and salaries, we were close to hysterics.

Dyed-in-the-wool bureaucrats at the Department of Personnel found nothing amusing or even vaguely funny. They wanted to see for themselves if this classification was really necessary in order to create specific job titles. So we took them to visit our treatment facilities to meet and interview the directors of the treatment programs, their counselors, and the Urine-Surveillance-Specialists-To-Be.

We explained to them the duties of the position, what was going on in the field, and the necessity of monitoring clients in a treatment program. "If people aren't watched closely," we stressed, "they can contaminate or dilute their urine samples." Pointing out the various clever ways that this could be accomplished, we amazed the personnel staff with stories of clean black-market urine for sale on the street at ten dollars an ounce.

"Even if someone is watching carefully," I said, "black-market urine has often been injected into the bladder of an individual who could not take the risk that he would either be dismissed or lose privileges in a program."

Unique scams were employed by devious clientele to use clean or black-market urine. In one treatment program, the director brought in a counselor and a Surveillance Specialist and had them explain how they had been observing a black guy for months as he peed three times a week into a plastic cup. The results always came back negative. Yet, they were told by other clients in the program that this person *was* abusing drugs. So, the director himself decided to watch, and much to his chagrin, observed the black male peeing through a white dildo attached to a small hose. The hose was running up through his pants to his underarm where there was a squeeze-ball squirting out the black-market urine.

The director reprimanded his staff members. How was it possible that they had observed a black guy for six months without noticing that he was peeing through a small white prick, and a dildo at that? They confessed that they were "dick-sight" weary and had lost track of color, size, and texture. Their attempts to gain favor by discrediting the myth of the black man's penis size proved futile.

Realizing the seriousness of the problem, the Department of Personnel reluctantly approved the job classification of Urine Surveillance Specialist. However, due to severe over-projections and funding cutbacks, we were unable to hire enough Urine Surveillance Specialists to warrant setting up a job classification.

It was then determined by the fourth head of our agency that the responsibility for urine surveillance would be that of the treatment counselor until such time as there was adequate funding. The counselors protested. Even though they were the lowest paid health specialists in the state, doing one of the toughest and most dangerous jobs in the field, their responsibilities had now increased.

We encouraged the programs to use therapeutic rather than punitive measures in the event of a positive drug screen. Taking our advice, the programs established protocols where clients or patients, instead of being thrown out of a program, would lose specific privileges. In the methadone program, this meant more counseling, more random urinalysis testing, and no take-home medication.

❑ ❑ ❑

BALTIMORE, MARYLAND
July 9-10, 1986

The confusion and controversy surrounding Len Bias' death continued. I had to be acutely aware of every issue, even those remotely involving Bias. The media, legislators, the College Park task force, and other agency heads were calling for information and direction. This could create the kind of scrutiny I didn't relish, especially with my baggage; and the Chemical Girl. Although I had to admit that the Bias death and its aftermath intrigued me.

On July 9, the assistant medical examiner, Dr. Dennis F. Smyth, announced that Bias had died as the result of freebasing cocaine. This statement contradicted the original finding of the autopsy performed by the chief medical examiner, Smyth's boss, Dr. John E. Smialek, who said Bias had died from *snorting* cocaine.

Smyth's finding was based on redness observed in Bias' trachea that the assistant medical examiner said was caused by the inhalation of heat, possibly from a water pipe found in a Dumpster near Bias' dormitory.

The state toxicologist who tested the water pipe reported that it showed no traces of cocaine. Nevertheless, he added that this was normal when freebasing at maximum efficiency.

Also recovered in the Dumpster were straws containing cocaine residue that were apparently used to inhale the drug, as well as a glass vial containing cocaine chips or pellets, a popular form of freebase cocaine called crack. Although the Dumpster was used by an entire dormitory of approximately 200 students, everything found in it seemed to be traced to Bias' death.

The chief medical examiner, Smialek, was on vacation. Smyth stated that he had corrected the chief medical examiner's statement that Bias snorted cocaine that fateful night.

The next day, the *Baltimore Sun*, in an article about a dispute over Bias' method of cocaine ingestion, quoted a Miami pathologist who said that snorting cocaine should not be ruled out regardless of Dr. Smyth's evidence. Dr. Roger E. Mittleman, the associate medical examiner for Dade County, Florida said that he believed there was no evidence of any kind to support the freebase hypothesis.

Smyth argued that the level of cocaine found in Bias' blood, 6.5 milligrams per liter, was far too high to indicate that Bias had snorted the drug. Dr. Mittleman countered that he had seen many cocaine deaths among people who had snorted the drug where the blood levels of the drug were much higher than 6.5 milligrams. Although he agreed that the redness of the windpipe was interesting, noting that he had never encountered it with cocaine, the fact that five milligrams of cocaine were found in Bias' stomach indicated to him that the cocaine had been snorted.

"If you snort it, some of it can find its way into the stomach because the esophagus is next to the trachea," explained Mittleman.

Mittleman, who had published a number of studies related to cocaine deaths, performed at least one cocaine-related autopsy per week. The State of Maryland reported only sixteen cocaine-related deaths from 1983 to 1985.

Smialek, still out of town, could not be reached for comment. He had originally said that intravenous drug use and freebasing were ruled out in Bias' death. Dr. Smyth said that he could not explain the difference between his and Dr. Smialek's findings.

Prince George's County State's Attorney Arthur "Bud" Marshall said that his office was looking into the possibility of freebasing, but they also believed that Bias had snorted the drug.

❑ ❑ ❑

BALTIMORE/NEW YORK
July 10-12, 1986

I received a message on my answering machine from Holt's wife Shelia in San Diego informing me that Holt was in the coronary care unit of New York's Saint Vincent's Hospital in Greenwich Village. She told me that they thought he may have had a heart attack, but not to worry.

I *was* worried. Holt and I had been friends for nearly thirty years, and he was one of the few guys whom I once thought would be able to control his drug usage–every junkie's dream.

However, everything began to change as his freebasing increased. He had telephoned a few months ago and said, "Ted, for the first time in my life, I've lost control. I'm taking cocaine alone in the closet while guests are in my house, and I don't want to share. I suspect that they are greedy and just want my dope."

Several weeks after this call, Holt phoned again, proudly stating that he had been drug-free for a week and was feeling great. He was now on a health-food kick. "I'm never ever going to eat meat again, and I've started drinking wheatgrass juice. By the way, I recommend that you try it too, since you're so concerned about your rate of deterioration."

After Holt's wife called, I contacted his sister who was a doctor in Baltimore. She gave me the phone number of the coronary care unit, and said that Holt had been trying to get in touch with me for the past couple days. I called Holt, who told me that he was feeling better. The doctors had conducted a series of tests, and he was to have a catheterization the next day to determine whether there was any blockage. If they found a blockage, they would either do an angioplasty or bypass surgery. They were still not sure whether he had actually suffered a heart attack.

I asked him how this could happen to a health freak. He said, "I'm here in New York with my girlfriend, Christine. Oh, by the way, don't forget, if my wife calls again, I was with you up until just a few days ago, and I date no woman in New York. I think she suspects I have a girlfriend.

"Anyway, Christine and I had just had some wheatgrass juice and were on our way to her loft. We walked up three flights of stairs, and then we 'went at it' in the stairwell. She started blowing me, even though I told her that somebody might walk by. After all, this is New York, so we should just go up to her loft.

"I laid down on her bed and she continued to blow me. You know how you're supposed to feel good during oral sex? Well, for some reason I started getting these chest pains. They began in my stomach and then went up into my chest, and it felt as if an 800-pound hippopotamus was bouncing up and down on top of me. She was really into it and refused to stop until I finally had to slap her on the side of the head. I told her to get me to a hospital fast.

"When I got here, I felt a little bit better, although my chest pains persisted. During the interview with the doctor, I told him about my long history with drugs. First of all, after his cursory examination, he couldn't believe that someone who had done drugs as long as I had was in such good physical shape. But when I told him that I had freebased coke regularly, he explained to me that under certain circumstances, cocaine can bring on a heart attack. You've told me about this, Ted, but I never listened to anything you said.

"So they put me in the intensive care unit and then moved me into coronary care. So, here I am. If you can come up, it would be a kick. I'm sort of scared. But there's been no pain for the last two days.

"My parents are coming and my girlfriend's here now. My wife's flying in tonight, and I'm afraid there could be some kind of confrontation. How about coming up here to referee?"

I flew to New York, taxiing over to Saint Vincent's, and walked into the middle of a huge argument just as Holt had predicted. It was like a scene in a Fellini movie.

Holt was in bed in his coronary care cubicle. His parents, brothers, and sisters from Baltimore were in the room, along with his girlfriend and wife. Everyone was loudly chastising and berating Holt. The nurse, unable to do anything, went to a phone and called security. I explained to the assembled group that if Holt had really had a heart attack, they were all placing his life in extreme jeopardy. And if he hadn't had a heart attack, this noisy argument would definitely give him one. But no one seemed to give a fuck.

Everyone was angry with Holt. His wife was furious because of the presence of the girlfriend. The girlfriend was mad at his wife. The parents and siblings were mad at both the girlfriend and the wife. His family said Holt had never listened to them when they asked him to reform his lifestyle. The nurse and a security guard finally arrived and threw everyone out but me.

Holt then confided to me that he may be having an arrhythmia, or perhaps an anxiety attack, or maybe another heart attack.

The nurse called the emergency room doctor to come upstairs immediately. The doctor concurred with Holt that he was only having an anxiety attack. He refused to give Holt drugs because of the catheterization which was scheduled for the next morning.

While the doctor concluded his examination, I flashed back to Holt's life twenty years ago as a neophyte drug smuggler:

BALTIMORE/PARIS/MOROCCO/THE BALEARIC ISLANDS/
THE MIDDLE EAST/AFGHANISTAN/PAKISTAN/INDIA
1963-1967

In May 1963, Holt met a wealthy coed named Joanna who attended American University in Washington, D.C. She paid his way to join her in Europe. However, while in Paris, they had a falling-out, and Joanna left Holt broke and alone when she suddenly returned to the United States.

At six feet tall and a slim 170 pounds with long, straight jet-black hair, Holt was rather good-looking. He had no trouble finding another rich American woman to support him. Within thirty-six hours, he had met Valery Verdi from Chicago, who took him to North Africa where they spent three months together. She returned to the U.S. in October, but he stayed behind.

Holt spent time with expatriate American writers, artists, smug-

glers, drug users, hippies, playboys, and many foreigners living in Morocco. It was a fun place to be, and he frequently traveled from Casablanca to Tangier and from Rabat to Marrakesh. To Holt, these cities were right out of a 1930s movie. Yet, by the mid-'60s, life began to get tough in Morocco. A revolutionary ferment was spreading throughout North Africa and life became difficult socio-politically for people like Holt. The tourists stopped coming, and everyone who lived there started looking for a new haven. They tried Corfu in the Greek Islands, but it was overrun by tourists. Holt and people like him just wanted to hang out in the Mediterranean where the weather was great most of the time. They investigated the Balearic Islands. The Island of Majorca was already exploited. Formentera was just a rock where a lot of hippies lived in tents, and Minorca didn't interest them.

The island of Ibiza, which was first made fashionable by Europeans in the early 1960s, was starting to boom, yet it was still a cool place where one could be left alone and not bothered. First, a few people, including the Living Theater group, went there, and then more people began to come. Pretty soon there were a few hundred people who gravitated to Ibiza from Morocco; an international group made up of Dutch, French, Brazilians, and Americans who could afford the lifestyle. They either had money or wheeled and dealed in money, and stayed on the island from April to early August. Then they went to Paris in the fall, and back to Ibiza to rest.

Ibiza became a haven for expatriates. It was an untouched paradise, although already in bloom. Only a hundred miles off the Levantine Coast of Spain, it attracted a lot of beautiful young people. Life was always on a first-name basis between the many leftover beatniks, potheads, con men, actors, hippies, and novelists.

When Holt arrived in Ibiza, he rented a house in the Old Town, and dealt primarily with the New York smuggling element. As tactless and obnoxious as some New Yorkers were, including Holt, their Eastern sensibilities were offended by the New Orleans drug dealers.

Holt never liked the New Orleans group from the time he lived in Mexico. In 1961, he turned them in to the local Mexican authorities because they were creating a bad reputation for other drug smugglers from North America. They were too obvious and kept their operation wide open. There were also a number of serious incidents in Mexico involving peasants and their children who unwittingly took LSD after accepting, with trust, handouts they received from the Louisiana people.

Holt's group bought houses on Formentera in which to store their dope. They didn't want to keep it in Ibiza because they worried about bringing "heat" to the island. But the Louisiana dealer contingent didn't care. As a result, there were always hassles between Holt's New Yorkers and the dealers from Louisiana.

By mid-August, the tourists overwhelmed the island, so Holt and his band left. First they went as tourists to the Greek Islands, and then to the Middle East for the drug harvests. Later they went to both the Near and Far East.

Holt's good reputation in smuggling circles was based on his high-quality drugs. To acquire that quality required traveling over half the world, visiting small farmers in several different countries. Once he made contact, he would have to stay for a while, no matter how monotonous it became. This was the reason Holt flew to remote places such as the northern Indian town of Srinagar. At the foot of the Himalayan Mountains, Srinagar was a breathtaking city where the stars seemed at arm's length, particularly if, like Holt, one was usually high on opium. He lived in Srinagar for three months to make a score. Staying high was his way of not going nuts.

In the old days, the Indians had an interesting way of harvesting hashish. They ran through the marijuana fields wearing leather vests wiped with honey so the pollen would stick to their vests. This was hashish, which they molded into blocks or sticks. When Holt saw this process, he said, "This is not good quality product control."

He informed the natives that the procedure needed great improvement. Holt created what he believed was an agricultural revolution, and equated it to the invention of the wheel. He introduced large garbage bags. He showed the farmers how to put them over the plants, tie them tightly around the stems, and shake vigorously. The bags would thus retain much more hashish pollen.

Naturally, Holt soon had the status of a god. He reveled in it, sitting in the villages of Morocco and Lebanon while women gently tossed flowers on him.

After frolicking on the Greek Islands, Holt's initial smuggling route included Lebanon. It was here that he would purchase high-quality hashish. Called 'golden red hashish,' Holt always believed it was superior dope, even better than the Nepalese temple balls, particularly in terms of the ultimate high. Nepalese temple balls were formed by hand into perfect little balls. They were very precisely made and brought a good profit. When Holt worked Leba-

*non, he would go to Baalbek, two hours north of Beirut, to culti-
vate farmers and try to entice them into selling him their best hashish. Beirut was Holt's favorite city in the world. It was a great
place to gamble; an international playground.*

*After Lebanon, Holt's next stop was Afghanistan. He would fre-
quently take friends and laborer "mules" along with him. They would
go into the mountains to meet the small farmers and smoke their
hashish. When the farmer said that his hashish was the best anywhere, Holt would give him hash he had acquired from other countries. Since the farmer had never been out of his country, he had
never experienced other hashish. This usually encouraged the proud
farmer to bring out his special bag. His first bag was always good
dope, but the secret special bag was superior hash, which was the
only hash Holt wanted to buy. There was usually not a large amount
to purchase, but it was always of outstanding quality.*

*In Afghanistan, Holt was introduced to the chillum, an instrument
used to smoke hashish. The chillum was kept lit with charcoal and was
used in a smokehouse where everyone got high. The carbon dioxide
produced by the charcoal brought on an even crazier euphoria.*

*Holt also bought drugs in Pakistan. There, the hashish and
heroin were stored in government warehouses. It was of inferior
quality, but helped Holt to supplement his load. In Lahore, Pakistan, Holt was once forced to be a mule to carry drugs across the
border. Although it was dangerous and outside of Holt's principles
to carry large quantities of drugs, this was an emergency and an
exception. He had to move some dope into the Golden Temple area
of India in order to supplement a load of hashish to a buyer who
was about to leave. Holt crossed the border on foot from India to
Pakistan, and had to hitchhike back.*

*When the local farmers realized what a fortune they could make
from Americans and Europeans for large quantities of hashish,
they wrapped the hash around rocks to create additional weight.
When Holt needed additional weight and could not get high-quality drugs, he would stuff heavy coins into the hashish. His consum-
ers thought it meant the hashish had the Government Seal of Ap-
proval, and believed they had something very special. A lot of these
coins became collector's items, and some customers even refused
to smoke this precious hashish. Soon after, coins became a mer-
chandising technique for many entrepreneurs in the drug smuggling business.*

At one point, Holt found himself alone in the province of Kash-mir by the Srinagar Lakes because the friends of a smuggler had told him that he would never score hashish there. To disprove their notion, Holt rented a houseboat and stayed there for three months. He passed the time by staying constantly stoned on the hashish he scored. During rare lucid moments, Holt bought lots of goods like shirts and material that he sent back to the U.S. to be stored until the day he returned and went legitimate–or so he hoped.

❏ ❏ ❏

After the doctor left, I brought Holt up to date on what was going on in my life, and he eventually calmed down. The nurse was just about to check his vital signs when his wife and Christine began a shoving match in the waiting room.

The next day, I hung around until after the catheterization. Holt was pretty scared since there was a slim chance that he could die during the procedure, which involved injecting a dye through the arteries via a tube inserted in the groin area. If there was any arterial blockage leading to the heart, it would be apparent in the x-rays. As it turned out, there was no blockage whatsoever, and Holt's internal structures were in amazingly good condition.

Though I was relieved for my friend, in a way I was pissed off. Somehow it didn't seem fair since I knew how he had abused his body with drugs for years, rarely exercised, and had a very poor diet. Even though he was eating a hot dog every day, there wasn't an ounce of fat on his body, and his cholesterol level was under 150.

As it turned out, Holt was having heart spasms, which is not an uncommon condition. He blamed the spasms on getting off drugs and eating healthier foods. "As soon as I get back to San Diego," he decided, "I'm resuming my daily regimen of junk food and dope!"

Chapter 7

Lifting his head up from the sand chair to sip a frozen daiquiri, the Deputy asked, "Why do you continue to refer to Lola as 'the Chemical Girl?'"

I explained briefly, "Besides the fact that she drinks more than you, uses all sorts of prescription, over-the-counter, and illicit drugs to get up, to calm down, and to function, she's also caught up in other facets of the technical, chemical world of the 1980s. The Chemical Girl lies in tanning booths year-round. She can have or not have her period by the way she manipulates her birth control pills. She uses diuretics, laxatives, cigarettes. Her life is managed solely by chemicals."

❏ ❏ ❏

The next day, the Deputy and I were waiting in city hall at nine a.m. to meet with the mayor of Ocean City. He was a little disturbed with us, but we didn't know why.

His secretary came out and chauffeured us into the mayor's office, where he had two tee-shirts designed by our COPYIR staff hanging over the edge of his desk. One said *SLEEP WITH A LIFE-GUARD* and had a huge pack of condoms airbrushed on it. The other was a picture of a big animated prick wearing a holster with two guns telling its buddies, *"COVER ME, I'M GOING IN."* We quickly figured out why he was upset.

❏ ❏ ❏

I considered the Deputy to be an indiscriminate fucker. He'd fuck anyone–a fat chick, a thin chick, an old chick, a young chick. It didn't matter what they looked like. In his mind, getting his "nut" or having an orgasm was as important as anything. It used to kill me to see him in action because he *could* score with pretty women, but his philosophy was "the easier, the better."

We were at the Ocean Club, probably one of the prettiest bar-restaurant-nightclubs in the country. It was located right on the beach at 50th Street in a setting reminiscent of a postcard. The front deck led out to the sand where, during the day, a Calypso steel band played. After dinner, the inside was packed with tourists and locals listening and dancing to outstanding Top 40 bands. The age range at the Ocean Club was thirty to sixty years old, as opposed to the Paddock and Samantha's under-thirty crowds.

The Deputy was talking to a very pretty girl named Karen near the bar by the entrance, and I picked up bits and pieces of their conversation as I stood nearby. She told him that she'd been arrested a couple of times for driving while intoxicated (DWI), and showed him scars on her forehead, chin, and knee from a drunk-driving accident. I walked away for a while to check out the action at the back tables and returned, picking up again on the conversation. She'd also been jailed five times in California, Colorado, New York, Florida, and Maryland for other drug-related offenses. I moved over to the other end of the front bar to watch a baseball game on one of six televisions mounted near the ceiling across the top of the wall.

I returned a half-hour later and overheard Karen telling the Deputy that she had a lot of bisexual friends and that she'd fucked a couple of them. I could see that this got the Deputy very excited. The girl was pretty, for a change, and loose, just his type. Twenty minutes later, she was telling him how she had shot up cocaine and heroin from time to time. That was it for me.

"Can I see you for a second?" I asked the Deputy.

"Not right now," he responded firmly.

"I need to see you *immediately*," I pleaded.

"Okay, but this better be important," he said menacingly.

I pulled him off to the side. "You know, after two hours of overhearing this girl's arrest and prison record, how she's shared needles, and fucked bisexual guys anally…I mean, what's going through your head? You think she may *possibly* test positive for HIV, have AIDS-related complex, or even AIDS? Where in the fuck is your mind? In your pants?"

"Well, yeah," said the Deputy, "it is in my pants. Come to think of it, though, you might be right. Uh, what do you think I should do?"

"What do I think you should do?" I asked incredulously. "Are you fuckin' suicidal? Get the hell away from her!"

"Yeah, but," he said, "she's good-looking and you're always accusing me of fucking dogs.…"

"Hey idiot, you wanna fuckin' die? Walk away from this one."
Thankfully he did.

❑ ❑ ❑

We drove south to the Paddock Nightclub on the lower end of
Ocean City at 17th Street and Coastal Highway. In its heyday, this
was the only place to be, and it still had great bands. The average
customer was now a little rougher and a lot younger, though. The
Deputy struck up a conversation with a fairly heavy young lady
from Pittsburgh, and I went over and complimented him on being
so indiscriminate.

We caught up with some other state health department employees–Shane, John, and Joey. They had come to Ocean City that
night for the Maryland Association of Counties Conference and
asked to stay with the Deputy and me in our hotel room. It would
be quite crowded, but we had worked with these guys for many
years, and they were a lot of fun to be with. The bullshit was always great. After forty-five minutes, we drove back to the Ocean
Club, and by now, the possibly AIDS-contaminated Karen had
vanished. The Deputy brought along the fat woman he had picked
up at the Paddock.

After partying for a while, everyone except the Deputy grew
weary and decided to head back to the hotel to catch some sleep.

Around seven in the morning, the Deputy was pounding on
the door. He had lost his key. We let him in, and although very
tired, we listened to his amorous tale of the night with the heavyset
girl. The Deputy always tried to find the positives in women regardless of their often hideous looks.

"Guys," he said, "you won't believe it. The chick was great.
Had the prettiest tits of any woman I've ever been with."

We laughed knowing he'd find some reason to praise her. "What
did you do?" asked Joey. And that was all the Deputy needed to
begin his lengthy discourse.

"Well, her girlfriend left and we didn't have a car, so we walked
out onto the 50th Street beach at the Ocean Club. She was staying
with some girls in one of the big condos around 120th. We decided
to take a long, romantic walk. After a few blocks, I convinced her
to do a little skinny-dipping. Right outta the cold water, I fucked
her in the sand around 63rd Street.

"Afterwards, we went back into the ocean and cleaned off, dressed, and then kept strolling. We got up to 80th Street and I got horny again, so I screwed her a second time in the sand. This time for a while longer, and I don't think she was real gung-ho at that point. She wanted to get to her condo and sleep, but I told her that there was nothing better than making love in the sand."

We were rolling in hysterics now, trying to picture the Deputy and this chick with their wet clothes and sand in every crevice of their mismatched bodies while she tried to get away from him. The Deputy was a very horny guy who loved to screw over and over again, and the fat girl obviously didn't share his infatuation.

"Well," he said, as he paraded around the room looking for dry clothes, "somewhere around the Sheraton I got horny again, but she didn't want to screw, so I let her blow me. Nothing was happening from that, so I pushed her back into the sand and screwed her again. She started crying so badly that I didn't get to finish her off. When she finally calmed down, we walked up the beach to the front of her high-rise condo. For some reason or another, *she* suddenly got horny and wanted to make love again in the sand.

"It wasn't as if I was on empty, but dawn was approaching, and I figured enough's enough. But she pleaded, 'You get on the bottom this time and let me dig *your* ass into the sand.' And let me tell you something fellas, you were right. She was a little on the heavy side. On top of that, her friends, who were all staying on the third floor, came out on the balcony, saw what was going on, and started screaming down to her. She leaped up, started crying again, and ran inside.

"And guess what? She took my underpants with her, and my socks. I guess as souvenirs. That's why I ain't wearing any underwear or socks."

❑ ❑ ❑

BALTIMORE, MARYLAND
July 17, 1986

I returned from Ocean City to attend a friend's son's bar mitzvah party. Although I had been separated from Candy for almost a year, she phoned, pleading for me to pick her up and take her to the bar mitzvah. She felt she'd be uncomfortable if she had to walk in alone. She acted as if she were the only woman who had ever been separated in the history of Baltimore. Like a fool, I acquiesced and picked her up at her office.

I was looking forward to confronting Candy about some funny feelings and coincidences I'd been experiencing–like being watched or spied upon. Still, I'd try to make pleasant whatever I could of the night. I knew I'd see a lot of friends there who would be uncomfortable with Candy's presence, but what could I do? At least I had a good tan and was feeling very confident.

The bar mitzvah was great. My friend Kligerman had been fairly successful in the carpet business, and had invited about 250 of his closest personal friends. The food, drink, and music were the best. And the fact that his son only made sixty-four mistakes reciting his maftir gave everyone something to joke and laugh about during the evening's grand festivities.

I was amazed at the amount of alcohol consumed at Jewish bar mitzvahs and weddings today compared to twenty or thirty years ago. Perhaps one of the main behavioral changes during the Jewish population's assimilation into gentile culture was the increase in the number of alcoholics and alcohol abuse.

Normally, Candy would not have shown up for this function since my friends disgusted her. If she did decide to make an appearance, she arrived late, greeted a few chosen people, told me how much she hated almost everyone there, and left early. At her worst, she would have done all of this, *and* alienated the wives of a few of my friends while she was at it. Instead, she decided to hang around me as closely as she could. It was as though we were Siamese twins.

Every time I slowed down she banged into my back, almost knocking me into whomever I had stopped to talk to. And God forbid I should forget to introduce her to someone. She'd say, "You're doing it on purpose and being rude to me. I don't know why you aren't treating me nicer. Why can't we go out and date and have fun?" After numerous years of a very shaky marriage, a few "leaves of absence," and now a permanent separation, she wanted to date and have fun.

A couple hours later, I was just too uncomfortable and decided it was time to go. Candy was on me the entire time and all she did was complain. I dropped her back off at her office. However, before I even put the car in park, she began whining again about how I wasn't being kind to her.

She couldn't accept the pending divorce. I told her that most people don't talk when they're separated, or they communicate through their lawyers, and as usual she wanted to argue the point. But that was Candy, and since she had decided to completely ruin my night, I decided I'd have to fuck with hers, too.

"I have a feeling that I'm being followed," I said. "Either you or some detective you hired has been following me for the past few months, and it's annoying me quite a bit."

Candy acted shocked and insisted that she was purposely leaving me alone, giving me space.

"Instead of eleven months," I said, "you're acting as if it's been eleven minutes since we separated! Also, I had a little problem after we first split up that I forgot to mention. Someone slashed all of the tires on my car, and the leading suspect is you!"

She completely freaked out. I told her that the policeman had said it was "a woman's work." She swore on *my* life that she didn't do it, and that worried me. I insisted that she swear on her own life or someone whom I didn't care about, but not mine.

That was enough arguing with her for the evening, so I bid Candy adieu and drove back to my apartment to make a few phone calls. When I left my apartment a little later, as a precaution, I took my sister-in-law's three-year-old brown Jaguar sedan she had left at my place for my parents to use.

Leisurely, I drove to Jan's, contemplating how long I would stay and what time I would return to the Eastern Shore. I also thought about the Chemical Girl.

As I turned into the driveway of Jan's apartment complex, I immediately spotted Candy to my left in her royal blue Corvette. She didn't notice me at first, but unlike James Bond, I stupidly screeched the car to a halting stop and stared directly at her with my mouth and eyes wide open. Recognizing me even in a different car, she started following me as I sped in and out of the complex, past the townhouses, condos, and apartments, and back out onto the main drag, Reisterstown Road. Candy was right behind me, and since she'd been an amateur race car driver in Texas many years before, I knew that there was no way that I could lose her. I didn't really know why I needed to anyhow, but I was still scared shitless.

I raced up Reisterstown Road towards the Baltimore Beltway, three miles south, when I noticed a strip shopping center on the right. Giving up, I pulled into the parking lot with Candy in hot pursuit. She parked next to me and wiggled her finger, motioning for me to get into her car. I shook my head "no," so Candy got out and slid into the front seat of my sister-in-law's Jaguar before I could find the door-locking switch.

"I've got you now, you bastard. I've got you cold! My detective has been following you. You may as well tell me everything. I want to hear the whole story now!"

Nervously, I answered. "I don't know what you're talking about. I'm just taking a leisurely evening drive, and what a coincidence that we ran into each other."

She didn't buy it, of course, and began screaming and yelling at me.

"Calm down," I said. "And please don't slash the tires on this car. It's my sister-in-law's, and she'll definitely turn you in to the police."

Candy again swore that she knew nothing about the tire-slashing, but added, "In my detective's report, he did mention that a white, male Caucasian slashed the tires on the night he followed you."

I reminded her that "white" and "Caucasian" meant the same thing, but she didn't seem to care. She said she knew all about the redhead, Jan, whom she referred to as "The Slut."

"It's terrible," she added. "This woman is young enough to be your daughter, and I consider that incest!"

This went over my head somewhat since we had no children, I wasn't that much older than Jan, and I was definitely not related to her. I pleaded with Candy to get out of the car. She wouldn't budge and said she'd grant me the divorce I wanted only if I owned up to having extramarital affairs.

"Tell me how long you have been dating this slut!" she demanded.

"I don't know what you're talking about," I said confidently.

Candy's detective was a former coworker from the Anne Arundel County Police Department, and it was his investigative work that had caught me. I was proud that it took a seasoned cop to hunt me down, considering I didn't know how she would benefit from this information, anyway. After all, I had left her the house and all of the assets. What more did she want? I asked her again to get out of the car, but she refused. So I got out instead.

I grabbed the keys, slammed the door, and began walking down Reisterstown Road toward the Beltway with no particular plan in mind. Candy leaped out of the car in hot pursuit, demanding that I stop so she could talk to me. I recognized the sound in her voice. It was the old physical-confrontational tone, and I knew that if she and I got into a hassle, fists would surely fly–mainly hers. Then she'd have me arrested, and really have me by the balls.

I decided to run for it, and run I did, even though I was still bedecked in a suit, tie, and dress shoes. It was hot, humid, and damp as I sprinted down the road. Fortunately, I was on a decline and it wasn't that difficult to run. Unfortunately, Candy ran after me. After a few minutes of sprinting in her high heels, she stopped, removed her shoes, held them defiantly up in the air, and yelled out, "Stop, you coward!"

I knew I was in trouble. Fearful, I increased my pace. Drawing from my jogging experience, I knew that, psychologically, if I was able to pull away from her, to swiftly increase the distance between us, she may not follow me. Hopefully, she'd think that she couldn't possibly catch up, and I knew that I could sprint faster than Candy.

The street came to an incline towards McDonogh Road, another 300 yards straight ahead. I started pumping my little feet as fast as they could go. I was flying now, and my heart was pounding. It felt like it was trying to jump out of my chest through my neck. I had three drinks in me from the bar mitzvah, and I knew that this would not increase my endurance. I figured it would definitely increase my risk of a major cardiac infarction, however, and I would die of a heart attack on Reisterstown Road.

For passersby, this scene probably looked a little bizarre, too. Here it was ten-thirty at night, and I was racing south on Reisterstown Road in a new gray suit pursued by a woman in bare feet, dressed to the "nines," with her shoes held high over her head, screaming for me to stop, and calling me a coward. Luckily, I was able to get a large enough lead on Candy, and she finally stopped chasing me.

At the peak of the hill, at McDonogh Road, when she could no longer see me, I took a sharp right-hand turn and ran into a complex of new buildings that housed a restaurant. But the restaurant was closed. I needed to get to a payphone as quickly as possible to warn Jan that Candy could be paying her a visit. Or maybe Candy had already killed her. I couldn't find a payphone anywhere and began to slowly retreat to my car. I used off-the-road guerrilla techniques, ducking behind some buildings, sprinting swiftly through a construction area, and then climbing a fairly steep grassy hill.

My suit was soiled from the sweat and construction debris, and I was trying not to get grass stains on it. When I got to the top of the hill, I saw that Candy was standing by my sister-in-law's car. Suddenly, she spun around, and I thought she had spotted me. I lost my balance and rolled down the hill, getting grass stains all over my suit. Startled, I began to run again, thinking that she might be in pursuit, and I ended up about a half a mile away, filthy.

Perspiration poured off of my face. I was drenched and close to having a panic attack. I tried to look at it in simpler, more positive terms; this *was* a good way of getting in shape. I ran back up to McDonogh Road and then across the street to another strip shopping center looking for a payphone, but there were none to be found outside. All the payphones were inside grocery stores and delis which were now closed. I made a mental note to write a nasty letter to AT&T asking how they expect people to call for help when they're in emergency situations and running around scared on northern Reisterstown Road.

By now I had run almost two miles in a circle. I tried to hail a cab, but the only taxis were airport taxis that wouldn't stop. I tried to take a bus and head north, back to where Jan lived, but all of the buses that passed were "Not in Service;" a wonderful practice late at night for people who might need transportation.

I saw some people pulling up to an automatic bank teller machine and figured that I'd be able to bribe a ride if I offered someone money to take me to a phone booth. Quickly, I ran over screaming, "Twenty dollars to anyone who can drive me to a phone booth!"

The late-night bank patrons looked at me terrified, peeling their cars out of the lot as fast as possible. I'm sure they thought I was trying to rob them. Furthermore, I must have looked even more disheveled and deranged than most crooks.

Frustrated, I decided to jog to Jan's. Shielded by trees and buildings, and praying that Candy wouldn't appear, I suddenly discovered myself across the street from the borrowed Jaguar. My estranged wife was no longer there, but I noticed a few undesirables hanging around the car. To my chagrin, the hood of my sister-in-law's car was up. As I raced across the street, dodging the traffic, the potential car thieves seemed to vanish. I closed the hood, relieved. My sister-in-law would have probably died if I had to tell her that the car was stolen. Then I thought, *What if Candy had opened up the hood and ripped out the distributor cap and all the wiring?*

Thankfully, the car started, and I sped over to Jan's. I didn't park in front of her house, instead I left the car a quarter of a mile away, just in case Candy the Slasher was lurking about. I ran to the apartment building and skipped up the four flights of stairs to Jan's place.

I had my own key, and when I let myself in, Jan was on the phone. Her father was also there, pointing a gun at my chest. I must have looked like a scary wreck. She hung up the phone and brought me a towel as her dad lowered the gun.

I asked her what had happened, and she said, "Your wife was here about an hour ago. She tried to get in from the main doorway downstairs, but I wouldn't let her up. One of the other tenants must have buzzed her in the security door. Two minutes later, she was at my door pounding, screaming for me to let her in while trying to turn the doorknob. I called my father, and he got here ten minutes later."

Jan's father brought a .357 Magnum over in a picnic basket. I thought that was overdoing it just a tad. Surely Candy could have been stopped with a regular .45.

I grabbed the phone and called my attorney, Ray, who had also been at the bar mitzvah. I woke him up, since it was now about midnight, and rehashed the story. Ray couldn't stop laughing. I told him I needed some fast advice, and he just continued to laugh. I explained that I was serious, but he still just laughed, and then berated himself.

"Damn it," Ray said. "I was going to drive down Reisterstown Road after the bar mitzvah, but instead I took a different route home. I would have given anything to see you being chased, in dress clothes, in ninety-five-degree heat, down Reisterstown Road, at ten-thirty at night, by Candy, waving her shoes high over her head."

I told Ray that I needed something to scare Candy with. Finally, he stopped joking and said, "Tell her the police were there when you arrived at the apartment. That you had to beg them not to file charges against her for disorderly conduct, attempted breaking and entering, and attempted assault." He laughed again, told me to call him in two days, and hung up.

I calmed Jan and her father, and then drove back to my apartment. Amazingly, I slid into bed and fell right to sleep. A year or two before, I would have been so anxious that I'd have packed up and left for Thailand immediately. But so much was happening in my life that this was just one more thing.

❑ ❑ ❑

BALTIMORE, MARYLAND
July 19, 1986

The Deputy and I were at Baltimore's Inner Harbor dining at Jean Claude's, a fine French restaurant where we sat outside overlooking the water. Afterwards, we went to the pier where the National Aquarium was located to see if Jan was working. I wanted to apologize for the ruckus Candy had caused earlier in the week.

The Deputy and others referred to Jan as the Shark Lady because she was the Dive Captain at the National Aquarium. It was her job to feed the fish and sharks, and clean the windows on the huge tanks that housed thousands of fish in the National Aquarium.

The fish knew when the Shark Lady was coming. The bigger fish always hung a few yards back waiting until she was in the water before slowly approaching her. But the smaller ones were a different story. Once Jan was submerged in the water with food, the smaller fish engulfed her in a flourish, some even nipping at her. She had to be very careful when this occurred, and it was a very paranoid experience because she couldn't see through the schools of fish at all. She had to be more than careful when the snapping turtles and the barracuda approached.

There were only a few sharks residing at the Aquarium, but they weren't of the dangerous variety. I once asked her why she wanted to perform such a potentially hazardous job, and she told me, "It feels like I'm visiting the Bahamas every time I dive into the tanks. I should be paying the Aquarium to let me go down there in the water to observe and learn and play with all of these exotic and beautiful fish that you couldn't find together any place else in the world."

Jan also liked to dabble in drugs, and she'd get high every now and then before going underwater. She even took LSD from time to time, tripping in the Aquarium.

❏ ❏ ❏

OCEAN CITY, MARYLAND

"Man, do you smell!" exclaimed the Deputy.

"That's fine," I said. "But I'd rather be cautious over there. It's only insect repellent. Stay away from me if the odor bothers you. I won't be offended."

"Yeah, but you'll be offending everyone else," the Deputy laughed.

After much ribbing about my paranoia regarding large insects, I had agreed to go with the Deputy, the Chemical Girl, and Tim Wood to the pony roundup on Assateague Island.

The Chincoteague Pony Roundup-Swim was an auction of ponies which occurred on Thursday during the third week of every July, with the actual swim taking place the day before on Wednesday. The swim attracted the most tourists and began on the Virginia side of the Assateague ending in Chincoteague, Virginia. The ponies lived on the Maryland-Virginia portions of the Assateague.

The purpose of the swim-auction was to keep the population of the herd under control. Proceeds of the auction benefited the fire department, which laid claim to ownership of the ponies. Legend had it that in the 17th century a Spanish ship wrecked off the coast and the ponies aboard swam ashore to Assateague. Originally, they were as large as farm horses, but over the years, their diet of salty marsh grass had caused them to grow smaller and smaller.

There were always numerous families in attendance since children all over the country had seen the movie or read the best-selling novel by Margarite Henry, *Misty of Chincoteague*. The green flies have a field day biting all these unsuspecting kids.

We drove over to Assateague Island in Tim's Ford Escort station wagon. Instead of putting on the air conditioning, all of the windows were open in the car. The scent of the insect repellent was the reason, but I didn't care.

"People can die from bee stings," I reminded them. "And I recently read a report that mosquitoes were carrying the AIDS virus in Miami. I don't really believe it, but you never know."

Tim Wood let out a whistle. "Ted, get serious. You got a better chance at being killed by lightning. The AP wire service, just the other day, in a report on the African Killer Bees, gave out the most recent National Center for Health Statistics data. It said that wasp, hornet, and bee stings account for about fifty deaths a year, whereas over a hundred Americans are killed by lightning."

"This AIDS shit bothers me," said the Deputy. "No one's sure of the incubation period or positive about how it spreads. I mean, if I gotta worry about mosquitoes, transfusions, saliva, tears, oral sex, anal sex, normal sex, food handlers, hospital workers, drug addicts, needles…gimme a fuckin' break!'"

"Christ," I called out. "You're with the health department. Do I need to send you to an AIDS workshop? Cut it out!"

We arrived on Chincoteague Island where the pony swim was to take place.

Tim gave us a brief history of the arguments over how the ponies arrived on the island. It could have been the English discoverers, the colonists, the Spanish shipwreck, or pirates. There was no hard evidence, only opinion and speculation.

"What's it fuckin' matter? They're here. What do you believe, Tim?" I asked.

"Hell, Ted, I'm a romantic at heart. I love the story of the shipwrecked Spanish Galleon. It seems the vessel was heading back to Spain from Peru with gold, silver, and these ponies..."

"Why ponies? Why not cocaine?" interrupted the Chemical Girl jokingly. "By the way, *Misty of Chincoteague* is one of my favorite stories."

"Ya know," said Tim, "they shot the movie here. That version had the original horses used to mine gold and silver in Peru. Since they were so small, they could move about in the mines after they were lowered in. To keep them from being scared of the dark, they were blinded."

"Jesus," I said. "They blinded the ponies and gave coca to the Peruvian slaves. Nice bunch of guys, the Spaniards."

"Wow," said the Chemical Girl. "This may sound strange, but..."

"Go ahead," I said.

"Well, with the cocaine, the darkness, the ponies...I mean, it sounds so...sensuous."

"Oh my God," said Tim. "I never heard it in that context before, young lady, but..."

We parked and joined the throng of visitors who had come to watch the pony event. It was very warm, so we looked for the nearest bar to quench our thirst. Within twenty minutes, the Chemical Girl had downed two and a half vodkas with cranberry juice.

Once back outside, I sprayed more insect repellent on my arms and face.

The Deputy laughed as I sprayed. "The mosquitoes won't get you here, Ted, but watch them green flies."

"You need to hire and train some cattle egrets," said Tim Wood.

"What for?" I asked. "And what are they?"

"They're birds that sit on the ponies and eat the flies and ticks off their backs."

"I'll buy you some, Ted," joked the Deputy, as Tim walked ahead with the Chemical Girl, "but, right now, we need to talk seriously."

"What's up?" I asked.

"You know," the Deputy whispered, "there're a lot of important people here today–lots of media, cops, and some government folks. And your little girlfriend's probably got more than a quarter ounce of coke in her purse. She's stoned on the Xanax, booze, and coke. We don't need this shit, man. Not only that, she's so whacked out, I saw her get bit by about five of those green flies so far, and she hasn't even flinched."

"Alright," I said. "See if you can get us a ride off the island. I don't want Tim to see this. And it won't do any good to talk to her while she's stoned, so don't even try."

❑ ❑ ❑

"I'm surprised you're going into Delaware, Ted," said the Chemical Girl.

"Why?" I asked as I drove north on Coastal Highway out of Ocean City into Fenwick Island, Delaware. We were heading to Rehoboth Beach to a fun and popular restaurant called the Blue Moon Café.

"They don't use the planes and fogger trucks to spray for insects like they do in Maryland," she explained. "And I know your fear of bugs."

"It's the bites, and I'm very allergic. What do you mean they don't use insecticides? I never knew that. Why?" I asked becoming slightly panicky.

"It's probably an environmental issue," she said. "I guess the Delaware folks are more concerned about the effects of inhaling the chemicals used to kill insects than the Marylanders. Hell, what's one more thing in the air to kill ya?"

"So if you live on the Delaware shore," I surmised, "you might get stung to death. And if you live on the Maryland shore, you might eventually die of cancer or something else caused by the insecticides. I'm for the Maryland way. What about you?"

The Chemical Girl laughed, took a drag from her cigarette, and pronounced herself a true Marylander.

"When I was a little girl, around seven or eight, my friends and I would chase after the trucks that sprayed the neighborhoods with insecticides. Back then it was different. Today they have the fogger trucks and loudspeakers warning people to stay inside. Fifteen to twenty years ago the trucks sprayed a mist over the lawns, and we would stand under it and scream for joy, enjoying the tingly feeling of the mist on our bodies. Nobody warned us of the dangers because they didn't know any better; although they had curtailed the DDT and some pesticides after Rachel Carson's book *Silent Spring* came out."

I remembered those trucks, but couldn't recollect whether I was ever exposed to the misty spray.

"Jesus, Lola! You're more of a Chemical Girl than I originally thought."

❏ ❏ ❏

BALTIMORE, MARYLAND
July 24, 1986

Following the Len Bias press conference, there was talk that perhaps someone had slipped the cocaine into his drink. I doubted that and asked some drug specialists about the effects of ingesting coke orally.

First, I called my friend, Ph.D. psychologist Michael Leeds in Oregon and he told me, "Cocaine is routed to the blood through the bloodstream and taken intranasally by snorting, freebasing, or smoking it. What is not absorbed through the mucous membranes would be swallowed or sucked down into the stomach.

"A gram taken intravenously would be fatal in the bloodstream. However, the rate of absorption through the gastrointestinal tract is much slower. The toxicity or fatal effects would vary depending on body weight and the metabolism of the individual."

Then I called Dr. Hank Knepper, a world-renowned drug expert, for his opinion. He basically explained that only a very small percentage of people ingest cocaine orally. Cocaine taken intranasally would produce the same amount in the stomach as if it were taken orally. Orally just takes much longer to find its way there. It depends on the amount taken, too.

Dr. Knepper continued by telling me that cocaine taken intravenously or freebased takes fifteen seconds to get to the brain, peaking in fifteen minutes; intranasally, ninety seconds to the brain, peaking in thirty minutes; and orally, two to three minutes to the brain with a sixty minute peak time.

Finally, I phoned my buddy, Dr. Mike Meyers, a physician in California, to see what he could add. Meyers was fascinating. As a medical student in New Jersey, he was discovered one day by a production company and ended up getting a major role in the movie *Goodbye Columbus*. He played Ali McGraw's dumb jock brother in the movie that made stars of Jack Klugman, Richard Benjamin, and Ali McGraw. Later, he wrote a book called *Goodbye Columbus, Hello Medical School*.

Meyers moved out to the West Coast and became one of the top drug doctors in the country, treating all types of addicts, including celebrities. He was a great resource because he was always about two years ahead in possessing good information on new drug trends and patterns that would eventually reach the East Coast.

He said, "The percentage of people ingesting coke orally in this country is negligible. It's not impossible for someone to drink it accidentally or to be forced to take a fatal dose of cocaine orally. However, I would find it very unlikely.

"If three to five grams of cocaine are found in the stomach, it's safe to assume that much more was ingested and could be found in the tissue, blood, and urine. Samples should be taken of these. Cocaine, in amounts worth noting, could be found in the stomach only by ingesting it. And, in most cases, fatal doses would affect the heart and the brain.

"There have been cases in South America of drug runners swallowing these balloons or condoms filled with cocaine which burst in the stomach, but that's kind of rare in the United States. I doubt if Bias could have swallowed a lot of condoms full of cocaine without knowing it. Even if someone accidentally ingested cocaine, he would get very ill and probably stop ingesting prior to receiving a lethal dose.

"In a survey of callers at the '800' cocaine hotline this past year, it was noted that fifty-seven percent freebased, thirty percent took it intranasally, ten percent injected it, and the rest either ingested it or inserted it anally–that is, they presumably did that. Why? I don't know."

❏ ❏ ❏

OCEAN CITY, MARYLAND
July 25, 1986

The Prince George's County Grand Jury indicted, for cocaine possession and obstruction of justice violations, two of Bias' teammates, Terry Long and David Greg, and the mysterious Brian Tribble, all of whom were in the room with Bias when he died on that fateful June 19 night.

Long and Greg were never household names in college basketball, but were becoming well known for other reasons. They were both targets of the Prince George's County state's attorney, newspapers and television, and the University's alleged in-house scrutiny of the athletic department.

Attorney Allan Goldstein, who represented Long and Greg, was frustrated and agitated. But the angrier he became, the faster his legal genius rose to the occasion.

One weekend, I ran into Goldstein jogging on Coastal Highway in Ocean City. I joined him for a two-mile run.

Goldstein, breathing hard, spoke nonstop. "You could have looked at this thing in a very different context. You could have said that the problem at Maryland was that athletes kept dying, from whatever cause–Marfan syndrome or an overdose of drugs. So far the University of Maryland has lost three top basketball players.

"Owen Brown died in a pick-up game in February 1976 at Xerox Corporation where he worked. Chris Patton was still playing at Maryland in April of 1976. He was told that the dunk rule was now legal in college basketball, so he went out on the court with a friend to practice dunking and he died. Both basketball players were autopsied and found to have Marfan syndrome, a circulatory disorder that targets taller people.

"People wanted to believe that the same thing had happened to Bias. Others believed that cocaine did them all in.

"Marfan syndrome is easy to see. It's a swollen artery with a big hole in it, and it gets stretched so thin that it bubbles and explodes. I think it was clear from the autopsy that Brown and Patton blew out their hearts. On the other hand, Bias died of an electrical problem.... Well, you should know more than I do.

"About a month before Bias died," continued Goldstein, "there was an article in the *New England Journal of Medicine* on random cocaine deaths. Somebody mentioned it to me. I thought it would be interesting to use in a case, but I put it aside, thinking nothing of it. Then I was listening to the medical examiner talking about Bias. I said, 'Son-of-a-bitch.'"

Chapter 8

EASTON, MARYLAND
July 26, 1986

After a visit to the Talbot County Addictions Office in Easton, Maryland, heading west to Baltimore, we stopped at the Tidewater Inn for lunch. The Deputy was meeting an Eastern Shore man who had two collector's item duck decoys that were supposed to be hot or stolen.

J.B. was an oysterman from Smith Island. Rumored to be in his late thirties, he looked about sixty years old. Weathered from the sea, and smelling like he'd just shucked a thousand oysters, J.B. carried the decoys in a loose brown sack.

The Deputy peeked into the sack and asked, "How much?"

J.B. thought a bit and whispered, "Five hundred."

I looked at the Deputy and he smiled.

"J.B.," the Deputy began, "I think you're goofin' on me. One, I don't think they're hot. Two, I don't think they're worth that price, hot or not. And three, I don't think they're genuine."

Outraged, J.B. told the Deputy, "Fuck you. I'll take 'em to someone who's a real collector, and a gentleman."

The Deputy didn't flinch. "J.B., if you need some money, just tell me. Don't bullshit me. I'll give you seventy bucks because I've always done business with you and your family. But if you want to be an asshole, lose my number!"

J.B. stood up, grabbed the sack, and stormed out of the lunch room.

"How do you know the decoys weren't legit?" I asked.

"Hell, I don't know for sure," the Deputy said. "But J.B.'s daddy sold me a couple fakes years ago when I was working the racetrack. Ever since then, I accuse all the oyster boys of goofin' on me."

We ate in silence for a while, and then the Deputy spoke. "If he's outside when we leave, I may offer him a hundred for both of them. It would give me an even thirty first-class decoys, if these are real."

"How will you know if they're genuine?" I asked.

"There's a professor at Washington College in Chestertown who verifies them for me. I've got maybe ninety, all told, and over two dozen are the real thing. That is, they were made by the best. I've bought them from all over the East Coast. I'm more proud of those ducks than my train collection, but don't tell our buddy, Ron. And I keep the real fine decoys under lock and key in a chest with a few mint train sets in Junior's room under his bed."

❏ ❏ ❏

BALTIMORE, MARYLAND
July 26, 1986

Ron commuted from Baltimore to his office at the FDA headquarters in Washington. He loved hookers, especially the young ones who populated South Broadway and Fells Point in East Baltimore. He'd been "dating" these girls for more than twenty-five years and had never had a problem with a social disease or with the police–until recently.

Ron Epstein even ran with prostitutes while he was married, although he claimed to have had permission. Because his wife would not leave the house, he'd go out alone every Friday and Saturday night.

As for social diseases, Ron was so obsessed and neurotic over catching something that, even in the '60s, he wore two rubbers to work. He did catch crabs in 1966, so he went to his friend, Harry, a barber in West Baltimore. In the middle of the barber shop, before six customers, Harry made Ron drop his pants to investigate. Then Harry took the cleaning spray for the hair clippers and sprayed it on Ron's testicles. It worked. The crabs went away. However, Ron says he never grew pubic hair after that again.

One Friday night, Ron was cruising around Fells Point when he spotted a pretty woman on the corner of Pratt and Broadway Streets. He drove by a couple of times, then parked his car and approached her. "Hi. What's your name?" he asked.

"Mary," she replied. She was blonde, in her early twenties, wearing a jean outfit which showed off her very nice, trim figure.

"Are you a cop?" asked Ron.

"No," she answered. "Are you?"

"No. I'm just a guy who wants to talk. Let's go over to Moana's, the bar across the street, and talk."

Moana's was a homey little place, formerly a bar for Norwegian sailors who visited the Port of Baltimore. Later, Moana bought it and the place became a lesbian-trick bar. Lesbians would hustle businessmen by pimping their "girlfriends" to the guys who came by for action. Ron loved it. To him it was the ultimate in domination–fucking a confirmed lesbian.

At work, Ron dressed typical yuppie, but while cruising on weekends, he dressed down. Old, worn outfits, oversized clothing, and someone's discarded McDonald's name badge on his overcoat. Ron didn't want to get ripped off in these bad neighborhoods. The clothes and badge signaled that he was a minimum-wage slob. He fit in wonderfully and loved every minute of it.

He only hung out on weekends, considering it taboo to run around during the workweek, and calling weekdays "school nights."

"What do you want to talk about? Do you want to go out?" the young blonde pried.

"We'll talk about it over at Moana's. Yeah, I want to go out," Ron whispered.

"Do you have thirty dollars?" she asked.

"Sure," said Ron.

"What do you want to do?" she asked.

"I don't know. Maybe a half-and-half," Ron answered cautiously. A half-and-half was a blow job and a screw. You got only one shot or ejaculation. If you came during the first half, it was over.

Mary touched the top of her head, and suddenly two ordinary-looking guys were on either side of Ron, moving him against the wall, showing him their Baltimore City Police badges, and quickly handcuffing him.

"You're under arrest for soliciting," said Officer Mary boldly.

"You can't do that!" cried Ron. "I asked if you were a cop and you said no. That's entrapment."

"You're a liar," said Officer Mary.

A police van was summoned, and Ron was placed in the van. If it hadn't been for the nature of the predicament, he would have enjoyed being handcuffed.

Ron was taken to the Southwestern District Police Station on Eastern Avenue where, before the desk sergeant, still handcuffed, his pockets were emptied. The search was routine until the police found rolls of cash in several of Ron's pockets, along with dozens of condoms, cigarettes, and matches.

A little background on Ron is relevant here. Somewhat neurotic, Ron became tense when he received his monthly checking statements, so he canceled his checking account twenty years ago.

His savings were maintained by his father, who was afraid that Ron would spend all of his money on hookers. Ron knew that any money he gave his father he would never see again, so he cashed every fourth paycheck and carried the tens, twenties, and fifties with him wherever he went, day and night. Naturally, he wore clothing with lots of deep pockets.

The police were startled to find more and more money as they searched Ron. Some in his front pants' pockets, more in his rear pants' pockets, and a whole lot more in one of his shirt pockets. All secured with thick rubber bands.

Curious, the police stopped their search and congregated around the brass rail at the sergeant's desk to observe and tally Ron's money. When the figure came to more than $7,100, one of the cops cried out, "Well, well, well. We've got ourselves a drug dealer, boys. Let's find his drugs."

And with that, while Ron's hands were still handcuffed behind his back, the police strip-searched him. Like the handcuffing, in another situation, Ron would also have enjoyed the strip-search. They didn't find anything more than a brown paper bag with a garter belt and stockings. To the snide suggestion of one cop that he was a fag, Ron replied that he enjoyed dressing up the girls he met, asking them to change in the bar's ladies' room before they went somewhere else for sex.

Ron was permitted to re-dress before being taken to the station's lockup, a series of aisles with jail cells on either side. Ron was allowed to keep the four packs of cigarettes he had with him, but was not allowed any matches or his belt, which kept his oversized pants up. The police *did* let him keep an overcoat with a fur hood that a friend had given him to stay warm while he negotiated with street whores during the cold Baltimore winters. But since Ron always felt cold, he even wore the overcoat in the summer.

Allowed one call, Ron phoned my apartment around ten p.m., only to get my answering machine. Frustrated, he left a message demanding that I come down immediately and spring him.

They told Ron he would appear before a commissioner after a fingerprint check, and then he could go home. While Ron awaited the fingerprinting and mug shots, he acquainted himself with his surroundings.

Many of the cells were empty, but they were filling up fast. At first, Ron was alone in his cell, which had a sink that didn't work and a toilet. The small, slender cell also contained a very narrow, metal-framed cot with a mattress made of three wooden planks. There were no linens or pillows. *This is no place for a nice Jewish boy to spend the night*, thought Ron. *If my parents or my work supervisor find out, I'm dead.*

After settling in his cot, Ron became more aware of all the noise from the other inmates. One guy kept screaming that he was sick, another pissed out of his cell, while a third kicked at the metal walls of his cell. Then Ron got his first cellmate–a huge, bearded guy with a metal-studded leather jacket. He sat down very close to Ron and glared at him.

"What'd you do?" Ron asked fearfully.

"Beat the hell out of a guy in a bar. I hope I killed the motherfucker," the cellmate replied.

"Why'd you do that?" asked Ron.

"He looked like a Jew," the guy said, staring carefully at Ron. "What's your name?"

"Abernathy," Ron lied, without batting an eye.

"Okay," said the guy, who then fell asleep on the floor of their cell. Ron immediately removed his Mezuzah and chain and put them in his pocket.

Finally, Ron was fingerprinted and photographed. He expected to see the commissioner right after that, but the hours rolled by, and no one retrieved him from his cell. Ron did speak to the guy in Cell Number Five, the cell opposite his, after his first cellmate saw the Commissioner and was released on his own recognizance.

Ron was in Cellblock C, Cell Number Two.

"Hey, C Number Two, you got an extra cigarette?" asked the guy in Cell Number Five.

At first Ron gave the guy cigarettes, but stopped when he became afraid that he'd run out.

"Hey, 'Two,' gimme a cigarette. C'mon, Two, I know your face!" screamed Cell Number Five, shortening Ron's official designation to a nickname.

But Ron refused to give up anymore cigarettes. He had asked a guard to light one for him and was chain-smoking a pack at a time, and they were going fast.

Cell Number Five began yelling. "Two, I've memorized your face, and when I get outta' here, I'm gonna kill you! You hear me? I'm gonna kill you!"

Ron freaked out. He'd been in the cell for several hours and was feeling like the guy in the movie *Z*, who was held incommunicado for six years. He started screaming for the guards, "Help, help! This guy's gonna kill me! Help!"

Two guards rushed into the cell. They pushed Ron against the wall and removed his shoelaces and the thick braided string in his coat hood.

"What are you doing?" cried Ron.

"We don't want you to kill yourself," the heavier guard said.

"Kill myself," said Ron. "For what? Trying to fuck a decoy cop? The guy in Cell Number Five is threatening to kill me."

"Calm down, buddy, or we'll have to restrain you," said the smaller guard. They left the cell as Ron began to pace around, holding up his pants and trying to keep his shoelace-less tennis shoes from falling off his feet.

Subsequently, Ron threw cigarettes into Cell Number Five. Although Ron smoked incessantly, he never inhaled, and would go through six packs a day.

Ron also talked to some of the other inmates for a while. One of them yelled out, "Hey, Two, what're you in for?"

"I tried to pick up an undercover vice cop and she busted me," said Two. Ron now loved his new nickname.

"Fairy. That's nothing," the guy said.

And no one talked to Two after that until he yelled out, "Yeah, but I grabbed her head and made her blow me in my car until the other cops came and rescued her."

"My man," another inmate screamed, and all of the other inmates, whom Ron never saw, became fast friends for the rest of the night.

Ron's fingerprints didn't transmit the first time, so they had to be re-sent. By that time, the commissioner had gone home.

As it turned out, Ron had to spend the rest of the night in his cell, in the company of an older, violent, smelly man who was arrested for what he called "howling at the moon." Thankfully, he fell asleep at the other end of the narrow cot, resting partially on Ron for hours. Ron was afraid to wake him, although the stench was overwhelming.

Finally, nature called. Quietly, Ron moved away from his cellmate to the toilet, lowered his pants, and sat down. Unfortunately, the old guy awoke and said in a nasty voice, "Hey, none of that in here. Not while I'm still inside."

Ron was scared. "But I've got to go. I can't help it!"

The old guy stood up. He looked menacing. "Don't you dare go! If you shit, I'll kill ya! Understand?"

Ron was a wreck. He stood and pulled his pants up. He'd have to hold it in for the next couple of hours. Oh, how he hated the decoy prostitute cop, Mary.

The next morning, Ron went before the commissioner, an attractive black woman who looked at Ron as though he had a loathsome disease. Ron, in turn, tried to look up her dress, since she was wearing sexy high heels and stockings.

The commissioner explained to Ron that he was being charged with a criminal act that carried a $500 fine or a year in jail. Upon hearing this, Ron threw up. A kind cop gave Ron some paper towels to wipe himself with, and Ron was released on his own recognizance. A trial date was scheduled for a month later.

I arrived at the jail, having received his message when I stopped home after returning from the Eastern Shore the next morning. The cops and Ron were counting his money for the third time as Ron nervously tried to re-lace his shoes.

We went to breakfast where he ran immediately to the restaurant bathroom and remained there quite a while. I also called him Two for the next few weeks.

Ron went home and prepared for his trial by practicing a reformed, repentant speech, and by considering giving away most of his possessions.

❑ ❑ ❑

COLLEGE PARK, MARYLAND

At the College Park task force meetings I attended following the death of Len Bias, rumors were rampant. The best story dealt with the allegation that Bias may have snorted six grams of eighty-percent-pure, dealer-quality cocaine the night that he died. Another rumor speculated that Bias frequently abused cocaine, and that he even sold it during his matriculation at University of Maryland. It was also suggested that he and a couple of other players had become sophisticated enough to know when not to use the drug. For example, if Bias had an upcoming physical by the National Basketball Association (NBA) or if there was a random urinalysis about to take place by the Maryland athletic department, he and his pals usually had enough advance notice to be sure that their bodies were clean when tested.

Cocaine leaves the system in twenty-four to thirty-six hours, and in many cases, with certain diuretics or after a great deal of strenuous exercise, it can leave the system within twelve hours. It was difficult in the early days of the Maryland drug urinalysis program for the athletic department to hide from players when the random tests were scheduled. There was always a day or two's notice from the NBA when a prospective professional player had to report for a random physical, which included a drug screen.

People believed that Leonard Bias was the quintessential student-athlete who represented a drug-free, clean-cut role model. Like many other big-time college athletes who lived for the adoration of their fans and were used to instant gratification, it was not difficult for Leonard and others like him to be seduced by cocaine. The positive aspects of cocaine ingestion were similar to those felt while playing in front of cheering fans.

As a former mediocre intercollegiate athlete, I was well aware of the problems of athletes who took drugs. Drugs often enhanced their capabilities on the field and calmed them down or motivated them off the athletic field.

Initially, it was disheartening at how naive some of the task force members seemed believing that athletes were being scrutinized unnecessarily. They spoke of their days of participation in intercollegiate and high school sports. Based on their recollections, they felt that drug abuse among athletes was rare. The innocence of a few brilliant and experienced academicians, elected officials, and others was amazing. Unfortunately, a number of people with great academic and intellectual skills seem to have little, if any, street sense.

The final report of the College Park task force was an excellent document coordinated by the chairman, former U.S. Attorney General Ben Civiletti. Had the University of Maryland adopted the recommendations of the task force, sought and received or reallocated funding for it, and marketed the task force's charge properly, it would have become the benchmark for colleges and universities all over the country.

Unfortunately, very few of the recommendations were adopted or implemented. The University also failed to publicize the fact that they were one of a handful of colleges and universities which had implemented a drug testing program. While it was not state of the art, it was head and shoulders above ninety-nine percent of the programs in the country.

❏ ❏ ❏

BALTIMORE, MARYLAND

I'm really not sure whether the Chemical Girl viewed me as a personal therapist, father figure, drug counselor, or sex toy. It didn't really matter what her interest in me was because she was such a fascinating woman–childlike, tragic, brilliant, vivacious, and dangerous. Our verbal sparring and her honesty in confessing her innermost thoughts and secrets were invigorating.

In a restaurant near the office where she worked, I tried to explain to the Chemical Girl that there were alternatives to drug use, particularly cocaine and alcohol. She asked me to name three. So I named ten. "Physical, emotional, social, intellectual, philosophical, sensory, interpersonal, political, creative-aesthetic, and spiritual-mystical."

"So what? Who gives a fuck?!" she said. And she ordered another vodka on the rocks with a splash of cranberry juice that she used to swallow a large pill which reminded me of the now defunct Quaalude.

"What was that?" I asked. "A 'lude?"

"I'll never tell," said the Chemical Girl.

In the '70s, methaqualone, 'ludes, or Quaaludes were considered to be the most popular high among the middle- and upper-class druggies and recreational users. Originally manufactured as a sedative/hypnotic, methaqualone was prescribed by psychiatrists for people with suicidal tendencies. "Take a half of one of these when you feel out of control, and it will put you to sleep," the doctors instructed.

While they explained that it was non-toxic and non-addictive, they didn't tell patients that if they fought off sleep 'ludes would give them a nice high.

"I don't recall the actual high from the Quaaludes per se," remarked the Chemical Girl. "I always used 'ludes with alcohol and cocaine and they were great! Too bad they're off the market."

I debated whether I should give the Chemical Girl the latest information or not, but it just came rolling out of my mouth. "It's my understanding that there are bootleg Quaaludes that are much better than the pharmaceutical variety, and they're currently being manufactured by world-class chemists."

"Oh, yeah?" said the Chemical Girl excitedly. "Where? I'll go there!"

"On the West Coast, in the Far East, somewhere out there," I said reluctantly. I'd forgotten how much she traveled.

❑ ❑ ❑

BALI, INDONESIA

At precisely the same time that I was discussing Quaaludes with the Chemical Girl in Maryland, Holt was meeting a young entrepreneur in the drug export business, in another time zone, in another part of the world.

"Big Russell speaks highly of you, Benito. He's my man in Hawaii. I'm the man in California," Holt bragged.

Benito Wallace was his alias when he dealt with people like Holt. Benito was the leader of a Filipino gang which trafficked in bootleg Quaaludes and crystal methamphetamine (ICE). He was the middle-man for gang leaders in South Korea and Hong Kong who controlled chemists who developed 'ludes, ICE, and other synthetic drugs.

Benito and Holt were sitting in Gipper's Bar and Grill on Kuda Beach in Bali, Indonesia. Kuda Beach was the hottest stop for world jet-setters to frolic.

In a twenty-four-hour period, Holt had flown from Newport Beach in Orange County, California to San Francisco, to Hawaii, to Japan, to Jakarta, and to Bali to meet Benito who had just the day before flown from Taipei, Taiwan to Singapore, Hong Kong, South Korea, back to Hong Kong, and on to Bali via Jakarta. Both men had a great deal at stake. Expensive airline tickets were not among them.

Bali offered the opportunity to make an awesome score without running the risks that had in earlier times sent Holt to jail. He had set up an elaborate buffer system to protect and provide himself with the largest profits of all his partners.

Holt was dealing in the unknown with Benito, but he represented a new and expedient conduit for Holt's drug network. He was quite familiar with 'ludes, but he needed to learn more about ICE.

"Benito, my friend, crystal meth' is popular with motorcycle gangs, but not with my customers. Competition with the bikers might ruin my good looks."

Benito was looking out at the bathers in the surf, sipping a *Coca-Cola*. "ICE is different. Customers who like cocaine will love ICE. What's more, they'll need lots of 'ludes to bring them down. It's a natural marriage, Holt. I assure you."

□ □ □

After his release from jail, my friend Holt had curtailed his major drug dealing, and had mostly just ingested drugs for a couple of years. He was extremely knowledgeable about drugs, and I felt somewhat responsible because much of his current knowledge was gathered from discussions with me. Treatment personnel can often predict trends and patterns far ahead of police or enforcement agencies throughout the world. The fastest way to learn about new drugs is from a treatment program.

Holt was curious about a new drug known as ICE. He visited one of the health departments in Honolulu and had a conversation with an intake counselor at one of the island treatment programs. The discussion concerned some of the problems they were experiencing in Hawaii with crystal methamphetamine abuse. The intake counselor, Todd, was very quick to take a liking to him since Holt had told him he ran a number of private treatment clinics. He saw Holt as a direct route to a new job on the mainland, perhaps in California.

Todd advised Holt that the drug was referred to as "Crystal" in Honolulu, but in the rural areas of the Island, it was called ICE.

"Filipinos," said the intake counselor, "refer to it as 'Batu.' It's a Filipino word for rock. It's almost always smoked because the people don't know there are other routes of administration. It's odorless and pure. Ninety percent! Even the residue of the drug remaining in the pipe is very potent. A lot of users smoke the residue again and again."

"So what does it sell for?" Holt asked casually.

Todd thought for a while. "Well, it depends. I believe the going price for a gram is three or four hundred dollars. Actually, it's usually sold in tenth of grams or less that cost about fifty bucks."

"What's it cost for a gram of cocaine on the Island?" asked Holt.

"Oh, about a hundred dollars. But," said the counselor, "in terms of duration, cocaine lasts only twenty minutes. ICE, God knows, can last from seven to thirty hours!"

"Who uses the drug more than anybody here on the island?" asked Holt.

"It's interesting," Todd began. "Asians. Not just Filipinos, but Chinese, Japanese, Samoans. Any Asian. I'll tell you another thing that I've begun to observe–there's a far higher percentage of women who use ICE than men."

Holt knew it went against the grain of most drug use. Men always outnumbered women when it came to abusing drugs.

"So just how dangerous is the drug from a physical, mental, and emotional perspective?" asked Holt. He wanted to know the downside.

"Well," said Todd, "I suppose you could say it's similar to cocaine with anxiety, violence, and hallucinations. People can get a little psychotic; especially when they come for treatment. It's one of the biggest problems we're finding here. With most of my experiences, I had to have a doctor give these people medication. They scared the shit out of me.

"Like cocaine, we observed rapid breathing, heart problems, hyperactivity, and a rise in body temperature. And I'll tell you, there are a lot of car accidents. We've also observed that people who have smoked ICE are prone to violence."

"Is that so?" said Holt, just about ready to wrap up his interview. "Lots of violence, huh?"

"You bet!" said Todd. "There's probably as much violence associated with dealers who trade in ICE as there is with people who smoke the shit.

"Oh, one more thing. Again, like coke, you can get addicted to ICE fairly fast. I'm talking about people who get addicted to methamphetamines. And I'm not talking six months or a year. I've heard about scores of users who became addicted to ICE after their first use–their *very* first use!"

❑ ❑ ❑

OCEAN CITY, MARYLAND

I joined the Chemical Girl as she was leaving a tanning salon in North Ocean City on 129th Street and bayside. She was looking bronzer and bronzer, and ignored any comments I made about the dangers of ultraviolet rays. We got into her car, she turned the ignition, and the tune "Don't Play That Song for Me" by Aretha Franklin was playing on the tape deck. It was much too loud, but the Chemical Girl was oblivious to the noise and, as usual, still spoke in a very hushed tone.

She sang along with Aretha, *"I remember when I first met him, he kissed me and he walked away. I was only seventeen, I never knew he'd be so mean. He told me, 'Darling, I love you, baby, baby, baby,' you lied, you lied, you lied…"*

"Any guys ever lie to you like that?" I asked the Chemical Girl.

"All men are liars, Ted," she said as she reached into her handbag, took out two Valiums and a birth control pill and swallowed them down with a miniature of Absolut vodka that she had saved from one of her plane flights.

The Chemical Girl finished off the miniature and pulled the car out of the parking lot onto Coastal Highway.

"Men can't help lying," she said, "especially to women. But I don't give a fuck if they do. I expect it."

❑ ❑ ❑

"Feeling a little down?" I asked.

"Yeah, the demons are visiting," said the Chemical Girl.

The demons were her depression. At first I wasn't sure if the alcohol and/or cocaine had brought it on or not. But during the past few weeks she had confided that she had periodically suffered from depression since she was around twelve. That was about the time when the Chemical Girl began getting high–self-medicating.

"Mom was depressed. That's why she left me. So's my dad. So were my grandparents. They drank, too."

"That's a good family tree," I said sarcastically. I realized then that she never had a chance. "Did I ever tell you about the heredity factor in behavioral health, or about dual-diagnosis programs?"

"Save it, Ted," warned the Chemical Girl. "I've been in more therapy than you could ever imagine, and I've heard plenty of your lectures. I can take care of myself."

Maybe she could. In the early '50s addiction was recognized as a disease. Yet thirty years later, it was still in its embryonic stage. Defined as a chronic relapsing disease of the brain, with less than a thirty percent success rate, we were still just scratching the surface.

However, ties to mental health problems were closing in. True, in the sixties we needed to escape the umbrella of mental health to achieve legitimacy and credibility; but now it looked as if the real reasons for relapse were psychological disorders like anxiety and depression which triggered substance abuse. Whereas we used to think only ten percent of addicts had mental disorders, it appeared way, way higher. Dual-diagnosis programs seemed the way to go, treating mental health and substance abuse together. But the politics of the addiction field, mental health field, and support groups like A.A. and N.A. were fighting it.

Neither professional group wanted to merge. There was disrespect by mental health folks toward addictions counselors. And addiction professions feared being swallowed up again by the umbrella of mental health. There were also funding and reimbursement issues. The older A.A. groups, steeped in tradition, distained medication to alter addiction and psychological problems. Abstinence from substances was the only way in their book. Unfortunately, the addict is the one relapsing....

Chapter 9

The courtroom was packed by nine a.m. on the day of Ron's trial. However, not everyone was there hoping to see the scales of justice tip in Ron's favor. Other people had received summonses to appear in court for various offenses. Everybody had their own cross to bear.

So there was Ron and his lawyer, early in the morning, jammed on a long bench with rapists, murderers, and other degenerates whom society would soon deal with. In the first row of benches, with her fellow cops, was Officer Mary, all dressed up in a skirt and high heels.

"Look at that little tart," Ron whispered too loud. "I'd like to tie her up and fuck her brains out!"

"Shut up!" growled Ron's lawyer, Ira B. Booke, a feisty criminal lawyer originally from New York. "Do you want to go back to jail?"

At the mention of jail and the reminder of that horrible night when he was an inmate, Ron immediately calmed down. He wore a conservative camel sport jacket, rep tie, brown slacks, and shiny shoes. His hair, which he kept unusually short to begin with, had been carefully trimmed. He could have been another one of a dozen or so attorneys who were in court with their clients. But Ron was a defendant charged with a sex crime. *Solicitation for a lewd and disgusting sex act,* read the police charges. *Poor Officer Mary,* thought Ron. *She would've done fine in Puritan New England. They would have elected her local princess! Her husband had better be careful what he asks for late at night: "Gee, Officer Mary, could I masturbate on your belly?" might get him five years of hard labor instead.*

Ron nervously awaited his turn to appear before the judge as he watched his lawyer huddled with the prosecuting attorney and Officer Mary. Things appeared to be going well until she turned and glared at him and made a face of absolute disgust–like he had farted during an embrace–and then shook her head "no" violently. That's when Ron wet his pants.

A few minutes later, Ron's name was called and he sloshed his way up before the judge. He had been cautioned not to speak until his attorney nodded to him. After the prosecuting attorney read the charges, Ron was asked, "How do you plead? Guilty or not guilty?"

At that time, Ron's lawyer stated that he and the state's attorney had been discussing the best way to serve the interests of justice in this case. They agreed to stet the case. After a year, Ron's record would be expunged if he didn't get into any more trouble. He was fined $200 and was free to go.

❏ ❏ ❏

OCEAN CITY, MARYLAND

I asked the Chemical Girl how she could trust herself intoxicated and stoned so much of the time. We were with the Deputy on the Sheraton beach. She looked at me and sighed. "Trust myself? Why the fuck do I have to worry about trusting myself? I can't trust anyone else. The only one I *can* trust is myself."

She reflected a few moments and rolled over to sun the front of her already too tanned body. Looking up at me she said, "Wait a minute. Can anyone trust you? I mean, I know you're separated, but I get the feeling that you've run around some in your time. When you were married, did you cut out a lot? Huh? Did you cat around often?"

"It depends on the definition of 'much,'" I said. "I never went out hoping, trying for something to happen…but if it happened, well then it happened. It wasn't love; it was strictly biological and it never negatively affected my love for my wife Candy. Only she could do that."

The Chemical Girl was rubbing tanning oil seductively on her shapely thighs and legs as she asked, "What do you mean by that?"

"Negatively affected my love for her?" I repeated. "No affair, no tryst, no liaison, no anything could negatively affect my love for Candy, except what she would do to me or around me. That's what did it."

The Chemical Girl then asked me, "Would it have bothered you if you had known that she had been cutting out on you…? And, by the way, do you think she cut out on you, Ted?"

I thought about the answer before saying, "More power to her if she cut out…and yeah, I think when she was a cop, she was fucking another cop. And I think at another time, she was fucking some lawyer. But what the hell, there's nothing I can say about that. It's tit for tat."

The Chemical Girl was now gently oiling her well-toned arms and belly as she turned to the Deputy and asked, "And what about you, Big-Time? Suppose your wife was fucking around? How'd you feel about that?"

The Deputy's face reddened as he blurted out, "I'd kill her. She's the mother of my daughters. I'd definitely fuckin' kill her."

The Chemical Girl laughed. "You're a trip. You have a lot of nerve being such a hypocrite."

❑ ❑ ❑

The Deputy, the Chemical Girl, and I were laughing and carrying on as the sun drifted west past the hotel building. I leaned back on my sand chair and started feeling little prickly stings on my upper back. As I swung around, I saw a small insect fly away, but I couldn't tell what it was.

Later my back began to itch and I asked the Chemical Girl to take a look.

"Jesus, Ted, you've got some big red welts and lumps on your back. It's starting to look like the Rocky Mountains. Something bite you?"

I went into a panic. "Quick. Come with me to my room...."

"Oh, Teddy," cooed the Chemical Girl. "Does this get you hot?"

"No! I've got to get my bee sting kit and shoot it in my leg or anything might happen. You know I'm allergic to bees and wasps and things like that." The Chemical Girl and the Deputy were smiling.

"Calm down. It's just those green flies," insisted the Deputy. "The wind changed and they flew in from the bayside. They're the big ones that bite the shit out of you. They're not like bee stings, though. They're just real itchy and uncomfortable."

"I'm not sure what it was and neither are you," I said loudly. "It could have been anything. And I don't know about the effect of green flies on me. I hate green flies. I hate mosquitoes. I hate all insects. I turned to the Chemical Girl pleading, "I need to get up to my room now! Come with me please!"

We ran up the stairs to my suite at the Sheraton, bypassing the crowded elevators, and rushed into the bathroom to find my bee sting kit. Fortunately, it had not expired. I took out the hypodermic and jammed it into my thigh, shooting what was probably pure epinephrine into my system intramuscularly.

"There," I sighed. "I think I'm gonna be alright now."

The Chemical Girl was smiling. "Ted, you just shot a lot of stimulant into your body, and if you didn't need it, you're gonna be like a speed freak for the next few hours. Why didn't you just put some ice on it, lie down, and take an allergy pill? Or you could have even waited to see the reaction from the bites."

I shook my head. "Look, I understand bees, flies, wasps, mosquitoes, and all insects, and what they can inflict. I've even been to the allergy clinic at Johns Hopkins. I *know* I did the right thing."

Later in the evening, I didn't want to admit to her that I could not fall asleep or even doze. My eyes were dancing and I was totally wired for about thirty-six hours. It was obvious that I didn't need the epinephrine because all the green flies did were aggravate me and leave these tremendous welts on my back. The welts lasted for two weeks and itched constantly. I had the Chemical Girl apply large applications of calamine lotion, but to no avail.

❑ ❑ ❑

ROCKVILLE, MARYLAND

"Let's face it. It doesn't matter if the United States declared martial law and closed its borders to keep heroin, cocaine, and marijuana from being smuggled into the country. Nor does it matter if a drug eradication program destroyed all the crops. We still have the capacity to create and manufacture enough drugs in this county to satisfy every drugger's illicit appetite."

I was speaking at a drug abuse seminar in Rockville, Maryland. "Where there's demand, supply follows regardless of risk, and the U.S., which only represents six percent of the globe's population, consumes more than sixty percent of the world's supply of dope.

"In our country, there are world-class chemists and even world-class idiots who clandestinely produce synthetic drugs that are more potent than drugs already available and in demand on the black market.

"These are known as 'designer drugs,' a term coined by Gary Henderson, a pharmacologist at the University of California at Davis. U Cal Davis and the DEA lab in Falls Church, Virginia are the only labs in America that have sophisticated enough equipment to identify all designer drugs or synthetics of botanically-grown drugs.

"Designer drugs are analogs. By slightly altering the molecular structure of an existing chemical formula a new drug is created, and most of the time it's completely legal. For example, fentanyl is a narcotic-analgesic used in surgery. By slightly altering the molecular structure of fentanyl, a chemist can create an extremely potent form of heroin–anywhere from 100 to 30,000 times more potent than street heroin. On the street, this synthetic heroin is known as Persian or China White heroin. The major problem here for the drug dealer is dosage. It is impossible to determine a safe dose until human experiments are conducted. A dose the size of a pinhead could kill a junkie, so the fentanyl analog must be stepped on and adulterated numerous times.

"Hundreds of deaths have occurred in California since the introduction of synthetic heroin. Over twenty percent of the narcotics on the market are the fentanyl analog. Many users die the instant the needle is injected. Before fentanyl, another designer heroin, MPPP, a meperidine or Demerol analog was sold on the street as very potent heroin from Southeast Asia. It too caused deaths, along with symptoms of Parkinson's disease.

"Fentanyl has also become an enormous addiction problem among doctors, primarily anesthesiologists. Their specialty makes them so susceptible to addiction that it is considered an occupational hazard.

"But there are other designer drugs besides narcotics: PCP, LSD, bootleg Quaaludes, ecstasy, and MDMA. Ecstasy is an analog of an amphetamine and is being called the LSD of the '80s.

"Domestic pot farms, forced inside due to crop eradication processes, which incorporate new growing techniques, have developed a seedless sensemilla hybrid. This has dramatically increased the THC content ten to twenty fold.

"ICE is a crystallized form of methamphetamine which is ingested by smoking and is extremely addictive. Manufactured in Thailand, Hong Kong, and Korea, it was trafficked by Filipino gangs in Hawaii and quickly became the drug of choice on the islands.

"Easy to transport because it is odorless, tasteless, and colorless, ICE sells for more than cocaine. Since the high can last from two to fourteen hours, however, it is quite cost effective. Lots of bizarre and violent behavior results from crystal meth; and overdoses can lead to convulsions, coma, and eventual death.

"Regular methamphetamine, known as 'crank,' trafficked by outlaw bikers, and manufactured in mobile cook-and-go labs in recreational vehicles, is on the rise in rural America.

"This modern moonshine or designer drug is…"

A man in a three-piece suit stood up with his hand raised. "May I interrupt you, Mr., uh, Ted?" he asked.

"By all means," I said.

"Thank you," he began. "I must denounce your use of the term 'designer drug.' It only serves to encourage use or experimentation and makes a mockery of the problem. I…"

"Wait a second," I interrupted. "Who are you?"

"Sorry," the three-piece suit said. "I'm Phillips from the DEA. We prefer the term 'controlled substance analogs,' and I must insist that you use it. You see…"

"Hey, Phillips!" I shouted. "This is my lecture, not yours. You can make your point without insisting that I use *your* terminology."

Phillips stared up at me and gave me a wry smile. "Of course," he said. "Please pardon me. It *is* your lecture. Perhaps we should talk later."

"Thanks, Phillips," I said. "I can't wait. Let's see…okay…the designer drugs are usually sold compressed into pills, applied to blotter paper, in capsules, in plastic bags, or mixed with marijuana. Often they are peddled, disguised as heroin or cocaine.

"Designer drugs…"

Phillips abruptly stood up, turned, and stormed out of the room as I continued my lecture.

❏ ❏ ❏

BALTIMORE, MARYLAND

The Chemical Girl was very disturbed because a sugar deal with Brazil that she and Lo Ming thought was going to materialize had fallen through. She had allowed her boss to use her American Express card and now realized that she would never be reimbursed. The Chemical Girl was in serious debt. Lo Ming had not paid her salary for three months and she had exhausted her life savings– thirty thousand dollars spent over eighteen months for cocaine, chasing a high she could never reinvent or repeat.

We were together in her apartment in downtown Baltimore by the Inner Harbor. Even though she was despondent, her attitude was mostly upbeat, and her immediate desires were sexual. She offhandedly lamented over the money she had blown on cocaine over the past few months. Although she didn't regret her enjoyment from the drug, she could sure use the money now. But she was an eternal optimist and constantly explored that end-of-the-rainbow dream.

"Ted, a few months ago on a plane coming back from Switzerland, I was seated with a heavily accented gentleman who now resides in Ocala, Florida. He told me this wild story about a business he had moved from South Africa to Ocala; an ostrich ranch on which to raise and sell them. He said that every part of an ostrich has a tremendous value in the marketplace, including their toenails, feathers, and skeletal remains."

She asked me if I ever dreamt about leaving Maryland and moving farther south. I told her that I had lots of dreams.

"How much of love is sex?" I jokingly asked her, changing the subject. I'd repeat this question often.

"I told you, ninety-nine percent," she said adamantly.

The public perception of life in America was a fabrication conjured up by the media to project its newsmakers and celebrities. In this case, college basketball superstar, Leonard Bias. Immediately after his death, he was an All-American guy, role model, born again. But a sordid image was beginning to overshadow all that–an insatiable lady-killer and a drug abuser, given to hanging out in bad neighborhoods.

Perhaps it *was* sordid to the still-naive public, rather naive press, and holier-than-thou politicians looking for new heroes. But Bias was mainstream America in the '80s. After all, millions were using and abusing cocaine.

The Incidence and Prevalence Survey of drugs and alcohol conducted by my agency revealed that approximately 500,000 Maryland residents were addicts. One hundred fifty-three thousand were drug addicts, including 51,000 narcotic addicts; 250,000 were alcoholics; and over 90,000 people were addicted to both. This half million represented more than ten percent of Maryland's population. Extrapolated from treatment, arrest, and hospital emergency room records, the Incidence and Prevalence Survey included only addicts, not experimenters or social-recreational users of drugs.

ROUTE 50/EASTERN SHORE

The Chemical Girl left me a message saying she would be at the Sheraton in Ocean City the next day and could stay for only forty-eight hours before leaving for Hong Kong with Lo Ming.

As the Deputy and I were driving back to the shore, he asked, "Ted, do you think you should be hanging around with the Chemical Girl? I mean, she does a lot of dope and she's sure to get busted. If you were with her…"

I knew the Deputy had my reputation at heart, so I didn't argue with his advice. "I'm not worried," I interrupted. "It's the risk of our work, right? Besides, she doesn't do anywhere near as much dope as she used to."

"What do you mean?" the Deputy asked.

"Well, she's been heavily involved in drugs since her early teens, and used to be involved with some very shaky people. But she's changed." God, it was amazing. I was defending a drugger.

"How do you know that?" asked the Deputy. "She could be bullshitting. I think you're blinded by her."

He could have been right, but I believed she had been up front with me. Besides, I was aware of the dangerous people she once hung out with. "She told me that she had done it all at one time or another; every drug and combination available."

"Did she ever speedball?" the Deputy asked.

He could never understand why someone would try to balance the high of a stimulant with a depressant. He loved John Belushi and was unable to comprehend why he was shooting heroin and cocaine at the same time when he died.

"The Chemical Girl told me that she had shot both, but never at the same time. She saw it as a waste of good dope and a good high."

"I agree," said the Deputy.

"But," I said, "she speedballs with other things. First time I was with her she did coke, Xanax, and wine. I've also seen her chew Nicorette gum and smoke a cigarette at the same time. She lies in a suntan booth for an hour and then puts Retin-A all over her face."

The Deputy smiled and said, "Ted, that ain't the same as speed-balling. But it's funnier and more interesting."

OCEAN CITY, MARYLAND

The Deputy was still skeptical about whether the COPYIR program in Ocean City was working. I tried to appease him.

"Look at it this way," I suggested. "The toughest thing with any program is coming up with the acronym, and I think we did a marvelous job with COPYIR." He looked at me and shook his head as I continued.

"Your problem is only being able to see the financial and administration side of this work. Think again about the clinical or programmatic side. We've got some of our most qualified counselors out there. We only use the ones from the methadone programs who are accustomed to the really disruptive clients, and who have tougher jobs than some of the drug-free or alcohol-free outpatient programs. I'm sure it's going to be okay. But, if you're still concerned, c'mon, we'll drive over there and see how it's going."

We drove from the Sheraton on 101st Street all the way south into the old town of Ocean City to the Crisis Center. The Crisis Center operated from eight in the morning until twelve at night. From twelve midnight until eight in the morning, the COPYIR program operated out of the condo where we housed the staff.

It was about nine in the evening when we walked through the door of the health department annex on Caroline Street, a half a block off the Boardwalk. Seated around the table were three counselors. Two of the women worked for the Pimlico Hospital Methadone Program, and the third for the Glendale Methadone Clinic, which is not hospital-based. Both clinics were located in Baltimore City. They looked up and smiled as the Deputy and I approached, asking us why we had come.

"The Deputy wants to find out if the program's working. What's the log book show?"

Laura, a curly-haired, thirty-something black counselor, took out the log book and began to recite, "Well, so far today we've had eight calls. Four people wanted to know when the next A.A. meeting is. Somebody found a pigeon that broke a wing and wanted to know where it could be treated. A woman called who said her husband had beat her up and left the house, gone out drinking, and was due back in five minutes. For that one, we called the police. The others were drug related. Some kid had been given a cigarette to smoke and he knew it was laced with something and was trying to describe it to us. First he said he smoked it. Then he said he didn't. Then he wanted to know if we were confidential. Then he didn't care. He said he'd call back, but he never did. Another kid called about a friend of his who took some strange drug. Unfortunately, none of us could understand what he was talking about, and he said he was going to bring his friend in. We're still waiting for him to show up. Why don't you guys hang around and see what else happens?"

The Deputy spoke up, "Who were those people leaving out the side door as we were arriving?"

Carol, a slim brown-haired woman wearing owl-like spectacles, who was the director of the Pimlico program, answered, "They were from an N.A. meeting that had just broken up. The townspeople really don't want the folks from N.A. and A.A. in this part of town, and we're trying to keep the meetings intact. We're encouraging the attendees not to congregate afterwards or to smoke, but you know how tough that is. Hell, if it wasn't for the no-smoking, no-caffeine rules, Synanon would probably still be around today."

"Well," I said, "let's not aggravate anybody. Being a cult didn't help Synanon either. It was difficult enough getting the founding fathers of Ocean City to okay this place. It's tough on the mayor. He's got a hell of a job to deal with down here. I know the visibility of this kind of program is the last thing that he needs. And loitering creates visibility. At the same time, we don't have much choice. So if there's a problem with N.A. and A.A. meetings taking place here, see if we can relocate or add a meeting to one of the local churches or somewhere not as close to the Boardwalk. Maybe even a couple miles outside of Ocean City."

We were sitting in the lobby quietly watching a video on the television when the door flew open and a guy burst in who looked like he was a renegade from a '60s hippie commune. Tall and thin, he had several tattoos and very long, filthy hair tied in a ponytail. A three- or four-day-old beard covered most of his face, and although he was probably in his late teens, he looked much older.

He spoke up, "You the people I talked to on the phone before about my buddy? I think he needs some serious help." Laura called him over to sit down and asked him what the problem was with his friend.

"My buddy, Lou," he began, "he's sitting out in the car. I don't like to leave him out there too long because he's real fried, if you know what I mean. He was space-basing, and I think it got the best of him. I'm real worried because he's talking weird and acting real funny."

I asked, "What's space-basing?"

He looked up at me and then over at·Carol and said, "Who's this dude?" Carol told him it was okay, that I was the one who had started the program. She asked him to explain space-basing to all of us.

"Oh man, it's kinda…it's like the latest thing, you know. You take crack cocaine, spray it with liquid PCP, and smoke it. And, uh, I don't dig it, you know, because it's a funky kinda rush. It makes you feel real, real crazy. I tried it a few days ago. Bought it from those guys, them uh…uh…you know, the guys that come from the South who work on the farms?"

He was speaking of the migrant workers. There was a segment of migrant workers who trafficked in cocaine, crack, very potent pot, and tootsie roll or black tar smack, the brown heroin from Mexico.

"Anyhow, Lou took a few hits of the space-base, and first he was kinda quiet. Then we went into the Paddock Nightclub, and he pulled me over and told me he saw God up by the back bar. Now, I didn't see God at the back bar, so I asked Lou to describe him. He got pissed off, grabbed me, and told me to look real hard back there, that God was sitting right behind the cash register drinking a Coors Light beer. Well, I still didn't see God. Besides, what would God be doing in the Paddock Nightclub?"

I told the young man to bring his friend in and we'd see what we could do to help him.

"Hey man, he's acting awful strange," he said. "Lou can get real crazy. And even though he's not a strong kid, he's been doing some off-the-wall shit today man; like putting his fist through walls and stuff and putting cigarettes out on his fuckin' forehead. I mean he's acting a little stranger than normal."

The young man walked out and brought in his friend, Lou, who seemed a bit catatonic as he tried navigating his way inside, bouncing off a couple walls and into the sofa by the television. Reese, the other counselor, blond and petite, sat down, looked him in the eye, and asked Lou how he was feeling.

"Well," said Lou, "I'm feeling alright now, but…hey, who the fuck are these two guys here? I just talked to…my man here said there was just women here."

He was staring intently at the Deputy and me now, and was growing paranoid and edgy. Reese told him not to worry and calmed him down for a few moments as I walked over, shook his hand,

and asked him to tell me about his experience with God at the Paddock Nightclub.

"Look man, I ain't fuckin' crazy, but God was there. He was sitting to the right of the cash register. He was drinking a Coors Light beer, and I tell ya, I think he was loaded, and I don't think it was the beer. I think he'd been doing something else because he had a fuckin' glassy-eyed look, and he was acting very, very strange."

"You mean," I asked, "God was stoned, drinking a Coors Light, and acting peculiar at the Paddock Nightclub?"

"Yeah, that's about the size of it," said Lou.

"How did you know it was God?"

Lou stared at me. "Hey, motherfucker, you don't think I know God when I see him? And, you don't think I know when somebody's stoned? And man, you would know that it was God because he looked like God."

"Well, what does God look like?" I asked softly.

"What does he look like? What kind of fuckin' question is that? I mean, God looked like Jesus, except he had on a three-piece suit and was wearing his hair like my buddy here, in a ponytail. But it was cleaner, and he had them thorns, you know, on top of his head. And he also had on them fuckin' John Lennon glasses. But you could tell he was stoned. You could see his eyes right through his glasses.

"So anyhow, I walked over to him," Lou continued, "and I told the bartender I'd have a Coors Light, and you know, give God a drink on me. So the fuckin' bartender called over these two bouncers, and they threw me the fuck out of the place. And I'm gonna tell you something, God did not move. He let them throw me the fuck out, and that pissed me off 'cause I was buying him a drink…. Hey, man, I don't like the way that guy behind you's lookin' at me!"

As soon as he said that about the Deputy, Lou leaped up, knocked me aside, and went for the Deputy's throat. The Deputy grabbed Lou and tried to hold him, but Lou broke loose and bolted out the door. He ran into the street and right into a parked car. He got up, turned around, and began screaming and babbling incoherently.

The Deputy, Lou's friend, and I followed Lou out and tried to subdue him. He was extremely strong for such a frail-looking young man, and he fought us off as hard as he could. The ladies came outside and joined in, trying to grab arms and legs and pin him down. Once we had restrained him, I told Reese to call the police and the paramedics to see if we could get Lou into Peninsula General Hospital in Salisbury.

The ladies were a little uptight about bringing the police into this action since one of the reasons that COPYIR began was to keep these kinds of kids from being arrested. However, the circumstances called for some type of law enforcement here, at least until the paramedics arrived, just enough to keep the young man from injuring himself. We brought Lou back into the Crisis Center and sat him on the sofa.

Carol came over and began to speak to him. She had a very soft, caring voice, and it seemed to calm him. A young college student masquerading as a rent-a-cop for the summer came in. After we briefed the student, we managed to convince him not to call a paddy wagon. He helped us by handcuffing Lou so he wouldn't hurt himself, which was as big a concern as his hurting someone else.

I asked the cop if he had heard anything about this space-basing, and he said no. Then I asked Lou's friend how much of this new drug he had seen.

"I ain't seen much of it. It's out there, but not many want to fuck with it because it makes you real kinda crazy and off the wall. Some guys stay whacked out for hours and hours, others for a couple of days. I seen this girl who did some, and she ain't been right since. She's been bouncing off the walls for about a week and a half. So it's kinda getting a bad rep, you know. I'm not sure if it's gonna be popular, but you people better do something about it. You better get the word out, you know."

An ambulance arrived and the paramedics rushed in. There was a psychiatrist who was doing an internship riding with them, and he gave Lou a dose of medication to sedate him. We thanked the doctor profusely, since most hospitals do not want to deal with druggers, especially those who exhibit violent and bizarre behavior. As the ambulance pulled away and headed across the bridge towards Salisbury, I told the Deputy that he could put his fears to rest. "I think this COPYIR program might work."

He straightened his collar, nodded in agreement, and said, "Let's go get a Coors Light."

❏ ❏ ❏

The Chemical Girl was making another cocaine buy from Backfin Molly. Instead of a gram, she was purchasing a quarter ounce to save herself about a hundred dollars. Backfin Molly met her in North Ocean City on 78th Street at BJ's on the Bay, a popular pub to locals and tourists. The ladies ordered two Bud Lite drafts and sat outside on the deck to watch the sunset. It was a beautiful sight on any clear summer evening.

"This is what got the real estate going on the bayside," said Backfin Molly. "It's the sunset versus the beach and the ocean when you're selling property here."

The Chemical Girl knew that along with the cocaine, any dealing with Backfin Molly included talk of real estate, women's lib, and Ocean City as a way of life.

The Chemical Girl wanted the cocaine very badly, but she also knew that the heat was on in Ocean City. Undercover police were everywhere in the summer. The rent-a-cops were seasonal and not local police, and were, therefore, extremely difficult to spot.

"You need to go out on your own, girl," said Backfin Molly. "Quit countin' on men. They can't be trusted. Be independent...."

"Yeah," said the Chemical Girl, "and be upright and be strong. What's the matter, Molly? Not getting any cock lately?"

"I hate men," said Backfin Molly. "I wish I had a cock. I'd fuck every guy who ever fucked me over!"

"I don't think I'd want a cock like that," said the Chemical Girl. "But it'd be great if I could have a real cock inside of me all the time. Just fathom that, driving around with one, sitting in a meeting with one. God, that'd be so great!"

Backfin Molly broke up laughing. "You slay me, girl. All you think about is sex. Let's cruise on down to the Ocean Club."

The ladies settled their BJ's check and strolled out onto the parking lot. They decided to take Backfin Molly's vehicle for the short drive there.

"How come you're so moody today?" asked the Chemical Girl.

"Shit! I lost a big sale," said Backfin Molly.

"Why?" asked the Chemical Girl, as she lit up a cigarette and placed her feet against the dashboard.

"'Cause of the fuckin' ocean. I had a rich elderly couple from New Jersey ready to buy an oceanfront townhouse on the beach up at 142nd Street. But the beach erosion since their last visit scared them off.

"You know, it used to be that the Army Corps of Engineers, after the hurricane of '33, would build these rock jetties to protect properties on the ocean. The jetties caused more sand to go up onto the beach making it ten times as wide as before. But over the years and after a couple more devastating hurricanes, the beach has gotten smaller."

"How much was the sale for?" asked the Chemical Girl.

"Three hundred and seventy-five thousand dollars. That's all," whined Backfin Molly sarcastically. "I coulda used that commission."

"That's too bad," said the Chemical Girl, snorting cocaine off the knuckle of the index finger of her left hand.

Chapter 10

OCEAN CITY, MARYLAND
AUGUST 7, 1986

The Deputy and I were having lunch at the Sheraton bar with Dancing Dave. We were discussing the Deputy's duck decoy collection and how he'd always been into collecting things. Mainly, he liked to say he did it for investment purposes, but I thought that it was basically more of a hobby.

The Deputy reminisced about his first form of collecting things for investments, going back to his first marriage. He told us a story about how he collected prized tropical fish, and that he had the finest pair of large, beautiful, breeding veiled angelfish anywhere.

"They were prolific breeders," he said, "and they gave me many hours of pleasure. One night I came home pretty late, and as I walked into the living room, I see my angelfish bouncing up and down on the Oriental rug. My wife had knocked over my fifty-gallon aquarium. Not only did it ruin the rug, but also the hardwood floor in the living room. Later, the basement ceiling caved in from the water damage.

"I was terrified that the angelfish wouldn't survive, so I ran to the kitchen, opened the refrigerator, and took out the top of the butter dish. I dipped it in some toilet water, scooped up the fish, and rushed them to a buddy's house."

The Deputy was smiling now. "The fish survived, and I made some money off of the sale of their offspring, but the marriage didn't make it."

Dancing Dave asked the Deputy when he began collecting duck decoys. The Deputy explained that when he used to work at the racetrack, his boss would take him duck hunting. "One day," he said, "we went to my boss' farm, and he showed me his duck decoy collection and water fowl carvings. It got me interested immediately. I saw it as a great investment and was mesmerized by how the art and the craft had come about."

Dancing Dave told the Deputy that when he was growing up in Delaware, his daddy not only collected duck decoys, but also carved them. For his family, hunting and trapping was more of a case of survival than anything else.

"We lived near Bombay Hook about fifty miles north of here," reflected Dave. "It was a big game reserve. Today, all kinds of carvers and photographers go there to take pictures. It's a very beautiful sight to see when the birds are migrating south."

The Deputy was very interested. "You say your father made his own decoys besides collecting old ones? About how many years ago was this?"

"Well," answered Dave, "this was back when I was growing up in the '40s and '50s. He collected them even before then from all around the area. I bet he made himself forty or fifty ducks and about twenty-five geese. He displayed them sitting, standing, perching, fucking, whatever. Sometimes he would trade them off for food, ice, bread, or fish. And he used a special paint so the water wouldn't eat the paint off 'em."

I was growing bored, but the Deputy was growing more fascinated, and he and Dave continued to discuss the decoys.

"Ducks land in seniority," explained Dave, "and they also have a thing about black ducks that are always last to land. I never saw a black duck or a gray duck land in front. After the ducks would land, there'd be no more leadership. But there'd be leadership up there in the sky and when they were landing. The leaders would fly in and break the water to make it easier for the other ducks. My daddy had string attached to the duck decoys so that they wouldn't float away down the river, and they were in the same order that the real ducks were in. The biggest and brightest were the leaders. If you shot the leader of the real ducks, the others panicked and were easy to kill. The toughest to kill were geese though. You know, big neck, small body, very tough to kill."

I walked out to the rest room as Dave continued to mesmerize the Deputy.

"It was funny to watch the ducks and geese," said Dave. "They'd talk to the decoys and mill around 'em. Of course you didn't want to shoot them when they were by the decoys or else you'd destroy the decoys. So what you had to do was to either shoot the ducks when they were landing or when they were taking off.

"Remember, it was no art or hobby then. We were killing ducks and geese 'cause we needed to eat. But they were only good to eat in the wintertime."

Dave was boasting now. "You know, man, I could survive if society was destroyed because I could trap and hunt. Know what I would do? I'd just go right back to Bombay Hook. I mean, I'd rather be a beach bum in St. Thomas to tell you the truth, and I'm working on a deal now, but…"

❑ ❑ ❑

OCEAN CITY, MARYLAND
August 7, 1986

It was early evening and the Chemical Girl was already intoxicated.

"How many drinks did you have so far?" I asked, pissed off.

"Have you seen the keys to my car?" she asked as though she hadn't heard the question. She began to slip into a one-piece white dress, no signs of underwear anywhere. The Chemical Girl looked over at me and said, "Let's see, my girlfriend Molly and I had two Bloody Marys for breakfast. Then we drank some beers on the beach. I can't remember how many. And I sipped about four Stoli's with cranberry juice over lunch.

"Later," she added, "we went to the Ocean Club and had a frozen daiquiri. About a half an hour ago, I had some more Stoli."

I shook my head. "Why don't you cool it out and stay in tonight. Give the alcohol a rest."

"Okay, I'll give it a break," she said. "Before I go out, I'll do some coke. Before bedtime, I'll take two Xanax. Ted, don't lecture me. If it weren't for people like me, you and the Deputy wouldn't have jobs!"

I told the Chemical Girl that I wasn't going out. I thought I'd spite her, but she didn't care. She lived for the night. It was ten p.m. and humid outside when she stormed out of the Sheraton Hotel suite. She didn't return until seven a.m. the next morning and slept until one p.m. I guess I showed her.

❑ ❑ ❑

BALTIMORE, MARYLAND
August 11, 1986

The secretary of health had a bad back, and the only relief she was getting was from acupuncture treatment. She asked if we had ever tried it for addictions.

We tried everything in Maryland, as I'm sure treatment personnel in other states had, too. Since there was no modality of treatment giving better than a thirty percent recovery rate, and that depended on how we defined success, it didn't matter if it were inpatient, outpatient, transcendental meditation, dance therapy, or stand-on-your-head therapy. If it worked for some people, we'd find a way to use it.

Many years ago, I asked Dr. Chen, who had just come to America to work on his Harvard Ph.D., to visit Baltimore to explain the benefits of acupuncture treatment for addiction. We had heard that several Hong Kong neurosurgeons had been inserting acupuncture staples with electrodes passing through them into the ears of patients with neurological problems. They had inadvertently discovered a new way to reduce an addict's craving for opium. Several of their patients had told them that after the acupuncture treatment, they no longer had the desire to smoke opium.

I was fascinated by the concept, so I went to Man Alive, the second oldest methadone maintenance program in America. It was located on Charles Street, a few blocks from our office. I presented a proposal to the director, Richard Lane, offering acupuncture treatment for some of the clients. He said, "It sounds like a great idea, Ted. Why don't you go out into the waiting room to see if anyone is interested?"

I was very excited as I pitched it to the dozen or so addicts who had crowded the lobby waiting for methadone. After explaining how successful the acupuncture treatment was, they all looked at me strangely. Some started to walk out the door. I stopped them, asking "What's the matter with you? What are you scared of?"

One guy answered hostilely, "I don't want any electric needles stuck in my fuckin' ear. And I don't want to be used as a guinea pig."

I was surprised. Again I asked, "But what are you afraid of?"

One man laughed, another got angry, and they both agreed in unison, "We don't want nobody sticking any needles anywhere in our bodies."

I said, "But I don't understand. That's all you ever do. You shoot dope all the time with needles, but you don't want an acupuncture needle stuck an eighth of an inch into your ear?" I guess I said this a little too loudly, since three other guys ran out the door, terrified that they were going to be made a part of an acupuncture experiment.

I visited several other methadone programs. We had at least a dozen in the city at the time. I received the same negative reaction everywhere. It was unbelievable. Here were men and women, many whose veins had collapsed from the overuse of needles, who were frightened to have two tiny acupuncture staples placed in their ear, even though it could possibly end their addiction.

Of course, I was still missing the point—they simply didn't want to stop using.

□ □ □

BALTIMORE, MARYLAND
August 10, 1986

It was one-thirty a.m. and the Chemical Girl was on her way out of the country. I was visiting Jan the Shark Lady, my redheaded friend, when I received a phone call from Ron. In a frenzy, he frantically begged, "Please come to my apartment right away! Use my spare key you have to get in and bring someone with you!" I asked him what was wrong, but he would only say that it was a life or death emergency and to come quickly.

I advised Jan of the call and we hurriedly sped off in her van. Since the tire-slashing incident, I no longer drove my car to her apartment.

Ron had given me keys to the apartment garage and his unit. From time to time, I used his place when I temporarily left Candy, needed a place to take a woman, or just needed a nap–something Candy did not allow in our home. I pulled the van into the garage, and used the bypass key to get into the elevator and up to Ron's floor in this very security-conscious complex.

We entered Ron's apartment but didn't see him anywhere. After calling out his name, he shouted for us to come to his bedroom. The sight was unbelievable. Jan became nauseous immediately and ran into the bathroom to throw up.

Before I continue, I must digress a bit to explain how Ron got into the unusual predicament that Jan and I were observing.

Because Ron couldn't get off with women unless he paid them, he was heavily into prostitutes. Even when he had girlfriends, he had to give them money before he could get involved in any type of sex. Ron was into some very unique and exploratory sexual activities. When he found a prostitute who was very creative and innovative, he usually requested repeat performances. He spent any-

where from thirty to three-hundred dollars a night, usually on weekends, on hookers.

This was a Friday night. Ron had picked up his prostitute friend downtown and they had taken a taxi back to his apartment. He'd nicknamed this particular hooker "Dogface Alice," which was appropriate since Alice had a dog-like face. She was twenty-eight years old with a decent body and was into very kinky sex like Ron.

Alice was no longer a bodybuilder, having been recently banned from competition for stealing handbags from her competitors. She was also caught shooting heroin and cocaine. Steroids were okay, but heroin and coke were taboo.

Dogface Alice's jaws had grown another inch since she and Ron were in Atlantic City the prior month. She had stopped taking steroids, but her jaws continued to grow.

Ron liked to handcuff his girls before engaging in their bizarre sex scenes. Every now and then he even liked for the girls to handcuff him or tie him up and act as though they were raping him.

This particular evening, Ron had tied Dogface Alice to the bedposts and positioned her spread-eagled on her stomach. He wished to engage in what many sexual deviants referred to as "fistfucking" where the aggressor lubricated their entire hand and gradually injected each finger and eventually the entire fist into either the vagina or, in this case, the asshole. It didn't seem to me to be a very comfortable act, and I couldn't understand how people got off by forcing objects, limbs, hands, organs, and even gerbils into the rectum. But then again, it was their sexual preference, and I tried very hard not to be judgmental.

Usually, before Ron got into a crazy scene with the prostitutes, they would do drugs. Ron and Dogface Alice had a preference for cocaine, and were pretty much wired on this particular evening. Since Ron, who was fifty, lived in an apartment complex where the youngest person next to himself was over sixty-five, he was always careful not to make a great deal of noise. He feared being evicted from his apartment, and for that reason, among others, he used a ball-gag on the hookers.

Sparing the details, Ron eventually got his fist up Dogface Alice's ass. However, her sphincter and internal muscles unexpectedly locked onto Ron's fist, and he could not remove it from her rectum. He tried hard and pulled mightily, but to no avail. Despite the ball-gag, her muffled screams elicited enough noise that Ron

*became petrified that the nosy old woman next door would call
Security. And if that happened, he'd surely be thrown out of the
apartment and his parents would find out. It would probably even
make the newspaper and he'd lose his job.*

*Ron couldn't move from the bedroom since Alice was tied and
handcuffed to the bed. He only had one free arm, and after trying in
vain for twenty minutes to break his fist free, he gave up and called me.*

After Jan had vomited and reluctantly returned to the bedroom, I
asked her to assist me in pulling Ron's fist out of Dogface Alice's ass.
It was a very bizarre scene, but I was so caught up in trying to pry
them loose that I was only vaguely aware that this was not the place to
be for someone in my position. Ten minutes of pulling, prying, and
trying to muffle their cries with pillows proved fruitless. I advised Ron
that we needed to get them both to a hospital immediately.

Pimlico Hospital was a mile and a half from Ron's apartment.
Jan and I dressed them as best and as quickly as we could. For Ron
we were able to slip on a pair of pants and pull a shirt over his head
and one arm. For Dogface Alice it was another story. Although we
tried to clothe her, all we were able to do was throw two blankets
over their backs to cover them.

We found the handcuff keys and removed them and the ropes,
but they were still very much attached. They could walk as a tan-
dem, but Alice was in tremendous pain. At one point, we even
contemplated leaving the ball-gag in her mouth to prevent her from
screaming out, but decided against it. Once removed, she cursed
and threatened Ron viciously and continuously as we snuck them
into the hallway, down the elevator, and into Jan's van.

We parked in the hospital parking lot and started to drag the
team out of the van, but Ron resisted. He was adamant that he was
not going into the hospital.

"I can't go in there!" he insisted. "There might be some of my
mother's friends convalescing or other people in there who know
me. There are doctors, nurses, and patients in that waiting room,
and it's just too embarrassing. Get a doctor out here to the van!"

I went into the emergency room and explained to the head nurse
that we had a somewhat complicated emergency. Without going
into detail, I said that it was imperative that a doctor or a very
experienced nurse come out and try to alleviate the problem inside
the van. The nurse shook her head no.

"No one walks out onto the parking lot," she insisted. "This neighborhood has become very bad. Riffraff often try to rob, kidnap, or get drugs and money from doctors and nurses. You have to bring the patients inside."

I returned to the van to explain, but Ron only ordered me to go in and try again without divulging the problem. This went on for the next twenty minutes until Dogface Alice swore that she'd start screaming for the police if we didn't take them into the hospital.

So with blankets awkwardly covering them, Jan and I, with great difficulty, walked Ron and Dogface Alice into the waiting area of the emergency room. It looked as though we were with two people who had on an old-time horse's Halloween costume. It evoked gawking stares from everyone.

It was very early on a Saturday morning and many locals from the surrounding neighborhoods were there to be treated for various wounds, illnesses, and drug overdoses. However, it sobered up many a folk as they observed Dogface Alice and Ron who resembled the rear of a horse. We told the waiting room audience that they were rehearsing for a play and there had been a slight mishap.

The people were trying to imagine what went wrong, and I doubt if anyone in their wildest dreams or nightmares could ever figure it out. I went back to the head nurse and escorted her to the pair, lifting the blankets. I thought the nurse would pass out, but instead she bit her tongue, nervously laughed, and yelled out, "Alright, let's go!"

The nurse hurried us into one of the rear emergency rooms away from the other patients and placed Ron and Dogface Alice on an oversized hospital bed in a kneeling position. A physician of Indian descent appeared shortly, and although he had probably seen a lot in his day, his eyes could not defy the bewilderment and shock when he pulled back the curtain.

In what seemed like seconds, the entire nursing, physician, and orderly staffs had found a reason to peek into the room. It became the talk of the hospital within minutes. People in the waiting area tried to fabricate reasons to get a look, almost creating a mini-riot. Security was ordered to guard the corridor doors and the room where the doctor was working feverishly to remove Ron's fist from Dogface Alice.

Eventually, after using a hypodermic muscle relaxant, Ron's fist was freed, causing screams of anguish from the pair. Ron's hand immediately cramped up and Dogface Alice was suffering from severe pain. This sent the security guards scurrying in, although they probably just wanted to see what the furor was about.

More doctors and nurses appeared, and Ron was mortified.

Dogface Alice was still livid. Jan and I simply sat there and stared at the unbelievable scene. Urinalysis and other tests were performed, and Ron and Dogface Alice were educated on abusing drugs...and fists.

I refused to give my name, explaining that we were simply neighbors helping out. Jan went to the bathroom to vomit a couple more times.

After cleaning up Dogface Alice and Ron, they were prescribed antibiotics and given tetanus shots. I prayed that there were no newspaper or TV reporters around. I could see the headlines–*State Drug Chief in Bizarre Sex Scene, Film at Eleven.*

Once the doctors and nurses finally left the room, Dogface Alice informed Ron that she expected a bonus or she would call the police immediately. Having no cash on hand, Ron borrowed a hundred dollars from me to keep her quiet. He was still terrified that there was a nurse, doctor, or patient who might know his mother, and hoped that the confidentiality statute would stick so he wouldn't have to sue the hospital.

Jan and I eventually sent Dogface Alice home in a cab and dropped Ron off at his apartment. I lectured Ron to refrain from fist-fucking, hoping that he had learned a lesson. It was now three-thirty a.m. and the long day and unnerving scene were finally over. Ron didn't leave his apartment for over three weeks.

❑ ❑ ❑

August 11, 1986

I told the secretary of health about Ron and his fist-fucking episode, and she said, "I can top that!" This was amazing since I didn't think anyone could top Ron's story.

When the secretary was a nurse, she worked in an emergency room. Late one night, a woman came rushing in, pulled her aside, and told her she had a little problem. The woman explained that she had been peeling potatoes in the nude when the telephone rang and had sat down suddenly on a kitchen chair to answer it. Not realizing that one of the peeled potatoes had fallen on the chair, it slid up her vagina and got stuck.

The secretary was flabbergasted and could not imagine that something like that could actually happen. She summoned one of the residents who spoke briefly to the woman. The resident doubted the story, but asked the secretary to prep the woman for an examination.

"An Idaho potato, which is usually half long and skinny and half fat, isn't something that could easily just slide up a woman's vagina," the resident explained.

In the end, the potato was really there, and he was able to remove it. But guess what the secretary told me? It wasn't peeled.

❏ ❏ ❏

HONG KONG/SHANGHAI/DETROIT
August 11-17, 1986

The Chemical Girl's latest trip to Hong Kong and mainland China was typical, although traveling with Arthur Lo Ming was anything but typical. Their flight on United Airlines, originating in Baltimore, found them in first class swallowing down the potent sleeping pill Halcion with champagne.

In Osaka, Japan they switched to Cathay Pacific Airlines. Often during these trips, they missed their scheduled connections due to Lo Ming's vanity. He spent a considerable amount of time in the bathrooms primping, spraying his hair, shaving and washing his face, and applying makeup to hide his acne scars. Then he had to have his $900 shoes shined.

The Chemical Girl lived in constant fear that their drugs would be found, since it was common for Arthur to pass out in the plane's bathroom from the alcohol and altitude. Her heart would skip a beat, this time from fear instead of cocaine, when the stewardess would say, "Mrs. Lo Ming, your husband has passed out in the bathroom. Please come with me." The Chemical Girl was always mistaken for his spouse, to Lo Ming's delight. It gave him the courage to grab her ass frequently. And with both hands! God, how it annoyed her.

Upon their arrival in Hong Kong, Lo Ming's disdain for waiting had them taking a limo into town without their luggage. Lo Ming would pay someone at the hotel to retrieve the bags later.

Lo Ming and the Chemical Girl brought their own drugs, courtesy of Lo Ming, who felt that providing drugs to the Chemical Girl would soften her up for his amorous advances. The strategy never succeeded, however. Lo Ming was a notoriously cheap drunk and drugger, whereas the Chemical Girl could ingest huge amounts of dope and alcohol before inebriation set in, if it ever did.

Before and after dinner at the Peninsula Hotel, Lo Ming and the Chemical Girl snorted coke. During dinner, they drank vodka and champagne. At the popular hotel disco, more coke was consumed.

After hours, back in their elaborate hotel suite at the Meridien Hotel, Valium, coke, vodka, and Xanax were ingested. Lo Ming would strip down to his boxers and crudely advance upon the Chemical Girl. She maintained enough distance, occasionally sprinting and jumping away from Lo Ming's lunge. Fortunately for the Chemical Girl, within twenty minutes, Lo Ming had characteristically passed out. Each night, he would try again to no avail.

❏ ❏ ❏

"There's not one part of the ostrich that can't be turned into a profit," the Chemical Girl told an inattentive Lo Ming. "Even the corneas and the long, flirty eyelashes are exploitable. The corneas are sold to medical schools, and the eyelashes go to manufacturers of false eyelashes. Also, Arthur, consider this: You get two hundred dollars for the feathers; seven dollars a pound for the meat, which is considered to be a delicacy in Europe and Africa, and there's at least a hundred pounds per adult bird; twenty-five dollars or more per square foot for the hide for a minimum of three hundred ninety dollars a bird; thirty to fifty dollars for the shells; and then there's the miscellaneous stuff that sells for jewelry and curios such as the feet and the claws. So, what do you think?"

Lo Ming hadn't heard a word. "Get me Ritchie in Zurich. I want to ask him about the fertilizer deal," he ordered.

❏ ❏ ❏

Lo Ming and the Chemical Girl flew into Shanghai, China by way of CAAC Chinese Airlines, whose planes were Russian Aleutian models known to be somewhat heavy and unsafe. Although security in Red China was extremely tight and unfriendly, Lo Ming still brought cocaine with him in matchboxes in his jacket pockets. For him, the chance of screwing the Chemical Girl was worth the possibility of years in a Communist prison.

Lo Ming was closing in on a major liquid latex deal. The liquid latex was manufactured in Thailand and shipped to China in metric-ton drums. Naturally, the Chemical Girl was excluded in any face-to-face meetings since this was where the real corruption took place. The Chinese would never trust her, or any woman for that matter.

Liquid latex had become extremely valuable on the open market since the AIDS scare. It was the base ingredient in the manufacturing of latex examination gloves, which were produced in a factory in Dalian, China.

Hundreds of thousands of dollars exchanged hands in Lo Ming's dealings in the Orient, including dealings with the banks. These "fees" were a way of life and business in the Far East. In Western culture, they were considered to be bribes.

While Lo Ming conducted business at all hours of the night in unspecified locations in Shanghai, the Chemical Girl would help herself to the cocaine matchboxes and then be chauffeured around the city by the banker's son and his driver. She had met the banker's son, Zhen, while he was in the States, and had taught him to drive and obtain an American driver's license, a major status symbol in China.

In Shanghai, they stayed at the first luxury high-rise hotel built there. Still under construction, the new Sheraton was first class. The front of the building was enclosed in glass from top to bottom and was in stark contradiction to its surroundings–dreary, dark, half built, industrial, and depressing, with parts of the city resembling a war zone. The Chemical Girl escaped the depression with warm local beer, Xanax, and cocaine.

Lo Ming had no fear of wheeling and dealing in the Far East, especially Red China. Bribery and corruption were easy there. Nobody fucked with China. Nobody.

❏ ❏ ❏

Usually when Lo Ming and the Chemical Girl returned to the States, they carried large sums of money which they didn't want to declare.

Since they had used up all of their drugs on the trip, they were only concerned with the $300,000 in cash that they were bringing in. The Chemical Girl could not carry any noticeable weight on her body due to her close-fitting dresses, and Lo Ming would not allow her to wear jeans or slacks, ever.

Because security at Detroit's airport was tight, the Chemical Girl had insisted that Lo Ming carry all the cash through Customs.

It was good instinct on her part since her baggage was thoroughly investigated and she was subjected to a humiliating strip-search.

"Damn it, Arthur. That's the last fucking time I go with you through Detroit!" she cried.

"Put your hair back up," he said. Lo Ming insisted that the Chemical Girl present a sophisticated image with him, and he loved her hair up, as it was worn in traditional Oriental culture.

"Fuck you, Arthur!" she cried. "And the next time I get prodded by some jerk-off custom agent, I'll personally shove the cash up your ass while you're in a drunken stupor!"

❑ ❑ ❑

Charles Lefty Driesell was the quintessential Southern cornpone coach. He was tall and bald, walked with a slight stagger, and was very charismatic. An excellent recruiter, Driesell had changed Maryland's early '70s basketball program. Despite his prediction of making "Maryland the UCLA of the East," a quote that came back to haunt him, he'd done a remarkable job.

I liked Lefty. He was personable, charming, and funny. When the Bias incident hit, I felt sorry for Lefty and defended him against his detractors. But as time passed, a different image of Lefty began to appear, and respect for Coach Driesell was quickly slipping away. Not because of Bias' death; that wasn't Lefty's fault. Nor was it because of the incidence of drug abuse among some athletes.

But it was obvious that the Lefty of the 1980s had become a different coach, recruiter, and administrator than the Lefty of the 1970s. Times had changed him, and so had his assumption of power and influence.

Most of the players didn't like Lefty, yet I'm sure that Bias had a special relationship with him. Athletes who were marginal players felt that Lefty was a phony. They noticed he was your best friend one day when it suited him, and the next day he acted like he didn't know you. Perhaps, though, that was how Lefty motivated the players–his psychological strategy.

Chapter 11

I glanced up from my desk to find a huge black guy with a big smile on his face standing in my office. All I could see was black, and beautiful white teeth. It was my old friend, the former Major Dorsett, who had worked with me in the early '70s in the Drug Abuse Administration.

"Hey, Ted, how ya doin'?" Major Dorsett shouted. Any comment out of Major Dorsett always seemed very loud, but it was a jovial kind of shout.

I invited him to sit, and we caught up on some old times for about a half hour. Then he got to the point of why he had come.

"Me an' some people have some backers with some serious money who want to open up a private drug rehab program for executives in the Caribbean."

"Major," I said, "that sounds like a great idea, and I wish you all the luck in the world. Anything I can do to help, I will. But it sounds awfully expensive...."

"Ted," Major Dorsett interrupted, "money's not a big object here. What I came for was to ask if you would consider serving as the executive director of the program. You can make a lot of money. Besides a good salary and some other perks, I might be able to get you a piece of the action. You fill a certain number of beds and anything over that you get a percentage of each of those additional beds. With your reputation, with all the people you know, and the magical way you handle the media, you'd be a great asset to us. We'd really love to have you. Think it over for a minute or two."

I sat for a while and thought about the Major's proposal. Over the last few years, I'd received a number of job offers, but I always felt secure with the state job and figured I could retire in about ten more years if I could survive being on call twenty-four hours a day. But the days were getting longer and the field of drug abuse was getting crazier and more discouraging.

"What kind of salary and perks are we talking about?" I asked. "And when would I share in a piece of the action?"

The Major gave me that big smile of his again, and answered, "Ted, the salary starts at $100,000 a year, probably twice what you make now. You get a car and an apartment on the grounds of the facility, and many other perks. You can hire and fire anybody you please, not like with the government. If you're interested give me a call in the next three weeks, and we'll talk about how much of the action you can get and how soon. Gotta run now. You take care. And don't forget to call!"

❑ ❑ ❑

As I mulled over his offer, I thought back to my earlier association with Dorsett. In the early '70s, we operated a methadone maintenance and detox program called ADAPT on Pennsylvania Avenue, near Mosher Street, which used to be the black entertainment district in Baltimore. It treated, at its peak, over twelve hundred patients a day. Fearful of the neighborhood and of the clients, many counselors and administrators refused to work there.

Major Dorsett had no such fear. He had done several tours of duty in Vietnam, was a decorated veteran, and a specialist in karate. The South Koreans in Vietnam, some of the most ferocious and merciless fighting soldiers in the world, had instructed him in karate.

So Major Dorsett and Sadie O'Rourke, one of the few social workers who was experienced in addictions, ran ADAPT.

There were always arguments and confrontations among the patients in the program. We had security guards around the clock, yet the clients were neither afraid nor impressed by a show of force. We were also concerned that the police might conduct covert surveillance at ADAPT. Following an addict was an easy way for them to make an arrest, but this involvement would have severely violated patient confidentially. The strongest statute for confidentiality in the country was in force in the drug treatment field. We had constant battles with the police and in the courts about violations of confidentiality and surveillance conducted outside of the methadone programs.

Major Dorsett, in his first few months of running ADAPT, solved many problems. He was respected and feared by the patients and clients in the program, as well as the police and the staff. He ran a very tight ship. With the exception of failing to convince a counselor whom we had sent down from our headquarters office to unlock the door of his office and go home, Major Dorsett didn't experience many setbacks. The counselor sent to ADAPT had never been exposed to narcotic addicts and dealers who loitered around the clinic, or to their confrontational attitudes. He became so terrified by what he saw and the patients on the program who approached him on his first day of counseling that he locked himself in his office. He barricaded the door and refused to let anyone in other than to open it briefly for meals, staying there for twenty-six days before he finally got up enough nerve to leave the building. He resigned and became a door-to-door pots and pans salesman.

Major Dorsett was returning from graduate school early one evening when Margarete, a very petite black woman, approached him. She had been thrown off the ADAPT program for having a number of dirty urines and for pulling a knife on one of the counselors when she failed to get one of her girlfriends accepted in the program. Margarete had been given a number of chances and had lost many privileges and was finally dismissed by Major Dorsett for the knife-wielding incident. She was extremely upset that she could no longer receive methadone and went back to the streets to buy it illegally–methadone that had either been stolen from treatment programs or sold by a client on a program from their take-home dosage.

Margarete strolled up to Dorsett and begged him to let her back in the program. He told her that she didn't have a prayer of being readmitted, and that he didn't want her loitering around the facility. She followed him up the street badgering him before beginning a violent argument. Major Dorsett stopped and turned around to face her. The confrontation became ugly and his voice rose. And then suddenly he was standing on his toes. Margarete had grabbed his nuts and held them in a deathlike grip. "Stay up on your toes, sucker, 'cause you're gonna lose your manhood if you don't put me back on this fuckin' program!" she ordered.

Major Dorsett, who had faced some very difficult obstacles in Vietnam, was speaking in a very high falsetto voice. He slowly began walking up the street, and the petite heroin addict kept her hold on his balls as they approached the front steps of the treatment program. As they entered ADAPT, Major Dorsett ordered everyone to stand clear as they walked back to the nurse who doled out the medication.

"Please give this woman eighty milligrams of methadone," Dorsett implored. The nurse stared at Dorsett who was still up on his toes, then looked at Margarete.

"But Major," she cried, "this woman's been put off of the program. You told me never to give her methadone again."

"Immediately!" screamed Major Dorsett. "Give her the dose of methadone right now or I'm coming through the cage after you!" he cried out again. The nurse finally took out the methadone, mixing it with Tang orange drink, which was the way it was dispensed, and handed it to the woman.

Still holding on to Dorsett's nuts, Margarete gulped down the methadone, thanked the nurse, and advised the major, "This wasn't just for one time only, you know. It's every day. And every time I don't get my meth, I'm gonna squeeze your nuts harder. And I'll find your nuts wherever you hides them." With that she was out of the door in a flash.

❏ ❏ ❏

"Hey, I just saw that old patient of yours duck away like he didn't want to see you," said the Deputy. "I'll bet he relapsed and is probably embarrassed." We were walking to lunch at Tyson's Place, a couple of blocks from our office.

"No," I said, "he's not trying to avoid me because he's dirty. It's actually because he's clean."

"Huh?"

"Look," I said dejectedly, "it's very complicated."

The Deputy was perplexed. "Ted, I don't get it."

"This is the only field of health," I said, "where the clinician is never appreciated after successful treatment, except in a few instances."

"You're telling me that because you got that guy on the road to recovery, turned around his life, took him outta the sewers that he thinks you're a pariah?"

I was astonished at the Deputy's use of the word "pariah."

I explained to him that during my first ten years in the addictions field it was very frustrating to discover that my few private patients, and some of the public clients I had taken an interest in, acted strangely towards me a year or so into recovery. Anytime I ran into them, they had little or nothing to say. This behavior astounded me since these were the same individuals who couldn't thank me enough early on.

Disillusioned, I approached treatment guru Dr. Sid Cohen and asked him about this phenomenon. "Sid, is it my breath? Was my clinical style offensive? What did I do to cause this reaction? I mean, we have so few successes in the field as it is."

Dr. Cohen sat me down and shook his head. "It's the curse of the addiction medicine field. After an addict is cleaned up and sober for a long period, their reaction to the therapist isn't all thanks, praise, cards, and flowers. The opposite occurs. Because you've seen these people at their worst–committing unspeakable acts, lying, stealing, robbing, abusing, whatever–they resent you. You remind them of their past misdeeds. And you've modified their behavior, which they look upon as a control issue. Therefore, it's natural for them to avoid you. But to us, as clinicians, it's very hurtful.

"If you stay in this field, get used to it; although many of us never do. Actually, it still pisses me off when I get that reaction, but what can I do? They thank you for fixing a broken leg, for driving away depression, for cleaning an infection, for bypassing a clogged artery…but seldom for this."

❏ ❏ ❏

BALTIMORE, MARYLAND
August 24, 1986

The nagging cough was still there. My dad finally convinced me to see another doctor. I went back to Johns Hopkins to see Dr. Michael Holliday who had operated on my broken nose years before, and who was considered one of the finest ear, nose, and throat specialists in the nation. I explained my cough to him. "Doc, it's gotta be AIDS. I know I'm dying."

He laughed, took a throat culture, and said, "It looks as if the infection is still around. I'll get back to you in about four days."

"Why will it take so long?" I asked. "The doctors at Instant Care prescribed an antibiotic immediately." He laughed again, told me to wait the four days, and discharged me from his office. I was sure it was AIDS.

After four days I called, still coughing and unable to sleep with that irritating tickle in my throat. I felt terrible. Doc Holliday informed me that the infection was in fact still there and that he would be prescribing a very potent and expensive antibiotic.

"What makes your antibiotic different from the doctor's at Instant Care?" I asked.

He explained that a throat culture should sit a minimum of seventy-two hours or longer. That way he could test different antibiotics to see how they reacted to my virus. In this case, at least three days were necessary for a physician to prescribe the correct antibiotic for the type of virus that was causing the cough.

"True," Doc Holliday continued, "you can get lucky about seventy-five percent of the time just by guessing at the right antibiotic. But in your case, this method can be extremely ineffective. Your cough would have continued until the right antibiotic was administered or until you became deathly ill. The longer the culture incubates the more different antibiotics we can test on it and the more accurate we are. You should be alright in a couple of days."

I picked up the prescription right away.

While I was in his office, Doc Holliday asked me how things were going. I explained that the cocaine problem was rolling, and he told me a story about his days in Vietnam in the late '60s that enlightened me to just how clever the Vietnamese were.

"Ted, the cocaine trade started years earlier. You could say it brought on a major heroin crisis in Vietnam with our GIs, in an indirect way. When fresh GIs from the States would deplane in Da Nang and Saigon and walk through those South Vietnam cities, they'd see the Vietnamese black marketeers. The marketeers would tell the young GIs that they were selling vials of cocaine.

"The Vietnamese knew about the horrors of heroin addiction in the United States. They knew there was no way they could sell heroin or opium for what they truly were. So they sold vials of heroin or opium to American soldiers under the guise of cocaine. The young GIs knew about cocaine from back home and because they had read magazine articles about celebrities who had used it. They believed it was both nonaddicting and nontoxic. They knew it was a great high for a recreational drug, so they purchased the vials very inexpensively.

"They snorted or smoked the so-called cocaine, and before long realized it wasn't cocaine. But they didn't give a shit. This started many U.S. soldiers on their way to heroin addiction. It was an escape from the tremendous stress and intolerable conditions of Vietnam. The U.S. Army reported that only a small percentage of soldiers were addicted to heroin. But in reality, the percentage was very high. It was quite scary.

"The vast majority of Vietnam vets cleaned up their acts when they got back to the States. Yet it was the marketing genius of the Vietnamese that helped skyrocket heroin sales and the spread of addiction. In some way, it probably helped America lose the war."

True to Doc Holliday's word, I recovered. Unbelievably, by the second day, the new antibiotic was working, and I felt a hundred percent better. It was a valuable lesson. Obviously, Johns Hopkins Hospital had better diagnosticians than the Instant Care Center on the Eastern Shore of Maryland. Shocking.

❑ ❑ ❑

I thought back to Vietnam, heroin, Nixon, methadone…and Jerry Jaffe. Dr. Jaffe was one of my few real heroes–a brilliant psychiatrist and academic researcher who was tapped by President Nixon in 1970 to head up the Special Action Office for Drug Abuse Prevention (SAODAP). Jaffe came to be known as The First Drug Czar of the United States. Urged by Nixon to curb the drug menace, Jaffe was concerned about the number of American soldiers returning from the unpopular Vietnam War who were frequent users of heroin.

Addict estimates for this cohort ranged from twenty to thirty percent of these servicemen. Jaffe influenced Nixon to greatly increase the number of federally-funded drug treatment programs. Within two years, nationwide methadone clients topped out at 80,000. Interestingly, expansion of drug treatment, normally equated with more liberal administrations, was one of Nixon's greatest accomplishments in dealing with curtailing violence and social disorganization.

Unfortunately, within a few years, the popularity and positive reputation of methadone was undermined by the public's belief that it was a cure similar to penicillin for pneumonia. Since methadone was only a form of treatment more like insulin for diabetes, this thinking was incorrect. As a result, the myth was created that methadone was dangerous and would produce even worse addiction.

❑ ❑ ❑

OCEAN CITY, MARYLAND

At the bar on the beach behind the Sheraton Hotel in Ocean City, the Chemical Girl swayed seductively to the steel drum band's rendition of "Red, Red Wine," a song of drinking and escape. Originally written in 1968 by Neil Diamond, the song had been re-released as a white reggae version by UB40. Clad in her pink bikini, holding a matching pink glass of vodka and cranberry juice and mouthing the words of the song, she confessed that she was named for her drinking escapist paternal grandmother–a Lola of a bygone era.

The first Lola Killen was born in 1918 to Nora and Alex Killen. She was of Dutch, Irish, and Cherokee Indian descent and grew up in Letcher County, Kentucky. Bordered by Pikeville, it was the site of the nation's most famous family feud, the Hatfields and the McCoys. Letcher County was also bordered by Hazard County where the show "Dukes of Hazard" took place. Lola was one of nine children and among the six who would die before the age of thirty-one. She had a passion for alcohol, as did her brother, Morgan, who died of liver disease as a result of abusing moonshine.

Alex Killen married Nora Wright around 1902 and fathered all nine children. The son of a full-blooded Cherokee Indian father and an Irish immigrant mother who died during childbirth, Alex was known for his irrational behavior and abusive drinking. His disdain for his stepmother was so overwhelming that he decided to kill her. He went to his father's house, and just as he was pulling the trigger of his gun, his father stepped in front of his stepmother. The gun fired, killing his father instantly.

Alex fled to the far western state of Washington where he hid out. His family would join him later. After a while, he decided to return to Letcher County with his family and turn himself in. He was sentenced to ten years in prison. While there, a fire broke out and Alex escaped the flames and smoke, but others were trapped inside. He went back into the prison to help rescue his fellow prisoners and guards, and punctured his lung during a fall. Because of his heroism and medical condition, he was granted a full and free pardon and released from prison. He died shortly after returning home.

Lola's mother, Nora, had a temperament similar to that of her husband. Early in her marriage to Alex, she caught him with another woman. Nora, armed with a twelve-gauge, double-barreled shotgun, met the woman near the railroad tracks. The woman ran, but Nora fired anyway, striking her in the ass. Fortunately the woman was wearing a thick fur coat that stopped the full impact of the birdshot. Unfortunately, the woman still had birdshot in her ass which had to be removed. Occurrences like this were common in those parts of Kentucky, but few were ever prosecuted.

To support her very large family when Alex was forced to flee after killing his father, Nora became involved in moonshining or "shining" as it was known–selling either illegally manufactured moonshine called "white whiskey" purchased in Kentucky or red whiskey purchased in Virginia which, unlike Kentucky, was not a dry state after the end of Prohibition.

Nora's oldest daughter, Bertha, helped her with the shining business. Not only did Bertha package the booze, she became pretty good at tasting it as well. On two occasions mother and daughter were busted for moonshining. Released after paying a fine, Nora and Bertha were warned that the next time they were caught, they would be jailed.

Nigger Fats, who ran the whiskey from the still where it was purchased to the home of Nora and Alex, delivered their supply in five-gallon crocks which cost fifty dollars apiece. This would be made into half-pint and pint bottles of moonshine, selling for three and five dollars respectively, a hearty sum during the Depression.

On one occasion, Combs, a friendly man who was known as the "high" sheriff of Letcher County, appeared at the house informing Nora and Bertha that the revenuers had caught wind of their operation and were on their way to the arrest them.

During this time, it was necessary for the feds to obtain a sample of the whiskey to make a case. Bertha began frantically breaking the five-gallon crocks and small bottles in an effort to pour the moonshine into the ground. The agents arrived while she was attempting to break the final, and very stubborn, crock. She viciously attacked one agent, holding him off long enough to try to break the crock several more times. Suddenly, she was struck in the head with a blackjack, knocking her into semi-consciousness, and the sample was secured. While the agents were attempting to place her mother Nora under arrest, Bertha came to and insisted that the whiskey belonged to her. She didn't want to see her mother, with so many young children, sent to prison.

Nora was fined $5,000 for having the business on her property, while Bertha was sentenced to three years in Alderson Federal Prison in West Virginia.

While serving her time, Bertha never forgot the person she learned was the informant, and vowed to seek revenge. Upon her release from Alderson, she went looking for Jeb McGee, the man who had sold out the family business. Bertha found McGee in a bar in Virginia. She approached him with a knife and swiftly stabbed him. To avoid being recognized and returned to prison, she did not remain on the scene long enough to determine whether she had killed him, but felt certain that she probably had. Bertha fled to Kentucky and later left her family for Baltimore.

Bertha had been married at one time. Family members found her husband dead of a gunshot wound, and it was declared a suicide. There was always some controversy as to whether it was in fact a suicide.

In her teens Lola married James O'Reily, a local coal miner. After her husband went to work each evening, she would visit the honky-tonks or speakeasies in a nearby town called Potter's Fork. These places were not really bars since Prohibition was in effect, and even after its end the area remained dry. After work, James would find her, and quietly and patiently take her home, remarking only that she was a mouse. No one ever figured out what he meant.

They had a son, Ronald, who sadly never had the opportunity to enjoy a family life with his mother and father. Lola's mother Nora feeling that Lola's free-spirited, unstable lifestyle made her incapable of raising Ronald, became his caretaker.

Before Ronald was two years old, his father was seriously injured in an automobile accident. James had a thirst for whiskey, too. The car he was driving plunged over Hayside Mountain in West Virginia where James and Lola were living at the time. James was placed in a body cast, and after a while, tired of not being able to move around, he had an uncle remove the cast prematurely. On crutches, he went out drinking, developed pneumonia, and died at the tender age of twenty-two.

Shortly thereafter, Lola followed in her sister, Bertha's, tracks and moved to Baltimore, Maryland. She lived on West Lombard Street and worked at Glenn L. Martin as a riveter during World War II. Lola was seldom home. She was living with a man named Thurman, who would later help care for Ronald, while seeing an older gentleman, Ray, on the side.

A short while later, Lola was diagnosed with tuberculosis and placed in a sanitarium where doctors performed the recently introduced radiation treatments. This left her with very little voice, and she was sent home to Kentucky with no hope for recovery. Bedridden and only able to whisper, she called for Nora's sister, Aunt Rose, to come to her bedside, confiding, "I'm going to die today. My only regret is that I have to leave my baby. But I've enjoyed every day of my life." Lola died later that day at the age of twenty-five.

Ronald witnessed the untimely death of his mother Lola. Although too young to fully understand the life and death of his father James, Lola remained in his memory—a party girl who loved him, but was never home, and who died when he was only five years old. Ronald would eventually name his daughter in her honor.

Ronald was raised by Nora and a couple of his aunts until he left Kentucky for Baltimore at the age of fifteen. He went to work at the Sparrows Point shipyards, received a high school diploma after attending night school, and began taking evening classes in Education at the University of Maryland, Baltimore campus.

Eva, a barmaid, who worked at Renee's Cafe across from the University, started dating Ronald. She became pregnant, but refused to marry him. She gave birth to an eight-pound baby girl and moved in with Ronald following her release from the hospital. Six months later, Ronald came home from work to find his baby daughter Lola alone and crying. Her mother had disappeared.

Several weeks later, Eva called. She told Ronald that she was never coming back and not to look for her. That was the last anyone ever heard from Eva.

Nora moved to Baltimore to help raise her great-grandchild, Lola. When Lola was teething, Nora rubbed moonshine on her gums to ease the pain and help her fall asleep.

Ambitious and determined, by 1966 Ronald had received his bachelor's and master's degrees in Secondary Education and was the Principal at Crestheights High School in West Baltimore County.

❑ ❑ ❑

"Dad always worries that I'm gonna end up like my Grandma Lola," said the Chemical Girl.

"Did he raise you most of the time?" I asked.

"Until my great-grandmother, Nora, died when I was ten or eleven. She took care of me with Dad, and then I lived with him until he moved to Minneapolis."

"When was that?" I said.

"Let's see. I finished high school," said the Chemical Girl between sips of her drink, "when I was sixteen. Then I went to work for Lo Ming, and Dad left town when I was nineteen, and I got my own apartment."

❑ ❑ ❑

"See the young lady there?" Tim Wood asked, pointing to a photograph. "She's a girl who's been dealing drugs for a while in

Ocean City, Dewey Beach, Fenwick Island, Bethany, and Rehoboth. She's a mid-level dealer with a pretty good size territory and lots of regulars. She's lived in this town for a long, long time." Tim had asked to meet me at the Plim Plaza Hotel. We were outside in front of the Plim on the Boardwalk, and he was showing me his latest set of photos. The young lady was Backfin Molly.

"You can't quite make out who she's dealin' with in this picture, but you can in these other two," said Tim. "Actually, I like this one picture best because you can see the Fenwick Lighthouse in the distance. If these weren't pictures that the police had asked me to take, I would definitely blow this one up and frame it."

I was getting a little antsy because I knew that Tim was driving at something; but he was taking some time getting to the point. "Tim, I've got to be back up at the Sheraton in an hour."

"Hold on, Ted," said Tim. "It could be I'm helpin' you here. Let me show you some other pictures. Here's that girl, Backfin Molly, again. Here she's dealin' drugs. You can't really make out who's in the picture here…"

"Tim," I interrupted, "what's the story? You working for the police? What gives?"

Tim smiled now and said, "I do favors for the police sometimes. And sometimes the police do favors for me. Now this operation isn't really like the big and sophisticated ones that have police photographers on the payroll and so forth. I mean, let's face it, Ted, the police are here to keep a lid on the town, to maintain crowd control. That's their main objective. All the other stuff is just ancillary. Still, they're very concerned about the drug and alcohol problems, even though, probably, a lot of the founding fathers and very influential people here can trace their family tree to the days of Prohibition and their involvement in illegal activities back then.

"You know what I got to show you some time, Ted," said Tim, interrupting himself. .

"No. What?" I asked.

"Some of the old photos. I've even blown up a couple of 'em from the old Rum Wars. This town was divided back then. We had people who were rumrunners, and they were held in very high esteem back then; many of 'em well respected.

"The Coast Guard stationed men here to enforce the law since the rumrunnin' took place all along the Atlantic. Some townspeople were put in jail, and when it filled up, my goodness, they'd put the prisoners up in a hotel and take care of 'em. There was a little violence that went with it, and millions of dollars worth of booze was confiscated. Sometimes it would mysteriously disappear, and sometimes they said it was destroyed, but...

"Actually, what happened back then, Ted, was that the rum and the booze would be brought in by water, and then it would be taken by horse-driven wagons across the island to the bayside. Trucks would pick it up and take it to big cities like Philadelphia, Baltimore, and Washington."

I still couldn't figure out what Tim was getting at. He took out more photos and moved closer to show them to me.

"Here's another shot of Backfin Molly dealin' drugs right outside of Samantha's. You can see one or two of the customers, but not all of 'em. *Here's* what I wanted to show you. These are part of my private collection."

I looked at the photos and immediately understood what Tim was driving at. They were shots of the Chemical Girl–three different scenes of her obviously buying drugs from Backfin Molly. I looked at Tim, speechless.

Never at a loss for words, Tim broke the silence. "Here are the negatives and the photos, Ted. I'm sure you'll find something to do with them. I think you better tell your lady friend that she best be very careful because the cops are gonna let Backfin Molly run loose for a little while longer until she leads them to who they really want. Either that or they'll pull her in. Then she's gonna have to roll-over on somebody 'cause Backfin Molly don't wanna go to jail. You know, she's got some kids and stuff like that, and they'll be easier on her 'cause she's local. They wouldn't be easy on your little girlfriend though, Ted; even though I assume she's just a user."

"Thanks, Tim. I owe you one. I have to get going. Thanks again. You're a good friend."

As I drove back to the Sheraton, I tried to figure out the best way to approach the Chemical Girl. Should I show her the pictures? Do I tell her that Tim knows? Would she then go and warn Backfin Molly? I was in a quandary because I didn't know what her reaction would be. At the same time, I wanted to protect her at all costs. I didn't want anything or anyone harming the Chemical Girl.

BOOK III

"The politicians and the media have their own interests. Their interests are survival, maintaining the bureaucracy, and developing news stories. There is a lack of any commitment of one discipline, or political group, or the media to addressing the drug abuse problem consistently and systematically. So that's where we are today. We drift along in this way."

Dr. John Ball
An authority on the social epidemiology
of drug abuse, and author of *The Effectiveness
of Methadone Maintenance Treatment.*

Chapter 12

I had to appear before a legislative committee reviewing the drug and alcohol budget. They wanted to discuss methadone maintenance and methadone detox programs again–always a controversial hearing.

One of the legislators who had been antsy during my discussion on methadone piped up and said, "Yeah, but aren't these heroin addicts, these IV users, aren't they the same guys shooting the dope and sharing the needles that are causing the spread of AIDS?"

"Yes, it's true that the fastest rising group coming down with AIDS today is the IV using population," I explained, "but we have an excellent outreach program that we have just begun on a pilot basis. It's called the SOAP Program, the Street Outreach AIDS Project."

I jokingly told him that we have to have an acronym for all programs, one of the toughest tasks in beginning a project. But he was impassive. I don't think he understood what "acronym" meant. Two other legislators were snickering in the back about AIDS. There had been a discussion by the AIDS Administration before my testimony, and since it centered on the homosexual population, many legislators weren't worried about it. Before I explained the SOAP Program, I decided to scare the two in the back of the room. I explained to the committee that everyone is at risk and that until the legislature stops looking at cutting programming and funding and looks at encouraging expanded programming, they're going to see a lot of deaths.

The giggling stopped and they began to listen. "Fifty percent of prostitutes are IV users and eighty percent of the sexual partners of prostitutes are IV users. Now I'm sure this doesn't happen, but let's say that during the session a legislator picks up a prostitute in one of the posh hotels in Annapolis. Somehow he contracts AIDS over a period of time. When that legislator dies, *then* we'll have the State Senator So-and-So Memorial Fund or Project or Program, and then we'll start receiving adequate funding. Once there is a major heterosexual death, you'll see some changes in public opinion."

As I was leaving the hearing room after my testimony, one of the legislators pulled me aside and wanted to know if it was true that you could get AIDS through heterosexual sex. I told him yes. He asked me, "But how about if it's just a blowjob?" I answered,

"Did you ever hear of bleeding gums?" He went pale and looked as though he might faint.

The SOAP Program was an idea that came to the Deputy and me while we were driving back from a site visit in Atlantic City following an AIDS-IV user meeting with John Brooks, the executive director for the Institute for Human Development, a multimodality treatment complex in the converted YMCA. We decided to recruit recovering methadone patients and train them in crisis intervention, prevention, education, referral, and outreach. We would put them out in the street where IV users congregate, and in and around shooting galleries where needles were shared.

The first thing that we needed to do was clear up the methadone program waiting lists since SOAP was mainly effective when there was easy and quick entry into the programs. This meant I had to increase the client/counselor ratio from thirty-to-one to forty-to-one, and in some cases forty-five-to-one.

Then we had to deal with the moral and ethical problems of taking recovering methadone clients and placing them in jeopardy by putting them into the community or environment where there would be that temptation for them to go back to using. We decided that we would provide additional counseling and more frequent urinalysis. If a member of the SOAP team had a dirty urine, he or she would lose their job as a street outreach worker, but would not lose their program privileges.

I would run the program for three months and pay the outreach workers $200 a week, since that was all the money we had. We also needed to implement a study to determine if we could change the behavior of the IV user in three months–a very difficult task.

I asked Dr. Bill McAuliffe, a brilliant clinical investigator and boyhood friend at Harvard University, to devise an impact study to see if we could change the IV user's behavior: Would the IV user come into treatment? Would they begin to practice safe sex? Would they use clean needles? Would they stop sharing needles?

I told Bill that we also needed to have the outreach workers trained in completing an evaluation process.

We put the SOAP team out in the streets, and after three months found that there was some significant change–enough for us to go to the governor and expand the program. Over the next few years, the program expanded throughout Maryland and was copied by dozens of other cities, states, and countries. It was the only viable AIDS prevention program that reached and impacted the IV using population.

We employed a couple of women in the SOAP program. It was difficult to send them into shooting galleries to talk to addicts, especially a cocaine shooting gallery where a woman might be repeatedly raped. Instead, we used them as liaisons and outreach workers with the prostitution community.

We encountered additional difficulties when the women visited the street corners to talk to working prostitutes. When the police were in the mood to round up prostitutes, they also rounded up the outreach workers. And the female SOAP members were also in jeopardy from the pimps. I explained the SOAP program to the police and made badges for the outreach workers to show to the police.

Then I spoke with a lot of people who ran bars on The Block, the adult entertainment district in Baltimore, and to a number of pimps I had known over the years. From a marketing standpoint, I explained that they should make sure that their hookers practiced safe sex. I asked them to try to get them off needles or at least encourage them to stop sharing needles and to help them get into methadone programs. As they listened intently, I also suggested that they should let their customers know this because if they didn't, they would lose them.

I thought I'd get killed or at least beaten up a couple of times trying to convince them, but my proposal to the pimps was pretty much accepted. Pimps, after all, have thousands of years of marketing experience.

□ □ □

OCEAN CITY, MARYLAND

"So," I said to Attorney Goldstein as we jogged past the Carousel Hotel, "Lefty went before the Grand Jury and came out smelling like a rose. It doesn't make much sense to me. At least not from what I was reading and hearing about Driesell."

I knew that Goldstein liked Bud Marshall, Prince Georges' County state's attorney a lot, even though he was an adversary as Long and Greg's attorney. Nevertheless, he felt that the state's attorney, in retrospect, had made a terrible mistake in permitting Driesell's attorney, the legendary Edward Bennett Williams, to appear in front of the Grand Jury. Otherwise, he surmised, Lefty Driesell might have been in serious trouble.

"It's unheard of to let a lawyer go before a Grand Jury," Goldstein shouted over the noise of the traffic. "Unheard of!

"But, what Bud Marshall observed was that a number of people who appeared before the Grand Jury talked about what a bad guy Lefty Driesell was. They closed the Grand Jury door and the witnesses said, 'Can we talk?' Then they badmouthed Lefty.

"Bud was neither a big basketball fan nor even a University of Maryland fan, but he got the impression through these interviews that Lefty Driesell was not a good guy. He wanted to get Lefty in the worst way. He believed that Lefty had committed a crime. When Lefty tried to send his assistant, Oliver Purnell, to clean out the room, he believed Lefty was obstructing justice, which is a crime."

"But," I said, "Purnell never went over..."

Goldstein smiled. "It doesn't matter. Marshall was thinking, *How am I going to get Lefty in front of the Grand Jury so that he waives immunity?* He knew this much. He knew that Lefty could not afford to be indicted. It was Lefty's Achilles heel. An indictment was just as bad as a conviction for a man in Lefty's position. The obstruction of justice statute is three years or a $10,000 fine.

"It's strictly my own theory, because Bud never told me anything. Marshall had to pay a price to get Lefty in front of the Grand Jury and persuade him to waive his immunity. Then Marshall felt he could indict him.

"First, an individual is given immunity automatically by law, but in order to persuade him to talk, he must waive his immunity. Otherwise there's no reason to call him. It does no good to put him in there and give him immunity if he is a target of the investigation because he would then come out clean. You must get him in there in such a way that he waives his immunity.

"Bud didn't have enough on Lefty to indict him. Yet he felt that if he got him in there, Lefty might contradict everyone else who came before him and the Grand Jury and then be indicted for perjury.

"So Marshall decided to make the trade. *I'll let Williams appear before the Grand Jury,* Marshall might have thought, *in exchange for Lefty coming before the Grand Jury and waiving his immunity. Opening him up to a perjury rap, I'll nail his ass on that.*

"What Bud didn't figure on was how great a lawyer Edward Bennett Williams still was. By the time Williams finished with the Grand Jury, they considered themselves the most important institution that stood between an honest citizen and an overzealous prosecutor.

"There's a saying that you can 'indict a tree' if you're a prosecutor before a Grand Jury; that you can get any kind of indictment you want. Yet Bud couldn't get them to indict Lefty no matter how much he wanted them to."

"Some people believed that Lefty was so charming that he manipulated the jurors," I said.

"I doubt he could have done it alone," said Goldstein. "If Lefty had retained a lesser lawyer he might have been indicted.

"It was Edward Bennett Williams' last move. He was an unbelievable lawyer. As ill as he was by then, Williams still outfoxed Marshall."

❏ ❏ ❏

OCEAN CITY, MARYLAND
August 26, 1986

"There're these long-legged, big-toed birds that sell for $3,000 called Struthio Caneus," the Chemical Girl told the Deputy as they belted down beers at the Ocean Club bar. "You get the same return as 150 head of cattle. They're ostriches. Ostrich-skin paraphernalia sells for $150 a belt, $450 a wallet, $1,600 a purse, $600 for less than top-of-the-line boots, and $3,000 a briefcase."

The Deputy listened intently. He had stopped staring at the two sixteen-year-olds in string-bikinis who were strolling by.

"An obliging female ostrich can produce anywhere from thirty to eighty or more eggs a year," continued the Chemical Girl, glancing at her notes in a black spiral notebook. "So if you've got twenty-seven females and the necessary males, it's possible that you can turn out one million birds by your eighth year in business."

"Is there much competition in this country?" asked the Deputy.

"A year ago there were no commercial ostrich ranches in North America, which is the world's leading consumer of ostrich hides and feathers," answered the Chemical Girl. "I've seen estimates today that there could be a couple of thousand around. In Florida, the number might be a dozen, but nobody really keeps count."

❏ ❏ ❏

"Ted," shouted Craig from behind the registration desk as I walked through the lobby of the Sheraton Hotel in Ocean City.

"Your estranged wife's on the phone. I was just going to take a message. Do you want to pick it up?"

I considered it for a couple seconds, knowing full well that every time I spoke with Candy, it made me feel uncomfortable and would usually ruin my entire day. At the same time, I knew that if I didn't talk to her, she was liable to drive to Ocean City and confront me about God knows what. "Okay," I said, "I'll pick it up out here on the lobby phone."

"Ted, I've been trying to reach you and I figured I could track you down at your old haunt," said Candy. She could track me down anywhere. "By the way, I saw your slut girlfriend the other day…"

"Oh yeah?" I interrupted. "Which one?"

"Don't be cute," said Candy. "The one I caught you with. You know the slut I'm talking about."

"You tracked me down here to tell me you saw some slut who you think is my girlfriend? Is there anything else?"

"The separation agreement. There're a couple issues we need to discuss before I sign, and I think you need to meet with your lawyer and bring him over to meet with mine. We'll try and resolve this thing as amicably as we can."

"What else do you want from me?" I cried. "I've given you everything." She had the house and all of the other assets. I just wanted to be free.

"Ted, I've been wondering how you got all your clothes and those other little knickknacks of yours out of the house? Did somebody help you?"

"Candy, I've gotta run right now," I said, wanting to close the conversation. "I've got a meeting and other business to take care of. I don't think my clothes, knickknacks, or anything else is of any concern to you. Can't we just discuss everything with the lawyers when I get back into town?"

"What are you afraid of?" asked Candy. "You think I'm gonna try and find out who helped you get everything out? I don't really care. That's your business. I'm not vindictive…"

"Then why do you want to know?" I interrupted again. "Why do you ask me so many questions? Just let up! I'd like to be your friend, but…"

"You can never be my fuckin' friend!" yelled Candy. "You were my husband and you left. You're a mother-fucker and nothin' can ever change that." Thankfully, with that, she hung up the phone.

□ □ □

It seemed almost surrealistic watching the Chemical Girl spin around on the merry-go-round at Trimper Amusement Park in old-town Ocean City. Actually, it was an authentic antique carousel, the largest and longest operating one in the country. Her eyes glittered by and reflected out to where I was standing.

Amidst the backdrop of darkness and white-crested ocean waves, she seemed to melt in to the sparkling animals attached to the bright, colorful lights of the carousel. The sound of the calliope took me back to a more innocent time.

The childlike ways of the Chemical Girl made her all the more endearing. In between barhopping, the beach, and sex; we'd take in the Ocean City amusement park scene as often as possible.

"I need to speak to you about something," I said, hating to break the magical moment. The Chemical Girl had completed her fourth exhilarating ride on the carousel. "It's about your friend, Backfin Molly."

"Yeah?" she asked. "What about her?"

"Look," I began, "I don't know or care about Backfin Molly. But I *do* care about you, and I also care about me. You must realize that you're somewhat of a risk to my career."

"What's the point, Ted? Spit it out!"

"Okay," I said. "Molly's the target of a big drug investigation. She's been heaty all summer. A friend of mine..."

"Who?" the Chemical Girl butted in.

"You don't need to know that," I answered. "Anyhow, this friend informed me that Backfin Molly's being watched very closely and that you've been seen in her company. Do you get what I'm saying?"

"Yes, Ted, I'm no retard," said the Chemical Girl. "Am I in trouble?"

"No," I said. "Not yet. But stay as far away from Molly as you can, and don't warn her. It's too late now. The next time you're with her, there'll be nothing I can do to help you. Understand?"

The Chemical Girl was silent as we walked out of the park towards Ryan's Landing, a restaurant on the tip of the inlet on the bayside.

"Listen," I said. "If there was something I could do for Molly, I would. But, it's just too late. Because she's a local they won't be too hard on her, and she might not take a fall if she gives up her source. That's how they play it."

The Chemical Girl slid her arm into mine and leaned her head on my shoulder as we entered the bar at Ryan's Landing.

"I'm famished," she said changing the subject, as always when she felt uncomfortable. "Let's eat!"

❏ ❏ ❏

SAN DIEGO, CALIFORNIA
August 26, 1986

Holt stayed away from drugs and unhealthy food for a while after his release from the hospital, even though he believed that being so healthy had caused the heart spasms. Before long he was back to engaging in a number of forms of substance abuse, except cocaine. He'd had enough scares with that. The paranoia, enhanced by freebasing for years and the heart spasms, had finally convinced him. He started smoking Persian White heroin again and returned to smoking grass and drinking Wild Turkey 101.

Still, Holt was in pretty good shape. He didn't have an ounce of fat on him and was tough and taut. Although in his mid-forties he had joined amateur basketball and volleyball leagues.

After returning from a trip to the Far East, Holt started feeling chest pains again and thought the heart spasms had returned.

He went to a specialist in Los Angeles, and during their first discussion about the chest pains, Holt mentioned that he also had a large mole growing on his back that he was concerned about. The doctor sent him to a colleague who removed the mole. The biopsy revealed it to be malignant. It was melanoma, pretty serious skin cancer, but they felt they had removed all of it. For protection, Holt was advised to undergo a battery of tests to see if the cancer had spread.

Holt was antsy to go to Cape Cod to meet his New York girl-friend, but decided instead to take the tests to relieve his anxiety. The tests revealed a mass on one of his lungs, and the cancer specialist would have to perform a more involved and serious biopsy to determine if Holt had lung cancer.

When Holt telephoned and frantically told me about his problem, his mood flipped from anxiety to depression. I asked him if the doctors felt that smoking had caused the mass. He told me that it had never come up in the conversation. Holt had smoked cigarettes since childhood, smoked marijuana for over twenty-five years, smoked heroin or "Chased the Dragon," and freebased cocaine; yet he didn't think it was necessary to tell his doctor, who surprisingly never questioned him about it.

A week later, Holt called back and told me that the biopsy entailed having a needle inserted through his chest and into his lung. Unfortunately, the needle punctured and collapsed his lung, causing it to fill with blood and rendering the biopsy inconclusive. Holt was experiencing constant backaches from the collapsed lung, and it was making him extremely nervous and anxious.

He said, "I've postponed going to the Cape again to meet my New York woman. I have my dear wife by my side now. They're going to do more tests while my lung heals. In the next test, nuclear dye will be injected through my body to see if it wraps itself around any possible melanoma."

I was worried and upset. I asked Holt, "If you have cancer, are you going to have chemotherapy or radiation treatments? You remember when Larry and Danny had cancer and decided to have radiation and chemotherapy? They never recovered. They just got sicker and sicker until they died."

Holt said the doctors would decide, but I argued with him because I thought it should be his decision.

"And by the way, Ted, thanks for being so positive," said Holt, sarcastically.

"If they say you're going to die, I'll take you to Thailand where you can die in a peaceful place you've always loved."

Holt felt that Thailand was a whorehouse and a drug store. He loved it there and asked me, "If it turns out that I *don't* have cancer, will you still take me?"

I said, "No."

Enraged, Holt hung up.

❑ ❑ ❑

OCEAN CITY, MARYLAND
August 27-28, 1986

Curious, the Chemical Girl asked, "So Ted, you're always asking me why I drink. Why do you drink?"

"I drink to be sociable," I answered. "One or two drinks are about all I can take because I don't like to be too high. I want to be in control of my senses. On occasion, I might drink to feel a little high or relaxed on purpose, but basically it's just a social thing for me."

She shook her head, bewildered. "That's one of the dumbest things I've ever heard. Why would you drink if not to get a buzz? I drink to get a buzz. I admit it. Most people I know drink to get a buzz, and they admit it. What the fuck is wrong with you?"

It was a dreary evening; foggy, rainy, and chilly for late August. We were lying in bed naked when she suddenly changed the subject.

"Ted, ostriches sell for $20,000 for a yearling pair and $50,000 for a breeding pair. They grow quickly and have these cute telescope necks. They look like they're walking on stilts, and they grow a quarter of an inch or more a day. With each added foot of growth, they gain up to $1,000 in value. As a matter of fact, the ranchers in Oklahoma are talking about switching from cattle to ostriches!"

"Why do you keep hocking me about ostriches?" I asked. "You're obsessed with them."

"I've done a lot of research," she said, "and I spoke to that guy I met on the plane. He sent me more information about the investment aspect and tips about working it myself in Florida."

"Look," I said. "It can't be that sure a thing. There must be some drawbacks."

"Okay," the Chemical Girl admitted. "One of the biggest problems with the ostrich is their diet. Nobody is certain of what and how to feed them. In addition to greens, they also eat catfish food, dog food, rabbit pellets, turkey grower, and even river gravel. Actually Ted, ostriches are birdbrains. They'll literally gobble up anything, including hardware. So after construction work at an ostrich ranch is completed, they have to meticulously sweep the entire ranch with a metal detector to make sure that they haven't left a single nail out there. Additionally, there's also the question of what percentage of protein to feed them. If it's more than twenty-two or twenty-three percent, their bodies can outgrow their legs and they become crippled."

"That's classic," I laughed. "Anything else?"

"Well," the Chemical Girl continued, "stress, bacterial infections, and overeating are the primary causes of ostrich deaths."

The Chemical Girl finished, for now, her ostrich pitch and decided to order room service. Her hotel bills were outrageous; but she insisted on eating, drinking, and residing only in the finest accommodations when she traveled.

She loved hotels and often told me that if she had her choice she would live in one. It didn't really even matter where the hotel was located. The Chemical Girl loved the way the staffs pampered her.

"Roughing it," she would sometimes say, "is slow room service."

□ □ □

The Chemical Girl pushed me out of her and rolled to her side. "Enough for a second, okay?" she said, gasping for air. "It tickles too much now."

"Alright," I said, pleased and relieved that the sex had finally ended.

The Chemical Girl had gone where no man would ever go–to the final frontier of nonstop, multiple orgasms; pleasure even too overwhelming for her at times.

I was tired...and a bit jealous.

"I love you," she suddenly blurted out. "Did I just say that? I hope you're not upset that I said that."

"No," I answered, "but I can't repeat it back to you because I've never been sure what love is. Do you really know?"

"Yeah," she answered confidently as if she had thought about it for years. "It's ninety-nine percent sex."

□ □ □

The Chemical Girl, the Deputy, and I were having breakfast at Dumser's on 124th Street on the bayside. They served the best creamed chipped beef on the Eastern Shore.

"You know, after all these years, I still have trouble dealing with people who experiment or who are addicts as far as quality control is concerned," I said.

The Deputy and the Chemical Girl glanced up. "What do you mean by quality control?" asked the Deputy. I saw the Chemical Girl smile.

"Why do people buy drugs from complete strangers and then ingest them like they were buying a sealed box of cereal at the grocery store or sealed aspirin in a pharmacy?" I explained. "What kind of sense does that make? They have no idea what's in it, what it's been adulterated with, what the adverse reactions might be, and whether it's really what they think they're buying. That's what quality control is and there is none."

The Chemical Girl spoke up, "Well, you figure that the people with the dope aren't dead and they're using it, too. And you figure that the dope is sold in such mass quantities and since you haven't heard about a lot of deaths, why worry about it? There's a code of honor, a code of trust."

"Come on, cut the bullshit," I said frustrated. "There've been many, many deaths over the years and many, many adverse reactions from illicit drugs. I can't believe people actually think the way you do."

The Chemical Girl responded, "But Ted, that's really what the people think. It may not be what they believe deep down, but they have to rationalize. They want the dope so badly, they have to rationalize that everything is going to be fine. Nobody would buy any drugs if they didn't feel this way."

"I still don't get it," I said. "It's like Russian Roulette."

"Let me put it another way," said the Chemical Girl. "When people choose a babysitter, they have no idea what kind of person they're hiring. They could be a serial killer, kidnapper, or a total fuck-up who could burn their house down. But they have to get out of the house to work or attend social affairs. It's similar to the desperation people feel when buying drugs."

"My God," I said. "You're comparing quality control in buying dope with hiring a babysitter. Unfucking believable!"

❑ ❑ ❑

My Chief of Research, Bud Hodinko, called me with the latest end-of-the-month program utilization data.

"Ted, the programs are filled to capacity. I'm afraid of waiting lists developing, especially in the methadone programs. Do you want to raise the client-counselor ratio again?"

"No," I said, as I slipped out of bed away from the sleeping Chemical Girl.

"Why is this happening in August, Bud?" I asked. "The programs always seem to fill up during this month. I don't get it."

"We've discussed this before, Ted. It's always August and the winter months. The winter months are easier to explain. Seasonal affective disorder (SAD), a form of depression when the decrease in sunlight is the greatest, generates a lot of substance abuse."

"Yeah, yeah," I said. "It would be cheaper to put all the addicts in suntan booths from December to March. But why August?"

After a long pause, Hodinko spoke. "According to the research I've perused, August is the cruelest month, and probably the most dangerous. It ranks first of all months for emergency room visits, and five percent are alcohol and drug related..."

"How many," I interrupted, "is the five percent nationally?"

"About a million," Hodinko responded. "Ted, I gotta run..."

"Wait!" I yelled. "How many emergency room visits in August for insect bites?"

"Hold on," he said as I heard the rustling of papers. "Okay, Ted. I don't know why you need this information but it's about 500,000. Talk to ya later." He quickly hung up.

"Oh, my God," I whispered.

Chapter 13

WASHINGTON/BALTIMORE
August 30, 1986

Ron was becoming even more nervous and depressed than normal. He went to his friend, Manny, in one of the divisions of the Food and Drug Administration where he worked and asked if there was anything new on the market for his increasing nervousness. Manny told him that there was an experimental miracle drug called Prozac which helped with nervousness, anxiety, and depression. It probably wouldn't be approved for another couple of years, and Manny didn't know if he could get any. Ron begged him, reminding him of the favors Manny owed him, and offered to get Manny a hooker. With that final enticing offer, Manny told Ron to return in a few days and he'd have fifty pills for him.

Ron explained the new information about Prozac to me, and I warned him about possible adverse reactions. "They can be very serious. Six percent of the population is allergic to something, and you could be part of that population!" But Ron never took advice and had always experimented with different prescription, over-the-counter, and illicit drugs; especially pills.

"Come see a doctor with me," I urged him. "Let him examine and assess you and see if there's something he can prescribe."

I knew that Ron was very cheap and never went to a doctor unless he felt he was on his deathbed.

"Let's go to Karl Roberts, my old college roommate. He's a good guy, and I guarantee he won't charge you a dime, Ron."

Ron finally agreed to go and met with Dr. Roberts on a Sunday when he was in his office doing paperwork. He didn't charge Ron after Ron's incessant whining about Sunday not being a legal business day. Ron was frank about his concern over his nervousness, depression, and obsession with hookers. He also told Dr. Roberts about his recent arrest. He went on to explain the source of his latest anxiety–problems at work. There were two female supervisors who drove him nuts. Actually, he had trouble dealing with women in any arena, except when he was dominating the prostitutes he paid to bring his fantasies to life.

Dr. Roberts was fascinated, and although I wasn't sure if he wanted to laugh or cry over Ron's story, he was a very good listener. He probably identified with Ron since Karl Roberts was also an extremely nervous individual. He told Ron that he should try to avoid stressful situations. Ron told him that he had already made his life less complicated, but was still extremely nervous and despondent.

After performing a cursory physical, Dr. Roberts drew blood in between his trips to his office to answer the phone, which seemed unusually busy for a Sunday. Every time Dr. Roberts left the office, Ron stole something from his desk or the shelves behind it. He even stole Dr. Roberts' photograph of his daughters, two very homely-looking teenage girls who happened to be wearing Ron's favorite–dresses and high heels.

Dr. Roberts told Ron that he should change his diet, and prescribed a mild sedative. "Although," Roberts added, "I think your anxiety is probably brought on by your depression."

We left the office and got into my car. Ron emptied his pockets. He had taken all kinds of medical samples, a stethoscope, the photo, and other office supplies. I asked him why he took the photograph.

He answered, "I'm going to put it on my desk at work, and maybe it'll keep those two bitches who supervise me off my back. If they think I've got two ugly daughters to deal with every day, maybe they'll identify with it because they're both so fucking ugly, too!"

Ron called a week later and told me that the new experimental drug that his friend "borrowed" from the FDA seemed to be working better than the pills that Dr. Roberts had prescribed.

"Once I take the pill, I'm not tired anymore. I feel up and happy, although I still get real nervous, but it's not like a sad nervous. It's more of a happy nervous. The only problem now is that I can't sleep well, and I'm hyped up too much. Sometimes I feel like my heart is racing. I've decided to take the pill every other day or only when I feel like my female supervisors are getting to me."

"Ron," I asked, "did the photos of Dr. Roberts' daughters do any good?"

"Nah," he answered. "As a matter of fact, it worked in reverse. They knew I didn't have any kids and thought I brought it in just to mock them. They even got some other bitch in the office to threaten to charge me with sexual harassment over the fuckin' picture. But the pills are working well."

❏ ❏ ❏

BALTIMORE, MARYLAND
September 3, 1986

The Deputy walked into my office looking haggard. I asked him if anything was wrong.

"Well," he said, "let's see. My wife's sister told her that she spotted me with a beautiful woman on the beach the weekend before last. I didn't know how to explain that it was the Chemical Girl and I was just keeping her company for you. Then I came home late Friday and Saturday night and my wife was waiting up. I gave her two Twix Bars from my briefcase but that's not what she wanted. Instead, she went nuts, throwing things and waking up Junior and the girls....Oh, and someone keeps calling the house and hanging up on my wife, and she's sure it's a girlfriend of mine. And last night, she found some panties in the back seat of my car."

I shook my head and asked the Deputy how much longer he thought his marriage would last.

"Ted, if I wouldn't have to pay more alimony and child support, I could afford to leave and take Junior with me. And if I had a chick like the Chemical Girl to play with full time, maybe I'd split anyway. But right now I can't afford another divorce, so I'm in for the duration I guess."

The Deputy sat down in a chair facing my desk.

"Something else I can help you with, buddy?" I asked.

"No...well, uh, maybe...I just wanted to get it off my mind and bullshit with you for a few minutes before I get back to work."

"Okay," I said.

"I was just reading these statistics," said the Deputy. "It says that there's more women harmed from getting battered by their husbands in the home than the combined muggings, rapes, auto accidents, and assaults on women outside of the home. And then it listed different places for battered women to escape to, like the House of Ruth in Baltimore."

"So, what are you getting at?" I asked.

"Well," said the Deputy, "what about husbands who don't hit women, but when their wives go off the deep end..."

I interrupted, "When you say wives, do you mean your three wives or are you talking wives in general?" I asked jokingly.

"Listen," said the Deputy. "I'm serious. I'm talking about wives in general. What I'm getting at is that I don't think it's right to hit a woman. But if a woman's coming at you violently, and you don't want to strike her, and you're afraid that if you subdue her you could bruise or hurt her, what are you supposed to do? Where are you supposed to go to get away from it? How are you supposed to handle it? How come no one ever talks about battered husbands and husband abuse? Why don't they call it spousal abuse since it could be a man or a woman doing the battering?"

"Well," I said, trying to end the discussion, "Perhaps I'll award a grant to a place for men to go. It'll be called the House of Ted."

"Very funny," said the Deputy, not amused. "I need to ask you something else. Something about AIDS. But, before I do, I have to tell you that I hate using rubbers or condoms. What is the shot of me catching it from a chick on a one-night stand or even a week-long stand? You've got to have some sense of this, and don't bullshit me, Ted. I know you've been attending seminars and conferences on this stuff."

I thought for a second and wondered how best to approach this topic with the Deputy. I figured I'd mix a little of my own philosophy with what I had absorbed from the seminars so far. It was still too early in the game, however, to make an accurate assessment on how AIDS was spread.

"I know I warned you to get away from that drug addicted girl in the Ocean Club that night," I said. "You could've caught just about anything from her–maybe even AIDS. The truth is we're just beginning to learn how AIDS is transmitted.

"But, if you want my personal opinion, I think it's much tougher to catch AIDS heterosexually. As long as you're the one who's giving and not receiving, if you know what I mean. Now, I should qualify that because we don't know what the women out there are doing. We don't know if they are sharing needles, and they are surely not going to tell you this when you pick them up. We don't know if they are fucking bisexual guys, and we don't know if they've had an AIDS-tainted blood transfusion. So there're a lot of variables to consider. However, I would say the odds are definitely in your favor if you don't use a condom and you're banging a chick, even if it's anal sex. But then again, I'm not a hundred percent sure. Maybe sixty-five to seventy percent. Maybe a little less. But that's the way I see it."

"You fucker," said the Deputy. "I don't know what the fuck you just said. Hell, maybe I'm immune to AIDS anyhow. I worry about you, too, Ted. The Chemical Girl's been around. And sometimes she's so stoned...."

❑ ❑ ❑

BALTIMORE, MARYLAND

The Deputy and I were visiting the Pimlico Hospital Methadone Program. Two women who worked at the COPYIR program in Ocean City had asked me to discuss partial funding of a modular building in which to establish an AIDS hospice.

I had known the ladies since I was a teenager, and I explained to them what had happened to Holt. Both women had spent some time with him in Mexico many years before. They were still fond of Holt and were also very interested in my account of his ordeal with the "White Lung Disease."

"Ted," Laura said. "Some of our doctors have found similar symptoms in a few of our drug patients. Maybe you'd like to talk to one of them."

I agreed, and within minutes, Laura had rounded up a drug doctor from the emergency room. We briefed him on Holt as he listened intently. He asked me a few questions and told me quite rapidly, "We've had several patients who developed severe hypoxemic respiratory failure with bronchiolitis obliterations organizing pneumonia after frequent freebase cocaine use."

"Whoa, Doc," I interrupted. "Speak English to me. I need to understand you in lay terms."

"Alright," he said, obviously frustrated. "You can die or become very ill from, for lack of a better term, what could be called 'crack lung.' This develops either from cocaine or adulterants like baking soda, or from deeply inhaling the smoke, or a combination of these. We see outward signs of pneumonia or other ailments resulting when poisons invade the lungs. With your friend, it could have been his history of smoking marijuana, opium, cigarettes, and finally, freebasing. He probably coughs a lot and loudly, maybe even coughing up blood, and has a chronic high temperature. He could die from either loss of blood or loss of oxygen. As for the mass..."

"Doc," I interrupted again, "how do you treat it? Will it recur if he changes his lifestyle?"

"We've been very successful in treating this with corticosteroids, and sometimes antibiotics work. In a few cases, we've seen spontaneous recoveries. As for your friend, Holt, I can't give you any assurances. I really must go now. Good day."

I was thinking what a pompous and abrupt asshole the doctor was as he turned around to face me.

"I wish I could be more helpful. Are you especially worried about his welfare?"

"Nah, Doc," I lied. "He's a great survivor!"

❏ ❏ ❏

SAN DIEGO, CALIFORNIA

Holt was positive he was going to die. The anxiety was so severe he went to see a psychiatrist, and then a psychologist, but neither helped. He tried group meetings like Alcoholics Anonymous and Narcotics Anonymous, transcendental meditation, and even read books on ZEN. Nothing worked.

Meanwhile, one of his doctors prescribed antibiotics, and amazingly, the mass in his chest grew smaller and smaller. At the time, Holt felt that his new low-cholesterol, meatless diet was what was actually helping him. He was also heavily medicated with tranquilizers. He promised God that if the mass disappeared he would change his ways, and even apply for a legitimate job.

When the mass finally disappeared, Holt was ecstatic. He quickly forgot his promise to clean up his life and get a steady job, and immediately resumed dealing Quaaludes and crystal methamphetamine.

❏ ❏ ❏

COLLEGE PARK/BALTIMORE
September 5, 1986

Returning from College Park after attending a subcommittee hearing on drug testing, I told the Deputy I was concerned about the Chemical Girl's obsession with the ostrich ranches, and he informed me that he'd also begun to research it.

"Ostrich imports from South Africa stopped last year," explained the Deputy. "It convinced a lot of people that this was a great new business opportunity; not just in Florida, but in Oklahoma, Texas, and other states. Ostriches are the largest birds in the world, growing up to nine feet and weighing about 350 pounds."

"Who gives a damn?" I blurted out, frustrated.

Undaunted, the Deputy continued, "In America, you can use the ostrich for many different purposes. The feathers are used in the fashion world, and they're also used as dusters to prep cars for painting. The hide, which is over twenty-six square feet, is very durable. It's used for boots, wallets, handbags, and other popular fashion and decorating items.

"And Ted," added the Deputy, "you'll love this part. Out in Nevada, these goony-looking birds with their twenty-five-foot strides run at Secretariat-matching speeds–up to forty miles an hour for pari-mutuel crowds!"

"You're as bananas as she is," I joked. "Give me a fucking break!"

But the Deputy went on, "Cowboy boots made of ostrich leather sell for $600. I heard that the comedian, Eddie Murphy, spent $250,000 for an ostrich-skin sofa."

❑ ❑ ❑

BALTIMORE, MARYLAND
September 11, 1986

The Medical Examiner showed me and other health department officials the final autopsy report on Bias. He also displayed x-rays of Bias' chest cavity and heart.

It was ironic that the ultimate athletic body could be destroyed so easily by an insidious drug, yet I had seen overweight, out-of-shape men and women ingest even more cocaine with nowhere near Len Bias' physiological damage.

Dr. Smialek began discussing the effects of cocaine on the heart and brain. "In the heart, coke causes spasms and constriction of vessels supplying blood to the heart, which reduces the blood supply and kills heart muscle cells. In Bias' instance, several muscle fibers in the heart had died in reaction to the cell death. One can conclude that the damage must have occurred days or weeks prior to his death. It *has* been confirmed that Len Bias was using cocaine well before his fatal dose."

The autopsy indicated that one blood vessel had a thickening of the wall, restricting the amount of the blood passing through the mantle. The repeated cocaine use damaged the internal lining of the blood vessel creating scar tissue and causing a very narrow channel. This made Bias more vulnerable to a heart attack, yet Bias didn't suffer what we considered to be a heart attack.

Smialek said, "Cocaine produces tremendous releases of catecholamine in the brain which generates excitability, causing seizures. And there *were* bite marks on Len Bias' tongue."

Had Bias continued to use cocaine and not died at College Park, he most certainly would have died in a game during his first year with the National Basketball Association.

One of the mix-ups after Bias' death, which was the prelude to a lot of litigation, was the lawyers' and others' misinterpretation concerning the documentation of cocaine in his stomach. Saliva that is swallowed ends up in the stomach. Bias hadn't vomited substantially, so the autopsy recovered ten milliliters of mucous in the stomach. There were no other fluids, nor was there food. It was perfectly reasonable to conclude that snorted cocaine would end up in the stomach. The mucous drips down the back of the throat and is swallowed. This would strongly indicate that Len Bias had ingested the cocaine by snorting it through his nose.

Several lawyers supported the notion that Bias was unknowingly given cocaine in a drink. These lawyers and others based their theory on a sophisticated multiplication process whereby the amount of cocaine in the stomach was multiplied by a thousand indicating "x" number of grams of cocaine ingested. Actually, the only people who knew that Bias had snorted coke did not come forward until after they received immunity. They were basketball players Long and Greg, and they were in the room with Bias at the time of his death.

It's nearly impossible to tell from an autopsy how much cocaine has been used, and it is not realistic to assume how much was ingested. It may have been the same quality that the police found in Bias' car, which was very pure. However, there was no way to be sure of the quality of the cocaine used in the dorm, nor to determine the quantity snorted.

The opinion from the autopsy report, which was signed on June 24 and again on July 2 by the medical examiner and the assistant medical examiner, basically gave this synopsis: "Leonard K. Bias, a twenty-two-year-old black male, died as a result of cocaine intoxication that interrupted the normal electrical control of his heartbeat, resulting in the sudden onset of seizures leading to cardiac arrest. The blood cocaine level was 6.5 milligrams per liter. Toxicological studies for alcohol and other drugs were negative. Due to the ongoing investigation of the circumstances surrounding the death, the manner of death is ruled undetermined at this time."

I had left a copy of the autopsy report on the bed in my hotel room in Ocean City, and the Chemical Girl began to read it one evening. Although the medical terminology made it extremely difficult to decipher, she started laughing as she turned to me and said, "Did you see this?" She was looking at the information regarding the genitourinary system. "It says the right testicle weighs seventeen grams and the left testicle, twenty grams." Giggling, the Chemical Girl continued, "Wow, one of his balls was bigger than the other."

I looked at her and smiled. Only the Chemical Girl could find something sexual in an autopsy report.

❏ ❏ ❏

BEDFORD, PENNSYLVANIA, ET AL
September 13-16, 1986

Ron and the Deputy were driving to a small town in Pennsylvania to attend a model train convention. The back of the pick-up, which the Deputy had borrowed from his brother, was filled with model trains that they would show, trade, or sell to turn a quick profit.

It seemed that Ron, instead of being tired after work, had started feeling so good about himself from the experimental pill, Prozac, that he had stopped isolating and started hanging out more often with the Deputy. He learned more about the Deputy's investments in collecting duck decoys, trains, tropical fish, and other items. By coincidence, Ron was informed by a coworker, Irving, that over the years when he was in the Navy, he bought a lot of model trains that were stored in his basement. The coworker planned to build an elaborate train set, but due to the dampness of Smith Island on the Eastern Shore where he lived, he was never able to get everything working together. So he wanted to sell all of his trains and tracks. The model train equipment was probably worth a lot of money, at least to a federal employee, but he didn't know how to go about properly advertising and selling it at a maximum profit. Ron put two and two together and informed the Deputy about the find.

Ron and the Deputy drove to Crisfield in Somerset County and then traveled by boat to Smith Island to view the collection of Ron's fellow employee. It was more than worth it since Irving had a myriad of collectors'-quality Lionel trains. The Deputy offered him $3,000 for everything, a mere fraction of the value, but Irving readily agreed to the sale.

A week later, they returned to Smith Island to pick up the trains. Since there was no way to take the borrowed pick-up truck over to the island, they rented a boat and hired a couple of workers from the island who helped them pack and clean up all of the tracks, trains, and other equipment that Irving had collected over the years.

It took a whole day, but eventually they returned to the Deputy's garage in East Baltimore County where they anxiously surveyed their cache. The Deputy said that he'd take possession since he had put out all of the money, and once his expenses were taken out, he'd split fifty-fifty with Ron.

Over the next few weeks, Ron and the Deputy made a number of small sales and were now ready for the big coup; a large train-swapping convention in Pennsylvania. The Deputy had not heard of this convention, but Ron swore up and down that he read about it in a flyer he saw in Washington. He had the address, time, and place. They packed up the remaining railroad memorabilia and drove to Bedford, Pennsylvania.

On the way, Ron became extremely anxious and began to hyperventilate in the truck, telling the Deputy that he was having chest pains. An ambulance passed by, and the Deputy suggested to Ron that they should follow it.

"Yeah," said Ron, "maybe we should. I'm not feeling real good to tell you the truth. I hope I'm not having a heart attack."

They stopped the pick-up truck, turned around, and caught up with the ambulance, following it to a hospital outside of Bedford. The Deputy rushed Ron into the emergency room, alerting the nurses of his chest pains. Again, Ron began to hyperventilate, and after thirty minutes, a doctor transferred him to the intensive care unit. Before the Deputy left, Ron whispered to him, "You think I should tell the doctor about this new drug and the other drugs I'm using?"

The Deputy told Ron he must tell them everything to get a proper diagnosis.

Ron asked, "Are you going to wait and see what happens to me?"

"No, you asshole," yelled the Deputy, "I'm going to that convention to see if we can sell anything and make a score!"

"But what about me?" pleaded Ron. "Shouldn't you wait here? What about my family?"

"Fuck your family," said the Deputy, who didn't believe Ron was in any real danger. "You dragged me all the way up here, and I'm going to try and find this convention. If you fuckin' die of a heart attack, don't worry. I'll see that your family gets your piece of the action."

The Deputy drove all over town but couldn't find the convention. He finally ran into a man with a yellow cowboy hat who knew about the model train convention. Unfortunately for the Deputy, the convention was held the year *before* in Bedford.

"Your friend," said the guy in the hat, "had probably seen the flyer and didn't look at the date. This is 1986. The convention was held in 1985."

Very pissed off, the Deputy immediately drove back to Baltimore, but not before the pick-up broke down three times. At one point, he had to be towed from an old bridge by an off-duty policeman who was also in a pick-up truck.

Left in the intensive care unit at the Bedford Memorial Hospital, Ron was finally discharged after three days. His hyperventilation and anxiety had induced a panic attack, but they could find absolutely nothing wrong with him. Ron was concerned and saddened that he had not heard from the Deputy. He wondered how much money they had made, and fantasized that maybe he had $10,000 coming to him.

After taking a bus back to Baltimore, Ron contacted the Deputy right away, who informed him that the convention did not exist. In addition, the Deputy told him he was taking another $500 off the top of Ron's share of any future sales for "aggravation fees."

After this event, Ron stopped taking Prozac and other pills, and swore to a life of abstinence. This lasted until the next weekend when a hooker promised Ron some very kinky sex if they could get high on whatever pills he had left in his medicine cabinet.

❑ ❑ ❑

BALTIMORE, MARYLAND
September 18, 1986

Dogface Alice, Ron's ex-bodybuilder and prostitute girlfriend, called me at my office in a panic.

"Ted, you gotta help me," Alice cried. "Ron's told me a lot about you. If I don't get into a drug treatment program in the next week, I'm gonna go to jail."

I tried to calm her down. "Alice, I've never heard of anyone being put in a jail for a first offense if they can't get into a program. What are you talking about?"

Alice was screaming now. "You asshole! The judge who found

me guilty of shoplifting said that if I didn't get into a residential treatment program, the only alternative was jail. And I'm not goin' to that women's center in Jessup, Maryland. You know what'll happen to me. Those black dykes will have a field day. I'd rather kill myself. If you don't help me, I swear I'll get you and that fuckin' nut, Ron, in trouble. He's told me some interesting stories about you."

I tried to talk some sense into her. "Listen, forget threatening me. It won't work. Was this your first bust, Alice? I mean, I've never heard of jail time for a first shoplifting offense."

"Asshole," she screamed louder, "I've been busted twelve times for shoplifting; the last seven times for stealing crabmeat. By the way, I've got about a dozen containers of crabmeat left. Are you interested?"

"No, Alice, I'm not," I answered. "I didn't realize you had been busted so many times. Who is your attorney?"

"Snyder's my lawyer. Daniel I. Snyder," she blurted out.

"You have Snyder call me, and I'll try to get you in a residential program, even though the beds are probably all filled. I don't want to see you go to jail, but Alice…"

"Oh, Ted, you're the greatest," Alice interrupted. "How about if I just give you about four or five containers of free crabmeat?"

"Alice, I don't give a fuck about the crabmeat," I said. "I don't want it. It's probably spoiled by now anyhow. Just have your lawyer call. Now, if I am only able to get you in a therapeutic community, you must realize that it's very confrontational. You may not like it, but it's better than jail. However, I'm going to try to get you into an intermediate care facility for twenty-eight days, and then you'll go to an outpatient program. If I can't get you in the residential program right away, I'll get you in an outpatient program first, and I'll call the judge and cool the whole thing out."

"Ted, I love ya!" screamed Alice. "Listen, give me your address and I'll drop off the crabmeat."

"Alice, just have your lawyer call me. I don't want any crabmeat….On second thought, drop the containers off at my office downtown. And I want you to promise me that you're going to see this thing through…and you better pray I don't get sick from the crabmeat."

"Okay, Ted. Anything you say. I'll call my lawyer and have him call you."

❑ ❑ ❑

BALTIMORE, MARYLAND
September 25, 1986

The Deputy's keys jingled ever so quietly as he opened the door to his home. It was five a.m. and still dark outside. After leaving a Twix Bar on a table by the door, he tiptoed into the bathroom and began to wash his hands and face. Then he washed his cock to remove the stench of sex left from the barmaid at Fat Daddy's Bar and Grill whom he'd been with for the past three hours.

He stripped down to his underwear, left his shoes in the bathroom, and tiptoed to the stairs. Suddenly, he saw dozens of tiny eyes on the steps staring out at him. *My God,* he thought. *What the fuck is going on? Are they rats or mice?* He wished that he had kept his shoes on.

Risking exposure and his wife's wrath, the Deputy hurried to the kitchen to search for a broom or a baseball bat to deal with whatever was behind the tiny eyes. But instead of a broom, he found a note from his wife on the kitchen table which read, *"Have a nice night. You'll be hearing from my lawyer in the morning."*

Fuck it, the Deputy thought. *I'll worry about that later.* He cautiously walked back towards the stairs and switched on the light. The Deputy gasped. On each of the ten steps were the neatly-sawed-off heads of his collectors'-item duck decoys. He began to sob.

❑ ❑ ❑

ANNAPOLIS, MARYLAND
September 30, 1986

An East Baltimore congresswoman beat the governor for the U.S. senate seat in the primary election. Publicity about the governor's war on drugs had not aroused media attention.

His strategy for an ambitious new drug abuse program designed to coordinate and finance a spending plan for treatment, prevention, enforcement, and education by means of an emergency deficit had failed to impress voters. Yet the first months following Bias' death had created a groundswell of national public relations alerting the public to the dangers of drugs as they related to crime, health, and the economy. Ah, the fickleness of the voter.

❑ ❑ ❑

One month later, the U.S. president unveiled a massive Federal Omnibus Drug Act as a direct result of Len Bias' death, although no one would admit that his death was the catalyst.

The treatment budget was announced at 343 million dollars. It was a start, albeit small, especially with an inadequate number of treatment slots and constantly growing waiting lists.

□ □ □

BALTIMORE, MARYLAND
October 22, 1986

I was talking on the phone with Wilbur Spikes, a stockbroker friend, whom I had once treated for cocaine addiction. "This may sound unusual, but tell me why I shouldn't invest in an ostrich farm. I'm trying to talk a couple of friends out of what I feel is a big mistake." Wilbur said he'd get back to me.

Two hours later, Wilbur called back. "Ostriches aren't too bright," he began, "even for birds. The male makes a kind of honking sound, like a moose with asthma, and the female does a lot of hissing. And these are not animals to fool around with even in captivity because they've got quite a kick. It takes at least three people to catch one, and an ostrich can beat you up pretty good. In Africa, ostriches have been known to kick the daylights, and even the life, out of marauding lions. As a matter of fact, a close relative of the ostrich known as the Australian Cassowary, or something like that, reputedly desires and eats human flesh."

"That's good information, Wilbur," I said. "Anything else?"

"Yeah," he said. "If the South African sanctions are ever lifted, the whole scheme could fall on its face because South Africa has more than enough ostrich farms to handle the world's demands."

□ □ □

Dogface Alice phoned, begging me to contact her attorney as soon as possible. "I can't reach him and I'm in serious trouble!"

I asked her what was wrong now, and she would only say, "I can't talk, so just please call my lawyer and try and get me out of this mess! I'm in the city jail!"

It took me almost seven hours, but I finally tracked down her attorney, Dan Snyder. He asked if I could meet him downtown.

At Central Lockup, we found out that Dogface Alice had been arrested once again for soliciting. Snyder walked off for a while and huddled with a cop friend of his.

"Oh well," I said to Snyder when he returned, "Alice is a prostitute and that's her thing. I can get her out of one jackpot, but I can't get her out of all these other predicaments. As a drug addict stealing crabmeat and selling it, I'll probably be able to get her into a treatment program. I don't know if she's still doing drugs, but violating probation is pretty serious. And then there's the prostitution thing on top of everything else."

Snyder pondered for a moment. "I'm not worried about the soliciting, the prior convictions, or even the violation of probation. Ted, when Alice was busted, she thought the charge was going to be solicitation and prostitution, which she could have dealt with. But Alice made a mistake. *You* may not think it was a mistake, and you might not want to get involved in this thing at all, but she compromised herself with something worse."

"Well, counselor," I asked, "what did she do? And, by the way, it sounds as if you should try to keep my name out of whatever it is."

Dogface Alice's attorney smiled, but quickly resumed his serious legal composure. "When Alice got popped, the police initially charged her with solicitation. In later conversations with the arresting officer, she told him that she had AIDS. So the cop not only charged her with prostitution, he also charged her with reckless endangerment."

"Jesus Christ!" I gasped. "Dogface Alice has AIDS?!" I thought about my friend, Ron, and prayed that he was still using protection, which he told me he'd been using since the '60s. Still, I was concerned about him. And I was worried about Dogface Alice and AIDS.

Attorney Snyder continued, "And guess what else, Ted? It seems that somehow this news was leaked to a local television station, and they already reported it on the afternoon news. Now the story's gonna be in the newspapers tomorrow with her name in it. And wait until the radio talk shows go on the air."

Sure enough, the next day there wasn't a talk show on AM or FM radio that wasn't flooded with callers' opinions on whether they should hang Alice right away, shoot her in front of City Hall, or bury her alive and destroy her blood.

Several television stations, in their journalistic endeavors, conducted polls and surveys reporting that ninety-nine percent of the public thought that Alice should be locked up and quarantined forever. They also felt she should definitely be convicted of the reckless endangerment charge.

The state's attorney for the city was having a field day trying to double-talk the press about what his office planned to do. And Alice was receiving large monetary offers from tabloids across the nation for her story.

I told Ron what had happened, and I thought he was going to have a nervous breakdown.

".I swear, Ted," said Ron, "every time I fucked Alice, I used not one, not two, not three, but four rubbers. As a matter of fact, the last time I was with her I was in the throes of passion, banging away at Alice from behind. But when I opened my eyes, she was already in the bathroom cleaning up, and here I was screwing the air, which, by the way, was one of the best orgasms I ever had."

After initially charging Dogface Alice with soliciting for prostitution and reckless endangerment, the city prosecutor dropped the second charge. Alice received a one-year suspended sentence and was ordered by the judge to attend AIDS seminars, volunteer with the local health department program for AIDS prevention, report twice a week to a probation officer, and stop stealing crabmeat. The judge added, "Alice, do you realize that you could kill your sexual partners?"

"Yes, Your Honor," said Alice remorsefully. "I'll never have sex again with anyone else. I swear it!"

Dogface Alice's request to do community work teaching bodybuilding to high school students was denied.

❏ ❏ ❏

COLLEGE PARK, MARYLAND
October 31, 1986

The day after the charges against Bias' teammates were dropped, Greg and Long were dismissed from the Maryland basketball team, and Bias' mystery friend, Brian Tribble, was again indicted. Head Coach Lefty Driesell resigned under intense pressure and assumed minor duties in the Athletic Department. He would be allowed to continue to receive his annual salary of $200,000 for eight years.

Chapter 14

BALTIMORE, MARYLAND
November 2, 1986

The Chemical Girl, the Deputy, and I were having lunch at The Biddle Street Station across the street from the State Office Complex. I had fifteen minutes to eat my shrimp salad sandwich before meeting with the College Park Task Force at the University of Maryland Baltimore Campus.

"Ostrich eggs are gathered like hothouse coconuts," said the Deputy. "They're deposited in cedar-lined incubators where the humidity is kept at a constant eighty-five percent and the temperature at ninety-seven and a half degrees. Like chicken eggs, they're candled at fourteen days to be sure that all is well with the embryo. Four weeks later, they go to the hatchery, and it takes about two days for them to hatch. Then they are taken to a brooder operation in Ocala, Florida. The baby chicks grow about a foot a month, and their value, again, rises about $1,000 a foot."

"I heard that there are presently no plans to market the low-cholesterol, high-protein meat of the ostrich because they're such great moneymakers. There's too much demand for live birds," the Chemical Girl chimed in.

"And, Ted," added the Deputy, "they're also real tough. They'll even take on a lion."

"Yeah, I heard," I said. "But if that's so, why do they stick their heads in the sand to hide? It almost reminds me of the way the two of you deny your addictions and probable bipolar conditions."

"Right," said the Deputy sarcastically. "Like you don't hide from your dysfunctional life, either."

To that, we all laughed nervously; mindful that maybe we were human ostriches...until the Chemical Girl enlightened us.

"Actually," she explained, "ostriches don't stick their heads in the sand. That's just a myth and a misunderstanding. When they sense that their nests may be threatened, they stretch their long necks against the ground to blend in with the sand; a sort of camouflage thing."

"Oh," I murmured as we sat quietly for a few seconds. I decided to add the recent information I had learned about these birds. "Let me tell you something. If the South African restrictions are ever lifted, all those big birds will ever be good for is eating!"

❏ ❏ ❏

I was lecturing at the State Penitentiary in Baltimore, something I did every three months, to a number of prisoners about drug and alcohol abuse and their alternatives. I included anecdotes that they could relate to so I could keep their attention, the span of which could be somewhat limited.

I had been going into the prisons for years. There was a time when it didn't affect me, and I didn't worry about it, feeling more like a savior to most of the prisoners. I was the main vehicle to getting them into programs that could help them get out of prison. But the older I got and the longer I lectured, the more fearful I became of being there. Looking out over the recreation area watching the prisoners, I asked a guard why it seemed that the prisoners were always moving in a sort of slow-motion jog. The guard answered, "You've always got to be movin' in here because once you stop, you're in big trouble."

Most guards hated the prisoners. The older guards talked about how the liberals in the late '60s ruined everything by granting prisoners rights. "Prisoners' rights," they would say. "That's what did it! That ended our control, our power. *They* run the prisons now, and we've become the inmates."

My agency always sought to implement new and innovative programs in the local jails and state penitentiaries. We started some excellent programs in the late '70s based on education and semi-treatment. But new programs were difficult to get off the ground with the negative attitude of the guards. They would say, "They've committed some horrendous crimes. They come into prison and get a high school equivalency or a college degree or even a master's degree. And we transport them to where they learn all this academic stuff, and we have to wait outside. Nobody pays for our schooling. Nobody pays for our degrees.

"We wait outside while these rapists, murderers, and thieves get their degrees. And if any of these guys have mental problems or drug or alcohol problems, we take 'em to where the treatment program is. We stand outside, and they get better. But if we want to get better, either our health insurance or our own money or both has to cover it.

"So why the fuck should we help with these new programs? We don't want to keep transporting these prisoners. The more movement, the more trouble."

I was ten minutes into my lecture. "Maybe I should digress and talk a little bit about *Coca-Cola*. Coca leaves were used as a flavoring agent for the early versions of the soft drink. It did contain a trace of cocaine, but not enough to do anything spectacular. It was more of a two-coffee effect. Today there are fifty milligrams of caffeine in *Coca-Cola* and similar beverages. But at the turn of the century, it was cocaine. So when you hear people say that in the old days they used to be hooked on cocaine because of Coca-Cola, it isn't so. It was a minimum dose with a minimal stimulant effect. Your grandparents and great-grandparents were not cokeheads.

"Let's talk about sex since that's on a lot of people's minds, especially here. Cocaine is a symptomatic antagonist or at least a dopamine antagonist. Small doses tend to improve sexuality, and the sensory mood changes seem to improve as well. As one gets into higher doses, there's a switch. Now there is ejaculatory failure and a loss of the ability to have orgasms. Eventually sex becomes a matter of disinterest due to the biphasic effect of cocaine."

I was interrupted by Prisoner Jack Borden. "Sir, please don't use those big words. I don't wanna fall asleep."

"Sorry," I apologized.

Borden was a three-time loser. Years ago, my Criminal Justice Division Chief, Joe Caskey, and I met with him at the Ex-Cel Therapeutic Community program. Back then, therapeutic communities were extremely confrontational. As punishment, they'd shave the clients' heads and make them wear signs which said *I'M AN ASSHOLE*. The therapeutic community length of stay was from eighteen months to three years, and Borden had six months remaining of a two-year stay at Ex-Cel. His alternative was a five-year sentence in jail. He notified Caskey that he couldn't take it another day at Ex-Cel and wanted to return to jail.

"Jack," I said, "don't be stupid. All you've gotta do is six more months. How can you choose five years in prison over that?"

"I'll tell ya how," cried Borden. "In jail I ain't gotta do nothin'. Here, I gotta work, clean, study, and be nice. I just can't stand it. Please send me back to jail!"

Caskey and I stayed with Borden for two hours trying to convince him to complete his time at Ex-Cel, but he wouldn't budge.
A week later he was back at the State Pen serving the alternative
five-year jail sentence.

❏ ❏ ❏

After leaving the State Penitentiary, I visited one of its "an-
nexes," Moana's Bar, where at least seventy-five percent of the
male and female patrons were ex-offenders. As a favor to Ron, a
regular in the bar, I had promised to speak to Moana about her
daughter Emily's cocaine habit.

I hated Moana's place. It was, at the most, ten feet wide with
about a hundred and twenty feet of bar. Dark, narrow, and filthy,
Moana's did not exactly attract the crème de la crème of Baltimore's
society. It was so bad that the mere presence of Ron and the Deputy,
who I spied at the middle of the bar, elevated their status to that of
British Royalty.

Moana wiped her eyeglasses with a dirty towel and told me of
her precious twenty-three-year-old Emily, who lived at home, stole
money, stayed out late, and ingested large amounts of cocaine.

Short, heavy, and frumpy, it was hard to imagine that years earlier
Moana was a featured attraction at strip joints on Baltimore's Block.
Her hair was now two tones of blonde and black, her facial hair needed
electrolysis desperately, and she wore so much white pancake makeup
that she could have been mistaken for a kabuki dancer.

After Moana's tale of woe, I gave her some tips on how to deal
with her daughter. I used the latest buzz words in the field: enabling, tough love, and codependency.

"Stop supporting her and bailing her out," I advised. "Throw
her out of the house and get on with your life."

"Suppose she dies or gets killed? I'd never forgive myself,"
said Moana, her voice cracking.

"Moana," I said. "She's gonna die or get arrested sooner or
later. You're not helping her."

Moana began to cry. "I know you're right, Ted, but she's all I got.
Lemme think about it, and have a drink on the house while you're here."

I walked to the center of the bar to join Ron and the Deputy. They
must have been drinking for a while since there were eight empty
bottles of Michelob in front of them which no one had removed.

"Ted," said the Deputy. "We couldn't help but overhear your clinical advice to Moana, and we think it's a crock of shit."

"Why?" I asked.

"Because you're a fucking hypocrite," said the Deputy, laughing with Ron.

"Why don't you two humor me and explain yourselves."

"Alright," said the Deputy. "You tell Moana to throw her kid out and cut her off 'cause she's enabling the girl and is codependent, like that's the only shot at redemption."

"If that's the case," interrupted Ron, "you, Mr. Therapist, are codependent and an enabler. And you don't practice what you preach."

I knew the guys were fucking with me, but I wasn't in the mood to hear their lecturing. "It's been a long day, and I only came here to do *you* a favor, Ron."

The Deputy was smiling. "Can't take it, huh, Ted?"

I stared at him and shook my head.

"Do you realize," said the Deputy, "that you are codependent and have enabled me, Ron, Holt, Candy, and most of all, the Chemical Girl?"

"Kiss my ass," I said as I walked toward the exit.

"Oh, Ted," yelled the Deputy, "I've got the answer for the College Park Task Force. Blame the University of Maryland for enabling the coaches, the Athletic Department, the students, the players, and Bias. And throw 'em all out!"

Driving away, I reflected on their comments. I hated it, but they were probably right.

❑ ❑ ❑

LOS ANGELES, CALIFORNIA
November 2, 1986

Holt went for a checkup at the hospital, and the doctor informed him that the mass was back. "It's growing at an accelerated rate," the physician explained. "I'm a bit concerned, so we're going to do a biopsy."

Three days later, the doctor called Holt and told him that the mass in his lung seemed more irreversible than it had previously. "We'll try large doses of antibiotics to start, but frankly, Holt, I can't assure you it's going to work."

Holt was very depressed, and was taking Valium and bootleg Quaaludes. He phoned me.

"Ted, I'm going to die. This time I think I'm really going to die!" Holt cried.

"Holt," I said in a calm voice. "Get a hold of yourself. Try not to be depressed, and don't give up. Remember, you said exactly the same thing the last time, and you were cured!"

"No, Ted, this time it's for real. I could just see the look in the fuckin' doctor's eyes. This is it. I'm going to die. I can feel it. You've always disapproved of my lifestyle and line of work, but drug dealing *is* kind of fun, and you never understood that. Anyhow, I'm real, real scared, Ted, and I need your help and support. Can you come out here?"

"Holt, see the doctor again in the next couple days and give me a call. Better yet, give me the name of the doctor and tell him I'm going to call him. Explain that I have permission from you for him to tell me about your situation, so we won't violate confidentiality.

"In the meantime, I'm going to check with some specialists here. I think you have White Lung Disease from smoking so much opium, cocaine, and grass. And God knows what else you've put in your fucking system. I know that they're starting to do a lot of research on illnesses like yours. Have some hope, man, and don't give up. Do you understand me?"

❏ ❏ ❏

November 6, 1986

Ron stopped by the Deputy's to play with the train sets and to find out how things were going with his wife. Outside, Junior raced up and down the street on the dune buggy desert rat with the dogs in hot pursuit. From behind the fence, Justice growled menacingly as Ron walked into the garage. Oh how that big dog hated Ron.

The Deputy was laying more train tracks as he joked to Ron, "For the past couple weeks, train track is about all I've been laying."

Ron had heard about the duck decoy disaster and the legal hassle with the Deputy's wife. Although his wife had left for a few days and hired a lawyer, the Deputy had decided to turn over a new leaf. He apologized to his wife, and they reconciled with the help of a marriage counselor.

"Actually, Ron, I couldn't afford another divorce right now with the kids and all. So we decided to see this marriage counselor twice a week together and once a week alone," said the Deputy.

"Now get this," the Deputy whispered. "The counselor is a good-looking woman, early forties, but looks younger, and has great legs. You'd go mad for her, Ron. Anyhow, the second time I was alone with her, she hit on me and we made it a little. No sex, but making out. This afternoon I'm meeting her at the Tip-Top Motel on Route 40. My wife's at her sister's with the girls, so it's cool.

"You can play with the trains and keep an eye on Junior while I'm gone. I'll only be two hours tops."

For the next hour and a half, Ron played with the train sets and drank beer. It was like a religious experience for him. After he finished he went outside to watch Junior, whom he'd forgotten about while engrossed in the trains.

When Ron emerged from the garage, Junior had finished driving the desert rat. He was pushing the go-cart up the pavement towards the garage when he saw Ron.

The mini-car had oversized tires on the rear and looked like a miniature California dragster. Its speed depended on the weight of the driver, and it had an eight-horsepower Briggs and Stratton motor.

"Wanna try it out, Mr. Ron?" asked Junior. "It's easy to drive."

"I don't know," Ron answered. "Go in the house and bring me out some beers, and then you can show me how."

Junior ran into the house as Ron explored the desert rat. He climbed into the seat and gently played with the steering wheel, brake, and gas pedal. The dog, Justice, was beside himself, barking and growling and leaping on the fence.

Junior returned and gave Ron driving instructions, and for the next half hour, he cautiously drove the desert rat up and down the cul-de-sac and drank more beer. Junior stood by giving directions and trying to keep the Deputy's stray dog collection from chasing Ron.

The Deputy was on his way back from his "session" with the marriage counselor. The Tip-Top Motel had hourly rates, but the Deputy was feeling his oats and decided to take the room for the night. He and the marriage counselor would meet again in the evening.

Ron had a nice buzz from the beer and was racing the desert rat up and down the street at about forty miles an hour. Justice's rage continued as he jumped and jumped at the fence. Before long he was up and over it.

Junior and the other dogs were startled as Justice took off after Ron. At first, he was oblivious to his angry pursuer. But as he turned the desert rat back towards the Deputy's house, he saw Justice approaching as fast as he could run. Ron panicked and the go-cart went out of control. Ron began to scream as Justice ran right into the desert rat, snapping at Ron's legs. The cart slammed into a curb and came to a halt as Justice leaped onto the seat.

The big dog began to maul Ron, who was dazed from fear, beer, and the accident. Justice was very strong and Ron was feeling faint. The canine attacked Ron's neck, severing the jugular vein.

The Deputy drove up to his house, saw the commotion, and began honking his horn. He screeched his car to a stop and ran towards the melee, but it was too late. Ron was already dead. Ones, fives, tens, twenties, and fifties floated about. Justice had ripped apart Ron's loot-filled pockets, too.

❑ ❑ ❑

November 8, 1986

Early in the morning, my ex- or estranged wife Candy called and asked to ride to Ron's funeral with me. Although Candy did not like Ron, or for that matter any of my friends, she had an excellent relationship with Ron's mother Rose. Rose looked upon Candy as the daughter she never had, and surprisingly Candy had a calming effect on Rose. After Ron's bizarre and untimely death, Rose needed intensive calming.

So against my better judgment, I took Candy to the funeral and, later, to the cemetery. The mid-fall weather was a warm seventy-eight degrees. As soon as I picked up Candy, she started on me. "Your behavior around town and in Ocean City is causing me embarrassment. You've been seen in public with those young sluts you date, and I want it to stop. Furthermore, I want to increase the life insurance policy I have on you, and…" Candy went on and on. I knew I would regret picking her up.

Ron's Jewish family chose an Orthodox funeral ceremony which was no big deal, except to Candy. Ron came from a large family and had many friends. Therefore, his parents not only had the usual eight pallbearers to carry his casket, but an unheard of number of a *dozen* honorary pallbearers to walk behind the casket.

Candy wanted to be a pallbearer, and even though Ron's mother agreed to it, the rabbi denied the request.

"Rose," he said, "no gentile or woman can be a pallbearer in an Orthodox Jewish funeral ceremony. It's against the Talmud, the law."

Rose reluctantly agreed. But Candy, known to be argumentative and clearly angry with all men, began a huge hassle in the funeral home. It ended only after Rose fainted for the third time over Ron's casket.

After receiving an earful from Candy on the drive over, and observing her confrontation with the rabbi, I knew that something else had to go wrong. According to my mom, bad luck always came in threes.

It was a forty-five-minute drive for the procession from the Levinson Funeral Home in Pikesville in northwest Baltimore City to the Petach Tikvah Cemetery in Rosedale in far eastern Baltimore County. The regular and honorary pallbearers tried to carry the casket peacefully from the limousine to the grave site, but confusion reigned. In their haste for a good spot by the graveside, people were tripped up, resulting in childish pushing and shoving.

Ron's grave was located at the far end of the cemetery near the fence overlooking the Beltway. Fortifying the fence were trees, bushes, and flowers. And fortifying the greenery were bees–wild, angry bees–the last of a late Indian summer. They hovered and buzzed around the gravestones as the mourners clumsily situated themselves for the closing service.

Seated in folding chairs in front of the open grave as the casket was slowly lowered into the ground were Ron's parents, uncles, and aunts. Candy, the Deputy, and I stood by Ron's mother.

Rose was no novice to funerals and cemeteries. Besides attending her family's and friends' funerals, she often attended funerals of people she didn't even know. She enjoyed them in a macabre way– sitting, rocking, shaking, and crying over total strangers. At the funerals of her close relatives, Rose would usually become hysterical, threatening to jump into the casket or grave with the deceased.

And now, with her son Ron dead, she began her usual funeral chant. "Take me too! Take me too, God! I've got nothing to live for now! I'm going with you, Ron! Here I come!"

Ron's dad held Rose tightly, even though he knew she would not actually jump in since she had never done it before. *We* also kept an eye on Rose, holding her shoulders now and then, but knowing that Rose wasn't taking the leap.

The bees were becoming annoying, flying around Rose's head, as the rabbi recited the Mourner's Kaddish. The Deputy, Candy, and I swatted and shooed them away. After a while, Candy pushed the Deputy and me back a bit and whispered, "You're both gonna get stung. Let me take care of Rose. I've got long-sleeved gloves on."

I thought to myself, *So that's why women wear long-sleeved gloves to funerals year-round.*

Rose rocked back and forth as the ceremony drew to a close. She was oblivious to the bees and to Candy's attempts at protecting her head against potential attacks.

Then, for the fifth time, Rose shouted, "Take me with you, Ron!" At the same moment that Rose was rocking forward and off balance, Candy attempted to swat away two bees. The back of her hand hit Rose's head with such force that she went flying out of her seat and into the grave, landing facedown on top of Ron's casket. She hit hard with a thud and was briefly knocked unconscious.

The mourners, in the midst of the closing prayer, suddenly went silent. It appeared as though the grieving Rose had actually leaped into the shallow grave. The Deputy and I witnessed the incident and tried to contain our laughter as Candy rushed over and began pulling Rose out of the grave.

Pandemonium followed, but everyone calmed down after Rose regained consciousness. She was totally unaware of what had just happened to her. Candy came over to us and threatened, "Don't either of you ever let on about what really happened or I'll kill ya! Let's get out of here."

Candy reached for my hand, but I knew what she had in mind and I quickly pulled it away. I started to say something just as I thought I felt a bee sting on my thumb.

"It looked black, and I think it was too thin for a bee," the Deputy commented.

"Christ," said Candy. "It looks like whatever it was took a helluva bite out of your thumb. Where's your bee kit?"

"I'm not sure," I said as we walked back towards the limousine.

Candy slipped over to console Ron's mom. As I watched, I began to feel very dizzy. Suddenly, my knees buckled in front of a gravestone with the name William Blank chiseled on the front.

The Deputy was speaking, "Ted, are you praying or what? Do you know this Blank guy?"

I looked up at him and opened my mouth, but nothing came out. I collapsed against the gravestone. My last thought was *heart attack*!

❑ ❑ ❑

November 9, 1986

I woke up in the intensive care unit of Good Samaritan Hospital, part of the Johns Hopkins Hospital Medical System. An elderly nurse was adjusting an IV tube as she explained, "Young man, you suffered a severe allergic reaction to a hornet sting, and you almost died. That handsome fella who works with you had to give you mouth-to-mouth or you would have been a goner. You're very lucky. Now, don't get upset that your body...and blood...look purple. You'll be okay."

I recovered for three days in the ICU during which time I was given a complete blood transfusion and other medications that brought me back to nearly normal. However, I itched like crazy, and it was very difficult not to scratch. For that reason, they kept my arms restrained, which was very unpleasant. Candy came by twice a day. She loved seeing my tied-down hands, but it scared the living shit out of me. I told the Deputy to warn Jan and the Chemical Girl not to come by for fear of a huge confrontation with Candy if she happened to pop in.

I stayed home for a day and a half before returning to work. During that time, I read more and more data and research regarding AIDS and grew increasingly alarmed and concerned. It wasn't just IV users, homosexuals, and bisexuals contracting AIDS. There were also a growing number of horror stories about people who had received blood transfusions and developed the disease. These were normal heterosexuals who had no involvement with drugs or homosexuality, nor had they had sexual contact with anyone with AIDS. Their cases had been traced directly to tainted blood transfusions.

Shaken, I considered calling Doc Honeybee and asking for something to tranquilize my mind. I was doubly concerned, of course, because the onset of AIDS could be months or years after a blood transfusion, or very quickly. Ron had once told me that when Dogface Alice was really desperate for money, she would sell her blood to a blood bank near The Block, Baltimore's adult entertainment area.

I tried to guess how many people like Alice had AIDS, HIV, or AIDS-related complex (ARC) and had given blood over the last few years. I read an article presenting some elementary findings that traced AIDS back to when the Tall Ships visited the U.S. in '76, and I thought, *God save me. There could be some chance, some small percentage, that one of the transfusion bags given to me contained the AIDS virus. Perhaps a sailor visiting The Block....*

❑ ❑ ❑

November 10, 1986

The Chemical Girl flew to Argentina with Lo Ming to discuss a fertilizer deal with a company in that republic. Things had not been going well for Lo Ming, and as usual, he was looking for someone to blame. He was also distraught over his suspicions that the Chemical Girl was running around with someone else.

During a layover in Miami on the return trip, Lo Ming got into a huge argument with the Chemical Girl because she was wearing her hair down instead of up the way he liked it. He also criticized her attire as he often did when he was distressed. Tired of his negative and controlling comments, she walked away, rushing off through the airport. Lo Ming was stuck with five pieces of luggage and could not follow her.

The Chemical Girl rented a car outside of Miami International Airport and drove up the Florida coast, inland, to Ocala. After a couple of phone calls, she located the gentleman she first met on the plane from Europe who told her about the ostrich farms. His name was Mellow McFrank. She told him that she was stopping by.

Upon her arrival, McFrank insisted that she stay over for a couple of days and take a look at his ostrich breeding farm. He would teach her about investment opportunities, and, perhaps, even offer her a small partnership if she was interested.

"You're a very pretty woman," he remarked, "but don't worry, I'm not interested in you for your looks. You're also very smart, and you've got a lot of connections that could make us both a lot of money."

McFrank was married to a short, heavyset German woman. She was very courteous, spoke little English, and treated the Chemical Girl like a daughter.

The Chemical Girl stayed at the ranch for a couple days absorbing everything that McFrank taught her about ostrich farming, marketing, and the potential profits involved.

❑ ❑ ❑

I flew to Los Angeles to meet Holt and his doctors. I had spoken to several top physicians at Johns Hopkins, Harvard, and various clinics about Holt's problem. None of them seemed hopeful that Holt could be saved.

Holt and I went to the doctor's office upon my arrival in Los Angeles.

"I'm going to be frank with you, Ted. I've already gone over this with Holt, but sometimes I don't think I'm getting through to him," the doctor said, glancing over at Holt. "The mass is growing at a very, very fast and alarming rate; faster than any type of cancer I've ever seen or treated before. Although we know that the root cause is not cancer, based on what Holt has ingested over time, it's doubtful that we can reverse it. I would estimate that he has approximately three months to live, and maybe even less than that. He should get his finances and will in order. I would like to keep him here to see if there's any chance of slowing the growth of the mass, but I don't want to give you *or* him false hope. I really doubt that anything can be done."

Holt was sobbing uncontrollably, but quietly.

"Doc," I said. "I've heard stories about people who lived for years with this type of disorder. Aren't there vitamins or injections he can use? Is there anybody anywhere in the world who can do anything for Holt?"

The doctor looked somber. "Ted, take a little walk with me while Holt gets control of himself."

We strolled slowly down the corridor of the hospital's terminally-ill wing, and for a while neither of us spoke. Finally the doctor said, "Ted, he hasn't got a shot at recovery; not a prayer. If he had only listened and stopped the drugs. But he began smoking crystal methamphetamine immediately after he improved the first time around.

"He swore he would straighten his life out. After doing ICE, he smoked the opium to balance out the powerful rush of the crystal methamphetamine. He's got so much going against him as a result of all that. It's really too late to do anything.

"He did tell me that you promised to take him to Thailand when he thought he was going to die the first time. If you still want to do that, you should do it soon. It's going to be a very rough few months for him, if he makes it that long."

I spent that night consoling Holt and his wife, and returned to Baltimore on a red-eye flight from Los Angeles that arrived at five-thirty a.m.

Chapter 15

BALTIMORE, MARYLAND
November 13-15, 1986

I knew the Chemical Girl had returned from her trip because her car was sitting in the parking lot beneath the condos where she lived. I stopped by her place near Baltimore's glittering Inner Harbor a couple times, but she didn't answer the door or her phone despite my repeated calls.

I felt certain that she was there. I could tell. I could feel it.

❑ ❑ ❑

The Chemical Girl finally returned my calls, inviting me over to her condo where we spent a relaxing evening. She seemed heavily sedated, was drinking a lot more than usual, and taking several tranquilizers at once. All she wanted to do was fuck, sleep, and drink over and over again. This went on for the next few days and, as usual, I couldn't get through to her how self-destructive she had become.

During infrequent lucid moments, she spoke about her hassles with Lo Ming. It looked like he would probably go out of business and that she would never receive all the money he owed her. His obsession with her and the realization that he could never have her also turned Lo Ming into a bitter and dangerous adversary. "He said he'd kill me if he couldn't have me. I hate him now, and I'm scared."

The Chemical Girl talked briefly about her trip to South America and Florida, but she was somewhat incoherent, and I didn't really want to hear about it anyhow. So we made love instead. All she wanted to do was to sleep and to fuck and to drink; and to sleep and to fuck and to drink.

❑ ❑ ❑

The Chemical Girl had been in the bathroom for a long time and when she came out, she was trembling. She came over and hugged me.

"Ted, I feel very shaky, my heart is racing like crazy, I'm nauseous, I can't eat, and I'm so tired. I just want to sleep all the time and never wake up."

"How long's this been going on?" I asked, afraid of her answer.

"Well, I guess it's happened before, but never like this."

I could feel her heart pounding through our embrace, and I knew it had zero to do with affection or emotion, but everything to do with alcohol.

"How come you've never told me about this before? Why didn't you say something?"

She was quiet for a while, and then she said, "Because I knew I'd get a fucking lecture out of you, Ted, and lectures aren't what I need right now."

I understood what she was saying. "I want you to see a doctor friend of mine. No lectures, no bullshit, no A.A. meetings; nothing like that. Maybe there's something physiologically wrong with you, something genetic," I lied. "Maybe like what happened to Len Bias' heart. With the amount of cocaine you use, perhaps that has something to do with this."

"Okay. If it comes back again, maybe I will," she sighed, "although I wish it would just go away. It's never been this bad for so long, and I'm real scared." The Chemical Girl started to sob, then she cried, then she whimpered. A few seconds later she crawled back into bed and fell asleep immediately. She slept for hours, and every now and then I checked her pulse.

While the Chemical Girl dozed, I called Doc Maco, the Medical Director of The New Hope Methadone Clinic. I had confidence in him as an addiction doctor, and he advised me to either bring the Chemical Girl to his office or have her come to the clinic right away.

When the Chemical Girl finally awakened from her deep sleep, I told her that I wanted her to call Dr. Maco for an appointment as soon as possible. She told me that she thought she was feeling better, and although her heart was still pounding and her hands were shaking, it wasn't as bad. She was still very tired, though. My instincts and experience told me it was alcoholism and that she was having delirium tremens (d.t.'s).

After about twenty minutes, the Chemical Girl, visibly shaken, picked up the phone and called Dr. Maco's office for an appointment.

"Ted, they can see me in an hour and a half."

"I'm going with you," I insisted.

"No," she said. "I'll go myself. I can make it. I'm a great driver you know, and I've never had an accident or a ticket."

"No way!" I said. "I'll drop you off and pick you up later. You are definitely not driving!"

❑ ❑ ❑

Three days later, I picked up the Chemical Girl from Baltimore General Hospital where she had been admitted from Dr. Maco's clinic located across the street. Before Dr. Maco released her, he spoke to me about her detox.

"I front-loaded her with Valium, ten milligrams an hour. She was in a twilight sleep for forty-eight hours."

"That seems like a lot," I said.

"Not really, Ted," replied Dr. Maco. "Most docs are too tentative at the beginning of a detox and then they overkill at the end. Their patients are sent home too zonked. It's because they don't know enough about addiction and addicts or the proper treatment for them."

He was right. Here it was thirty-some years after the American Medical Association had defined addiction as a disease and, except for maybe a handful, the medical schools still weren't mandating courses on it. Elsewhere it either wasn't taught or was only an elective, despite the fact that it was the number one public health crisis in America.

"Will she be okay?" I asked, concerned about seizures.

"Valium is long-acting, and your girlfriend understands that. She can quote from the Physicians Desk Reference (PDR). The Valium also helps with her Xanax problem. Unfortunately, the odds are that she'll still relapse. Oh, and the blood test indicated some potential liver dysfunction."

"I know relapse is a probability," I said.

"Hell, Ted. She's CIA."

"Huh?!" I asked, surprised. "She's with the government?"

"No. You're too close to this, Ted. You're not thinking like a clinician. CIA is the acronym for Catholic, Irish, and Alcoholic."

"Oh my God, Doc, you're right. You ought to see her family tree–a classic study in heredity and alcoholism," I said.

I remembered the twin studies from Sweden where twins separated at birth were brought up in different environments and still became alcoholics. And recently there was a study showing a twenty-five percent chance of addiction from each parent, grand-parent, aunt, and uncle. The Chemical Girl never had a shot.

"Do you love this girl?" asked Dr. Maco.

"I dunno…I'm not sure," I stammered.

"You love her. Don't bullshit me," said Maco. "Just be careful, Ted. She may not be good for your career."

❑ ❑ ❑

BALTIMORE, MARYLAND
November 18, 1986

The Chemical Girl called me. "I just got back from the doctor's. When they did the second blood test, my liver checked out fine. And the rest of my physical examination was okay, too."

I asked her, "Well, so what does he think?"

"Fuck, Ted, you know what he thinks! He says I drink too much, but he's the first person who ever said it in an easy-to-understand way. And he says I have to cut back…well…actually, he said to stop drinking and drugging completely. If I don't, he said I'll either die or wake up one morning and not know who I am."

I told her that I was sure it would work out alright. I knew she didn't want to hear a lecture or an I-told-you-so or a clinical speech. Hell, no addicts I ever talked to about addictions, drugs, or alcoholism paid much attention to the spoken word.

Later that evening, the Chemical Girl and I made love slowly and, for me, carefully. I don't know why, but after her medical scare, I thought any hard sex might be detrimental to her.

A half hour after our lovemaking, she strolled over to the refrigerator, removed a bottle of Stoli vodka from the freezer, and casually poured herself a drink.

"God! What's the matter with you?" I asked flabbergasted. "After what this doctor just said…"

"Ted, don't worry," she interrupted. "It's just a little drink. I can't cold-turkey this. That's impossible. You know I don't want to die. I'm not going to kill myself. I can handle it. And don't you fuckin' dare say, 'Controlled use is the dream of all junkies,' or I'll kick you in the nuts."

❑ ❑ ❑

BALTIMORE, MARYLAND
November 19, 1986

The Deputy's wife slammed the phone receiver down. Her face grew bright red as she burst into tears. After a few minutes the crying subsided, her breathing steadied, and she calmly reflected for a few minutes. Before long, a devious-looking smile spread widely across her face.

The Deputy and his son were in the garage playing with the trains when the Deputy's wife reminded them that they were going shopping and out to eat a quick dinner with her. Although the Deputy and his son didn't want to go, they knew they had to give her *some* time. So they turned off the sets, left the trains where they were, and headed for the car.

The three of them piled in and the Deputy's wife drove to Eastpoint Mall where they had a nice, but very quiet, dinner at Ruby Tuesday's. Junior strolled off to the bathroom, and as soon as he was out of hearing range, the Deputy's wife hissed to him, "You son-of-a-bitch. I heard about you and the marriage counselor."

"What are you talking about?" the Deputy asked innocently.

His wife smiled at him for what seemed like minutes. Then she answered, "You motherfucker, you never stop, do you? You can deny it all you want, but it isn't going to matter. I guess I'm going to have to learn to live with it because unfortunately I *do* love you. I'll just have to accept it, but I'm not feeling too hot right now. Do me a favor and take the boy to that movie he's been wanting to see. I'm going over to my mom's, but I'm not going to tell her about this. I just want to relax and shoot the breeze. If not, I may go out and have a drink or two. Just spend some quality time with your son, okay?"

The Deputy decided that there was no need to pursue the conversation. "Okay, I'll take him to a movie. I really don't know what you're talking about, though. If you want, I won't see the marriage counselor again, and we can find another one."

"Look. I don't want to discuss it any further. It's finished business," she insisted. "Just take Junior to the movies, and I'll pick you guys up around nine-thirty. If I'm later than nine-forty-five, take a cab and I'll meet you at home."

The Deputy agreed, and his wife left. Twenty minutes later, as the Deputy and Junior laughed at the coming attractions before the movie at Eastpoint Mall, the Deputy's wife returned to their home. She walked calmly to the lower level of the garage and found an old baseball bat. Then she walked back up the stairs to where the expensive and irreplaceable train sets, treasured model train memorabilia, and tracks were kept. They were all collector's items, worth thousands and thousands of dollars.

She switched on the sets and watched the trains whiz by. With a smile on her face, she took the baseball bat and began smashing the moving trains, the bridges, the little stop signs, the blinking lights, and the tracks. She destroyed everything in sight before retrieving more trains and other equipment that were packed away. Unwrapping them slowly and placing them neatly on the tracks, she smashed them with the baseball bat, too. The Deputy's wife continued until she had trashed everything–every single piece of the Lionel train collection and the other antique train pieces that the Deputy had accumulated and invested in over the years. The train memorabilia was to be the bulk of the estate that the Deputy would either leave to his children or sell for his own escape and running-away money.

After slowly walking back to the house, the Deputy's wife went to Junior's room and pulled the locked chest out from under his bed. Junior didn't even know its contents. She busted the lock with a sledgehammer, removed thirty more pieces of very rare trains, equipment, and track, and smashed them to smithereens. Then she began to laugh and laugh and laugh....

❑ ❑ ❑

The Chemical Girl was talking on the telephone with me, sounding more excited than I had heard her in a long, long time. She seemed alert, alive, and sober.

"Ted, the doctor told me that my immune system was fucked up. He said that the alcohol and drugs had played havoc with my body and my mind, and that what he saw happening to me usually appears in much older addicts. Maybe it's because I have that Irish drinking gene and overdid it a little bit. Anyhow, he's a vitamin freak. I know that most physicians aren't, but he named some special vitamins I should get, so I went to a health food store on Charles Street and spent almost $400."

"You spent what?" I asked incredulously. "Why would you spend that kind of money? Where did you go? What store?"

"I think it was called The Green Earth. The owner, Buzzy, said he knew you very well, and he gave me a discount. Anyhow, I took all these vitamins, and maybe it's psychological or something, but I feel really healthy. I even went out and jogged a half a mile, and I haven't run in a long time. So, what do you think?"

I told the Chemical Girl that I thought it was great even though I knew Buzzy was known for taking advantage of people. He was an old friend who once informed me that the CIA and FBI were killing off celebrities, and making it look like they overdosed. I didn't want to discourage her, though. After all, every now and then I took vitamins and minerals. I didn't know whether they did me any good physiologically or psychologically, but I would try almost anything that promised good health.

I was quite sure that her immune system must have been in really bad shape because of the way she abused alcohol and dope during the short time I knew her. I was also concerned that, statistically, addicts averaged five relapses, and that didn't mean that they stopped abusing chemicals after five. That was just the average. There was no way that I could picture the Chemical Girl cleaning herself up for good.

❑ ❑ ❑

BALTIMORE, MARYLAND
November 20, 1986

A couple days later, the Chemical Girl was still gung-ho on vitamins. She was born-again, and chatted constantly about it. We'd been over her place for two hours, and even the lovemaking was a little more active and innovative than usual.

Against my better judgment, I let her convince me to swallow some very large vitamins. I had no idea what I was ingesting, and after about fifteen minutes, I felt like vomiting. I didn't know why the manufacturers couldn't make those good-tasting, chewable children's Flintstone vitamins for adults, too. Vitamins in their pure form sucked. But I wanted so badly for the Chemical Girl to remain drug free, and I did not want to discourage her vitamin use. So I bit the bullet *and* the vitamins and went home nauseated.

Two hours later, I began feeling a little funny, and it wasn't ha-ha funny. It was more like the funny feeling I felt after being stung by a hornet, and I noticed that my body was turning pink. *Maybe I had been bitten by a spider or some other insect in the house,* I thought. I wasn't sure, so I got my bee-sting kit and injected myself in the thigh with the epinephrine. Nothing happened and I panicked. Grabbing my keys and sprinting to the car, I drove as fast as I could to Pimlico Hospital. I was sweating profusely, fearing that I might die.

I parked the car illegally outside the emergency room entrance and ran in. I explained to the intake nurse what had happened, but from the knowing look in her eyes, it was obvious she already knew. My pink skin had become red as she directed me to a rear cubicle and summoned a doctor. I tried to methodically explain to the doctor what had occurred and my previous allergic reactions, but I really didn't know what had happened.

The doctor was Greek, although I thought he was an Arab. Over and over again, I tried to explain to him what had occurred. He was speaking in broken English, and I wanted to smack him in the mouth. Why was it that everybody who worked in the emergency room either spoke in broken English or no English at all? I was positive that some Americans must still work in hospital emergency rooms somewhere in the United States. I wasn't prejudiced, but I was desperate for the doctor to comprehend what I was saying so I could be treated.

We reviewed the last twenty-four hours, even though I was fairly sure that some hairy-assed fucking spider in my apartment bit me in the behind; or that a bee or wasp left over from the summer had stung me; or worse yet, maybe another hornet got me. I had not mentioned the Chemical Girl or anything that transpired at her place because it was none of their business. But then I figured, *What the hell, maybe it will help.*

"Look, Doc. I was with my girlfriend and we were into some very insane lovemaking. I don't think *she* stung me, but if she did, it was worth it. Oh yeah, and she gave me some vitamins, although I don't think that would have done it. I've taken vitamins before."

The doctor raised his eyebrows and asked me if I could find out what kind of vitamins I took. I requested a phone and called the Chemical Girl, who thankfully answered on the first ring. I explained to her briefly what was going on and told her to tell the doctor what each vitamin was. He was on the phone with her for quite a while. I felt like shit and was really starting to worry, and I knew I didn't want to go through anything like the hornet sting again. The doctor finally hung up and told me that he was going to give me some injections.

"I think that your girlfriend," he said in broken English, "didn't realize that one of the vitamins she give you could cause you such harm. And I have seen only in extreme circumstances people die from it."

"Die from it!" I cried out, still confused by the doctor's accent. "Are you kidding me? What did that fucking whore give me?"

The doctor smiled as he gave me an injection and said, "She give you some bee pollen in form of vitamin. Lots of people take it. Bee pollen has very stimulating effect upon them. But there are people who have allergies to this. It can result in very severe allergic reaction, and that is what you are having. If you had not been stung by hornet earlier this year, you would not be like this. We take care of you, though. Do not worry."

I thought I was going to pass out and told the doctor so before grabbing him and pleading, "Whatever you do, no more blood transfusions. If you have to, at least find out who donated the blood first. I don't want to get AIDS. No whores, no junkies, nobody who had a transfusion before; like some jerk like me...oh my God, I'm gonna be sick." And with that, I threw up all over the doctor.

Forty minutes later, I was released and went home to my apartment. Whatever the doctor had given me worked and I felt much better, even though my skin was still flushed. A little more brown in my face and I could have passed for a guy with a great Florida tan.

❏ ❏ ❏

OCEAN CITY, MARYLAND
November 24, 1986

It was late November and the weather had changed dramatically. Cold and raw outside, it was sleeting and the wind was picking up. The Deputy and I were once again at the Sheraton in Ocean City. We had attended a daylong meeting with officials from the Eastern Shore counties and the mayor of Ocean City. The topics of discussion included a cocaine detox program to be set up next summer in one of Salisbury, Maryland's health department clinics, and the results of the effectiveness of the COPYIR program and the probability for continuing it.

After the meetings, the Deputy and I had dinner in the hotel bar before retiring to our rooms. I was exhausted and fell asleep watching television. Around midnight, I got up and returned a couple phone calls. Then I dialed the Deputy's room, but there was no answer.

I decided to peruse the Sheraton's nightclub where I figured the Deputy might be. As I walked through, I saw a scattering of about thirty patrons listening and dancing to a band called "First Class." The band had just finished its next-to-the-last set and announced that they'd be back in twenty-five minutes. At the far corner bar lit with blue lighting, I spotted the Deputy drinking a Coors Light. I sat down next to him.

"How long have you been here?" I asked.

"I guess for the past hour or so," answered the Deputy. "This band's real good, Ted. What's up?"

I told him I just felt like relaxing, and asked if he was still upset over his wife trashing his beloved train sets.

"My wife and I are history!" he growled. "There's no point in going back. If she's gonna take a baseball bat and whack out the train sets, she'll do the same to me one night while I'm asleep. I don't need this shit. I'm trying to figure the best way to get out. That cunt!"

"Easy does it," I said.

We sat in silence until his anger subsided, and after a while, we joked a bit about failed marriages. Then we began reminiscing and philosophizing.

"Have you ever been in love? *Really* in love?" I asked.

"I don't know," answered the Deputy. "We've talked about this before, ya know. What is love? What is romantic love? I know it changes over time, and sometimes it's just lust, or biological, or sexual."

"The Chemical Girl says that love's ninety-nine percent sex," I announced.

He continued, "I'm not so sure, Ted. That's what she says, but what about you? What do you see in her? Sex or more than that?"

"If love is what I think it is," I answered, "then I've been in love a few times. Short-term puppy love mostly. I think I might have been in that kind of love with Candy. And I was in love with a couple other girls before her, but there's something different about the Chemical Girl. She's so vulnerable and childlike, but unfortunately very fucking self-destructive. Yet she's such a free spirit. It's very refreshing.

"She's kind of like her grandmom Lola, whom she was named after–an escapist and risktaker. The Chemical Girl is always longing to be hugged and held. I never liked to do that with any other woman, but I always want to hug and hold onto her. Maybe that's romantic love. What do you think?"

"I can see it, but it's self-destructive for you, too," the Deputy responded.

"You still haven't answered me," I said. "Have *you* ever *really* been in love? Christ, you've been married three times. You're always telling me how you love this chick and that chick."

"I fell in love one time," he admitted. "At least I guess it was that feeling of love. You know what I mean? Remember I told you about a place where I used to hang out in Western Maryland years ago called 'Loonie's'? It was outside of Westernport in Garrett County, all the way up past the Maryland line in West Virginia. Even though lots of Western Marylanders hung there, it was on the West Virginia side as I recall.

"Loonie's was a private club disguised as a bar and restaurant. You had to be a member to get in. It was open twenty-four hours a day, and most of the clientele were people who worked at the Kelly-Springfield tire plant when it was in its heyday years ago. There was *lots* of action. That plant was the key to the economic survival of that part of West Virginia and Western Maryland.

"Man, you'd go up there and walk into this place, and no matter what time of day or night it was, it was mobbed with hundreds of women; and, of course, a lot of men, too. Every fifteen minutes before eight hours had passed, everybody would scatter, empty the place. Half an hour later, it'd be filled up again with new people. Then, fifteen minutes before the next eight hours went by, all *those* people would leave and a new group of folks would arrive. The new group would stay until almost eight hours later, and then they'd leave, and it would begin all over again."

The band began their last set and the Deputy was right. They were great. No matter how down one might have felt on this bleak, cold, raw November night, there was something about their music that lifted you up. Even the alcohol couldn't dull my senses.

The Deputy continued with his Loonie's love story. "You see, there were different shifts. The housewives of the guys working at the Kelly-Springfield plant were there with the guys who just got off shift. The women would wait until their husbands went off to work and haul-ass to Loonie's. Then, right before their husbands' shift ended, they'd split so they'd be home when their husbands arrived. The husband wouldn't know that his wife had been at Loonie's because people in places like Western Maryland, West Virginia, and Kentucky were very closemouthed. Nobody told anybody about any-one else's business.

"Anyhow, I'm in Loonie's one afternoon, Probably the four-to-twelve shift, and I notice this woman. I know if I tell you she was gorgeous, you're just gonna say the usual, 'Yeah, you tell me about all those chicks, and they end up with asses as big as a Phila-delphia pie wagon with the doors wide open.' But, Ted, let me tell you, she was in a league with the Chemical Girl and the Shark Lady. She was beautiful with one long braid of blonde hair that hung down her back past her knees. She had a body that was al-most close to Candy's when you first married, but she was slim-mer. So I'm watching her, and I see her look over at me, but I don't respond. You know me. I'm going to find a chick that's easy, and she looked like too big of a challenge.

"Well, I had to be in Garrett County for a few days on business, and two days later I'm back in Loonie's, and there she is again. I was sweating and my heart was beating very fast when I looked at her. Finally, after I'm there about four hours, I nervously walk over and ask if I can buy her a drink. She looks me up and down and says, 'Sure. My name's Carolyn,' and we start a conversation.

"She told me that her husband worked at the Kelly-Springfield plant, she had two kids, and she had moved to West Virginia with her parents when she was about eight or nine years old from Ten-nessee. She couldn't have been more than twenty-five or -six years old, and she hoped one day to move to the big city of Baltimore. Can you believe that? Baltimore was the big city to her, like New York or L.A. She realized that she'd have to start off slow, like going to Cumberland first, which was the biggest city in far West-ern Maryland. Then maybe she'd move on to Hagerstown, which is a little bigger, before she could finally settle in Baltimore. She wasn't real worldly, Ted, like most women from that area.

"Anyhow, she asked me if I ever get to Baltimore and I said, 'Yeah.' That *really* impressed her. I told her a little about myself, and I could see she was definitely interested. Before she left Loonie's to get back home before her husband got off his shift, she was holding my hand on top of the bar and kinda sweet-talking, almost cooing to me. Suddenly, the clock above the bar sounded around quarter to twelve, and she was gone."

Kinda cooing, I thought. *Hmm.*

"I went back anxiously the next day during the four-to-twelve shift, but she never showed up, and I was sick and heartbroken. I stayed there six fuckin' hours, Ted, *six* fuckin' hours drinking, but she didn't return. The next day I eagerly went back again, waiting and waiting, and she didn't come back that day either.

"I wasn't going to disappoint myself and go back the next day, but something told me to go. Around six o'clock, I walked into Loonie's and there she was sitting at the bar. She smiled, called me over, and asked me if I was staying close by. I told her I was registered at The Oakland Motel on the Maryland side, and she said, 'Let's go.' Just like that. 'Let's go.' We drove hurriedly in separate cars to the motel, and for the next three hours, I fucked her every which way but Sunday; or maybe it was the other way around. The time flew by and at eleven-fifteen p.m., she said that she had to get back home. Before she left, she told me that she'd meet me at Loonie's the next day, and for me to get there about four-fifteen p.m. so we'd have more time."

First Class had really been cooking, and the band leader, a young surfer-boy-look-a-like named Danny, addressed the small gathering. "Last call folks, and please tip your bartender and waitresses generously. Last song, too, so here we go!" They played the old Gap tune "Early in the Morning." It was ten minutes until two which meant that the song could only go for another ten minutes before closing time. But the song didn't end at two a.m. It went longer, and grew louder. It was a shame that there was no one to dance with because the rhythm called out for it. The lyrics were stimulating and the melody seductive. Instead, all I could do was listen to the Deputy's story and fantasize about the girl from Loonie's while the song played:

Oh, I missed your kiss when you were gone
I was young and foolish, didn't know what I was doin'.
Didn't know what I'd lost 'til you were gone.
Oh, I missed your lovin' when you were gone.
Now I got to get up early in the morning to find me another lover.
Well I got to get up early in the morning to find me another lover.

The Deputy continued. "We made passionate love for six or seven hours the next day. Believe me, Ted, I know I loved this woman, and I'm sure it wasn't just the sex. I asked her if she would run away with me, although I was married at the time. But, hell, when wasn't I married?

"'I'm not ready to run away,' she said to my disappointment. 'I've only had one other affair besides you, and I *do* like my husband. He married me when I was just a teenager, and it was more or less arranged by the families. I didn't have any say in the matter, but he provided for me and took care of me, and my kids are still young, too. But one day I'll visit Baltimore and look you up. My husband is going to be off for the next couple days, so, unfortunately, this'll be it for us.'

"I asked for her phone number, but she wouldn't give it to me, saying she couldn't take the chance. But she did say, 'Just stop at Loonie's whenever you're travelin' through. Maybe I'll be there, maybe I won't. But that'd be the only place to find me.'

"I reluctantly said goodbye and went back to Baltimore fantasizing that she would change her mind. I thought about her so much that for the next three or four months, I drove weekly all the way out to Loonie's in West Virginia. The first trip, I caught up with her, but it was right before her husband was gonna be off the next day or two. Because of my work, I couldn't stay with her more than one day. But, it was great."

The music continued:

Now I got to get up early every morning, 'cause the early bird always catches the worm.

Now I gotta get up early in the morning, got to make up for the lesson I learned.

Got to find me a lover who won't run for cover, find me a lover who won't run for cover.

Got to get up early in the morning to find me another lover.

Now I got to get up early in the morning to find me another lover.

"After that, I never saw her again. I couldn't find her. When I'd ask somebody at Loonie's about her, no one would say anything. A couple guys even told me to be real quiet and not to ask so many questions. Plus, I was always fearful that I'd say something to the wrong guy who might tell her husband, or even *be* her husband. These were tough, devoted, loyal men; people *I* wouldn't even fuck with. So after a while, I stopped driving out to Loonie's."

I was now focusing on the song.

I was young and foolish didn't know what I was doing, didn't know what

I had lost 'til you were gone.

She had a pretty face, drove men wild, I even wanted her to have my child.

Got to get up early in the morning to find me another lover.

Now I got to get up early in the morning to find me another lover.

"Two years later, I had to be in Western Maryland on business," said the Deputy, "and I rushed over to Loonie's, but again she wasn't there. About a year after that, I was in West Virginia, drinking in the hotel with some golf buddies, and I became very anxious. So I drove over to Loonie's bar. Recognizing the bartender who'd waited on us when we first met, I pulled him to the side and told him that I really needed to see her. He whispered to me, 'Partner, let me tell you somethin'. You ain't never gonna see her again. Her husband was feelin' real down and got all drunked up in here one night. He'd lost his job at the plant, got to swearin' and cussin', and stormed out. He went home in a rage and shot her, the two kids, and then blew his brains out.'

"I was dumbfounded. 'Oh my God!' I said, 'That's unbelievable.' But the bartender simply said, 'No, my friend, it ain't unbelievable. It ain't the first time it's happened up here and it won't be the last.'"

Early in the morning, find me another lover.
Early in the morning, find me another lover.
Early in the morning, at the break of day, everything's gonna be alright.
Early in the morning, at the break of day, everything's gonna be alright.
Early in the morning . . .

The story and the music boosted me to such highs and plummeted me to such lows that I began feeling dizzy. It was the first time I'd ever truly felt sorry for the Deputy. Usually he was so lucky and resilient, and able to bounce back easily from adversity, that he never evoked sympathy. He was more like a caricature. But now, listening to his love story, he suddenly became human....

❏ ❏ ❏

BALTIMORE, MARYLAND
November 27, 1986

I sat with Dr. Hodinko, a very quiet, unassuming, and brilliant guy. He ran the Research Center at the Alcohol and Drug Abuse Administration, and was always coming up with simple, comprehensible, and very special data that even I could understand and explain. It gave our agency and public relations department excellent credibility.

We were reviewing the increased cases of AIDS beginning around 1976, when the Tall Ships first visited New York, to the present time, about nine years later. Then we looked at the increase in cocaine use over that same period of time. Initially, we reviewed Maryland data only, but then we started looking over the national statistics. And what became intriguing was that it looked as though there were two perfectly parallel lines–the rise in AIDS and the rise in cocaine use.

I asked him what he thought. "Do you consider it a coincidence?"

As usual, in his cautious manner, he said, "I'll have to study it more."

But I was excited by the feeling that there was a definite correlation here between AIDS and cocaine and possibly stimulant use, and I wanted to talk about it; maybe even to the press.

Hodinko cautioned me, "Why don't we just start working on publishing a paper about it?"

❑ ❑ ❑

The Deputy walked into my office. "Ted, I don't think the money the governor promised is really available."

"Well, technically it's not available," I agreed. "According to the governor, he was going to fund these new initiatives with a deficit appropriation. Then he'd get the legislature to go along with it or maybe find it in a budget surplus."

The Deputy interrupted, "I have some trouble with that logic. The *new* governor may not want to go along with it. The current governor may have already allocated the surplus, and I don't know how the legislature is going to react."

"So, what are you telling me?" I asked. "I've already started two new programs, and announced a few others. They've appeared in the media. We've sent award letters out to grantees, and we've entered into contractual agreements. Are you saying there may be no fucking money?"

"Yeah," answered the Deputy. "That sums it up pretty good. But rumor has it that there might be a new infusion of funds. There could be some brand new federal money coming down the pike as a result of this Bias thing–much more than the president's new Omnibus Drug Bill. I've got a feeling that, politically, things might have turned around enough that there may be some big federal dollars coming our way. And, if it comes, it may be retroactive to the federal fiscal year, and we could still be okay. We may not have to worry about the deficiency appropriation."

❏ ❏ ❏

A couple weeks went by, and the Chemical Girl was losing interest in vitamins, but still attending A.A. meetings with some regularity. The Deputy was missing work or leaving early, probably dealing with his never-ending domestic problems. I did the usual and covered for him.

❏ ❏ ❏

BALTIMORE, MARYLAND

I was having dinner with the Chemical Girl at Sabatino's, a restaurant in Baltimore's Little Italy. "I'm taking my old buddy, Holt, to Thailand to die. I may stay there a while, but I'm not sure yet. I'll still help you out financially, though, when I can."

Sabatino's Restaurant served Southern Italian cuisine and was the largest restaurant in Little Italy. The tables were arranged closely together, and it was always noisy and pleasant at "Sab's." It had been a fixture in Baltimore for many years, and out-of-town celebrities often made it their first stop.

The Chemical Girl was very much alive and vibrant on this particular evening. She didn't seem at all sorry or sad about my impending departure, which disappointed me a little.

She told me that she didn't need any money because Lo Ming had given her a decent settlement for her silence about his business dealings; along with a veiled threat. Furthermore, she informed me nonchalantly that she and the Deputy were moving to Ocala, Florida or somewhere south next month to enter into a partnership with the ostrich farmer she had visited after severing her ties with Lo Ming.

"Ted, I spoke with this guy on a number of occasions in the past few weeks, and explained the deal to the Deputy. He's separating from his wife and taking a leave of absence from his state job."

"You...and the Deputy?" I stammered. "I can't believe it! What about me and you?"

The Chemical Girl laughed. "Cut me a fucking break, will you, Ted? You and me aren't going anywhere. You're still seeing that red-headed chick Jan, you come and go as you please, and you still hide out from your ex-wife. *And*, you're fucking anal and uptight as shit over my lifestyle. Besides, you've just told me you're running away, probably from yourself, with that junkie asshole Holt, who's gonna die in Thailand. The Deputy and I are strictly business partners."

The Chemical Girl mimicked me, "And what about you and me? Ha, ha, ha!"

We ate in silence for a while as I digested her remarks along with a Bookmaker salad and Sab's popular house dressing. The Chemical Girl ordered another Pepsi, and I acknowledged the fact that she appeared clean and sober.

"I haven't had any drugs or alcohol since I drank that glass of vodka after coming home from the hospital. That was my only relapse," she boasted.

"Actually, I wouldn't define that as a relapse. One drink is more like a slip," I said.

"They wouldn't say that at A.A.," she countered.

"No," I agreed, "they wouldn't. They're too steeped in the old traditions. A slip is new jargon for addiction clinicians. They're minor and usually situational."

"Like how?" the Chemical Girl asked.

"Say a guy is clean for ten years. Then one day his wife leaves him, he gets fired, and his car breaks down on the expressway. In despair, he goes to a bar, has four or five drinks, and gets drunk. However, the next day and long after that, he never drinks again. That's a situational slip…at least to me and other more enlightened clinicians. But, like you said, probably not to A.A."

"So how do *you* define a relapse?"

"The best example is what happened to Dr. Bob, one of the founders of A.A.," I answered. "In 1935, surgeon Bob Smith and stockbroker Bill Wilson vowed to keep each other sober through a set of steps developed by Bill. These steps evolved into the cornerstone for all self-help groups. It started in Akron, Ohio and came to be known as Alcoholics Anonymous or A.A."

"What happened next?" asked the Chemical Girl.

"Dr. Bob went to a week-long Atlantic City convention, got smashed the whole time there, and when he returned to Akron, was still very drunk. Bill Wilson came to his aid, even giving him a beer to steady his hands during a surgery Bob had to perform. It was the last drink he ever had. *That* was a relapse."

As we were leaving the restaurant, we bumped into Lo Ming and another man who were entering Sabatino's. He smiled at the Chemical Girl and glared at me, not saying a word.

"Isn't that a coincidence," said the Chemical Girl looking ashen. She sensed danger. Having seen the man she both feared and loathed, there was no doubt in my mind that he would kill her if she crossed him. Or that he'd do the same to anyone else who got in his way.

❏ ❏ ❏

I didn't know what to think or feel about the Chemical Girl and the Deputy. Was it anger, betrayal, or self-pity? With no answer coming to mind, I packed my luggage.

❏ ❏ ❏

PHUKET, THAILAND

Holt and I sat peacefully on the Patong beach in small bamboo sand chairs. We looked at the sun shining brightly on the sea off the west coast of Thailand, in a beautiful resort called Phuket. Every now and then we would bullshit a little and then sit quietly soaking up the awesome rays. There must have been countless cancer-causing agents in those rays. Not that it mattered to Holt–he was dying. Whacked out half the time, he didn't talk about his impending death except on a few occasions.

"How you doing, buddy?" I said to Holt. "You want a drink?"

Holt looked over at me, glassy-eyed. He'd been taking pills, but I didn't know what they were. I knew he'd been smoking opium he had gotten from Raymond, a friend who lived in Changmai, a northern province of Thailand. Raymond had met us in Bangkok where we stayed at The Oriental Hotel for a few days before going to Phuket. We had been there for about two and a half days. It was the sort of place you'd want to live forever. Like Bali, it was one of the most beautiful resorts in Asia, and scores of Europeans vacationed there. I knew I would have to leave this paradise at some point, but Holt, on the other hand, would stay forever.

"Teddy-boy, this is such a gorgeous beach. I always loved to go to the beach with you. Remember good old Ocean City? It was fucking great years ago."

"Yeah, Holt, of course, I remember. I've been going to Ocean City for close to thirty years. The beach is still there, although erosion is eating away at it. The federal government is supposed to help with a beach replenishment program, but I'm not sure it will work."

"Ah," said Holt. "It ain't the same. Ocean City went plastic just like the other Atlantic Coast resorts. I want to remember the Ocean City of the late '50s and early '60s when it was a little-bitty, old resort town with a beautiful beach; although you can't compare it to the beach here. Yet thirty years ago if you and I had walked onto this beach, I'm sure I'd feel the same way I feel about this beach as I feel about Ocean City today."

"Ted, Ocean City was something else when we first went there, remember? We were among the only Jews there. You, me, Caps, and Sheldon might have made the count four. Amazing, huh?"

I smiled and said, "Holt, you're *not* Jewish. You were *never* Jewish."

"Ted," he smiled, "you're right. I don't know why I thought I was Jewish back then. Everybody else was denying that they were Jewish. At times, I did, too."

"Yeah, but Holt," I remarked. "you didn't have to deny that you were Jewish. You *weren't* Jewish. Where did you get this Jewish thing from, anyway?"

"I don't know," he said, now totally wasted. "It was probably from liking you and your pals so much. Also, I used to date a girl who worked for a Jewish Community Center in Atlanta, and I sold a lot of dope to her friends. Jews loved cocaine, Quaaludes, and anything I dealt them. *They* even thought I was Jewish. I guess because I was with a Jewish girl. I remember I even told *her* that you and I were the only Jews in Ocean City." We laughed and then fell silent for a while.

Finally, Holt said, "It's funny. I mean, Ocean City was about three or four hours away in those days. Now we're halfway around the world thinking about the same things. I've done a lot of traveling in my days, and you've done your fair share. You know, we're always traveling, always wanting to be somewhere different, but always ending up back home. Physically, home to me might be the West Coast now, but I really never considered anywhere truly home except Baltimore. It's always been tough to go back, though, Ted. After I got busted a couple times, I knew I could never make it there. Baltimore was always a big small town. Everyone knew everyone else's business. I would have loved to have stayed, but I couldn't give up my traveling for anything…especially the drugs that went with it."

I sat quietly, reflecting on what Holt had said, and realized he was right. We were always running away, only to return home. I had no idea what we were looking for or what we were running from or to. And I wondered why we did come back. Maybe, here on the beach in Phuket, I could think of a reason. *Perhaps I didn't need to go back this time,* I thought. Nah, I had to go back…but for the life of me, I couldn't figure out what the fuck for.

My eyes closed as the hot sun opened my pores. I tried to figure out what I *was* looking for. What kept us going, and why? The words to an old Bob Dylan song came into my head. *The only thing I could do was to keep on keepin' on*…and I thought about the Chemical Girl.

❑ ❑ ❑

Several days later, Holt lapsed into a coma. It was just after lunch, and I thought he was taking a nap. But the nap went on for hours. Even though I knew it was a drug-induced sleep, I felt he'd awaken soon. But this time something wasn't right, so I went to get the town doctor who lived at the Coconut Village Hotel. He told me that there was something seriously wrong with Holt.

"Doc, he's dying. He came here to die because he loves Thailand so much. He's been here many, many times. I thought maybe he had a month or two, although his doctor back home did say it could be only a matter of weeks."

The doctor stared at me and, in broken English, tried to explain that the sickness that brought Holt here may not have had anything to do with why he was in this coma right now. "It may be that he smoked too much opium."

An ambulance was called and Holt was taken to a local hospital. Two hours later, he was dead. I made funeral arrangements for Holt for the next few hours, making sure that his body would be taken to the northern province of Changmai where his buddy, Raymond, would see that he was properly buried.

After I got off the telephone with Raymond, I decided to check out of the hotel instead of spending a few more glorious days on the beach. I was ready to go home.

Chapter 16

Upon arriving back in the States, federal authorities stopped me at customs. They wanted to know my affiliation with Holt and his drugs, as well as with Lola, the Chemical Girl, and Lo Ming and their cash smuggling into the United States. They weren't buying my drug and alcohol confidentiality excuse.

I told them that Holt had died of complications from years of smoking heroin, and Lola from a drug overdose. She had been cremated, I explained. I concocted a story of how, by using a fake passport, she had joined me and Holt in Thailand via a European route. I had no idea where she really was, but I felt my story was better than telling them the truth. Something told me she shouldn't be found, by me and especially not by the feds, who were skeptical of my tale.

❑ ❑ ❑

I was taken upstairs by two Drug Enforcement Agency (DEA) agents who wore Windbreakers with the letters "DEA" embroidered across the back. They seated me in an office, instructed me to wait there, and asked if I needed anything. "How about one of your jackets?" I nervously joked.

I felt slightly dazed and bewildered and I knew I was in a serious jackpot. I tried to get my thoughts together enough to figure out what kind of legal representation would be needed to assess damage control. I always believed myself guilty since grade school, a trait inherited from my mother.

A new player walked loudly into the room. He was scruffy looking, and had I not been in an enforcement agency office, I would have definitely pegged the guy as a sleazebag dope dealer. There was no doubt that he was an undercover narc. He also assumed the role of supervisor to the two agents with the DEA Windbreakers. There was something vaguely familiar about him, but I couldn't quite pin it down.

"Ted," he began. "I can call you Ted, can't I?" I nodded in agreement, and he continued. "Your friend, Holt...sorry he's dead, and we have had that confirmed. But we know you're lying about Lola.

Your late friend, Holt, was trafficking in some new, strange drugs that are gaining in popularity. Do you know what drugs they were?"

"No," I said. "Listen. You know the field I'm in. You know there's a confidentiality statute that covers me. I mean, if you guys have any sense, you know I'm not a smuggler. I don't deal in dope and I don't launder or smuggle money. There seems to be a big misunderstanding here..."

The scruffy guy interrupted, "We'll be the ones to judge whether there's a misunderstanding, Ted, or whether you've violated any laws. It'd be best if you cooperate. All we want are answers to some questions about certain people. That's all. Let me ask you about Holt. He trafficked in bootleg methaqualones and ICE or crystal methamphetamine. I'm sure I don't have to explain these drugs to you, Ted. You've made it clear that you're in the drug field and have some degree of expertise. We also think Holt was dealing Ecstasy, and we know he was smoking and ingesting narcotics. Furthermore, the autopsy determined..."

I sat up straight with an incredulous look on my face, my blood pressure rising. "What the fuck do you mean an autopsy? So fucking soon? You guys went over to Thailand and dug him up to cut him open? You fucking ghouls!"

"No, we're not really ghouls," the undercover narc responded. "We're just trying to do our job. Let's say, for the sake of argument, Ted, that you're innocent; that you didn't know what Holt was doing. Or if you knew, he was your friend for years and you felt sorry for him. Whatever.

"Besides smoking cocaine, marijuana, and opium for years, what happened to Holt was that he didn't understand, at least early on, that twenty percent of the narcotics sold here on the West Coast are synthetic. I think he smoked some of the fentanyl analog, and that's probably what made the mass grow so big in his chest. Boy, you should have seen it. It was really fucking ugly.

"Holt may not have realized that it was synthetic heroin that he started selling. One of his buddies, a hell of a chemist, has already been 'turned around.' In fact, he told us all of this. But then, of course, people we turn around will tell us a lot of things."

"So, what is it you want from me?" I asked firmly. "How come you haven't read me my rights? And why don't I have somebody to represent me?"

"Well," said the narc, "we haven't really charged you with

anything, Ted. We're just asking you some questions. By the way, what would you call those drugs that Holt trafficked in?"

This guy was driving at something, but I couldn't figure out what it was. I didn't know if I should keep my mouth shut, which was usually the right thing for me to do, or let him know that I was basically an innocent.

"What do you mean, what kind of drugs were they?" I asked. "The classification, drug type?"

"Yeah, yeah. What kind of drugs are these? Ecstasy, synthetic heroin, ICE, and 'ludes."

"Oh," I said, "I see what you mean. They're, uh, they're basically analogs. They're a variation of real drugs, synthetic drugs called chemical analogs. You guys should be familiar with that term."

"Yeah, Ted, I'm familiar with it," he said with a grin. "And obviously, you've learned a little something, or you've come to your senses. I noticed you didn't use that fucking asshole term 'designer drugs.'"

I looked closely at the DEA agent. I knew I recognized him from somewhere, and it wasn't too long ago.

"You know, Ted," he said. "You used to tick me off a little bit, but…"

"Phillips!" I shouted. "You're the guy at my lecture who interrupted me. You stormed out! I knew that I fucking knew you…man, nice disguise," I equivocated.

"Yeah, it's me. Phillips. I'm Agent in Charge here on the West Coast, and it was a hell of a surprise to see you caught up in our net. You shouldn't run with such nefarious people. By the way, Ted, we know *Holt* is dead. But don't tell us that Lola died after traveling through Europe to get to Thailand. I mean, you're reading too many of those articles that say we're inefficient and incompetent when we're actually far from it."

I decided to remain silent. I didn't want to see the Chemical Girl get into any more grief. I wanted to see her have a little bit of happiness, even though I begrudged her happiness with the Deputy.

"We're going to let you go," said Phillips. "But we could have caused you a lot of trouble. I'm sure glad you didn't use that term 'designer drug.' It's a bad term; a very bad term. Maybe you can visit us out here sometime to lecture the boys.

"And, Ted, in case you're interested, we traced your former girlfriend to the southeastern United States. I know that's a big area, but then again, maybe you don't want to find her anyway."

"Why don't you leave her out of it, Phillips," I said. "Believe me, she's no longer doing whatever it is you think she did…"

Phillips interrupted, "How do you know what she's doing, Ted? Anything else you can give us?"

I shook my head no.

"I didn't think so, Ted.…Nah, I didn't think you could add anything. Besides, we've got bigger fish to fry. You like that term, Ted? It's an old Federal Bureau of Investigation term. Anyhow, go on. Get out of here, and get your luggage. Maybe we'll be in touch one day. Ya know, do lunch. Maybe at Sabatino's?"

❏ ❏ ❏

BALTIMORE, MARYLAND

It was starting to get darker each day, a sign that winter wasn't far off. An emptiness pervaded everything as I sat in my office. Holt and Ron were dead. The Deputy and the Chemical Girl were gone. Jesus, it was eerie.

The trouble with customs, the DEA, and especially Phillips were still too vivid to even consider it a nightmare. I felt very down. Maybe it was Seasonal Affective Disorder. Maybe I just needed some sunlight.

I didn't know what to do. Continue to work for the state? Go to work in the private sector in the Caribbean with Major Dorsett? Become a year-round beach bum in Ocean City?

I phoned Mellow McFrank in Ocala, Florida. "Hi. My name's Ted. I'm looking for a pretty woman in her mid-twenties named Lola. I'm also looking for her partner. They're getting into the ostrich business, and she visited with you a while back. Do you remember?"

"Whoa, friend," answered Mellow. "Lot's of people come by here wanting to make money with my breeding ostriches. But lemme think a second."

I described the Chemical Girl to him in more detail, and it jogged his memory. "Oh yeah, her. Nope. Haven't heard from her since."

"How about anything strange, you know, anything unusual? Like maybe in the last few weeks?" I asked. It was the kind of question that Phillips would have asked.

"Well, I dunno. There was this guy who wanted me to send him some breeders up to the Carolinas, to Myrtle Beach. I told him it might be too cool up there, but he insisted. Said he wanted to live there. Just moved there, I think. Wanted to be by the beach and the golf courses. So…"

"That's it! That's gotta be him! Thanks!" I interrupted. It had to be the Deputy and the Chemical Girl. I just felt it.

"Jeanette!" I yelled to my secretary, who came hurrying in.

"What's wrong?" she asked.

"I have to go on a trip. Use my comp time or annual leave, whatever."

"But, Ted, you just got back. Where ya goin'?" she implored.

"Road trip. Don't know for sure, and don't really care. I'll call you in a couple days," I said as I rushed down the corridor towards the elevator.

"Ted, wait!" Jeanette screamed. She came running after me, shattering my thoughts.

"What's wrong?" I asked.

"Ted, you're gonna lose your job. The new governor's transition team keeps callin'. They want to talk to you, and they're very impatient and demanding. You *do* serve at the pleasure of the governor, and…"

"Okay, okay. I'll call them ASAP, alright? Don't worry so much. You won't lose your job."

"Ted, I'm not worried about me. It's you. You've been through a lot. There's so much happening. And the people at University of Maryland keep callin', too, about Bias."

I tried to comfort Jeanette, but she continued. "I'm very, very worried about you. Why don't we go somewhere and talk. You know you can always confide in me."

I didn't know if I could really confide in her, although she had been my secretary for years. I didn't think what I had to say was any of her business, although she probably knew most of my business, anyway.

"Listen," I said. "It's just that things have been hectic. I'm not leaving. Forget what I said about going away. I'm not going to chase after a bunch of dreams. That idea was ridiculous to begin with.

"It's just that Ron is dead, Holt is dead, and the Deputy is gone. Not to mention what a drag it'll be not to see Len Bias in a Celtic uniform playing alongside the Bird. Nobody could have beaten those guys, not for years."

Jeanette stared up at me quizzically. "Who's the Bird and what are the Celtics?"

I managed a weak smile. "I already had dinner and I'm on my way to meet someone. Don't worry about me. I'll see you at work tomorrow. We'll take care of the new governor's transition team, the College Park Task Force, everything…. Oh, and get me some brighter lights in my office; real bright ones."

Jeanette had a pleading look, hoping I would change my plans and discuss this further, but I was finished. As an afterthought, she called out, "Ted, have you been okay? I know you were worried after you got stung, and then you went away. What about that?"

"Oh, shit," I mumbled. I hadn't thought about the transfusion in a while. It hadn't occurred to me that I didn't really know whether the blood from the transfusion was tainted with AIDS. Dogface Alice used to give blood when she needed money. At one time or another, most junkies I knew went to the blood bank. I had obviously kept the possibility of having contracted AIDS in the recesses of my subconscious. Like always, I brought my fears to the forefront and made myself a total wreck. Maybe I'd call the hospital tomorrow to see if they could trace the origin of that blood. Fuck, maybe I really didn't want to know. After all, no one was sure of the incubation period for AIDS I reminded myself. Why did Jeanette have to bring it up?

❑ ❑ ❑

I went home to my apartment and listened to my messages on the answering machine. There were several from the usual array of coworkers, friends, and family. Then there was a very unexpected call for this time of the year. It was Craig from Ocean City.

Craig managed the Sheraton Hotel and I had known him for years. He was the consummate hotel manager, and a computer programming genius. The message said, "Ted, call me immediately. I've got an important message that I can't leave on your machine." The message was the same three different times over a four- or five-day period. My inexpensive machine did not give the date or time of the calls.

I phoned the hotel, but Craig was gone for the night and wouldn't be back until seven the next morning. I called Pocomoke

City information where I knew he lived and got his home phone number. It was one a.m. when I woke him and asked what the important message was.

"Ted, great to hear from you…but not at one in the morning," he said groggily. "But I've got to tell you something that I'm not supposed to say over the phone. It'd be great if you could get down here, but I'm not certain if the message is important enough for you to make a six-hour round trip."

"Craig, I'm tired of playing this cloak-and-dagger game," I whined. "Unless this involves something that is detrimental to your or my health, safety, or welfare, I really need for you to give me the message."

There was silence on the line before Craig finally said, "Okay, Ted. Lola called and asked me to get you down here ASAP. She's going to call on one of the pay phones in the Sheraton lobby every day at three p.m. for a week until you answer the phone. She said it's not safe to call you at home. Of course, we're talking about it now on your phone, so…"

"Fuck it," I interrupted. "I guess I've gotta make the trip because it sounds pretty important. As much as I don't feel like a long drive, I'll see ya tomorrow."

❑ ❑ ❑

ANNAPOLIS, MARYLAND

On the way to Ocean City, I stopped in Annapolis and had breakfast with Attorney Alan Goldstein who updated me on the Len Bias aftermath and the political ramifications of the case.

Prince George's County State's Attorney Bud Marshall moved to indict Brian Tribble, Len Bias' friend, who allegedly supplied the cocaine that killed Bias. And although he was criticized for this move, he would have been dead politically if he hadn't done it. People were screaming for blood, and the state had to "give" someone to the public.

Marshall faced a brick wall to prove his case against Tribble; a case that Tribble won. Yet it wasn't Marshall who lost it. One of the best prosecutors in the State of Maryland lost the case. Interestingly, Marshall was defeated in his run for state's attorney by Alex Williams before the case went to trial.

"When Williams took over the State's Attorneys Office," said

Goldstein, "a close advisor gave him some brilliant advice. 'Go to Bob Bonsan, a former top prosecutor in Prince George's County, and let him run the office. You be the figurehead and the politician. That's what elected state's attorneys do. Have Bonsan handle the day-to-day administration of the office.' And that's exactly what Williams did.

"He lured Bob Bonsan from the U.S. Attorney's Office, which wasn't hard since this was a great chance for Bonsan to be a de facto prosecutor. He would make the decisions, and the first one he would make would be the Tribble case since Williams had no choice but to move forward with it. Williams had to get Tribble convicted for his involvement in Len Bias' death, so he gave the case to his number one lawyer, Bonsan. He was the best lawyer in the State's Attorney's Office, but he still lost the case.

"It was a fascinating trial with two excellent lawyers; Bonsan for the State and Morrow for Tribble. Bonsan may have made some miscalculations, but most jurists believed that the case could not have been won, anyway. The State really didn't have enough hard evidence. Long and Greg, Bias' roommates, never gave them what they needed, and the jurors reacted to that. To them, Long, Greg, and Tribble all played the same role. The jury thought Bonsan was trying to make a bum out of Tribble and acquitted him."

Chapter 17

I arrived in Ocean City by one p.m. As I entered the Sheraton lobby, Craig greeted me from behind the registration desk and pointed to a bank of three payphones, one of which would ring at exactly three p.m.

"I don't know what this is about, Ted, and I don't care. It's always great to see you. If you want, I'll give you a room for a few hours or you can stay overnight. No charge. You've spent enough time and money here, and it looks as if you need some rest."

I thanked Craig and registered to stay overnight. Craig was a romantic at heart, and booked me in suite 1409, the room where I first made love to the Chemical Girl. I decided not to take a nap for fear I would miss the call.

There were too many things to take care of and too many details to work out before I'd be ready for Major Dorsett's job offer and the Caribbean. I knew he'd be calling soon and that notice would be short, but I'd already made up my mind.

At exactly three p.m., the phone rang. I was trembling as I lifted the receiver off the hook. It was Lola, the Chemical Girl.

"Ted, thank God Craig got a hold of you. If I didn't talk to you this week, I may have never spoken to you again."

Immediately choked up, I tried to speak, but nothing came out of my mouth. I was crazier about the Chemical Girl than I realized, and had played it all wrong with her. Now all I wanted to do was make it up to her. After some brief small-talk, and before I could tell Lola that I was madly in love with her, she began telling me about what had happened to her and the Deputy.

"It was crazy the way things evolved," she said. "The Deputy and I just decided 'what the hell,' we might as well go into the ostrich business. I had the money from that little settlement deal I made with Lo Ming, and the Deputy had put some money away, too, although not much.

"Anyhow, we had enough to buy four breeders from McFrank in Ocala, but the Deputy didn't want to move to Florida. Since he used to be an assistant golf pro in Myrtle Beach, he felt the weather would be perfect for our venture. I didn't care. It was a beach scene to me, and I thought it would be a good opportunity for us...."

"Ted, I swear to you, I never fucked the Deputy. As a matter of fact, he met a girl here the third day after we arrived. He's with her as we speak, in a Holiday Inn on the beach.

"But, anyhow, we got down here, and, within days, McFrank shipped the ostriches, which cost a small fortune. The Deputy had to take out a loan because I was there under a false name. As you know, because of Lo Ming I have a bad credit rating.

"Next thing you know, everybody in the world started showing up at our front door. Here we're trying to be so clandestine and, out of the blue, who shows up, none other than Lo Ming himself. I don't know how he found me. He told me he'd made a big score and was going to go into an extremely lucrative hotel deal in New Zealand. He wanted me to join him, and offered me forty grand up front just to go. He told me the usual–I didn't have to fuck him, I'd just be his assistant. It was tempting, but I turned him down. He made me and the Deputy swear that we'd never seen him if we knew what was good for us. A serious threat, right!

"That night a second visitor appeared at the door; a detective working for the Deputy's wife. I think it was the third wife, but I'm not sure."

"Neither am I. I could never follow the Deputy's divorce agreements and obligations," I interjected.

The Chemical Girl kept talking, oblivious to what I had said. "Anyhow, this detective came to Myrtle Beach and met with the Deputy for a while before abruptly leaving. He didn't threaten us, but obviously whatever he said to the Deputy made him somewhat jumpy. The Deputy said we were going to have to sell two of the breeders because he needed money to take care of some personal obligations in Maryland.

"After our visitors left, the Deputy and I retreated to our Myrtle Beach hangout, a small bar on the beach. It was the first time in days that we had gone there. Later, we returned to the little ranch we were renting, and guess what? The ostriches had run off, and we had no idea where they had disappeared to. We notified the Sheriff's Office and the State Police, and talked to neighbors and people passing by. For days and nights we hunted, but we couldn't find the ostriches.

"They were gone, and who the fuck knows why or where? Because they were dangerous, an all-points bulletin was issued by the police. Well, while we were waiting at the ranch figuring what else could go wrong, a DEA agent named Phillips appeared at the door. He told the Deputy to sit in another room while he questioned me.

"He told me what happened to you when you came back into the country, and he said that he was going to look after you and me because he liked us. I didn't believe a word he said. Then he asked me a few questions about Lo Ming. I refused to talk about him, even though he had been here about a week earlier. Before Phillips left, out of nowhere, he gave me a fake ID and said, 'Young lady, get yourself lost.' Then he called the Deputy back in and said that it'd be best if we never mentioned that he was here, if we knew what was good for us. One more threat!

"So, by now, we've had two out of three threats on our lives the way I've got it figured. But, you know what? Unbelievably, I've got brand new ID, so I'm pretty happy, although we still didn't know what was fucking happening. We were just about broke, had all these threats on our lives, and the ostriches had run off. If they attacked anyone, we would be liable. And we were also trying to figure out what happened to you.

"In the meantime, there was a guy we met when we first came to Carolina. He's a very wealthy man about sixty-eight years old who was visiting Myrtle Beach to play golf with his buddies. He lives in Phoenix, Arizona, and his name is Dick Richardson. We used to see him at the bar where we hung out.

"Dick played golf with the Deputy a couple times when we weren't working the ranch, and took a liking to him. When he found out that the Deputy and I weren't cohabiting, he took an even greater liking to me. He's a multimillionaire widower with lots of businesses, and every night we sat around and talked.

"So anyhow, the Deputy and I figured we might have to return to Baltimore, or get jobs waiting tables. After the DEA agent left, we went to our hangout and ran into Richardson. Besides the money, Dick's not a bad-looking guy, either. He has silver hair, a real jovial personality, and a sort of red face. He noticed that we were kind of bummed out, and when the Deputy went to the bathroom, he asked me if there was anything that he could do for me–like did I need money or anything.

"I told him that the ostriches had run off, the Deputy had some problems with his ex-wife and kids, and it looked as if we were going to have to go back home. Naturally, I didn't mention you, Lo Ming, the DEA guy, or the detective.

"He said, 'I'll make you an offer. Live with me in Phoenix…no strings attached. I really enjoy your companionship. I know you love the sun and the water, and although we don't have an ocean in Arizona, we have beautiful weather. There's lots of partying, fun, and swimming pools. Since my wife died, I haven't really had anyone in my life. Everyone's always trying to fix me up, but those dates are only interested in my money; which I've got plenty of, my dear. You come and live with me in my house, and, of course, you'll have your own bedroom. I'll give you money, and you can open up your own bank account. If you're interested, tell me before I even offer a dollar amount.'

"'Tell you what else I'll do,' he said. 'I'll get the Deputy a job here as an assistant golf pro, buy him a condo, and help him out with anything he needs. Every now and then he can visit us in Phoenix. What do you say?'

"Well, Ted, what could I say? I accepted his offer, and I'm leaving for Arizona on Tuesday. I wanted to talk to you before I left because I didn't know what had happened to you, and I've been worried sick. I'm sure you're going to bring me up to snuff on what's going on. Anyhow, the Deputy still loves you and I still love you, but going to Phoenix is the best of all scenarios for me right now.

"I don't know what's going to happen to the Deputy, but he's very happy in Myrtle Beach playing golf. And I don't know what's going to happen with you, Ted. I love you and I know you love me, but I don't think we could have ever worked out because I know how disappointed you get with my drinking and drugging. I don't know if I can ever really completely stop. You know I like to live on the edge, and I don't think you could afford it or tolerate it. And even if you think you could, I really don't think we were meant to be, baby. I'm so sorry."

"Are you clean and sober now?" I asked.

"Well, to be truthful, I've had a few slips," she answered.

"A few slips is a relapse," I said.

"Yeah," she laughed, "and love is ninety-nine percent sex."

"Hey," I said, "how much of your love for me was just sex, anyway?"

She was silent for a moment and then answered, "Eighty percent."

"Great," I said. "I must be doing better.

"Lola, you're probably right. I guess we aren't meant to be. I'm fine, but I don't know if I'll stay with the state. I've got job offers from a few places running treatment programs, being a lobbyist, advocating for addicts, or maybe even going with the federal government. I'm not sure what's going to happen to *me* career-wise, but I wish you the best in the world. Give me your new name and address, and if my travels take me to Arizona, I'd love to look you up and see you again. You can always catch up with me by sending a letter or calling my office here with the agency, and they'll forward it to wherever I go."

There was silence on the phone and then the Chemical Girl said, "Okay, Ted. My new name is Ruth Goldberg. Can you fuckin' believe it? Ruth Goldberg. As Irish as *I* am. That's the name the DEA guy gave me. I guess he has a warped sense of humor.

"I'm going to keep the name, and I promise you I'm not going to marry this old dude. Please don't forget to write or call me in Phoenix. We'll be at 4210 Collins Avenue. I don't know the phone number or zip code, but I'm sure the number's listed under Dick Richardson. Just leave a message, and I'll get back to you. I love you, baby. I'll always love you. I gotta ring off now, but please take care of yourself."

And with that, the Chemical Girl was gone. I felt slightly empty and a little nauseous. I walked outside of the Sheraton onto the beach for some fresh air. It was bitterly cold as I strolled towards the Carousel, a half-mile walk.

I thought about the Chemical Girl, the Deputy, Lo Ming, me, and everybody else entangled in my life. I wondered how our lives would eventually end up. But mostly, I thought about the Chemical Girl and what kind of future we could have had. She was right, though. It would probably have never worked out. But damn, it was like a fantasy being with her. She was so young, so wise, so innocent, so addictive, so dangerous, so devious, and so…so sensual.

❑ ❑ ❑

BALTIMORE, MARYLAND
February 1987

I ran into Attorney Goldstein in Baltimore. He was defending a gambling kingpin in a wiretap case.

"Al, do you think there's anything that isn't known about what happened in Bias' room?" I asked, hoping that he would shed some new light.

"Clearly, we know that Bias had done cocaine before with Tribble," began Goldstein. "At least ten times that we know of from my guys, Long and Greg, who had partied at Tribble's house after the NC State game and a couple other times. They knew Tribble and they knew that Tribble hung out with Bias.

"But they didn't know where the cocaine came from that night, and they weren't sure whether Tribble was the only one who brought it in. Long and Greg truly never knew the specific facts about what happened in that room other than that when they entered the room, the cocaine was already there. Tribble cleaned it up after Bias collapsed, and some of the paraphernalia was dumped in the Dumpster by Terry Long…"

I interrupted Goldstein, "So there's a lot of unanswered questions about what took place in that room."

"It probably doesn't make any difference," said Goldstein. "We do know this much—Bias lived a double life. He was straight, clean-cut, antidrug, Mr. Hero by day, but after midnight…."

❏ ❏ ❏

A new administration driven by the governor-elect's motto *Do It Now!* had taken over the State of Maryland. Playing out the string until I was given the green light to resign by Major Dorsett, who had offered me the treatment job in the Caribbean, I was cautiously packing up my office and apartment. It was reminiscent of my slow escape from Candy, yet just as difficult due to the demands of the new bureaucrats who followed the victorious former mayor from the city.

I was in the underground garage of the state office complex at quarter to eight in the morning when I ran into the secretary of natural resources, Dr. Yeager. He had just come from the new governor's weekly cabinet meeting. The governor liked to have his cabinet meetings begin promptly at seven a.m., so he locked the conference room door at precisely that time. Anyone who arrived after seven was not allowed into the meeting. People would pound on the door, crying out to be let in, but to no avail. And these were prestigious people, secretaries of major departments whose budgets ran into the millions, maybe billions, of dollars. They had all kinds of graduate degrees after their well-known names, had staffs of several thousand employees, and impacted hundreds of thousands of people.

Dr. Yeager, a holdover from the previous administration, said that the new governor was a little disturbed by a radio talk show he'd been listening to. The governor loved to listen to call-in talk shows, and had heard two callers say that drug treatment didn't work. He said that several calls later, a gentleman professing to be a doctor stated emphatically that "It is true that treatment doesn't work. At most, it is less than five percent successful."

"So the governor wasn't in too hot of a mood this morning," said Dr. Yeager, "and he asked the cabinet, 'Why are we wasting thirty million dollars a year if treatment doesn't work?'"

I asked the secretary, who had been in the substance abuse field for years, had started one of the first city treatment programs at Johns Hopkins, and was an addictions consultant for the NBA, "Why didn't you speak up?"

"It just wasn't the right moment, Ted," he responded.

"Did the secretary of health speak up?" I implored.

"No."

"Has anyone spoken up at all?" I continued, somewhat exasperated.

"Yes. One of his staff said, 'Yeah, you're right, Governor. It doesn't work! We're wasting our money.'"

I was flabbergasted and frustrated. I could not believe that all these people who knew that treatment worked could be so intimidated by the new governor. But then again, that's usually what went on at the cabinet meetings if you got there on time.

The secretary of natural resources was getting into his car. He smiled and said, "I'm sure your phone will be ringing by the time you get to your office."

Sure enough it was, and on the line was one of the governor's three chiefs of staff who ordered me over to his office immediately. My office was in State Office Complex A and the governor's offices were in State Office Complex B, next door on the fifteenth floor. I ran over so fast that I was still carrying my overloaded briefcase that I had forgotten to leave in my office.

The chief of staff was in a somber mood. He motioned me into his office immediately, instructed me to sit, and rehashed what Dr. Yeager had told me.

"I don't understand. You know treatment works. Why didn't you say anything?" I asked pleadingly.

"It just wasn't the right time, but I'm sure you're going to take care of things," he stated matter-of-factly. "I want you to put together a position paper right away explaining how treatment works, why it works, and cite some examples. And then I want you to go on that talk show and rebut what was said."

I agreed, and he told me that he would have one of his aides get back to me as soon as possible. "Ted, you're to give Mr. O'Meara the position paper. He'll give you the name of the talk show host as soon as I get it from the governor."

I wasn't back in my office more than twenty minutes when I got a call from O'Meara. "Ted, get that position paper over to me as soon as you can. It was the Ken Lester talk show that the governor heard. You're to get on that show ASAP, and even if the governor doesn't listen to the show, some of his old cronies will. You can believe they'll let him know right away. This is top priority, so please don't fuck up!"

I called the Ken Lester show and was given a date to appear on the show ten days later. I then met with Bud Hodinko of my Research Division and explained to him why we had to put together, in twenty or thirty pages, a position paper explaining why treatment works.

Hodinko said, "Twenty or thirty pages isn't nearly enough, but I'll go through some of the research and some of your speeches, and together maybe we can come up with something tight-knit. It might have to be single-spaced, though."

I told him that would be fine and that we would work on it over the next couple of days.

Later that afternoon, O'Meara called again and asked me where I was with the position paper. I told him that it might take a few days, and he ordered, "Drop everything! Like I said before, this is top priority, and I expect it within two days!"

I hustled back to Hodinko's office, and within forty-eight hours, we came up with a twenty-eight-page, tight, concise paper on why treatment works.

After we had it typed, I rushed over to O'Meara's office and hand-delivered it to him. Without even looking at it, he tossed it hastily back to me.

"This won't work," he complained. "It's too long. Much too

long. And it doesn't look good, either. First of all, the lines have to be at least triple-spaced for the governor. It's got to be in bold lettering, maybe even all caps. It's just too, too long, Ted. The man just doesn't have the time. Get me something much shorter. Good day."

"But, O'Meara," I retorted, "you have to understand. We're talking about twenty years of research. We're talking about a multitude of lives over a number of years. You can't do that in less than twenty-eight pages."

He was becoming frustrated and a bit pissed off as he sternly ordered, "Just get it back to me and make it much shorter. And remember, it's got to be easy to read. *Very* easy to read. And hurry it up!"

I ran back across the street and told Hodinko, who just shook his head hopelessly. We prepared another more concise position paper, one that was hopefully easier for the governor to read. The next day, I walked in and handed O'Meara a ten-page, double-spaced, bold-lettered summary of why treatment works.

"Ted," he said, shaking his head, "this just doesn't work. It's still too damn long, and the governor doesn't have the time to look at something this wordy. He doesn't have the patience to go through this. Make it easy on yourself, Ted."

"O'Meara," I shouted, "what's wrong with you? Ten pages, double-spaced? Are you kidding me? Give me a fucking break! How am I going to explain this accurately in less than ten pages?"

O'Meara tried to play clinician with me, saying, "I know you've been doing a good job, and Ted, the governor's proud of you. We're all proud of the marvelous work you've done for the state. And you gave the city a lot of money for drug treatment when he was mayor. Why fuck up now? All we're asking for is a position paper on why treatment works that the governor can read and digest with ease. Be a good boy, Ted. Come see me tomorrow when you've got something better. I've got a meeting now. Ciao."

Instead of running on my tired legs, I calmly strolled back to State Office Complex A, went up to my office, called Hodinko, and explained to him that the position paper was still much too long. "Oh, and Bud," I said, "O'Meara said 'Ciao.'"

Hodinko had a great temperament. He chuckled and said to me, "Don't worry about it. Just go about your business. I'll work on it and try to get it down to less than five pages."

Later that afternoon, to my surprise and relief, Hodinko had put together an excellent position paper consisting of four pages of triple-spaced, bold capital letters explaining why treatment works. I rushed across the street and interrupted O'Meara. He was in a meeting with three gubernatorial aides over the proposed drunk driving laws that the administration was drafting. I threw it in front of him.

"Here. How's this? I'll bet you'll like this one."

O'Meara barely looked at the position paper. "Ted, buddy, it's still too long. It's four pages. Much too long!"

"O'Meara," I said frustrated, "do me a favor. Just read these four pages, and *then* tell me how many pages you want! What the hell are you looking for? I've got to go on that talk show shortly, you know? I need some help!"

O'Meara told me that the position paper had nothing to do with the talk show. "It may be used for a legislative briefing, and the governor will definitely read it, but this is just too long."

I went back across the street and met with Hodinko again. By the next morning, we had it down to two pages. I delivered it to O'Meara, telling him firmly, "I'm not leaving this room until you've read these pages and told me that they're acceptable!"

"Ted, baby," he said, glancing at the first page, "It's still a bit too wordy, but I'm going to go over it because you've made such a great effort. And by the way, I'm going to listen to you on Ken Lester, and I hope it's good."

I considered the show. Fear had kept me from thinking about it. Ken Lester was a far-right radical who loved to go after the local newspapers, legislators, and the governor. He even went after the Reagan Administration for being too leftist. I knew I was in for a hell of a time once I went on that show. But it couldn't be any worse than dealing with O'Meara.

"Ted, this isn't bad," said O'Meara, "but it's still too long. What I'm looking for is one page, bold letters. I do like the triple-spacing, however. It's better than double-spacing. Oh, and the governor likes bullets. He doesn't want to read long sentences or paragraphs. You know what bullets are, don't you? Get to the heart of the matter, Ted. C'mon, you're doing good, even though it's taken you over a week. Now get something back to me tomorrow because the governor asked my boss what was going on with it, and I had to cover for you."

"You had to cover *my* ass?" I asked incredulously. "I can't fucking believe you, O'Meara. You're driving me crazy with this thing. Now you want one page, bullets, triple-spaced? Why didn't you tell me this earlier? I swear I could fucking throw you out the window." With that, I stormed out of the room, went back to my office, and called in Hodinko.

"Bud," I said, aggravated, "one page, triple-spaced, bold, thick capital letters, and bullets, baby, bullets. Just quick lines, no sentences, nothing long, no paragraphs. Get it for me right away or I'm gonna go fucking nuts!"

I appeared on the Ken Lester radio talk show for more than an hour and a half. However, I barely got to the point of talking about why treatment works or to rebut what was allegedly said on the show that had upset the governor. Lester would constantly digress. He started talking about why the governor was supportive of the fifty-five-mile-per-hour speed limit when he knew the governor's driver drove faster than that. Then Lester said that the state should be drug testing all of the legislators, accusing many of them of being alcoholics and even drug abusers. He tried unsuccessfully to get me to agree with everything he said.

I was sweating bullets, and not the kind of bullets the governor wanted on the treatment position statement. I laughed nervously and changed the subject often. Finally, with ten minutes left on the show, Lester let me talk about why treatment works. Then he shocked me, saying he wholeheartedly agreed. He also kept me on for an additional twenty minutes while several listeners called in to discuss treatment.

The show didn't turn out nearly as bad as I thought it would. I was, however, afraid that the governor may come down on me for the fifty-five-mile-per-hour speed limit discussion, or that ten dozen legislators might go completely nuts fearing that they would be drug tested.

A day later in Little Italy, I was about to enter Sabatino's Restaurant as the governor was strolling out. He saw me and came over to shake my hand.

"Ted, Ted," he shouted, "I heard the Ken Lester Show yesterday. You were great, excellent! I'm proud of you."

"Thanks, Governor. I was just trying to rebut what had been said on his show about treatment that you brought up at the cabinet meeting. And I also gave O'Meara..."

"Whoa," the Governor interrupted. "It wasn't the Ken Lester Show I heard that on, Ted. It was the Paul Alan show on WBAF. That's the show I wanted you to go on.

"You know, Ted, you shouldn't take chances going on that Ken Lester Show. It's very dangerous. He's always trying to embarrass somebody. I mean, you could lose your job over something like that. It was a very ballsy move, but don't do that again. Get on that Paul Alan Show. I've been waiting for about three weeks now. You need to rebut it and attack while it's still fresh on the public's mind.

"By the way, Ted, weren't you supposed to give me some kind of position paper or statement about why treatment works? What's taking so long?"

Before I had time to explain, the governor's bodyguards were escorting him into his limousine. As I walked into Sabatino's, I felt totally ill.

The next day, I called O'Meara and explained to him that I had gone on the wrong show. He told me he was sure it was the Ken Lester Show, but that he would get back to me. I told him that he didn't have to get back to me because the governor had personally told me it was the Paul Alan Show. O'Meara told me not to worry, that he'd call back as soon as he had confirmed it.

A day later, O'Meara phoned and said, "You're right, Ted. It was the Paul Alan Show, so try and get on it as soon as possible. And the governor looked at your position paper and has written a note on it. Come on over and take a look."

I hurried over to O'Meara's office, not knowing what to expect. But when I walked in, O'Meara's secretary was beaming. "Look what the Governor put on your position statement."

I figured maybe the message would include kudos, or perhaps he wanted to promote me or maybe even give me a bonus. After all, he didn't know I was planning on leaving. I looked at what he had written, and all it said was "Okay." Not even "Okay" with an exclamation point. Just "Okay" period.

I got a date for the Paul Alan Show two weeks later, and when I finally went on the air, it was quite an experience. Alan let me give my views on treatment, and then he came at me from his perspective before fielding calls. We were only supposed to do an hour show but we ended up doing two and a half hours. It was a good show and I felt I came off well. Alan invited me to return any time I wished to discuss drug and alcohol issues.

❏ ❏ ❏

Several days after my appearance on the Paul Alan Show, I got a call from the governor's chief of staff, and later from O'Meara, telling me that the governor had heard the show and he thought that I'd done a nice job. An hour later, I resigned.

❏ ❏ ❏

PHOENIX, ARIZONA
July 13, 1987

It was six a.m. when the Chemical Girl arrived back at her home in Phoenix. She started the previous evening at the hotel bar at The Pointe with the elderly gentleman she shared a luxury semi-ranch with. Dinner followed at Avanti's restaurant in Scottsdale. Later, they shared a bottle of Taittinger champagne to celebrate the evening before, when for the first time, the Chemical Girl had shared his bed. The lovemaking was the first she had experienced in some time.

The Chemical Girl insisted that the old guy use a condom for protection. He thought it odd, but he was almost proud. Even though he was chronologically much closer to death than the Chemical Girl, she knew better. During a routine physical examination at the spa, she had found out she was HIV-positive. Since the incubation period for AIDS was still being hotly debated, she could only surmise as to how she had gotten it. From sharing needles long, long ago, or from unsafe sex? *And what about Ted?*, she thought. *He never used condoms. He had that altercation and possible blood exchange at the methadone clinic, not to mention the blood transfusion after the hornet's sting. He'd been bitten and stung by green flies, mosquitoes, hornets, and bees. Was it possible that insects could really transmit the disease? Should I call his office?*

She had been on drinking binges from the moment she arrived in Phoenix and was now using depressants. Her eyes were puffy and swollen, but otherwise, the Chemical Girl looked great. Her tan was a deep, deep golden brown, and her body had become even firmer from the rigorous workout regimen she'd been following at the fashionable Tucson spa, Canyon Ranch.

After the champagne, the elderly gentleman went home, while the Chemical Girl made her rounds of the bars and after-hours spots. She had become a familiar figure in these places over the past few months.

She didn't feel very drunk at six a.m. as she walked through the spacious house to the kitchen, popped open a Pepsi, and headed towards the pool. Still in a flowing black dress and wearing very high black heels, the Chemical Girl steadied herself on a chaise lounge.

The sun was just coming up and foretold of another incredibly hot summer day in Arizona. The previous week had an average temperature of 113 degrees–brutal to most, but not to the Chemical Girl. She was a throwback to the ancient Aztec sun worshipers. Opening her purse, she withdrew a beautifully ornamented pillbox given to her by Lo Ming. A multitude of pills in various sizes, shapes, and colors stared back at the Chemical Girl as she contemplated her needs and desires for the day.

First, she dealt with a headache of epic proportions. Migraines had been a way of life for the Chemical Girl since her teens, and the alcohol didn't exactly chase the head pain away. She removed a Fiorinal from the pillbox, swallowing the smooth, round, flat pill with a swig of Pepsi. Disdaining coffee, the Chemical Girl began every morning with the heavily-sugared Pepsi, although a Classic Coke also sufficed.

A barbiturate like Fiorinal could become a dangerous drug when taken in concert with alcohol. But warning labels didn't bother the Chemical Girl. She took out three half-milligram pink Xanax pills and ingested them. Xanax was a benzodiazepine prescribed for anxiety and not to be mixed with barbiturates or alcohol. But this never fazed the Chemical Girl.

The heat embraced her body as she closed her eyes. Even in weather this intense, she seldom perspired. *I'll nap by the pool for about an hour and then go inside to bed after the old man leaves for his golf game*, the Chemical Girl contemplated. Within seconds, she was in a deep sleep, dreaming of her beloved Ocean City.

❏ ❏ ❏

ARUBA
July 15, 1987

Pleased with my facility's inpatient success and recovery rate, I took the day off to relax on the beach. The two-week, intensive residential program was working well so far.

I spread my Skin-So-Soft, an Avon product, evenly on my body. I didn't use it for smoother skin or a better tan, but for repelling insects. Months earlier in Thailand, my late friend, Holt, had introduced me to it, and it was truly a great discovery. It made it easier for me to deal with bees, wasps, hornets, or other flying or crawling insects whose bites caused me terror, and sometimes serious life-threatening reactions.

Investors from the United States, Europe, Japan, and South America represented an excellent feeder network for the state-of-the-art inpatient addictions facility established on the breathtaking island of Aruba. The beds were filled and projections suggested profits in the not too distant future.

The outpatient program, a partnership with the government, was only doing so-so. By the docks, the natives began their drinking routinely at five-thirty in the morning and continued throughout the day. Attempts at intervention, treatment, prevention strategy, and aftercare were abysmal. Recovery rates wavered at around fifteen percent at best. Compulsive gambling was also a problem, but was not open for discussion by the government since casino gambling was an economic necessity in Aruba.

I was relatively happy taking in the hot South Caribbean sun on beautiful white Manchebo beach. Glancing at a day-old *USA Today*, I noticed a story datelined Phoenix, Arizona. My eyes immediately shot to the article as my mind was often on the Chemical Girl. It told of a woman who had been drinking heavily the previous night and had decided to sit outside and catch the rays of the early morning sun before the intense Arizona heat rolled in later in the day. She had fallen into such a deep sleep that she was outside the entire day and was completely dehydrated. Because she was unable to awaken, she had literally baked to death. Her name was Ruth Goldberg, a.k.a. Lola, a.k.a. the Chemical Girl.

I rolled off of my sand chair, curled into the fetal position, and wept.

EPILOGUE

"What there was left of us
Was all covered in dust and thick skin"

John Hiatt
The Most Unoriginal Sin

Lefty Driesell joined James Madison University as head basketball coach. President Slaughter, in a ballsy and hurriedly-thought-
out move, replaced him with Bob Wade. A legendary figure from
East Baltimore, Wade was a black, inner-city high school coach
who had led Dunbar High School to a national and mythical title in
the early '80s. The Maryland athletic alumni were extremely upset
at Slaughter's move. They would have preferred a Maryland alumnus for the position. Wade became the first black coach in the prestigious and highly competitive Atlantic Coast Conference (ACC).

Within three years, Maryland's basketball fortunes would again
rise and fall. An excellent recruiter, Wade took the Terps to the
National Collegiate Athletic Association (NCAA) tournament by
his second year. However, by Wade's third year he was fired for a
number of small NCAA violations, the greatest of which was providing transportation for a player to get to his classes. The NCAA
report sanctioned the University for not monitoring Wade's program more closely. In effect they were saying, "Don't hire any
more black, inner-city high school coaches. But if you do, you'd
better watch them closer than other coaches." In addition to the
sanctions against Maryland, the NCAA sanctioned Wade personally, as well as some members of his staff. Any school that hired
Wade might subsequently have received sanctions against its basketball program. It was a terrible decision by the governing body
of college sports against a truly good man.

Maryland, for cooperating fully with the NCAA investigation,
was given a surprising two-year probation period which included
bans from television and tournaments. It was an extremely harsh
penalty considering the lack of major violations and the fact that
the University bent over backwards to cooperate. Schools with far
greater violations that fought the NCAA got far fewer sanctions.

Former Chancellor Slaughter of the University of Maryland at
College Park was selected as President of Occidental College in
California. He also became President of an NCAA commission of
college presidents to clean up athlete academics, which was ironic
since Slaughter's athletic house at College Park was considered
very soiled.

Nineteen employees of the Maryland Athletic Department received two-week notices with no benefits or severance pay. They
took the fall because the Maryland athletic program was deep in
the red, and because Len Bias had died.

Every time the University of Maryland had a decision to make, and they could have gone the right way or the wrong way, they went the wrong way. Was it something in the nature of the people who were there, or was it something in the institutional decision-making process that bred such bad judgment?

❑ ❑ ❑

Bob Wade, who returned to the Baltimore City public school system, was replaced at Maryland by Gary Williams, the former head coach at Ohio State University and a Terp alumnus. He moved smoothly through the sanction years and guided Maryland basketball to ten straight NCAA tournament selections, a Final Four appearance in 2001, and a National Championship in 2002.

Lefty Driesell left James Madison University and finished his coaching career at Georgia State University. One of the winningest coaches in college basketball history, he not only won at least a hundred games each at Davidson U., University of Maryland, James Madison, and Georgia State, but he also took each team to the NCAA Tournament. Retiring in the middle of the 2002-2003 season, Driesell, enjoying a rebirth, was among the former basketball coaches and players honored in 2003 at the new Comcast Center at University of Maryland that replaced Cole Field House. Remarkably, Coach Wade wasn't invited.

❑ ❑ ❑

Oliver Purnell, the assistant basketball coach, who refused to clean out Bias' room became head coach at Old Dominion University and Dayton University. Recently, he was named head coach at Clemson University, only the second black coach in Atlantic Coast Conference history.

❑ ❑ ❑

A little over four years after Len Bias' untimely death, two other noteworthy incidents occurred in the Prince George's County area where Bias grew up, lived, and died. Brian Tribble, the mystery man in the Len Bias death, who allegedly supplied the cocaine that fateful night, but was acquitted by a Prince George's County jury, got into trouble again. In August 1990, in a bizarre set of events, Tribble was arrested in Maryland following a botched sting operation in the hotel where the jury deciding the fate of Washington, D.C. Mayor Marion Barry was sequestered. Although Tribble, a DEA target, who had supposedly gone to the hotel to purchase $120,000 worth of cocaine, escaped an FBI and local police manhunt, he later turned himself in to the feds in Baltimore. Tribble agreed to accept a prison sentence of ten years with no parole for his involvement in a cocaine drug ring that was rumored to have brought in more than a hundred pounds of coke over a two-year period.

Tragically, less than six weeks after this incident, Jay Bias, Len's brother, was gunned down outside a Prince George's County shopping center by a man and his friend who thought the younger Bias was flirting with his wife. After the shooting, Jay Bias was rushed to Leland Memorial Hospital in Riverdale, Maryland where he was pronounced dead. It was the same hospital where his brother Leonard had died.

❏ ❏ ❏

Dr. John E. Smialek, Maryland's chief medical examiner, who enjoyed overnight fame in diagnosing the cause of Len Bias' death, died of a heart attack in May 2001 at the age of fifty-seven. He was preparing his continuing seminar for homicide detectives when he collapsed at his desk. During his fifteen years of employment with the State of Maryland, he received national acclaim in forensic pathology.

❏ ❏ ❏

One of the two men accused of killing Jay Bias was ironically represented by Attorney Alan Goldstein, who had defended Bias' roommates, Long and Gregg. The client was found guilty and sentenced to thirty years in prison. Goldstein, who one year earlier was named Outstanding Criminal Defense Lawyer by the Maryland Criminal Defense Attorneys Association, appealed the decision.

While awaiting the appeal, the forty-eight-year-old Goldstein, an adjunct professor at Georgetown University Law Center, who handled some of the most publicized cases of the '80s, died of lung cancer on August 1, 1991.

□ □ □

Perhaps the final ironic and tragic twist to the fate of a State of Maryland-bred basketball player was that of Reggie Lewis. A member of the 1981-82 Dunbar Poets of Baltimore, which produced four NBA players (Lewis, Mugsy Bogues, Reggie Williams, and David Wingate), he was coached by soon-to-be-named University of Maryland Head Coach Bob Wade. The next year's team became National High School Champions.

Lewis attended Northeastern University, played against Len Bias in 1985, and was *also* drafted by the Boston Celtics. He became a premier professional player, had a twenty-one-point scoring average, and was the team's captain. Lewis was a blessing and benefit to his communities in Baltimore and Boston, and was highly regarded.

Suddenly in 1993 at the age of twenty-seven, Lewis died of a heart attack on the court. Although never proven and following publicized lawsuits, cocaine was suspected….

□ □ □

During the first year that I worked with the Drug Abuse Administration, we opened forty-seven different treatment programs around the state in twelve months. It was the last time that that process would ever go that smoothly and with that many programs without community opposition. Approximately thirty-five years later, despite the need for more treatment and the fact that not only does treatment work (decreasing crime, increasing productivity, lowering health costs, etc.), and despite the fact that we have learned more about how to operate programs with more efficiency and security, it's almost impossible to open new public or private treatment facilities at any level (in-patient, out-patient, or methadone maintenance).

This was echoed more forcefully by Dr. Vincent Dole (who passed away right before the publication of this novel) in an interview from *Addictions: Evolution of a Specialist Field.*

"A second major impediment is the attitude of the public. Communities refuse to have treatment programs in their neighborhoods even when there is a demonstrated local need. A community in New York rose in opposition to having a residential facility set up for orphaned babies. If they consider the babies a threat, how would they react to a clinic that treats addicts? In public health terms, we have reached a stage in the drug problem at which society is getting what it asks for."

□ □ □

Also in the book *Addiction: Evolution of a Specialist Field*, Jerry Jaffe, the first drug czar of the United States, and later acting director of the National Institute on Drug Abuse during the period of this novel stated, "It was the beginning of the AIDS epidemic, and we were trying to persuade the powers that be within government that addiction was a major vector in the transmission of AIDS. They were skeptical; they thought that this was another bureaucratic maneuver to get a piece of the AIDS money.

"And when people finally isolated the virus and showed that bleach could kill it, they would not let us disseminate that information. They said that would be the wrong message, and I considered this felonious — to know that you could tell people that with simple household bleach, they could sterilize syringes, since in our country many people did not have access to sterile materials. We were in a position to tell them how to kill the virus, but we weren't allowed to tell them."

Jaffe was originally appointed by Nixon in 1971 at the creation of the modern war on drugs.

□ □ □

Coincidentally, in 1986 when Bias died, famed journalist James Mills, who authored the books *Panic In Needle Park* and *Report To The Commissioner*, wrote the non-fiction story *The Underground Empire*. Rumored that several countries tried to suppress it, this voluminous 1,165 page exposé on the relationship between governments and criminal groups opened with the following words:

The inhabitants of the earth spend more money on illegal drugs than they spend on food. More than they spend on housing, clothes, education, medical care, or any other product or service. The international narcotics industry is the largest growth industry in the world. Its annual revenues exceed half a trillion dollars–three times the value of all United States currency in circulation, more than the gross national products of all but a half dozen of the major industrialized nations . . . .

□ □ □

Len Bias' death signified the watershed for the beginning, theoretically, of the final war on drugs. Following Bias' death, politicians finally sat up straight and took notice. More money and resources have flowed into the war on drugs. Still, the effort is not nearly enough and the war goes badly . . . .